A HAUNTING IN SILVER FALLS

ROCKWELL SCOTT

A HAUNTING IN SILVER FALLS

PART ONE

1

The small airport was out of date compared to the gleaming terminals she was used to, though not many local airports could compete with Chicago O'Hare. Kara Mills paused when she passed a poster advertising her city.

"Get Away to Chicago! Budget Fares!"

I wish *I could turn around and get away back home,* she thought as she looked longingly at the photos that portrayed the familiar soaring skyscrapers of downtown. She already missed the energy and excitement—and she mourned the potential summer vacation she could have had with her friends. Yet here she stood, exiled to a sleepy southern town for the whole summer.

Kara forced herself to move along from the poster. Staring at it wasn't doing her any favors.

She walked into the arrivals area and scanned the masses for her aunt's face. Even though she'd only met Aunt Adrienne a handful of times growing up, it was impossible not to notice her in a crowd. Sure enough, Kara spotted Adrienne waving enthusiastically near the exit. Her flowing caftan and abundance of clinking bangle bracelets helped her stand out among the conservatively dressed people. Kara knew Aunt Adrienne was in her fifties, but the woman had a brightness about her that made her seem much younger.

As soon as Kara was close enough, Adrienne swept her up in an exuberant hug. "It's so wonderful to finally have you here!"

"Hey, Aunt Adrienne," Kara said, then squirmed out of the warm embrace. She forced a polite smile.

Adrienne grasped Kara's shoulders and looked her up and down. "You've grown up."

Kara only shrugged. "I guess."

"How was the flight?"

"It was fine. Airport security though... I wasn't expecting all of *that*. Way more intense than it used to be."

"Well, I would think so," Adrienne said. "But can you blame them? It's only been a year since that horrible business in New York." She grimaced. "Did you check a bag?"

"Yeah."

As Kara waited beside the creaking baggage carousel, she subtly studied the other travelers. Everything about them seemed foreign. The men sported sturdy denim and worn leather boots that spoke of manual labor. Their hearty laughter rang loudly through the crowded space. The women wore modest sundresses with dainty floral prints, a far cry from the sleek blouses and power suits Kara was accustomed to, and their hair was almost uniformly swept into neat ponytails. There was an elderly woman in a wheelchair with immaculate curls clutching an expensive handbag. Despite her frailty, she still exuded an air that commanded respect from all around her—

she'd deemed herself worthy simply because she was the eldest person in the room.

These are my people for the summer, Kara thought with a sigh.

Kara perked up as she recognized her black suitcase bumping along the carousel, right at the front of the rest. When she went to grab the handle, she was taken aback as a nearby man swooped in and grabbed it for her, yanking it off the belt and setting it upright in one swift motion. He nodded and smiled.

"Oh, thanks," Kara said.

She wheeled the larger suitcase over to where her aunt waited. "You're welcome for making your bag come out first."

"What do you mean?"

"I manifested it," Adrienne said, as if it were obvious. "I focused my intention on your luggage being unloaded quickly from the plane. And it worked!"

"Ah." Aunt Adrienne couldn't be more different from Kara's mother—or anyone she knew back home, really. Any of her friends would have laughed at such superstitious nonsense. "Or maybe it was just random luck."

"No such thing as luck, my dear. We use our mental energy to shape outcomes." She tapped her temple.

Better start getting used to the spiritual stuff now, Kara thought. "Well… thanks for the magical luggage help, I guess."

———

AS THEY DROVE from the airport in Adrienne's battered sedan, Kara stared out the window as the scenery shifted from the outskirts of Jackson to the rural roads of central

Mississippi. Old farmhouses, sprawling fields, and the occasional country store or gas station dotted the landscape.

Aunt Adrienne tried to make conversation, asking about school and Kara's friends back in Chicago, but Kara could only summon up one-word answers and non-committal noises.

"So, tell me about this new man your mama's dating," Adrienne said. "What's the deal with him?"

Kara shrugged. "I don't know much. His name's Robert. He's a lawyer, and they met through work. They've been seeing each other for a couple of months."

"And they're already heading to Europe together?"

"Seems so."

Kara had Robert to thank for her current predicament. She still remembered the evening her mom had revealed to her that Robert had invited her for a summer abroad in Europe. She'd listed out their itinerary with excitement: Rome, Paris, Athens. Kara had been excited because what she'd heard was that she was going to have a summer of freedom—sixteen years old and *finally* deemed mature enough to stay at home for three solid months on her own. She knew she could handle it.

Then her mother had dropped the bomb. "I've already called your Aunt Adrienne and arranged things. You'll be staying with her while I'm gone."

And just like that, the summer of 2002 was ruined before it had even started.

"Well, I hope this one treats her right," Adrienne said after a long bout of silence. "She deserves it after all she's been through."

Ramshackle houses dotted the roadside, porches sagging and paint peeling. Scruffy dogs dozed in the mottled shade of towering oak trees draped in wispy Spanish moss. Fields of tall grass rippled in the breeze. Everything moved at an unhurried pace. There were no blaring horns or crowded sidewalks. *How can people stand living this... slow?* Kara wondered. Yet another tide of homesickness washed over her.

The car trundled through the small downtown area of Silver Falls, passing by a row of low brick buildings: a barbershop with an old-fashioned striped pole, a hardware store, and a diner.

"That's Barry's Barbershop," Adrienne said, apparently catching Kara looking at it. "He's been cutting hair in this town for over fifty years. Knows everybody's business too, so watch what you say around him."

Kara nodded absently as she gazed out at the sleepy storefronts. A group of elderly men sat in tipped-back chairs outside the hardware store. Kara couldn't help but feel they regarded Adrienne's car with suspicion as it passed by—which was strange, since her aunt had lived here for years.

"Oh, and there's Belle's Diner, which has the best fried catfish around. I cook most of the time, but we'll have to go there for dinner one night so you can try it."

"Mmhmm," Kara said, her mind drifting to the many new restaurants, cafés, delis, and bakeries that had just opened up near her neighborhood back home. She'd been looking forward to trying them out with her friends that summer. She could imagine all of them crowded around a table, talking and laughing over plates of avocado toast and matcha lattes. Silver Falls felt like another world entirely, and not in a good way.

They passed a trio of young girls clustered on bicycles in the street, long braids trailing behind them. Kara pictured her own friends again, wondering what they were up to. How Nina's pool party had turned out. If Ben had worked up the nerve to ask out Jada yet. Her real life felt so far away.

Then something occurred to Kara. "Why is it called Silver Falls? Is there a waterfall here?"

Adrienne chucked. "There used to be a long time ago, apparently. It was near Lake Silver, which still exists, and is just outside of town. That whole area is said to have been considered a sacred place by the indigenous people who settled this region."

"What about you? Do you believe the lake was sacred?"

"Of course! It was, and still is," Adrienne answered, as if it were ridiculous to even ask.

Eventually, they turned down a long gravel driveway that led to a large two-story house with a wraparound porch nestled among huge oak trees with thick trunks.

"Here we are," Adrienne proclaimed, parking in the yard near the porch.

Kara stepped out, the humidity and loud buzzing of cicadas enveloping her immediately. The buzz of cicadas was jarringly loud.

Adrienne popped open the trunk and hoisted Kara's luggage out, making it look even lighter than the man at the airport who'd taken it upon himself to assist Kara.

She's pretty strong for her age, Kara realized.

"We'll start with the tour," Adrienne said as she led the way.

Kara followed Adrienne up the creaking steps onto a wide porch adorned with wind chimes and potted plants. Her aunt heaved open the warped screen door and gestured grandly. "Welcome to your new summer home."

They entered a living room where old white curtains

8

blocked the cloudy sunlight. A lumpy sofa and armchairs were pushed against the far wall facing a simple fireplace. Kara ran a finger across a side table, frowning at the thick coating of dust that came away. In Chicago, dust never had a chance to settle, since her mother was adamant about cleaners coming over once a week without fail.

"Over eighty years old, but full of character," Adrienne said. "I hope it'll feel like home for you this summer."

"It's nice." Kara tried to make the compliment sound genuine. It seemed perfectly suited for her aunt, but Kara had always preferred newer-style homes.

"This is the dining room," Adrienne said, leading them to a space opposite the living room on the other side of the house's entrance area. It was mostly dominated by a massive table made of dark wood that looked more modern than any other piece of furniture Kara had seen inside. A cabinet flush against the wall presumably held dishes and china.

"And the kitchen is just off this way," Adrienne said, walking through a threshold connected to the dining room. The kitchen showed similar signs of age—peeling wallpaper, chipped countertops, and cabinets on crooked hinges. She opened a narrow door to reveal a pantry. "What's mine is yours. I wasn't sure what you were eating these days, so I put off going shopping. We can do that later. Now, upstairs."

Adrienne hoisted Kara's bag once again and started up the stairs near the front door.

"Aunt Adrienne, I can carry that—"

"Don't be silly. You're the guest here."

Mom never would've carried my luggage, Kara thought. Tracey Mills was many things—driven, ambitious, independent—but she definitely wasn't one to serve others.

On the second floor, Kara's assigned bedroom featured a bare bulb overhead and slanted ceilings. The bed's mattress visibly sank in the middle. Across from the bed was a wooden dresser, the top scarred with water rings. Kara couldn't help but remember how, when she was younger, her mother had chastised her every time she'd forgotten to use a coaster.

By far the most striking thing in the room was a wall-mounted shelf laden with a collection of crystals, each one different in size, color, and shape.

"You won't find *these* in a five-star hotel," Adrienne said over Kara's shoulder when she noticed her looking at the display. "I've arranged some protective stones to bring positive energy into your space. Rose quartz for love, citrine for healing, black tourmaline to absorb negative vibrations, and a few others."

"It's very nice. Thank you." While Kara didn't believe the "protective stones" had any of those effects, she could at least appreciate them as pretty decorations.

Adrienne beamed, then pointed down the upstairs hall. "The bathroom is that first door on the left. And the room at the end is me. Across from you is another bedroom, but I'm mostly using it for storage. And that pretty much wraps up the tour. I'll let you freshen up a bit. Once you're done, I have a surprise for you."

Kara had no idea what kind of "surprise" to expect, but taking a shower did sound good right about then.

After Adrienne went back downstairs, Kara extracted her toiletry bag and a change of clothes from her tightly packed luggage and headed for the bathroom. Like the rest of the house, it was outdated but functional. An antique clawfoot tub took up most of the space, surrounded by a clouded plastic curtain that badly needed replacing. Kara turned the faucet handle and water sputtered out a few seconds later. As steam filled the room, she peeled off her travel-rumpled clothes. The pressure from the shower head was weak, but it was piping hot, just how Kara preferred it.

After toweling dry and slipping into comfy shorts and a tank top, Kara returned to the guest bedroom, where she put her suitcase on the bed, unzipped it, and flipped it open. She meticulously folded her clothes into piles before transferring them to the old dresser. The top drawer, which she'd planned for her socks and under-wear, was stuck, not budging no matter how hard she yanked on it.

With a huff of frustration, Kara redistributed her belongings to the remaining functional drawers. As she tucked away the last of her toiletries in the bottom drawer, she wondered how long it would take before this place started to feel remotely like home.

Who am I kidding? she thought. *It won't.*

Hearing noises from outside, Kara wandered across to the bedroom window, which looked out over a sizable bit of land. Off in the distance, she could make out a neigh-boring homestead. There was a fenced pasture beside the distant house which contained a small herd of goats grazing and bleating to each other—the zoo-like sound loud enough to come through the window. Kara had a chuckle. The sight of livestock just roaming a few hundred feet away was wholly foreign to her city upbringing.

I hope they aren't this loud at night, Kara thought, real-izing she didn't know the first thing about goats.

Kara went back downstairs, feeling a bit more

grounded now that she'd unpacked. She found her aunt in the living room, practically vibrating with excitement.

"Are you ready for your surprise?" Adrienne asked with a playful grin.

Kara shrugged. "Sure, what is it?"

"Well, it happens to be thrift-store day—a little ritual I've developed that I'm quite fond of. I can't *wait* to take you to this delightful shop in town so we can hunt for treasures." Adrienne clasped her hands together.

Kara tried not to let her lack of enthusiasm show on her face. From what she had seen of Adrienne's home decor, their ideas of "treasures" were vastly dissimilar. But Adrienne looked so eager that Kara didn't have the heart to object. "That sounds... fun," she said, hoping she came across as sincere.

Adrienne and Kara's mother could not be any more different from each other. To Tracey Mills, shopping was a carefully planned expedition to department stores or boutiques, always with a specific purpose in mind. Going without a plan risked wasting both time and money. That, and Tracey wouldn't be caught dead in a thrift store. And while Kara was definitely less rigid than her mother, she couldn't deny that she took after Tracey more than Adrienne. Which meant she had a very long summer ahead of her.

"Wonderful. Let's head there now. The longer we wait, the greater the chance all the good stuff will be gone."

Kara sighed as she resigned herself to an afternoon of sifting through other people's cast-offs.

2

Kara eyed her aunt as Adrienne wove through the aisles and racks of Thrift Love, eyes darting around as she scanned all the stuff, seeming equally enthusiastic about every single item in the place.

Kara wrinkled her nose, still a bit bothered by the stale aroma of dust and age. She tried to busy herself perusing the shop's wares, just to give herself something to do, but she didn't expect to see anything there that interested her.

Mismatched plates were stacked precariously on a shelf, faded patterns barely visible beneath cracked glaze. Racks of clothing sagged under the weight of jackets and dresses in long-outdated cuts and fabrics. Kara briefly examined an ancient radio that looked kind of neat—like something out of a historical black-and-white film—but when she turned the dials, the device gave no hints at life.

At the heart of the cluttered shop stood a large, circular table, its surface entirely obscured by the haphazard assortment of items piled upon it. Kara drifted closer, and to her surprise so did Adrienne, as if something there was calling out to both of them.

An antique typewriter with jammed keys nestled against a tarnished silver tea set. Stacked books spanning decades and genres. An old chessboard with missing pieces. To Kara, it looked as if the table was a catch-all for the shopkeeper, who had yet to sort the items into their respective categories. If a customer was willing to dig through the pile and found something they wanted, then great—one less thing that needed to be sorted.

"Isn't this lovely?" Adrienne said as she held up a tangled necklace of wooden beads. She brought it closer to her neck so Kara could see how it looked on her.

Kara shrugged. "Yeah, it's... nice." It seemed like something her aunt would wear.

Adrienne smiled and returned the beads to the table. She started sifting through things, hunting for more "treasure."

Kara couldn't even begin to fathom what would catch her aunt's interest enough for her to buy it. She only saw junk: a taxidermy raven with beady glass eyes. A brass compass forever stuck pointing south. A chipped porcelain figurine of a ballerina.

Like some kind of purgatory of objects, Kara thought. "What are you looking for?"

Adrienne only smirked. "You're missing the point. *We* aren't looking for anything. We're making ourselves available for whatever's here that's searching for *us.*"

"Oh." Kara figured that made sense... in an "Adrienne" sort of way.

Adrienne continued sorting through the pile. She paused as she uncovered an old baseball, its once pristine white leather now yellowed with age. Tracing her fingers

14

along the red seam, she murmured, "Oh, the stories this ball could tell."

Kara watched her aunt turn the ball over and over, inspecting it closely as if hoping to find a faded autograph that increased its value.

Or maybe she thinks it'll start talking to her.

"A young boy might've owned this ball and used it when he played with his friends. Or it was a home-run ball in a high-school game."

"Right…" To Kara, it was just an old, dirty baseball. She half expected her aunt to claim she could divine the ball's history just by looking at it long enough or holding it in her hand.

"There's *definitely* some positive energy inside this," Adrienne said, nodding resolutely.

"Energy?" Kara asked.

Adrienne fixed her eyes on her niece from across the table. "Oh yes. This ball carries the memories of the good times it helped create. I can feel it."

Kara only stared at her aunt, though Adrienne didn't seem put off by her niece's skepticism.

"Energy is everything and everything is energy, Kara. Remember that."

"Sounds a bit too circular," Kara said.

"Exactly. I'm glad you get it."

"Maybe. They never taught that in science class."

Adrienne scoffed. "Be careful about believing everything they teach you in school." She set down the ball and moved on to a vintage ink pen. "This wrote letters that changed lives," she declared, inspecting its chipped nib. "It sealed some important deals in its time, too."

Kara held her tongue. In her opinion, the history of everything on that table—and in that store—was likely far more ordinary than Adrienne imagined. Still, her aunt's whims were oddly endearing… even if Kara herself was too pragmatic to share in them.

The bell above the door jangled as a stern-looking woman marched into the shop, lugging a large cardboard box.

"Oh!" Adrienne pulled herself away from the table and rushed to the woman. "Let me give you a hand with that, Debra."

"I've got it," Debra replied curtly, despite obviously struggling with the weight as she brushed past Adrienne. She heaved the box onto the central table with a *thud* that rattled everything else on the surface.

"New donations?" Adrienne asked, peering eagerly at the box.

Debra gave a brisk nod. "Just dropped off this morning." She went behind the nearby counter that sported the cash register and started flipping through some paperwork, keeping her back to Adrienne.

Speaking of energy, Kara thought as she glanced back and forth between the two women. There was near-palpable tension coming from Debra. *This woman is not fond of my aunt.* Debra was thin with shoulder-length, straight chestnut hair with a few strands of grey that stood out; her mouth seemed perpetually stuck in a frown.

Adrienne started sifting through the box of new donations, outwardly oblivious to how the other woman felt about her. Though Kara had a feeling Adrienne knew.

If she's so perceptive about the energy from a baseball, then she should be able to sense that.

The bell jingled again as a teenage boy pushed himself

into the store, also carrying a box, larger and bulkier than Debra's.

"Over there, Cole!" Debra called out sharply from behind the counter. She gestured to an empty space on the floor near the entrance. "Put it right there."

Cole shuffled over and set the box down heavily where the woman had indicated. He straightened up, rolling his shoulders to relieve the tension from carrying the awkward load.

He had a lean, athletic build, evident even beneath his loose-fitting plaid shirt. His unkempt, dirty-blond hair fell across his forehead. He turned, then seemed to notice for the first time that there were customers in the store. When his eyes landed on Kara, he appeared transfixed, unable to peel his gaze away. Kara saw his Adam's apple bob as he swallowed nervously.

The moment was broken by Debra's sharp voice. "Cole! I need you to unpack and sort those donated clothes from yesterday."

Cole jumped, as if snapped out of a trance. "Y-yes, ma'am," he stammered. He disappeared into a nearby side room, turning on a light as he went inside.

Kara watched him go, amused by the encounter. She could tell instantly that the country boy had been intrigued by her presence. It probably wasn't often that there was a new face around Silver Falls.

Kara was surprised to find herself equally intrigued. *You rarely meet guys like him in Chicago,* she thought. At first glance, he seemed rugged and fashioned by manual work—unlike the boys in her high school who were more polished and refined. To her, boys like him existed mainly in pop-country songs and movies, not in her daily life.

And she didn't even *like* country music. Still, she couldn't deny her curiosity.

Lost in her own world, Adrienne hadn't seemed to notice the exchanged glances between Cole and her niece. She only continued rummaging enthusiastically through the donation box.

"Oh my," Adrienne said, eyes wide with delight. "Kara, you *must* come see this."

Kara shuffled over to her aunt, expecting another mundane item deemed as treasure. Instead, she recoiled.

Adrienne held a foot-tall statue. The figure's body was so thin that it was nearly skeletal. Its bony arms hung rigidly at its sides, hands curled into gnarled claws. Most striking was the mask—its leering grin stretched unnaturally wide, and slanted eyes seemed to peer out with malicious glee.

"Ugh," Kara said, unable to help herself.

"This has a *very* old energy," Adrienne muttered to herself, staring at the thing with wonder.

Debra closed a filing cabinet drawer with a metallic scrape. As she turned, her gaze fell upon the leering statue and she let out a shriek—the papers in her hands dropped to the tiled floor, scattering.

"It's okay, Debra," Adrienne said, the other woman's reaction finally taking her attention from her discovery. "It's just a statue."

Debra's face contorted in revulsion as she gaped at the idol. "What *is* that thing? Was it donated?" Despite her horror, it seemed some morbid fascination prevented her from looking away completely.

"He's cute," Adrienne said.

"He is *not*," Debra spat. "He looks like the devil."

Adrienne cast a knowing glance at Kara that Kara felt

she was expected to decipher. Perhaps Adrienne was amused at Debra's immediate assumption that anything remotely from another culture was of the devil. To Kara, that made sense. If the number of churches they'd passed on their way from the airport was any indication, the general population of Silver Falls was probably a God-fearing bunch.

"Well, someone in this town must've owned him at one point," Adrienne replied. "I'm guessing the stuff in this thrift store is dropped off locally, right?"

Debra scowled. She didn't seem to like the thought that anyone in her town would ever keep such a thing inside their home.

"How much?" Adrienne asked.

"You want it?" Debra asked, her eyebrows shooting upwards. "Just take it. Get it out of here."

Adrienne shot her niece a look, one that seemed to say they'd just gotten themselves a great deal.

3

"Like I said, you never know what's going to call out for you in there," Adrienne told Kara as they left the air-conditioned store and walked into the blazing heat of the parking lot. She still cradled the statue like a baby.

"I think I preferred the baseball," Kara said.

"The baseball was intriguing, true, but there's a different energy in this piece—one much older and wiser. We could learn a lot from it."

Learn? Kara wondered. She'd assumed her aunt was just going to put the figure on a shelf. *Learn what? And how?* She couldn't fathom how Adrienne believed this thing was anything more than rock.

When they got into the car, Adrienne tried to pass the statue over to Kara. "You can have the honor of holding our new friend."

Kara recoiled. "No thanks, I'm good."

"Now you're starting to sound like Debra," Adrienne said before letting out a playful tut. "Don't tell me you have superstitions about this little guy, too."

The statue's carved grin seemed to grow more sinister in that moment, as if inviting Kara to touch him.

When Kara didn't respond, Adrienne said, "Well, we can't make him ride in the trunk. He's part of the family now."

"Maybe I just have to... get used to him," Kara mumbled.

Adrienne leaned over and deposited the statue onto the floor at Kara's feet, then started the engine.

As they pulled out of the parking lot, Kara couldn't resist glancing down at the sculpture. Its empty stone eyes seemed fixed on her. A tingling chill crept up her legs, so she shifted, angling her feet away.

"So, what's the deal with that lady back there?" Kara asked, mainly to distract herself from the statue's gaze. "The one who runs the thrift shop."

Adrienne glanced over. "You mean Debra? Yeah, she's never been too fond of me."

So I was right, she isn't clueless, Kara thought. "Why?"

"Being the good Christian woman she is, my spiritual beliefs don't sit well with her."

"Oh." Kara remembered the display of crystals in the guest bedroom. Those rocks would probably set off alarm bells in Debra's religious worldview. She'd likely condemn them as pagan idols or, at the very least, New-Age nonsense.

Not sure I believe they work, either, Kara thought. *Maybe Aunt Adrienne's right. Maybe I am more like Debra than I think...*

"Church on Sunday isn't for everyone," Adrienne said. "And unfortunately, some of those churchgoers don't care for the non-church folks like myself. But it's alright, I pay her no mind," Adrienne continued breezily.

"That's kind of sad, actually," Kara said.

"A couple of years ago, Debra sent the pastor from her church to my house," Adrienne recalled with amusement. "He tried to get me to accept Jesus Christ as my lord and savior and all that."

Kara's mouth fell open at the audacity. "What did you do?"

"I had to gently but firmly tell him that I appreciated his concern, but I was quite settled on my spiritual journey."

Kara shook her head in disbelief. "I don't think I could be as nice as you in that situation." Religion had never been her thing. Back in Chicago, she'd been invited to church by a handful of people over the years. She'd gone one time, then quickly decided it wasn't for her; she agreed with her mother's negative assessment of organized religion, and also agreed that the answers to life's big questions were to be found in science. After that single church visit, she'd begun politely declining any and all invitations to Sunday morning services. She could tell that the friends who'd invited her were disappointed, but they thankfully hadn't pressed the issue. They *definitely* never would've sent a preacher to her doorstep. If they had, Kara knew it would have really gotten under her skin, and she certainly wouldn't have handled it with her aunt's grace. "So even after that, you kept shopping at her store?"

"Sure. Why not? There's always something great to find there." Adrienne glanced down at the "new member of the family" between Kara's ankles before returning her eyes to the road. "Plus, it's good to support a local small business. The woman has had her work cut out for her ever since her husband passed away about a decade ago. I don't want her to struggle any more than she already has. Our beliefs may be different, but she's just doing what she thinks is right."

Kara felt a swelling respect for her aunt, who'd remained unruffled by Debra's animosity and still supported the woman's business. *There's no way I could be so nice to someone who openly didn't like me.*

"I don't see the need to meet anger with more anger," Adrienne explained. "Negativity breeds more negativity. But if you counter it with positivity, sometimes minds and hearts can be changed."

"I guess that makes sense," Kara said.

"Saw you making eyes at that boy back at the shop," Adrienne said, shooting Kara a knowing glance.

"What?" Kara felt her cheeks flush—she'd assumed her aunt had been too engrossed in her new statue to notice. "No I wasn't."

"I'm just messing with you," Adrienne chuckled. "Even though he's Debra's son, you have to admit he's cute."

Kara shrugged, trying to act casual. "I guess. Not really my type."

"Opposites attract, and all that."

"Maybe in the movies," Kara said, "but this isn't a movie."

She shifted in her seat, suddenly remembering their silent passenger. Almost involuntarily, her eyes drifted down. Its hollow gaze remained fixed on her, as if it had been listening to every word.

4

Back home, they climbed out of the car into the still, summer evening. Cicadas buzzed from the nearby trees.

Inside, Adrienne made a beeline for the fireplace and reverently centered the statue on the mantel.

Kara watched uneasily. She'd hoped her aunt would tuck the unnerving figure away somewhere else. Instead, it held court over the living room like a prized possession. Its hollow stare swept from corner to corner, as if claiming ownership of its new domain.

Adrienne admired the statue for a few more seconds before turning to face her niece, oblivious to her discomfort. "You ready for some dinner?"

Kara nodded. The hunger had settled in during the drive home.

As soon as Adrienne headed off to the kitchen to cook, Kara went upstairs to her bedroom, where she retrieved her textbooks. She'd brought her full set for the coming year's classes—Biology, Chemistry, Pre-Calculus, AP Literature, and AP US History. Just looking at the stack gave her a swell of motivation. Her friends had made fun of her for studying over the summer, but she didn't care—she was determined to get a head start before the school year began. This was a key part of her earning and keeping a high GPA. That, and she'd heard from others that junior year Chemistry was incredibly difficult—a head start would be invaluable.

She brought the books down to the living room, where she sank onto the sofa and opened her Biology textbook. She read and reread a section on cellular reproduction, mouthing the steps silently. *Prophase, metaphase, anaphase, telophase.* She'd reviewed that part a few days before her flight but still didn't quite have it down. In the kitchen, cabinets opened and closed as Adrienne prepared dinner.

Amidst the sounds of chopping and sizzling oil, Kara struggled to focus, reading the same paragraphs repeatedly. The fine hairs on her neck prickled and her gaze drifted up to the statue leering down from the mantel. Though unmoving, its carved eyes seemed to track her every shift and fidget.

This is so stupid, Kara thought. *It's just a statue.*

Despite trying to convince herself, she changed seats from the sofa to a nearby recliner and angled the chair in such a way as to put her back mostly to the statue... which only helped for a few minutes. She still sensed the watchful presence.

Giving up, she closed her textbook.

Maybe I'll be able to focus better in my room, she thought. *Or on the porch.*

Adrienne appeared in the doorway, wiping her hands on a dish towel. "Food's ready."

"Awesome," Kara said, standing quickly, happy for an excuse to leave the living room.

As she left, she cast one more glance at the statue, as if some invisible force drew her eyes to it.

She froze.

It had rotated slightly. As if turning to watch her go.

No way. Kara blinked. *It was like that before, right?* She wasn't sure. She couldn't remember. But somehow it *seemed* to be in a different position.

I'm just being paranoid, Kara told herself, and with that, she went into the dining room. She settled at the table as Adrienne emerged from the kitchen bearing two steaming plates.

"Vegetable stir-fry."

Kara inhaled the savory aroma. The rainbow mixture of snap peas, bell peppers, carrots, and broccoli over brown rice looked both healthy and appealing.

Adrienne disappeared back into the kitchen and returned with two glasses of creamy white liquid, which Kara eyed suspiciously.

"Goat milk," Adrienne explained. "Straight from nature, with no chemicals or preservatives."

"From the neighbors?" Kara presumed.

Adrienne seemed impressed. "How did you know?"

"I have a good view of their animals from my bedroom."

"Have you ever had goat milk?" Adrienne asked.

"No." In Kara's experience, milk only came in bright cartons from the grocery store.

"Give it a shot. You'll feel like a whole new person."

Not wanting to seem ungracious, Kara took a tentative sip. It tasted sweeter than she'd expected, with a tangy undertone. She nodded approvingly at Adrienne, who seemed pleased. Kara doubted she'd drink the entire glass, though. It was… strange.

"So what were you reading out there?" Adrienne asked before taking a bite of stir-fry.

Kara swallowed a piece of broccoli. "Oh, just reviewing some biology. I like to stay ahead for next year's classes."

Adrienne tilted her head, looking both puzzled and concerned. "You brought your textbooks? For summer vacation?"

"Of course," Kara said matter-of-factly.

"Honey, summer is for taking a *break*," Adrienne said gently. "You need to give that big brain of yours a rest."

"I like to be prepared. And also review some stuff from last year, so I don't forget it all."

Adrienne studied her niece for a moment. "Well, I think you deserve a little R&R while you're here. Your mother was the same way when we were in school— always trying to get ahead and stay ahead. I watched her burn out a time or two."

"And she hasn't changed," Kara said. "A time or two" was putting it mildly. Kara had seen her mother burn out many more times. *But she should be fine for a while after these three months in Europe,* she couldn't help but think.

She appreciated her aunt's sentiment, but her study habits were ingrained. They gave her a sense of control and purpose.

"I… know this isn't where you wanted to spend your summer," Adrienne said, her voice gentle yet earnest. Kara paused, her fork hovering over the plate. She looked up, surprised by the sudden change in tone. "I just want you to know that it means the world to me that you're here, even if this wasn't your first choice." Adrienne's eyes were kind, her smile tinged with sympathy. Kara opened her mouth to protest, but Adrienne raised a hand. "It's okay, you don't have to pretend. Silver Falls isn't Chicago, and I also know big cities are more your speed. And I'm sure being stuck out here with your weird aunt wasn't how you envisioned your summer vacation. But I'm grateful to have this time with you."

Kara looked down, realization dawning—her aunt had seen right through her lackluster mood, her distracted politeness. Still, she appreciated Adrienne's honesty, and found her sincerity touching.

"Thanks, Aunt Adrienne," Kara said softly. "I know I've been kind of... pouting since I got here. But really, I'm glad we have this chance to hang out."

Adrienne beamed. She reached out her hand, palm up on the table. Kara took it, and her aunt gave it a small squeeze as they shared a smile.

5

A piercing rooster's crow jolted Kara awake. As she blinked in the muted dawn light, it took a moment to get her bearings in the unfamiliar bedroom.

Another screeching call came from outside, and Kara realized the rooster must live on the neighbor's property. She stifled a groan. *Getting woken up by a rooster at dawn is the most country thing ever.*

Downstairs, Kara wandered into the kitchen. The scent of fresh coffee lingered in the air, but the room was empty. A mug sat half-full and abandoned on the counter, telling her that Aunt Adrienne had gotten up even earlier.

Kara checked the living room, where early-morning light filtered through the curtains. There, she found no sign of Adrienne.

Is she not home? Kara wondered. She pulled aside the curtain to check if her aunt's car was parked in front of the house. When she looked, though, she spotted Adrienne on the porch, sitting lotus-style on a cushion, meditating while facing the rising sun.

Not wanting to disturb her, Kara sank into the worn couch. The living room felt eerily quiet, so Kara instinctively scanned the room for a television, but didn't find one. *She doesn't own a TV? How did I not notice that before?*

Back home, the TV was a great way to fill any silence with mindless chatter and flashing images. But here, Aunt Adrienne seemed content with stillness and quietude.

Without a TV, the only thing in the room her eyes were drawn to was the statue on the fireplace mantel. She shifted and averted her gaze. The silence felt heavier now.

This is ridiculous, she thought.

But as irrational as it was, her discomfort only grew. Kara stood, decision made. She'd go upstairs, get back in bed, and maybe read for a bit as she waited for Adrienne to finish meditating.

Just as she turned toward the stairs, though, the front door creaked open. Aunt Adrienne breezed in, barefoot and clad in a loose, flowing dress. "Good morning, sweetie," she said. "Sleep well?"

Kara paused on the first step. "Yeah. But the rooster was… unexpected."

"You'll get used to him," Adrienne said as she walked toward the kitchen. "How about some breakfast? I'm thinking blueberry pancakes."

"Can't say no to that." Kara followed Adrienne, suddenly excited by the prospect of food.

A few minutes later, Adrienne started cooking. "Could you grab the blueberries?" she asked as she whisked eggs and milk together.

Kara went to the fridge, where she found the berries on the bottom shelf. She carried them over to the counter, enjoying how the smell of melting butter in the pan filled the kitchen.

"You know," Adrienne said, "after we finish breakfast, I thought we could do something outside before it gets too hot."

"What did you have in mind?"

Adrienne grinned. "You'll see. I think you'll enjoy it."

Kara couldn't help but frown. The last time Adrienne had taken her on a little excursion, they'd returned with the monstrosity in the living room.

———

KARA SQUINTED against the glare of sunlight bouncing off the windshield. As they cruised down the road, the trees on either side became an endless sea of green that blurred together.

"I admittedly don't get as much exercise as I should, but when I go for my walks, I like to do them before it gets too late in the day," Adrienne said.

"Makes sense," Kara said. The sedan's air conditioning already struggled to keep up with the Mississippi heat, and Kara could feel sweat beading at the nape of her neck. "And where exactly are we going?"

"To Lake Silver. Because you're spending some time here, I figured it should be one of the first things you see. Since our town is named after it."

They came to a stop in a small gravel lot several minutes later. As Kara stepped out of the car, the loud *crunch* of rocks under her feet echoed in the quiet of the wooded area they'd arrived at.

"There's a shortcut to the lake right there, but short-cuts are never as much fun," Adrienne said. "Let's go this way." She gestured toward a wooden sign displaying "Nature Trail" in faded letters.

Kara followed her aunt. The path was narrow, forcing them to walk single file. Branches reached out from either side and threatened to snag her clothes.

"Watch your step," Adrienne called over her shoulder. "These trees are hundreds of years old, so their roots are everywhere."

As if on cue, Kara's foot caught on a gnarled root protruding from the ground. She stumbled and barely managed to catch herself before she face-planted into the dirt.

They continued on, following the trail markers deeper into the woods. The canopy overhead grew denser. Despite the shade, Kara could feel sweat trickling down her back. The air was thick, humid, and felt like it clung to her skin. She swatted at a mosquito that buzzed near her ear. Fallen twigs cracked underneath her sneakers.

"Would you say you're the outdoorsy type?" Adrienne asked.

"Eh…" Kara contemplated how to respond to that. "Usually swimming pools and tennis courts. Not so much actual… woods. With the bugs."

"We're communing with nature, dear. Opening ourselves up to the energy of the earth. The bugs have every right to be here with us."

Of course you'd see it that way, Kara thought. Still, she had to admit that being surrounded by towering trees and the soft sounds of the forest was… different. And not necessarily in a bad way.

Their hike continued for about fifteen minutes longer, and Kara was surprised when she started to get winded. Stepping over roots and avoiding thorny plants made the hike more challenging than she'd expected.

As they rounded a bend in the path, the trees opened

up, revealing a vast expanse of shimmering water. Lake Silver stretched out before them, its surface a mirror reflecting the cloudless sky above.

"I come here often," Adrienne said as she settled onto one of the nearby benches. "It's peaceful in a way that you can't find anywhere else in town. And in a way, I feel like the lake remembers the distant past. Things humanity has forgotten over the generations."

Kara sat down beside her aunt. Adrienne had told her yesterday that she also believed the lake to be sacred, just as the Natives had. To Kara's eyes, it didn't seem to be anything special. The brown water and the shore's muddy edges gave the perimeter a swampy look.

It's still nice, though, Kara thought. *Definitely peaceful.*

"I come here when I need to think, or when I'm seeking guidance," Adrienne continued. "Sometimes, if you listen closely enough, you can almost hear the whispers."

At that moment, Kara could only hear the combined sounds of no less than ten different species of insects.

"And I make sure to get here early because by noon, this place will be filled with teenagers swimming, shouting, and drinking. And also it gets hot." She sighed.

They sat there together in silence for a while. The mid-morning heat bore down on Kara, but she didn't mind. It didn't take her long to embrace the tranquility that the lake offered.

Aunt Adrienne might have a point, she thought. *Maybe I don't spend enough time just... sitting.*

That would have to be something she'd have to change once she returned to her normal life in Chicago.

———

THAT EVENING, Kara sat on the living room sofa, idly flipping through a dog-eared paperback she'd found on the bookshelf. Adrienne had been upstairs in her bedroom for quite some time, but eventually came down and took a seat in the chair beside the sofa.

"That's a good one," she said when she noticed the book Kara held. She then grabbed a magazine from the small table between the couch and chair, flipped it open, and started reading.

Kara tried to refocus on the pages, but the silence of the room soon became too much for her. She shifted and looked around, wondering how her aunt could tolerate so much quiet.

"What's wrong?" Adrienne asked, having noticed Kara's shuffling.

"It's so… quiet."

Adrienne smiled. "Isn't it nice?" Kara didn't respond. "Oh, right. You're used to all the city noise."

"Yeah… but it isn't just that. Don't you own a TV?"

Adrienne's eyebrows shot up. "You like TV?" She set her magazine aside and got up from the chair, then disappeared down the hallway that led to the back of the house.

I like TV? Kara wondered. *What kind of question is that? It's just something people do.*

Adrienne returned lugging a twenty-inch old-school television, which she lowered onto the coffee table facing Kara. Kara watched, amused, as her aunt unraveled the cord and plugged it into a nearby outlet.

"So you *do* own a TV," Kara said. It was one that had both a VHS player and a DVD slot built into the base. "Why don't you keep it in here like a normal person?"

"Because I don't have much use for it, so it usually lives

in the spare room." Adrienne brushed the dust off the top of it.

Kara's brow furrowed. "But don't you watch the news?"

Adrienne looked genuinely confused by the question. "Why would I want to watch the news?"

"To know what's going on in the world? Mom and I watch it every single night back home."

"Oh, honey," Adrienne said, shrugging. "If there's something important, I'll hear about it. I don't need a TV to tell me."

Kara stared at her aunt, baffled. "What about big events? Like 9/11?" Not even a year later, the memory of that terrible day was still fresh.

"That's what I mean. People were talking about it in town. How could I *not* have heard about it? In fact..." Adrienne thought for a moment. "Yeah, that was actually the last time I watched the news."

Kara wasn't sure how to respond. The idea of not being constantly connected to world events seemed... wrong.

But before she could formulate a reply, Adrienne had moved on, rummaging through a nearby cabinet while saying, "Who needs news when you can watch a good movie?" She pulled a VHS tape from the cabinet. "*Harold and Maude.* It came out in 1971 and still holds up."

Kara squinted at the worn cassette cover. "Never heard of it."

"I figured. That means you're in for a treat." Adrienne slid the VHS into the player.

As Kara's aunt settled into the couch beside her, Kara couldn't help but feel skeptical about an old movie her eccentric aunt loved. *It's probably going to be weird and boring.*

The film began, and Kara found herself drawn in despite her initial reservations. She was both shocked and entertained as young Harold staged elaborate fake suicides and attended strangers' funerals. And then there was Maude—vibrant, quirky, and full of spirit, even with her advanced age.

"I see why you like this," Kara said during a quiet moment about an hour in, glancing at her aunt.

As the story unfolded, Kara found herself captivated. She laughed at Maude's antics, marveled at her free-spirited approach to life, and had a lump form in her throat at the film's bittersweet conclusion.

When the credits rolled, Kara sat in silence, processing what she'd just watched. "Yep, you were right. That was good."

Adrienne nodded, a knowing smile on her face. "Like I said, beats the news any day." She leaned forward and pressed the rewind button so the tape would be ready for the next time she wanted to watch the movie. "And it's a great reminder to be true to yourself even when the rest of the world thinks you're weird."

"Yeah," Kara said, though she didn't think her aunt needed the encouragement.

After the tape was rewound, Adrienne unplugged the TV, wrapped up the cable, and started carrying it back to its hiding place, as if leaving it in the living room would create too much temptation. "Let me know when you're ready for more cinematic works of art. Until then... I'm heading to bed."

6

Once again, Kara was woken up by the neighbor's rooster, the shrill crows pulling her out of her sleep.

So... this is going to be an every-morning thing, she thought. *Great.*

She tossed beneath the quilt, the old metal bed frame creaking at the slightest movement. As she settled onto the limp pillow again, an unnerving prickle skittered down her neck. She had the feeling of unseen eyes watching.

Now alert, Kara scanned the shadowy room. Her gaze landed on the dresser across from the bed. Dread curdled in her stomach.

The statue from the thrift store was leering back at her.

Kara shot upright. Her breath came in shaky gasps as she looked into the hollow stone eyes.

How the hell...

She flung the blankets aside and picked up the tank top she had been wearing the previous day, which she'd discarded onto the floor before going to sleep. She threw it over the statue, covering its face. Perhaps it was foolish, but she felt much better now that the statue's gaze was no longer upon her.

Then Kara stormed out of the bedroom and marched down the staircase, fuming.

What kind of sick joke was that? she thought. *Why'd Aunt Adrienne put it in my room?*

Kara looked through the living-room window; Adrienne was meditating in the same spot she'd been in yesterday morning.

Kara stepped out onto the porch, the air already humid. Adrienne's eyes were closed, face serene, as she drew in long, steady breaths.

As irritated as she was, Kara didn't want to interrupt Adrienne. Yet before she could slip back inside, her aunt spoke without opening her eyes.

"Good morning," she said, voice calm. "Was it the rooster again?"

Adrienne's composure only frustrated Kara more after the unsettling start to her day. "Are you trying to mess with me?" she demanded sharply.

Adrienne opened her eyes and looked at her niece, surprised. "What do you mean?"

Kara huffed. "That *statue*. It was in my room when I woke up." She suppressed a shudder at the memory.

Adrienne's brow furrowed. "I didn't put it in your room, I promise. I wouldn't do something like that to you."

Studying her aunt's expression, Kara felt her initial anger dissipate—she sensed her aunt was telling the truth.

Which left one question.

"So if you didn't move it... who did?"

"Show me," Adrienne said, standing up.

Kara went back inside, Adrienne following close behind. She paused in the living room to check the fireplace mantel, as if to confirm that the statue was no longer there.

"Huh," Kara heard her say.

Upstairs, Kara stopped in the open doorway of her bedroom, allowing Adrienne to enter first. Her aunt went to the dresser, where the tank top draped over the statue created a vague, unsettling silhouette.

"There," Kara said, a note of vindication in her voice. "I woke up and it was just *there*. Staring at me."

Without responding, Adrienne lifted the shirt off and studied the statue's face. Kara held her breath, half-expecting the figure to have changed or moved, but it looked the same as it had earlier.

Then Kara felt her eyes go wide as a terrifying thought struck her. "Someone was in the house last night!" she blurted out. "That's the only thing that makes sense. Did you hear anything that sounded like someone breaking in?"

But Adrienne only turned back to Kara with a thoughtful look. There was a hint of a smile on her lips.

"Why are you smiling?" Kara asked, alarmed. *What am I missing here?*

"I *knew* it," Adrienne said.

"Knew what?"

"There's a spirit inside our statue."

7

Kara blinked several times. At first, she didn't think she'd heard her aunt correctly. But then she realized this was indeed Adrienne she was speaking with. *Of course* the woman had come to that conclusion.

"A spirit?"

"Yes!" Adrienne's voice spiked upward with excitement. "The spirit that lives within this statue moved itself into your room while we slept."

Kara stared incredulously. "What? You think the statue just got up and walked in here by itself?"

"It didn't walk, no. But its energy—its spirit—can clearly transport the vessel it inhabits," Adrienne explained.

"That's impossible," Kara scoffed. "There has to be a logical explanation." As the words spilled out, she realized there was no way her aunt would actually agree with her.

Adrienne just flashed her a small, knowing smile. "Open your mind, Kara. There are mysteries in this world beyond what we can see and touch. And *definitely* beyond what's in your science textbooks."

Kara crossed her arms, gaze flickering between her aunt and the statue. There was no rational justification for what had happened. Yet believing the object had moved itself, guided by some kind of spirit? That was absurd.

Wasn't it?

"Well, can you ask it to not sneak into my room while I'm sleeping?" As long as her aunt had made her mind up, Kara knew she had no choice but to play along.

Adrienne didn't respond, just picked up the statue and cradled it in her hands. She looked down at its masked face, almost expectantly, as if waiting for it to speak out loud to her.

Kara grimaced, put off by the connection she thought she saw blossoming between her aunt and a… statue.

She brushed past Kara and went downstairs, then to the living room. Kara followed and watched Adrienne return the statue to its previous place on the mantel. She took a few steps back and studied it with her hands on her hips like it was an object in a museum.

"I would've thought having a spirit attached would mean we should get rid of it," Kara said, hopeful.

"Don't be silly, Kara, you can't get rid of it. Spirits have a way of imprinting onto objects, and once they do, it's nearly impossible to separate them," Adrienne explained. "They choose things that are meaningful to them. Look at this little man." She gestured toward the statue. "He's clearly from a different time. He could be centuries old, perhaps even millennia. The spirit could've been inside there for a thousand years by this point." As she spoke, her eyes lit up more and more, as if the prospect excited her and gave her energy.

"I guess I meant get rid of the statue itself," Kara ventured. "I'm not trying to… kick a spirit out of its home. Just… I don't want to be freaked out. You know?"

"There's nothing to be afraid of, Kara," Adrienne said. "As long as we treat him with respect, then we'll be fine."

Kara didn't like the sound of that. "What happens if we don't?"

"Why wouldn't we treat him with respect? Why *wouldn't* we welcome him into our home?"

Kara stared at her aunt, her skepticism warring with an unsettling feeling in the pit of her stomach. Adrienne seemed almost delusional in her insistence about this so-called spirit.

Adrienne must've deduced the thoughts that were surging through Kara. "I understand your doubts. But there are more dimensions to this world than you realize. If you open yourself to them, you'll see."

Kara bit her lip. Arguing would get her nowhere. "Well, possessed or not, I don't want it in my room again tonight," she said.

"And I think I know just how to make sure of that."

Adrienne swept past her and into the kitchen, leaving her alone with the statue.

What is she talking about? Kara thought.

Adrienne returned to the living room a moment later, carrying a small plate topped with two pieces of bread in one hand and a glass of water in the other.

"What's all this for?" Kara asked.

Adrienne put the bread on one side of the statue and the water on the other.

"You're *feeding* it?" Kara asked, incredulous.

"They're offerings," Adrienne said. "It's a way to welcome the spirit into our home. To be honest, I should have thought to do this yesterday."

"And the spirit will… take these offerings?"

"We can only hope."

"It must not be too picky if you're only giving him bread and water."

"The specific offerings aren't as important as the intention behind them. It's a symbolic gesture, an invitation to exist harmoniously together."

Kara had a hard time imagining the statue coming to life in the middle of the night to eat the little snack that had been laid out for it. Yet her aunt seemed completely serious.

"Have you done this before?" Kara asked.

Adrienne glanced over at her with a small smile. "No, not exactly. But I feel like I've been preparing for something like this my whole life."

"Preparing how?"

"Well, I've read many, many books and accounts from people who work with spirits. Learning about how to commune with them, welcome them, and gain their wisdom." She ran a gentle finger over the statue's oversized, masked face. "I guess you could say I've been educating myself, so that if I ever had the honor of hosting a spirit in my home, I'd know exactly how to make them feel comfortable. And now I finally do."

Kara shifted as she listened. Her aunt spoke about this supernatural stuff in such a matter-of-fact manner—as if it were normal. "And the books told you that leaving it bread and water would do the trick?"

"Like I said, offerings are just a symbolic way of showing respect and good intentions."

Kara was still uneasy, but clearly this meant a lot to Adrienne. With a sigh, Kara resigned herself to going along with her aunt's eccentric notions, at least for now.

"And that food will keep him out of my room tonight?" After all, that was the main thing she cared about.

"Almost certainly," Adrienne said, giving a firm, resolute nod.

8

Kara's eyes fluttered open as the rooster's crowing traveled in through her bedroom window.

Doesn't he ever sleep in? Or take a break? Kara thought. Another, more unwelcome notion quickly followed it—*the statue.*

Suddenly, she was wide awake as her mind went to what had happened the previous morning.

She hesitated. A sense of foreboding kept her frozen in place.

I have to look eventually, she told herself. She had no idea what she'd do if that dumb little statue was perched up on her dresser again.

All at once, she mustered the resolve to sit up and look across the room.

No statue.

She let out a slow breath, heart thudding in her chest. She'd made it through the night with no supernatural intrusions.

Kara got up and went downstairs, where her eyes shot

to the fireplace mantel. The statue stood in the same place it had when she'd gone to bed. She hesitated at the foot of the stairs as she stared at the statue. The plate and cup were still on either side of it, but Kara was too far away and the morning light in the room wasn't yet bright enough to answer the question lingering in her mind. She felt compelled to get closer; once she did, what she hadn't wanted to see was confirmed.

The bread was gone, with only a few crumbs remaining. The water glass was empty.

Kara sighed. She was reminded of when she was a kid and her mother would encourage her to leave cookies and milk for Santa. She'd wake up the next morning to find them gone, allegedly eaten by the big man himself. But in reality, they'd just had been a midnight snack for her mom.

I don't believe that Aunt Adrienne would do this, Kara thought. There was no way the woman would get up in the middle of the night to eat the offerings just to mess with her niece. It didn't make any sense.

But a spirit inside the statue consuming the offerings made even less sense.

Kara stepped out onto the creaky wooden porch, where the morning dew still clung to the planks beneath her bare feet. Once again, Adrienne sat cross-legged at the far end, eyes closed, facing the sunrise. Her hands rested on her knees, palms upturned.

Kara hesitated, not wanting to disturb her aunt's meditation. But after a moment, Adrienne's eyes opened and landed on her niece, as if she'd been waiting for her to wake up.

"Come sit," Adrienne said, patting the space on the porch next to her.

Kara obliged, lowering herself down beside Adrienne and tucking her legs beneath her. She glanced uncertainly at her aunt, whose eyes were still alight with enthusiasm.

"Did you see?" Adrienne asked.

Kara nodded, but her aunt seemed oblivious to her discomfort.

"This is a good sign. It's a spirit of peace, not malice. We have nothing to fear."

"Then why does it have to live in such a creepy statue?"

Adrienne gave her a look. "Don't be like that. We still don't know where that statue or the spirit came from, but as I said yesterday, we can assume that whoever made it lived a long time ago. Of course they'd have a different aesthetic than we do nowadays."

"I guess." A part of her wanted to ask Adrienne if she had indeed removed the bread and water herself, but she held back. She had a feeling that question might offend Adrienne. Plus, deep down, she already knew that wasn't the case. "At least he wasn't in my room again," she said instead.

"I told you the offerings would work."

"So what happens now?" Kara asked.

"We give him more." She stood.

"More?"

"Oh yes. You wouldn't stop feeding a baby, would you?"

Now she's comparing this thing to a baby, Kara thought. *Why can't she just adopt a cat and be normal?*

Kara followed Adrienne back into the house. She watched as her aunt lifted the plate and glass from their places next to the statue.

"Normally, I would've done this first thing in the morning when I got up, but I wanted you to see for yourself that the spirit accepted our offering," Adrienne explained as she carried the dishes to the kitchen. She returned with fresh bread and water, which she placed on either side of the statue the same way she had the day before.

"There. That should keep our new friend satisfied." She gave the object an affectionate pat on its misshapen head.

"So you just... do this forever?"

Adrienne shrugged. "We'll have to pay attention and see how the spirit responds in the coming days and weeks."

Weeks. For the first time in her life, Kara actually had the thought that maybe it would be better if her summer vacation flew by. School sucked most of the time, but at least it was predictable—and without spirits.

The robotic ring of the house phone sounded from the kitchen.

"Only one person who'd call this early," Adrienne said.

Kara watched her aunt disappear into the kitchen.

"Hello?" Adrienne answered. "Good morning, Glenda."

Kara drifted into the dining room, where her aunt stood at the threshold of the kitchen. For some reason, even though the landline was cordless, Adrienne remained near the cradle, leaning against the doorway.

"Of course, I'd be happy to come get it. No trouble at all. Actually..." Adrienne turned and glanced at Kara. "My niece arrived the other day, so I'll send her over to pick it up instead. I'd love for you two to meet."

Who am I meeting? Kara wondered.

"Alright, great. She's coming now," Adrienne said, then hung up. "That was Glenda Norris, our neighbor just across the way. It's their barn you can see from your window. She has some fresh goat milk for us."

"You want me to go and pick it up?"

"Would you mind? Glenda and her husband Ed are getting on in age, and that field between our properties has a bunch of ditches and holes. I don't like the thought of them walking through it. And even better, it'll give you a chance to meet them."

"Sure," Kara said. Frankly, any excuse to get away from the unsettling statue was welcome.

"Great. You head over for the milk and I'll start breakfast. It'll be ready by the time you're back."

9

Kara went upstairs and changed. By the time she was ready to head out, Adrienne had started cooking breakfast as promised, the first smells beginning to fill the house.

She left through the front door and went around to the back. Even though it was still early, the morning was already hot and humid, and she knew it would only get more intense as the day wore on.

Kara reached the overgrown field that stretched between the two properties, filled with long grass and weeds. There, she recalled Adrienne's warning about the uneven terrain and trod cautiously. More than once, she stepped about an inch deeper than she'd anticipated, which threw her off balance. She agreed with her aunt—walking through this would definitely be treacherous for older folks.

But they're raising goats, so they still must be in decent shape.

She saw a small barn in the distance and heard the

muted bleating as she drew nearer to the neighbor's property.

Less than a minute later, Kara spotted a woman waiting along the fence line. She wore jeans and an oversized flannel shirt, and her snowy hair was swept into a tidy bun. As Kara neared, she could make out the deep wrinkles that creased the woman's face. Despite her age, though, her light eyes were lively and alert.

"You must be the niece. I'm Glenda. Welcome to town." She smiled and held out her hand.

"Kara Mills," she replied, shaking the offered hand. "Nice to meet you."

Two grocery bags were beside the woman's ankles, each containing what appeared to be a liter-size mason jar of milk.

"Adrienne can't get enough of this stuff," Glenda said. "She loves it."

"I tried it for the first time the other day," Kara said.

Glenda brightened. "And?"

"It was good." That was a slight fib. It hadn't been *bad,* but like almost everything else that had happened to her that summer, she knew it would take some getting used to —and she'd likely forget about it entirely once she was back home.

"I'm glad to hear that. I may be able to spare some more jars now that I know there are two of y'all over there. How long are you staying?"

"The whole summer."

Glenda blew out her breath. "Well, I'll see what I can do." She gestured to the bottles at her feet. "I can't promise there'll be enough, because I'll have to let Martha dry up for a couple of months so we can breed her again. Adrienne should remember that, but remind her for me, will you?"

"Sure," Kara said, making a mental note.

"How's Silver Falls treating you so far?" Glenda asked.

"Pretty good." Another fib.

"Where are you from?"

"Chicago."

"So this is *very* different for you."

"Oh yes," Kara said, chuckling. "But it's nice."

"I bet you've never milked a goat before, have you?"

Kara felt her smile falter as she sensed where this was going. "I haven't."

"Want to try?" Glenda seemed very excited by the prospect—Kara knew she'd feel guilty if she declined.

I moved south for the summer, so I might as well, right? she thought.

With a nod, Kara followed Glenda. As they made their way across the field, she noticed a large male goat with shaggy brown fur gazing at them.

"That's Ed the Goat," Glenda said. "Not just Ed—that's my husband's name. Ed the Goat."

"You named your goat after your husband?" Kara asked, amused.

"Yes. They look alike."

To Kara, the goat *did* have an uncanny resemblance to a scruffy old man, with his scraggly beard and hunched posture.

As they continued on, Kara noticed a rooster come strutting across the field, his brilliant red comb bobbing atop his head.

"That's Rocky," Glenda said, seeming to notice Kara's reflexive scowl. "Let me guess—he doesn't let you sleep in."

"Not at all," Kara said, her frustration slipping out before she could suppress it. A flash of panic coursed through her at how rude she might have sounded.

Glenda chuckled. "He's pretty good about making sure everyone in earshot's up at the crack of dawn."

Kara relaxed as she realized Glenda wasn't offended—in fact, the older woman seemed to share her sentiments.

They reached the small barn, where Glenda slid open the door and led them inside. The smell reminded Kara of a petting zoo she'd visited as a kid—earthy and pungent, with hints of hay. A handful of goats wandered about, nosing in corners for stray bits of food.

Glenda took a nearby white goat by the red collar it wore around its neck and ushered it toward a raised platform with metal fittings along the sides. "Alright, Martha, let's show our new friend here what you've got."

Kara watched as Glenda struggled to lower herself down to her knees beside the milking platform. The woman's joints audibly creaked when she settled onto the barn floor. Martha munched away at the food in the platform's trough, which distracted her enough to keep her still.

Once situated, Glenda took Martha's udder in her wrinkled hands and massaged it. After several seconds of that, Glenda wrapped her fingers around the goat's teats and squeezed in an alternating, rhythmic manner, squirting thin streams of milk into the metal pail below. Even though the woman had struggled to get low enough to do the work, there was deft precision in her hand movements, likely honed after years of practice. The milk made a light splattering sound as it hit the bottom of the empty bucket.

"Easy, right?"

"Seems simple," Kara said.

"You want to try?" Once again, the hopeful tone in the woman's voice kept Kara from declining.

"Sure." Even a month ago, she'd never have imagined herself milking a goat on a sweltering Mississippi morning. Part of her wanted to laugh at the absurdity of it all, while another part felt a strange excitement at trying something so far removed from her normal city life.

Glenda went to stand and give Kara room to take her place, but wasn't strong enough to get all the way up.

"Oh, here," Kara said, offering Glenda her hands. Glenda braced herself against Kara and managed to get upright.

Kara wondered how often Adrienne—or anyone else —checked on the Norrises. With Glenda struggling to even get down next to the milking stand, she might not have many goat-tending years left in her. Now she understood why Adrienne hadn't wanted Glenda walking all the way over to her house to deliver the milk.

Kara got into the same position Glenda had and took the soft, warm udder in her hands. She emulated what Glenda had done, but her uneven movements gave her away as a beginner.

"Don't be afraid, you won't hurt her," Glenda encouraged, so Kara started tugging harder. Streams of milk began shooting into the bucket.

If only my friends could see me now, she thought. *They'd never believe it.*

Though the experience was new and strange, there was an unexpected satisfaction in the motion. Kara settled into the repetitive task and found it almost relaxing. It also felt good to take care of Martha, giving her something that she needed.

After a minute or two, her forearms began to burn from the unfamiliar movement, but Kara persisted, determined to fill at least a decent portion of the pail. The goat seemed unbothered, munching her food as Kara worked.

"You're a natural," Glenda said—Kara had a hunch she told that to everyone she taught how to milk a goat.

When her arms could take no more, Kara gave a final squeeze and let the teats go, flexing her cramped fingers. She looked down at the several inches of milk she had collected, feeling a small sense of accomplishment.

"Well?" Glenda asked with an expectant smile.

"It's… actually kind of fun," Kara said.

"Working with goats will keep you young, that's for sure. Come anytime. We'll be happy to put you to work."

Kara straightened up and gave Martha a pat. "Aunt Adrienne's never going to believe I did that."

"If she doesn't, tell her to give me a call. I'll back up your story."

———

KARA MADE her way back through the overgrown field, the two mason jars of goat's milk heavy in her hands. The sun had risen higher now, and beads of sweat quickly formed along her hairline.

"There you are," Adrienne said when Kara stepped inside. The air conditioner was a welcome relief. "I was starting to wonder if you'd gotten lost."

"I milked my first goat!" Kara said as she set the jars on the counter, unable to keep the hint of pride from her tone.

Adrienne paused and looked at her, impressed. "You've only been here a few days and you're already a farm girl."

"Well, not quite." Although Kara couldn't deny the sense of accomplishment. She flexed her fingers, still feeling the odd sensation of the goat's udders, so different from anything she'd touched before.

They sat down to eat. Adrienne had made eggs, sausage, and biscuits served with—of course—goat's milk.

"Do the Norrises have any family around?" Kara asked as they ate. "Or anyone else who visits them regularly?"

"They have two adult sons. One's up in Memphis, the other in Birmingham, I think. They only visit once a year or so. Why?"

"When she was showing me how to milk one of the goats, it looked kind of hard for her. I had to help her stand up."

Adrienne's expression clouded with concern. "They've had goats ever since I've been living here, but yeah, eventually all that physical work takes a toll."

"I'm thinking of going back tomorrow morning," Kara said. "Just in case they need a hand with anything."

She'd surprised herself with the statement. So far, her life had more or less been devoid of manual labor; instead, her efforts had been entirely focused on school. But she felt herself wanting to accept Glenda's offer of coming back anytime to be put to work. She couldn't study all day, every day, after all. Also, getting out of the house—and away from the statue—wasn't a bad thing.

A slow smile crept over Adrienne's face. "I think they'd appreciate that very much."

"Might as well. As long as Rocky's around, it looks like I'm going to be up early every morning anyway."

10

After breakfast, Kara had helped Adrienne clean up the kitchen, then returned to the dining-room table for another session with her Biology textbook. She refused to study in the living room as long as the statue's watchful eye was there. Kindly spirit or not, it was off-putting. She could've moved the whole operation to her bedroom, but she didn't like that either. To her, the bed was for sleeping, not for studying.

She didn't get far before her phone chirped with a text. She flipped it open, the lime-green backlight glowing. The message was from her friend Olivia.

'How's the south treating you?'

Kara grinned. She went to type out a response, then hesitated, remembering her mother's warning before she'd gotten on the plane in Chicago.

"Don't run up the cell phone bill," she'd said.

Even though each text message cost only a couple of cents, Kara had learned the hard way soon after she'd gotten her own cell phone that they added up fast. Still, she needed to catch up with her friend.

'Can u call me? Free incoming.'

It was a strategy Kara often exploited—incoming calls to her cell phone were free. And since Olivia's parents didn't care how much they spent on their phone bills, it was always better for Olivia to call her instead of the other way around.

"Hey, Liv," Kara answered.

"I was starting to think you'd fallen off the face of the earth."

"Of course not. But it's been… interesting here." *And that's putting it lightly,* she thought. With the phone pressed to her ear, Kara went upstairs to her room and shut the door behind her.

"Interesting good or interesting weird?" Olivia asked with a hint of amusement.

"Both, I guess?" At once, she thought about the surprising amount of fun she'd had working with the Norrises… and the thrift-store statue that made her uncomfortable. She chose to tell her friend about the goat milking. Olivia could barely stop laughing.

"And what *else* are you doing besides milking goats?" Olivia finally managed.

"You know, summer stuff. Going for hikes. Watching old movies. Studying."

"Trying to 'get ahead.' "

"You sound like my aunt. She also thinks it's weird that I'm studying over the break."

"Your aunt's right, Kara."

"Maybe. Anyway, what's going on back home?"

Olivia filled Kara in on the details. The new deli had had its grand opening the day before, and Olivia was disappointed to report that it wasn't as great as they'd predicted. She tried to spin it as if Kara wasn't missing out on much… but it didn't quite work—even if the deli had turned out to be lame, Kara had wanted to discover that *with* her friends instead of hearing about it later.

Nina's beginning-of-summer pool party had been a hit, and somehow about twenty more people had shown up than were actually invited. *Well, Olivia exaggerates, so it was probably more like five,* Kara thought.

Olivia reported that her older brother had gotten laid off from his job at the auto plant and was stressed about finding new work.

"But yeah, that's about it. You're not missing much."

"Right," Kara said, not feeling like that was the case at all.

"Anyway, I have to run. You *are* planning to come back for junior year, aren't you? Or are you going to drop out of school and milk cows for the rest of your life?"

"Goats," Kara corrected. "And no. I'll be back in a couple of months. Promise." She laughed.

They hung up, and Kara returned downstairs to the dining room to resume studying. After about five minutes of reading, Kara realized she was still smiling from her conversation with Olivia. *Guess I didn't understand how badly I needed to hear from home,* she thought.

The landline phone rang with a loud trill, yanking Kara out of a paragraph on cellular respiration.

Adrienne, who'd been rummaging around in the kitchen, was close enough to answer it after only one ring. "Hello?" she said into the receiver, then turned to face Kara.

For a brief moment, Kara thought it might be her mother calling to check in, but Adrienne's expression told her otherwise.

Adrienne held out the phone. "It's for you."

"Who is it?" Kara asked.

Her aunt didn't answer. She only shook the phone as if beckoning Kara to come and take it. There was the faintest hint of a smile on the woman's face.

Kara walked across the dining room to the entrance of the kitchen, where the phone's cradle was affixed to the wall. *I literally just talked to Liv,* she thought. *Who would be calling me now?* Besides, none of her friends at her aunt's home phone number. Taking the phone, she raised it to her ear. "Hello?"

"Hi, Kara?" a male voice on the other end said, then cleared his throat.

"Yeah…"

"Hey, this is Cole. Cole Turner. From the thrift store. That my mom owns. I… saw you there the other day."

"Right. Hey."

"How are you doing?"

Kara could detect the nervousness in his voice. "I'm good. And you?"

She heard some shuffling footsteps just on the other side of the wall in the dining room—her aunt was eavesdropping.

"I'm good too." He cleared his throat again after a few more seconds of awkward silence. "Hey, so, I was thinking… since you're new here in town, that maybe you were bored. Or didn't know anyone or were looking for something to do. Would you want to go out and grab dinner tonight? There's a burger place that's really popular. I… think you'd like it."

"Umm. Sure," Kara found herself saying.

Why not? she thought. Cole had seemed harmless enough. Maybe having a new friend around Silver Falls would help the summer pass by faster.

"Great," Cole said—she could immediately tell he was relieved. "Uh… can you drive?"

"I don't have my license yet." That had been a huge fight between Kara and her mother. She'd turned sixteen in April, so all she had to do was take the test at the DMV to get her license, but there hadn't been time to go down there yet between the end of school and her mother's busy work schedule. Kara had wanted to get her license before traveling to Silver Falls, but her mother had refused. Now, she'd have to wait until after summer was over.

"Oh, no problem. I can pick you up."

"Okay," Kara said. "Do you know where my aunt lives?"

"In this town, everyone knows where everyone lives," he said with a small chuckle.

"Makes sense."

"Anyway, see you at seven?"

"Sure."

They hung up. As soon as they did, Adrienne appeared around the door, a knowing smile on her face. "Sounds like someone has a date."

"It isn't a *date*," Kara said.

"He's picking you up. Pretty sure that means it's a date."

"Why were you listening?" Kara shot back. Then she paused. "Oh—is it okay if I go? I mean, I didn't ask you first. Maybe you had something planned…"

Adrienne scoffed. "You don't need to ask me. I'm not your mother." With that, she returned to the kitchen to finish whatever she'd been doing before.

———

KARA STOOD in front of the bathroom mirror later that evening and brushed a few stray curls into place. She had opted for her dark green blouse that felt dressier than her normal t-shirts and tank tops, but not so fancy that it screamed "I'm on a date."

After a final glance to ensure everything was in order, Kara headed to the living room to wait for Cole's arrival. There, Aunt Adrienne was curled up on the couch, immersed in a book. She peered at Kara over her reading glasses and smiled.

"Don't you look lovely," Adrienne said. "I'm sure Cole will be quite smitten."

Kara sat in the armchair next to the couch, trying not to fidget. Her attention was once again involuntarily drawn to the statue perched on the mantel. As usual, its carved eyes seemed to follow her.

If nothing else, a night out is a good way to get away from him for a while, Kara thought.

Five minutes before seven, Kara heard tires coming up the gravel road that led to the house.

"Sounds like he's here," Adrienne said.

She stood up from the armchair. "I'll be back by ten," Kara said. "I have my phone if you need me." She held up her silver flip phone before slipping it into her pocket.

"I'm not your mother," Adrienne said for a second time that day, then returned her attention to her book.

The screen door squealed as Kara stepped out into the muggy evening. She was still trying to get accustomed to the wall of southern heat she encountered every time she left the air-conditioned home.

Cole had already gotten out of the truck and was walking up toward the house. He paused when he saw Kara come out.

"Hey." He nodded with a nervous smile.

"Hey there," Kara said as she walked the rest of the way down the porch steps. Up close, he had an easy-going demeanor, though she sensed his nerves beneath the surface.

As they approached Cole's lifted pickup, he darted ahead to chivalrously open the passenger door for her.

"Thanks," Kara said. Because of the towering height of the wheels, she had to step up onto the bulky tread plate and grasp the handle to hoist herself into the seat.

Cole ensured her feet were inside before closing the heavy door. He circled the hood to the driver's side and hopped in beside her, then turned the key in the ignition and the engine hummed to life.

"Is this your truck?" Kara asked, running her hands over the smooth leather seat. Everything about it looked brand new.

"It kind of belongs to the whole family, actually," Cole replied.

"It's really nice." Kara took in the polished dashboard and the faint new-car scent. "You don't see too many trucks like this where I'm from."

"And where's that?" Cole asked.

"Chicago," Kara said.

"Wow, Chicago." Cole let out a whistle. "I've never been. Only seen it in movies and stuff. What's it like?"

"It's fun," Kara said, her thoughts briefly turning to her friends and what they might be doing at that moment.

They'd laugh if they heard I was going out with a country boy right now, she thought.

Cole turned the truck off Adrienne's gravel driveway and onto the main road that would bring them into town.

"I've never even left Mississippi before," he said. "I bet Chicago makes this place seem pretty dull."

"I haven't seen much of Silver Falls yet, since I've only been here a few days, but it seems nice," Kara replied, trying to be diplomatic.

"It's really small. Everybody knows everybody," Cole explained. "Which can be good and bad, I guess."

He kept both hands positioned at the bottom of the steering wheel as he navigated the rural highway. After about five minutes of driving, a handful of buildings came into view.

"Main Street's just up ahead," Cole noted. "Duke's is the name of the place I was telling you about on the phone."

Kara gazed out the truck window as they drove down Main Street. The structures were a mix of old and new, with no real cohesion to the architecture. Some were built from weathered wood that looked to be from decades ago. Others had a more modern brick façade.

"How long has your family lived here?" Kara asked.

"Oh, a couple of generations, I think," Cole replied. "My grandpa started up the thrift store back in the '60s."

They passed a red-brick building with a bell tower that Kara guessed was one of the town's churches. The tall glass windows glowed from the light inside.

"That used to be the main church, but they've since built a brand new one, and it's much bigger, more modern," Cole said when he saw Kara looking. "You're welcome to come with us sometime. If you want."

"Thanks," Kara said, though she doubted she would take him up on that. Unlike burgers, church wasn't really her thing. Kara suddenly recalled the story Adrienne had shared about Cole's mother sending the local preacher to

Adrienne's house to confront her about her spiritual practices.

Like mother, like son, she thought.

"Here we are," Cole said, pulling the truck into a diagonal parking spot in front of a beige building. In an ornate red script, the sign read "Duke's Diner: Best Burgers this side of the Mississippi."

Cole held the door as they entered the cozy interior of the diner. Kara eyed the shiny leather booths and checkerboard tile floors. Behind the lunch counter, gleaming milkshake machines stood ready to serve.

A cheery hostess with a blonde ponytail greeted them with a bubbly, "Oh! Hey, Cole." The hostess's welcoming smile faltered a bit as her gaze landed on Kara. Her eyes flicked between them, clearly trying to place who the unfamiliar girl with Cole was. "For two? Inside or out?"

"Outside please, Amanda," Cole said.

As they followed the hostess, Kara couldn't help but wonder if she'd witnessed the beginnings of some gossip. In a small town, any new face would draw attention and speculation.

It's actually nice of him to risk that for me, Kara realized.

They passed through a door marked "Patio Seating" and into a cozy fenced-in patio. Mismatched tables and chairs were scattered across the area. Several ceiling fans spun lazily, stirring the humid air.

Kara sank into one of the seats, its metal curlicues pressing into her back.

"Good to see you, Cole," Amanda said, touching his shoulder as she walked away.

"Friend of yours?" Kara asked.

Cole only shrugged. "There's only one high school around here," he said.

"Is everyone going to hear from her about how you were eating with some girl from out of town?"

"Almost definitely," Cole said, smiling widely and laughing for the first time that evening. His teeth were perfectly straight.

"Thanks for enduring that for the sake of entertaining me," Kara said.

Cole only shrugged. "They can say what they want. I figured you seemed cool, so I wanted to hang out."

Nice of you to think that, even though we've never spoken before, Kara thought as she grabbed one of the menus and scanned the listings. There was a photo of the diner's signature burger—a towering behemoth with two beef patties slathered in melted cheese and topped with crispy onion rings. She wondered if she could even open her jaw wide enough to bite it.

"That cheeseburger looks intense," Kara said. "Think I could handle it?"

"Absolutely not," Cole said, earning a laugh from Kara.

The Light Duke seemed a bit more her speed. Smaller, and only had one patty.

A waitress with blonde hair pulled back into a ponytail bounced up to their table. "Hey Cole," she greeted warmly. At first, Kara thought the hostess had returned, but when she looked closer, she could just barely tell that this was a different girl—another cheery blonde.

"Uh, hey Elise," Cole replied, rubbing his palms on his jeans.

"How's your summer going so far?" she asked, shifting her weight to one leg. Without waiting for a reply, Elise turned her peppy smile toward Kara. "I'm Elise, nice to meet you."

"Kara. Nice to meet you, too."

"She's visiting from Chicago," Cole explained. "I'm showing her around town a bit."

"Oh, nice," Elise said, although Kara could tell that Elise's interest had immediately disappeared. "Y'all ready for something to drink?"

Kara ordered a water and Cole a sweet tea. Elise wrote it down and walked away, long ponytail swinging.

"I had no idea she worked here too," Cole said. "Must've just started. She wasn't here the last time I came, which was like two weeks ago."

He said something else, but Kara didn't hear it, as she was distracted by the busy patio area. She noticed quick, sideways glances cast her way from the other diners. At the next table, a couple eyed her curiously before leaning together to whisper to each other. A server balancing plates on his shoulder did a double-take as he passed. Kara shifted, self-conscious under the weight of all these fleeting yet obvious looks.

"You okay?" Cole asked.

"Yeah," Kara said quickly.

But Cole held her gaze, concerned. "Are people looking at you?"

Kara nodded, surprised he had noticed.

"Sorry about that. Folks around here just… aren't used to new faces. You're probably the most interesting thing to happen to Silver Falls all summer."

He grinned good-naturedly and Kara couldn't help smiling back, charmed by his awareness.

Elise returned with their drinks a few seconds later. "One sweet tea, one water."

After they ordered burgers, Cole unwrapped his straw. "You gotta try the sweet tea here. It's the best in town," he insisted, sliding the frosted glass towards her.

Kara took a polite sip and barely suppressed a wince at the cloyingly sweet, syrupy drink.

"More sugar than tea, right?" Cole grinned.

"Think it's a little too much for me," Kara slid the cup back to the other side of the table and sipped her water to cleanse her palate.

"So..." Cole began, fiddling with the paper wrapper from his straw. "Your aunt seems nice."

"Do you know her well?" Kara asked, feigning a bit of ignorance—if Cole's mother didn't want to speak to Adrienne when she came into the thrift shop, then she doubted Cole did either.

He shook his head. "No. She comes into my mom's store every week or so. But they don't chat much. She's always been nice to us, though."

"I got the impression that your mom and my aunt don't really get along," Kara said.

Cole let out a nervous laugh. "I guess that's how it is, yeah. My mom's real religious—goes to church every Sunday, reads the Bible every night." He paused. "Well, I guess I *also* go to church every Sunday and read the Bible. But she thinks Adrienne is into some weird stuff."

"What kind of 'weird stuff'?" Kara pressed, and Cole squirmed and hesitated to answer. "Come on, just say it."

"Witchcraft, mostly." The words sounded like a confession.

Kara smiled and rolled her eyes. "She's a spiritual woman, that's all."

"I always tell my mom that it's none of her business what other people believe in," Cole said. "That they can live their lives the way they want."

Kara searched Cole's face, wondering if he *actually* told his mother that.

"That's basically what it comes down to," Kara said.

"Are you close with your aunt?" Cole asked, seeming as if he were trying to change the subject.

"My mom and Adrienne aren't super close, so we only visited her a couple of times when I was younger. I think they might've had some kind of falling out a long time ago. I don't know the details, but I bet if I asked Aunt Adrienne, she'd tell me."

"That's too bad. Family should stick together," Cole said.

Maybe that's true in your world, Kara thought. For her, that just wasn't the case—she was quite independent from her mother. Since her mom worked late, Kara was often alone in the evenings and spent most weekends out with her friends. Kara even got the impression that her mother preferred it that way and was proud to be raising a self-sufficient daughter.

They had a few more minutes of small talk before Elise appeared, balancing two loaded plates on a tray. "Alright, one Light Duke and one Double Duke combo." She laid the food on the table.

Kara eyed her burger, suddenly quite hungry. She lifted the bun, noting the perfect griddle marks on the beef. Cole grabbed a ketchup bottle and doused his fries before handing it to Kara.

She then bit into her burger. Savoring the smoky flavor, she decided Cole was right—this was probably one of the best burgers she'd ever had.

"Speaking of the stuff my aunt believes in..." Kara took a napkin from the dispenser and wiped a small amount of secret sauce from the corner of her lip. "So, you remember that statue your mom sold to us the other day?"

"Is that what Adrienne picked out? I didn't see."

"Yeah, she got this little... tiki-looking thing. I don't know what it is, exactly."

Cole shook his head. "I've been unloading boxes of donations for my mom for years. You'd be surprised at some of the stuff that comes in." He rammed a fry into his mouth. As he chewed, he asked, "What about it?"

"Well, she really likes it, I guess. She's almost been treating it like it's a third member of our household. She's even... talking to it."

Why am I sharing this with him? she thought as the words came out. *Probably because I just need to tell someone about the weird stuff. Get it all off my chest.* Kara realized why she was talking about it: she was looking for validation. The whole situation with the statue was unsettling, and she needed another person to confirm that it was, indeed, strange.

Cole's eyebrows shot up in surprise. "That's... interesting."

"She's convinced that there's some kind of spirit inside of it."

Cole shifted in his seat. "A spirit? Like a ghost?"

"I'm not sure what she thinks, exactly," Kara admitted. "But yeah, something like that."

Cole shook his head, seeming skeptical. "That sounds pretty far-fetched to me."

As Kara took another bite of her burger, she could see the discomfort and disbelief written plainly on Cole's face. *He doesn't like talking about spirits,* she realized. She'd been about to mention the bread-and-water offerings, but after seeing Cole's reaction, she decided against it.

"It's far-fetched to me, too," Kara said, and Cole relaxed. *That's enough of that topic,* Kara thought, making a mental note for herself. The last thing she wanted to do was alienate her first—and likely only—friend in town.

"Do you play any sports at your school?" Kara asked.

Cole's eyes lit up. He almost seemed to forget about his burger for a few minutes as he began talking about baseball, going on and on. Eventually, he caught himself. "Sorry. I'm rambling."

"No, it's interesting."

"What about you?" Cole asked.

"Tennis, when I get the chance. But I think I've found a new hobby, believe it or not." Cole gave her a questioning look. "Milking goats."

Cole stared at her for several long moments, trying to decide if she was joking or not. When he realized she was serious, he burst out laughing.

As the evening wore on, their conversation drifted to easier topics—favorite movies, school subjects, and funny stories about their friends. When Elise brought the check, Kara reached for her purse, but Cole insisted on paying. "My treat," he said as he counted out cash from his wallet. "I'm glad you came out tonight." As they stood to leave, Kara realized she had enjoyed herself more than she'd expected.

Maybe I am starting to adapt to this town, she thought.

11

The streetlights were sparse outside of town. Cole focused on the road ahead, one hand resting casually on the steering wheel while country music played softly on the radio. It was just after nine o'clock.

As she looked at him, Kara felt grateful—he'd shown her a fun time. In a way, she wished the evening didn't have to end. But she also had a small amount of guilt at leaving her aunt alone for so long.

"What'd you think of Duke's?" Cole asked.

"It was very good."

"I'm sure you have much better in Chicago," Cole said. "But still. You can't come to Silver Falls and *not* go to Duke's."

"Thanks for taking me out tonight," Kara said after a moment. "It was nice of you."

Cole shifted in the driver's seat, as if he'd suddenly become nervous. "Yeah, no problem." The casualness in his tone sounded forced. "Maybe, if you want… we could do it again?"

"I'd like that."

"Do you have a cell phone?" Cole asked. "So I don't have to call your aunt's landline next time."

"I do."

Cole leaned toward the side, fishing his small silver phone from his pocket. He flipped it open and handed it to Kara. "Put your number in."

"Oh, look." Kara held up her own phone to show Cole, who took his eyes from the road just enough to notice that the models were the same.

"That means we must have the same carrier."

"Yeah," Kara said. There was nothing better than finding out that she and someone else had the same carrier. That meant they could call and text each other for free after nine o'clock at night, and all weekend.

Since they had the same phone, Kara knew exactly which buttons to press to add a new contact. She saved her number, flipped the phone closed, and handed it back to Cole.

The truck slowed so Cole could turn down the narrow gravel driveway leading to Adrienne's house. Kara felt a prickle of unease as the porch came into view. The home seemed darker than normal. Then she saw that Adrienne's car wasn't parked out front.

Cole also noticed. "Where's your aunt?"

"I... don't know."

Kara caught Cole giving her a concerned look. In that moment, she realized she'd given away her anxiety about being alone in the house.

With the statue.

"She must've just gone out to pick something up real quick," Kara said, forcing herself to sound casual. "I'm sure she'll be back soon."

Cole pulled the truck up near the porch, where they hesitated in silence for a minute. Kara could see the conflict written on Cole's face. She could tell he didn't want to leave her alone if she was nervous, but was also trying to calculate how to ask to stay with her without appearing too forward or inappropriate.

"I'll be fine, I promise," Kara said, attempting to reassure herself just as much as him.

"You sure?" Cole asked. "I can wait. You know, if you don't want to be alone."

"She'll be back."

"Well. If you get scared... give me a call."

"Will do. Thanks again."

With that, she threw open the truck door and hopped down, stumbling a bit because she'd forgotten how high up Cole's truck was from the ground.

Kara went around the front of the vehicle and gave Cole a wave as he eyed her through the driver's-side window. She could tell he was still unsure about leaving her there alone, his eyes searching her face for any sign that she wanted him to wait.

A minute later, Kara watched as Cole's truck reversed down the driveway before disappearing into the night. She stood motionless on the porch for a moment, listening to the sounds of the crickets and frogs in the surrounding woods. The nighttime melody didn't calm the nervousness churning within her. She hesitated and stared at the dark windows. She went to use her key... but found the front door unlocked.

Kara stepped inside and immediately flicked on the switch, flooding the living room with light, which did little to put her at ease. She headed for the stairs, but somehow felt her eyes drawn to the statue, still perched on the mantel.

Except the room wasn't as Aunt Adrienne had left it.

The plates that had held bread and water just that morning were now shattered on the floor. Broken ceramic was scattered about, along with the pieces of bread. The rug had dark spots where the water had soaked in.

Kara's breath caught in her throat as she stared at the broken dishes. She backed away from the living room, unable to tear her eyes from the statue leering at her from its perch. Her mind raced, grasping for some logical explanation, but nothing made sense.

Kara whirled around and rushed for the front door, nearly stumbling on her way. She burst out onto the porch, frantically scanning the darkened road—Cole was long gone.

She gripped the porch railing so hard her knuckles burned, struggling to steady her panicked breathing. "It's fine, it's fine," she whispered to herself. But the mantra did little to calm her racing pulse.

The rug was still wet, she thought. *This happened recently. Probably after Adrienne left.*

She couldn't bring herself to go back inside.

To her relief, headlights appeared in the distance a moment later, cutting through the blackness that pressed in from all sides. Kara stood motionless on the porch as the twin beams drew nearer. She recognized her aunt's sedan, which bumped over the uneven gravel of the long driveway before pulling to a stop in front of the house. The stress that had built up began to release.

Adrienne emerged from the car, her arms laden with

grocery bags. "Didn't expect you to be back so early," she called up. "I went out and got us some ice cream."

Adrienne climbed the porch steps, then stopped dead in her tracks when she caught the first sight of her niece. The woman set the bags down and turned to face Kara. "What's wrong?" she asked, though her tone suggested she already knew.

"The statue," she began, her voice strained.

Adrienne's expression remained neutral. "Oh." She placed a hand on Kara's arm before going to see for herself, leaving the grocery bags on the porch. Kara watched through the screen door window as her aunt disappeared into the living room.

A few seconds later, Kara followed Adrienne inside. Adrienne studied the scene with interest rather than fear. "It seems we have a restless spirit in our midst."

"Restless?" Kara doubted anyone would call a child "restless" if they'd thrown a plate off their highchair and smashed it into pieces.

Adrienne nodded. "And maybe a little troubled, too." She turned toward her niece. "But we have nothing to be afraid of. All spirits need is understanding."

"Understanding?" Kara asked. "Are you sure?" *Restless and troubled don't sound like a good mix.*

"I know what we have to do," Adrienne said. "But first, why don't you rescue the ice cream from the heat before it melts?"

Kara nervously chewed her lip, far from convinced. But she managed a small nod, not wanting to argue. She went back outside and retrieved the plastic grocery bags Adrienne had set down on the porch. She brought them to the kitchen, where she placed the tubs of ice cream in the freezer. The outsides of the containers were already wet with condensation from the humid night air. As she worked, the knot of anxiety in her chest loosened, though only a little.

Kara made her way back to the living room and stopped short when she saw Adrienne coming down the stairs. Her aunt held a beaded necklace, running her fingers over the intricate pattern of colored glass and carved wood baubles.

"What's that?" Kara asked.

Adrienne smiled, her eyes distant. "It was a gift, long ago. From someone very special." She stepped closer to Kara, holding the necklace out for her to examine.

Kara turned it over in her hands. It almost seemed to hum with energy. Each bead was unique—swirls of turquoise glass, rose quartz, and hand-carved oak.

"It's beautiful," Kara said. She meant it—the necklace looked homemade and radiated both love and care. "But why…"

Adrienne took the necklace back. To Kara's surprise, her aunt stepped over to the fireplace mantel and laid it at the foot of the statue.

"What are you doing?" Kara stared in disbelief. "You can't be serious."

"This necklace carries loving energy—it will help soothe the spirit. Bread and water were just basic sustenance," Adrienne explained. "I suspect this spirit would appreciate something of more value."

Kara couldn't believe that Adrienne was offering up something so precious and sentimental. "You think it'll eat it?"

Adrienne chuckled. "Honestly, dear, it's hard to say. Spirits are unpredictable. It might take it, wear it, or even return it. What matters most is the *intention* behind our offering."

Kara couldn't help but imagine coming downstairs the following morning to find the necklace dangling around the statue. "Will it give it back to you when it's... done with it?"

Adrienne only shrugged. "Maybe."

"But it means so much to you."

"And now it can serve a new purpose. Possessions are merely objects, temporary in nature. What matters are the connections and memories they represent."

"I don't know..." Kara crossed her arms. "That thing smashed your plates. What if giving it the necklace just encourages it to be... more destructive?"

"I think he'll be very appreciative."

Kara sighed. Her aunt had made up her mind—arguing wouldn't do any good. "If you say so."

"Come on. Help me clean up this mess, then we can have some of that ice cream."

They worked together to sweep up the shattered glass and bread from the carpet. The whole time, Kara felt the statue's hollow gaze following her every move.

12

Kara awoke to the now-familiar crow of the neighbor's rooster. As her eyes adjusted to the dawn light, her gaze darted to the chest of drawers across the room. Even though it had only happened once, the statue's sudden appearance had stuck with her. Relief washed over her when she saw the statue hadn't come to visit again.

Then the events of last night came flooding back.

The rejected bread and water. The necklace. Had it been accepted?

I don't even want to know, she thought. But she'd have to get up eventually.

Kara threw off her blankets and got out of bed. As she descended the stairs, she found herself treading lightly, as if afraid to disturb the heavy silence that filled the house. The morning sun cast shafts of light across the hardwood floor. All was still. She peeked into the living room toward the fireplace.

The statue remained where it had been. Kara's chest

tightened when she saw the empty spot on the mantel where the beaded necklace had been last night.

There's no way. Kara moved closer. She scanned the area below, hoping the jewelry had simply fallen onto the floor, but there was no sign of it. *I refuse to believe that Adrienne is doing all this to play a trick on me,* Kara thought.

No matter how hard she tried to rationalize it, she couldn't deny what she was seeing. The statue—or whatever force it harbored—had accepted Adrienne's offering. And now it was gone.

Kara looked out the nearby window. Adrienne was, as usual, outside on the porch, meditating while facing the rising sun. Kara watched as the woman sat with legs crossed and eyes closed, back straight, and hands resting on her knees. Adrienne's face was serene, the faintest hint of a smile on her lips. The morning light cast a warm glow on her skin. Kara knew her aunt must've checked to see if the statue had accepted the necklace as soon as she'd woken up.

How is she still so calm?

Kara decided not to interrupt the meditation and instead turned from the window and headed upstairs to shower and change.

The hot water did little to ease the heaviness that had settled upon her. As she dried off and got dressed, Kara's mind kept going to the missing necklace.

Once ready, Kara made her way back downstairs, where she heard Adrienne piddling around in the kitchen.

"Good morning," she said. "Let me guess. The rooster."

"Yeah."

"As long as you're up, I might as well make breakfast. I was thinking waffles."

Despite the earlier tension, Kara felt her stomach rumble at the thought. "That sounds great, actually."

Kara followed her aunt around the kitchen, handing her ingredients as she cooked a batch of waffles from scratch. The scent of vanilla and cinnamon filled the air, mingling with the sizzling batter on the iron. Kara found the familiar motions of cooking soothing, a welcome distraction from the elephant in the room, which Adrienne did not mention. As long as she wasn't saying anything about it, Kara decided she wouldn't either.

They worked in focused silence, the only sounds the *clink* of bowls and *hiss* of batter hitting the hot iron. Then an idea occurred to Kara—the Norrises. That would be a good way to get away for a bit.

She felt guilty, but couldn't deny that it was true. *I just don't think the house is being enough for both me and Adrienne's beloved statue,* she thought.

By the time the waffles were ready and they sat down to eat, Kara had made up her mind. "I was thinking of heading over to the Norrises' again today," she said. "To help out some more with the chores."

Adrienne glanced over with a smile. "Yeah, you mentioned wanting to do that. Well, I think that's very kind of you. I'm sure they'd appreciate it."

Kara felt a swell of relief. She'd wondered if Adrienne might protest, or say that she already had plans for them—more hiking, more shopping, more old movies. Or maybe she'd catch on that Kara was looking for a reason to get away from the house.

"It's nice to see you making connections here," Adrienne said. "The Norrises are wonderful people."

THE MORNING SUN beat down as Kara crossed the open field separating the two properties. She could already feel sweat coating her back as the humid summer air clung to her skin.

As she approached the wooden fence marking the boundary, Kara unlatched the gate and let herself in, then made sure to securely close it behind her. She spotted Rocky the Rooster strutting near the chicken coop.

"I swear you're getting louder every morning," she muttered as she passed.

Ed the Goat was grazing under a shady tree. He lifted his head to gaze at her with his horizontal pupils before returning to his breakfast.

A few mornings ago, Glenda Norris had been waiting for her with the milk. Today, however, Kara didn't see the woman around. She headed for the barn to check there, pulled open one of the large wooden doors, and went in.

A stooped figure of a man was inside, and he paused when he saw the unfamiliar face. "Morning, young lady," he said in a gravelly voice. "I think I know who you are."

Kara figured this was Ed Norris, Glenda's husband. "Good morning. I'm Kara, Adrienne's niece. Are you Mr. Ed?"

"Yep, that's what I thought. And yeah, I'm Ed. Nice to meet you. Glenda told me you were a natural when it came to milking Martha."

"I'm not sure about that, but it's nice of her to say," Kara said.

Ed grinned. He wore overalls, a flannel shirt, and a weathered ball cap and sported an impressive white beard. His blue eyes were lively and intelligent. Kara had to admit the grumpy-looking goat did bear an uncanny resemblance to his namesake. "Don't tell me y'all drank all that milk already?" he asked. "Did Adrienne send you back for more? Well, that's fine. I'm sure we have some up at the house. I'll go check—"

"Actually, I just… wanted to see if you needed any help with the work this morning."

Ed looked her over appraisingly as a slow smile spread across his face. "Aren't you sweet. I won't say no to some extra assistance." He gestured with a gloved hand. "Why don't you start by giving Martha her breakfast? You know how?"

"Seems simple enough." Kara grabbed a nearby bucket of feed and filled the goat's trough.

"See, nothing to it," Ed said when she was done. "Over here next." He went to a row of plastic buckets hanging on the wall. "Gotta make sure everyone has fresh water first thing."

Kara listened intently as Ed showed her how to detach the buckets, dump out any old water, and refill them from the hose outside. The goats crowded around as soon as she returned the freshly filled buckets to their pens.

"Next up is food prep," Ed continued. Apparently, the goats ate a careful mixture of several things. In a closed-off section of the barn, Kara measured and combined various grains, seeds, and nutritional supplements as Ed instructed and supervised. It was a lot of information all at once, so much of it went over Kara's head. Still, Ed praised her work.

"We'll set this aside for tomorrow," Ed told her when they were done. "Next up, it's time to deal with the chickens. Cranky bastards, though I can't help but love 'em."

Kara walked beside Ed as they made their way across the field toward the chicken coop. She welcomed the older man's easy conversation after the strange events of the past few days.

"So, whereabouts are you from?" Ed asked.

"Chicago," Kara replied.

Ed let out an impressed whistle. "Welcome to our little corner of the world. You're spending the whole summer with Adrienne?"

"Yes, sir."

They reached the coop, where Ed showed her how to carefully open the door to make sure none of them escaped and replace the feed and water for the clucking hens.

"You try now," Ed said, taking a step back to give Kara space.

Kara tried to mimic Ed's slow, steady movements, but the moment she reached for an empty water container, a particularly bold hen pecked at her knuckle.

"Ow!" Kara drew her hand away. The hen had left a small red mark, but hadn't broken the skin.

"They do that," Ed remarked. "I mentioned they were cranky. You all right?"

"Yeah. Didn't hurt too bad."

"You're tougher than you look, that's for sure. Glenda still shouts curse words whenever she gets got, but don't tell her I told you."

Kara couldn't help but smile. She was thankful for the distraction the morning's chores provided. Not only that, there was something comforting about being surrounded by the animals, whose routines were so simple and predictable compared to the bizarre events that had been unfolding at her aunt's house.

The work wrapped up around noon, by which time

Kara had worked up quite an appetite. Her stomach rumbled.

"I appreciate the unexpected help," Ed said. "Feel free to drop by anytime."

"It was fun, Mr. Ed," Kara said, and she meant it. "I'll come over again sometime for sure."

As she headed back toward her aunt's house through the field, she slipped her cell phone from her pocket, flipped it open, and typed out a quick text to Cole Turner.

'I just did a bunch of chores in the barn next door.'

Despite the charge being slapped onto her mom's bill, she smiled to herself as she sent the message, figuring that Cole would appreciate it. But as her gaze rose to once again look at her aunt's house, her thoughts went to what was inside, and her smile vanished.

13

Walking up the steps to the front porch, Kara examined the mark left by the hen on the back of her hand. Luckily, it no longer stung. In a way, she felt she'd earned a badge of honor. As she entered the kitchen, Adrienne looked up from the soup simmering on the stove.

"Well, don't you look like a proper farm girl," Adrienne said.

"If you say so."

She grabbed a glass from the cupboard and filled it with water from the tap, taking a long drink to wash the dry feeling from her mouth.

Despite her stench and the fine layer of dust and hay strands clinging to her clothes and skin, Adrienne wrapped her arm around Kara's shoulders and pulled her in for a quick hug. "I'm proud of you for helping the neighbors. I know they appreciate it too."

"It's actually kind of fun. Don't be surprised if I go back tomorrow."

Adrienne grinned. "Your mother is never going to believe this. *And* you're just in time for lunch."

She ladled out two bowls of soup and they sat at the table. As they ate, Kara's phone chirped with a text message. It was a response from Cole. She flipped it open with her thumb and pressed the button to view the new message.

'Barn chores sound like hard work. You could be at the beach instead, haha.'

'After all this, the beach is boring to me now.' Kara grinned as she sent the text. She thought about the cell phone bill piling up, but she honestly didn't care—she doubted her mother would notice during her jaunt through Europe with Robert.

Once they'd finished eating, Kara excused herself to go shower and change. The hot water was glorious on her skin, washing away the morning's grime. After toweling off and changing into a clean outfit, she felt renewed. In a way, the work she'd done had been successful in *almost* helping her forget about the little nuisance lingering downstairs in the living room.

The brief recollection of the statue was enough to inspire Kara to find a reason not to go back down. She eyed her backpack of textbooks sitting on the floor near her bed.

Perfect way to spend the afternoon, she thought. *I haven't been studying nearly as much as I wanted to.*

Kara settled onto the bed, crossing her legs and spreading her textbooks out in front of her. She opened her Chemistry textbook, the subject she felt most uncertain about going into junior year. She flipped through the first couple of chapters, skimming the headings and diagrams, her mind only half-absorbing the information.

A buzz from her phone immediately pulled her attention away. She glanced at the screen to see a new message from Cole. Unable to resist, she opened it.

'You know, I've never been to the beach.'

Kara was taken aback. *Who's never been to the beach?*

Normally, she turned her phone off and didn't respond to messages at all when she studied, but what Cole had said captured her attention more than Chemistry had.

'How have you never been to the beach? I thought that was a pretty common family vacation?'

She set her phone down, intent on ignoring any further messages so she could focus. Her eyes returned to the pages in front of her, rereading the same paragraph three times before her cell chimed again.

'Mom doesn't like it, so we never went. We don't really take vacations. She spends all her time working at the shop.'

Kara frowned. *No vacations?*

'The beach is overrated anyway :p' she replied.

They texted back and forth for a while, responding to each other quickly. Kara's focus was absorbed in her text conversation with Cole when a series of *thumps* and shuffling noises came from the ceiling. She glanced up, eyebrows furrowing together as she listened. More scuffling echoed down.

Thumb poised over the keypad, she waited to see if the sounds would stop, but they continued. Curiosity finally pulled her attention away from her phone.

Setting it aside, Kara climbed off the bed and crossed the room. She poked her head out into the hall and looked up. The attic door in the ceiling was open, the folding ladder extended down.

"Aunt Adrienne?" she called out. "Everything okay up there?"

"Oh yes, I'm fine," Adrienne's muffled voice filtered down.

Kara hesitated for a moment, listening to her aunt rummaging around. Whatever she was doing sounded like hard work. *Maybe she needs some help?* Kara climbed the ladder until she could see into the attic. It was a small, cramped space packed full of cardboard boxes, old furniture covered with sheets, and various knick-knacks. Adrienne was on her knees, sorting through one of the larger boxes. She glanced up when Kara popped her head into view.

"I didn't mean to disturb you," Adrienne said. "I figured you were studying. I promise I was trying to be quiet."

"You weren't bothering me," Kara said, remembering that she hadn't really been studying at all. "But now I'm wondering what you're looking for up here."

"Oh, just some old things." Adrienne gestured vaguely around her.

To Kara, the answer felt evasive. *Something else to give to the statue?* she couldn't help but think. Her aunt's attention was already drifting back to the contents of the box.

"Do you need any help?"

"No, no, you go on with what you were doing," Adrienne said distractedly, unfolding a yellowed linen cloth. "I've got it under control up here."

"Okay. Well, if you change your mind, just holler."

"Will do, sweetie. Thank you." Adrienne flashed her a brief smile before returning her focus to whatever she held in her hand.

Kara descended the ladder and returned to her room.

A bit odd, Kara thought. She picked her phone back up, thumbing open Cole's most recent message, which she hadn't seen yet.

'I always figured it would be nice to travel. Germany or Japan are the two places I want to see. But we don't have the money right now.'

'I understand,' Kara typed. *'I think my mom is visiting Germany with her boyfriend this summer on her trip to Europe.'*

'Crazy how she didn't invite you. Maybe we should go together and not invite our moms, haha.'

'Let's do it.' Kara grinned at the idea while also knowing that a trip like that actually happening was far-fetched. But still, it gave her something to entertain her mind with since Chemistry had utterly failed to keep her attention.

———

THE NEXT THING SHE KNEW, the last remnants of a dream were slipping away as Kara awoke. For a moment, she was disoriented, but then realized she'd fallen asleep. The fatigue from the morning's manual labor had crept up on her.

Rubbing the sleep from her eyes, she grabbed her phone and checked the time—nearly 6 p.m. She had two messages from Cole, the first one having come minutes after her last reply over three hours ago.

'At least your mom likes to get out of Chicago and see some new places. My mom, not so much. She'd be happy if she never left Silver Falls for the rest of her life.' The second text had appeared about an hour after when she hadn't replied. *'You there?'*

"Kara! Dinner's almost ready," Adrienne called from the kitchen.

"Coming!" she called back.

She then took a second to type out a reply to Cole. *'Sorry, I just woke up. I must not be used to all the physical activity from this morning.'*

Kara slipped her phone into her pocket and made her way downstairs, the savory aroma of roasted chicken wafting up to greet her. Her stomach rumbled.

In the kitchen, Adrienne was tossing a salad. "Let me guess. You fell asleep."

Kara gave her a sheepish look. "Yeah... I was more tired than I realized. But it smells amazing in here."

Soon, the table in the dining room was laden with food—roasted chicken, mashed potatoes, fresh salad, and warm bread. Adrienne and Kara took their seats catty-corner to each other.

"This looks wonderful, Aunt Adrienne," she said. "You've been spoiling me since I got here. Mom almost never cooks."

Adrienne waved her hand dismissively. "It's just nice to have someone to cook for again."

"Again?" Kara asked, catching the implication. Adrienne stiffened, clearly realizing her slip. "Who were you cooking for before?"

"Ah, it's been a long, long time."

"Come on. Who was he?"

"I'll have to tell you about it some other time."

Kara opened her mouth to ask again, but held back her words when she noticed an uncharacteristic wave of sadness cross her aunt's face.

Oh. There was something serious, she realized.

Kara's mother had mentioned that Adrienne had had

boyfriends in the past, some of them long-term. But of course, her mom hadn't bothered to learn much about them—she had a very low awareness of anything outside of her immediate priorities and concerns. The way Adrienne lived, Kara assumed her aunt had been on her own for quite some time. Now she wondered what had brought about her current situation.

"So, how did the studying go?" Adrienne asked, fast to change the subject. "Still boggles my mind that you study over your summer break. When I was your age... no way."

"Chemistry's going to be tough," Kara said after chewing and swallowing—she was already making quick work of the chicken and potatoes.

"I'm sure you can handle it," Adrienne said. "But I'm glad you got the nap in. That means you'll be ready for tonight."

Kara paused with her fork halfway to her mouth. "What are we doing?"

"It's a surprise." Adrienne flashed a smile.

Kara frowned. Somehow, she figured her idea of a surprise differed very much from her aunt's. "I'm... not sure I like the sound of that." The last "surprise" had brought them to the thrift store—and the statue.

"I think you'll be into it," Adrienne said. "It's definitely going to be a *lot* more interesting than Chemistry."

Nervousness fluttered through Kara's stomach.

14

After dinner, Kara carried the plates to the kitchen sink and started to scrub them. It had become her usual routine after they ate; if her aunt cooked, then the least she could do was wash the dishes. She scrubbed hard with the hot, soapy water, and when the plates and glasses and silverware were clean, next came the pots and pans. Adrienne's house didn't have a dishwasher, but Kara was happy to pitch in.

The whole time she worked, though, Adrienne was curiously absent. Usually, she would come in to lend a hand, but not that evening. The window above the sink that looked out over the side yard was completely black. The summer night had fallen.

Once she'd finished, Kara dried her hands with a kitchen towel and wiped up the water that had splashed onto the countertops. She hung the towel on the oven handle and checked her phone. She had a message from Cole.

'What are you doing tonight?'

Kara hesitated for a moment before responding. She

wondered if he was trying to invite her out somewhere, or if he was merely asking to keep their conversation going from earlier.

'My aunt says she has something planned, but I don't know what it is.'

She sent the text and closed her flip phone with a *click*, in a way wishing she could go out with Cole again—if only to get away from whatever her aunt intended for them to do that night.

Kara went through the dining room to the foot of the stairs near the front door. She spotted Adrienne in the living room, kneeling on the floor beside the fireplace, the statue looming above her on the mantel. Two cardboard boxes sat nearby, flaps folded open. Kara figured the boxes were what Adrienne had been searching for in the attic earlier.

"There you are," Adrienne said, glancing up with an eager smile. "Come have a seat."

Kara lowered herself down onto the couch. "What's all this?" Even though her aunt was only searching through the boxes, she still found herself uncomfortable at the sight of Adrienne kneeling before the statue. It almost looked like she was worshipping it.

"I know you noticed my necklace was gone this morning," Adrienne said.

So this does *have to do with the statue,* Kara thought, disappointed. But she figured they'd have to address it eventually. Between working with Ed Norris in the barn and texting Cole Turner, she'd done a good job of distracting herself—though those distractions wouldn't occupy her mind forever. "Yeah. I did."

"Well, I think it's time we learn a little bit more about our guest."

Kara didn't like where this was heading. "What do you mean?"

"I want to communicate with the spirit that's inside the statue."

Kara pressed her lips together. Something uncomfortable roiled in her chest. "I don't know…"

"Come on. Doesn't that sound interesting? Aren't you curious?"

"I'm still not too sure what to think about all this."

Adrienne's face softened. "I know all this 'spiritual' stuff is a little outside your element. You *are* your mother's daughter, after all. But if you're so committed to learning about Biology and Chemistry, then I think you should also familiarize yourself with the *other* side of our reality—the one scientists refuse to touch."

Maybe they refuse for good reason, Kara thought. "Is it safe?"

"If you know what you're doing," Adrienne said, which didn't bring Kara much comfort—she remembered Adrienne saying she'd never actually experienced a spirit before, and that all her knowledge had come from reading books.

Besides, what's the point? What's there to gain from doing this?

"Here, help me push this," Adrienne said, standing and gesturing toward the coffee table. Together, they pushed it to the far side of the room, its legs scraping on the floor.

Kara watched with unease as her aunt rolled up the rug, revealing the hardwood floors beneath. There was now a cleared space on the living-room floor. Adrienne set the rug on top of the coffee table in the corner.

She then pulled out the large, dusty tome from one of

the boxes and flipped it open to a bookmarked page, revealing an intricate symbol.

So this is really happening, she thought.

Next, Adrienne took a piece of black chalk from the same box and began copying the symbol from the book, her hand gliding in practiced strokes. Kara took a few steps closer and studied the image on the page: a large circle filled with strange shapes and unfamiliar symbols. It reminded her of something she'd seen in a horror movie one time—a film she'd endured rather than enjoyed after her friend Jen had dragged her to the theater. In the movie, a cult had performed rituals around a similar-looking circle.

Kara watched with growing apprehensiveness as Adrienne carefully chalked the elaborate circular design onto the hardwood floor. Despite its complexity, she was doing a pretty decent job of reproducing it. Once finished, Adrienne stepped back to examine her work, nodding with satisfaction.

"This is what's known as a magic circle," Adrienne explained, gesturing to the pattern. "Circles like this have been used for thousands of years as a way to communicate safely with spirits."

Kara stared at the foreign symbols and shapes, trying to decipher their meaning. "How does it work?"

"It helps contain and focus spiritual energy. Its design is very precise—each symbol has a specific purpose." Adrienne pointed out a few of the key markings. "This one here represents the four elements, while this next one amplifies psychic abilities. And here, these symbols invoke protection."

Protection? Kara thought. *From what?*

Adrienne went on, clarifying the function of several

more arcane shapes. Kara listened intently, her skepticism still holding strong during this rare glimpse into an ancient, esoteric practice.

"It's also crucial that the circle is aligned with the four cardinal directions." Adrienne gestured toward the front door. "That's north. And east is that way." She pointed at the window that looked out onto the porch. Just on the other side was the spot where she did her sunrise meditations each morning.

"Why does it matter?" Kara asked. In a way, she felt that if she could ask a question her aunt had no answer for, then perhaps that would be a clue that all of this was nonsensical. If she couldn't explain it, then maybe there *was* no rational explanation.

But Adrienne knew her stuff. "The four cardinal directions correspond to the four elements—earth, air, fire, and water. They also represent key energies in our world," Adrienne said. "Facing north taps into the elemental power of earth. It grounds and stabilizes us. East connects to the element of air and the potential for new beginnings. South represents fire and the raw force of power and action. Finally, west links to water and intuition."

Kara took in the bizarre information with curiosity but also skepticism. She had to admit, her aunt had done her research on the topic. The reasoning sounded almost scientific in its own strange way.

"By aligning with the cardinal directions, the circle connects with those fundamental elemental forces and enhances the power of the ritual," Adrienne concluded.

"So because you have this circle facing north, that means we want earth?" Kara asked, eyeing the northern portion that faced the front door.

"Yes."

"Why earth?"

"That's what my gut tells me."

And now you lost me, Kara thought. To her, citing a "gut feeling" was just another way of saying that you were making this up as you went along—that you were only doing what you felt like doing.

Adrienne seemed to sense that Kara didn't particularly resonate with all this.

"I know it might seem arbitrary, but there *is* logic behind it," Adrienne explained. "Each spirit has an affinity for a particular element that resonates with their energy. When I tune in, I intuitively sense this presence is ancient, primordial, and deeply connected to the earth. The statue itself is hewn from stone. It's hardy and enduring. That points to an earthy essence. So, I believe facing north will help awaken and invite our friend."

"But how can you know that'll work if you've never spoken to it before?"

Adrienne smiled. "That's the wonder of intuition. When you're attuned to the unseen forces around us, you discover an inner guidance that reveals the way."

Kara was silent as she thought about this.

"What do you think about Robert? Your mom's new boyfriend."

She shifted her weight, caught off guard. The question seemed to come out of left field. She and her mom had never really discussed him in depth, and she'd only spent time with him a few times. "He… seems nice enough," she said.

Adrienne tilted her head. "But what does your *intuition* tell you?"

"My intuition?"

"Yes. When you're around him, how does he make you

feel?" Adrienne prodded. "Is there a sense you get about him that you can't quite explain?"

Kara thought for a moment. She pictured Robert's easy smile, his booming laugh. On the surface, he was charming and generous; after all, he was funding her mom's entire European vacation.

Yet there had always been something about him that rubbed Kara the wrong way. An intangible feeling she couldn't articulate.

"I guess I… don't totally trust him," Kara admitted. "And I'm not sure why. He hasn't done anything wrong."

Adrienne nodded. "Maybe not, but your intuition is telling you something important. You're picking up on things beneath the surface that your logical mind can't grasp."

Kara frowned. She hadn't thought of it that way before. "I figured I was just being judgmental and rude."

"Not at all," Adrienne said. "Our intuition is there to guide and protect us."

"So you're saying I should trust how I feel, even if I can't explain it?" she asked.

"*Absolutely,*" Adrienne said. "Always and forever. I realize it's easier said than done, but your intuition is your inner guide. It taps into truths that go beyond the physical world that our senses show us."

Kara absorbed this perspective. She'd heard that there was wisdom in following one's gut instincts, but still, she struggled with that. To her, most situations needed to be carefully considered and evaluated.

"I really am grateful for the bonding time we're getting here," Adrienne said.

Summoning spirits together is bonding? she wanted to ask, but refrained. *Can't we just watch more old movies?* But she could see in her aunt's face that she truly was enjoying all of this. Adrienne likely felt she was imparting some important and valuable life lessons—ones Kara couldn't learn from her mother or her narrow-minded textbooks.

Kara watched as Adrienne chalked one final symbol onto the floor about a foot away from the north side of the circle. It was a smaller circle containing an equilateral triangle.

"What's that one for?" Kara asked.

"This is the most important part," Adrienne explained. "It's for the spirit—the space we've designated for him to manifest within. It represents containment and protection and amplifies spiritual energy. By combining the two shapes, we create a defined area where the spirit can enter our plane of existence."

Kara studied the simple yet precise design. In the context of everything else, it made sense that there needed to be a space specifically for their potential supernatural visitor.

Adrienne set the chalk on the fireplace mantel and brushed the remaining bits from her fingertips. Then, she picked up the little statue from where it had rested on the mantel for the past few days and cradled it like a fragile child. She placed it within the smaller circle she'd drawn for it. She adjusted it so that it faced toward the center of the larger one.

Adrienne straightened and surveyed their handiwork with satisfaction. "Only a few things left to do." She returned to the box from the attic and started taking out identical-looking wax candles. "Here, help me put these around the room."

Kara eyed the candles apprehensively as Adrienne handed them to her one by one. Still, she indulged her aunt, placing them in various spots on the floor and on tables. Next, Adrienne gave her a book of matches, and she lit the candles.

When about a dozen candles were burning, Adrienne flipped the light switch off. Their sudden plunge into near darkness was unnerving, the flickering candlelight casting ominous shapes across the walls. The chalk circle seemed to glow, its arcane symbols rendered even more mysterious in the unstable light. The statue maintained its endless scrutiny over the proceedings, shadows seeming to cling to its sharp features.

"Shall we begin?" Adrienne stepped into the center of the circle and beckoned for Kara to join her. "Come, stand here with me."

Kara hesitated. "I think I'll just watch from the couch."

Adrienne's expression hardened. "No, you must be within the circle's protection." Her voice had taken on a sternness Kara had never heard from her aunt before—it almost felt like she was being commanded.

"What's wrong with being outside of it?" Kara asked.

Adrienne's eyes flicked over to the statue before meeting Kara's gaze. "There are things we cannot completely control in the spiritual world. The circle shields us from uninvited intruders." She left it at that, not elaborating further.

Kara glanced between the statue and her aunt. She sensed she didn't have a choice—this wouldn't be over with until she complied. With growing trepidation, she stepped over the chalk markings and joined Adrienne in the circle's center.

Adrienne gave an approving nod and clasped Kara's hands in her own, lightly massaging her slick palms. "Good. Now take a deep breath and try to relax."

Kara inhaled, the smoky scent of candles filling her lungs.

"Empty your mind. We want to make sure we're open and receptive," Adrienne instructed.

Kara tried her best, pushing away the nagging thoughts and misgivings swirling in her head. She focused on her breathing, on the warmth of Adrienne's hands, and the candlelight. But she couldn't ignore the heavy, watchful presence of the statue, nor how the air seemed thicker all of a sudden. Somehow, being in the middle of the circle made her feel... different. As if she'd stepped into a completely different room.

Surely it's just my imagination, Kara told herself.

Adrienne placed Kara before her, rotating her so they were both looking northward—at the statue. Adrienne rested her hands on Kara's shoulders. Since Adrienne stood a full foot taller than Kara, their difference in height allowed an unobstructed view toward the north for both of them.

"First, the opening prayer," Adrienne whispered near Kara's ear. Her aunt then continued in a clear, steady voice: "We gather in this consecrated space to commune with the spirits beyond the veil. To all friendly beings of light and wisdom, we extend an open invitation. Lend us your sight, that we may glimpse hidden truths. Gift us your voice, that we may hear the secrets. Share with us your eternal knowledge, that we may grow in understanding."

Kara strained to focus on the words, to understand their meaning, but they drifted past her, muffled and distant. She felt oddly numb, probably from the sheer strangeness of it all.

Adrienne went quiet. The final echo of the prayer

seemed to reverberate around them before fading into the shadows.

Kara waited for something to happen, even though she wasn't sure what she was waiting for.

Adrienne whispered in her ear again: "Next, the invocation." Her voice was again steady and authoritative as it cut through the heavy silence. "Spirit dwelling within this vessel of stone, we call upon you. Manifest yourself before us, that we may know you."

Adrienne cast a glance down at the statue, which remained motionless.

"Ancient one surrounded in mystery, we open our circle to receive you. Honor us by unveiling your presence."

Again, Adrienne fell silent, watching the statue expectantly. The flickering candle flames seemed to still, as if the very air was holding its breath in anticipation.

Kara felt a nervous fluttering in her stomach. She wasn't sure what she'd expected, but the absolute stillness of the statue was somehow more unsettling than if it had moved. Its empty stone eyes gazed back at them, giving no indication it had heard Adrienne's summons.

After several long moments, Adrienne spoke again, her voice taking on a more commanding tone, as if trying to force the statue to respond: "By the names of the ascended angels, we call you forth!"

Kara realized she had closed her eyes at some point during the invocation. As she opened them, the room seemed subtly changed—the candle flames burning lower but brighter. The temperature had taken on a slight chill, as if maybe the air conditioner had been lowered. She peered into the gloom, almost expecting ghostly shapes to have materialized while her eyes were closed, but all she saw were flickering shadows moving against the walls.

The silence stretched on. It grew heavier with each passing second. She felt Adrienne give her shoulders a reassuring squeeze.

How long do we wait? Kara wondered. *It didn't work. We tried. Can we just pack it up and go to bed?* In that moment, nothing seemed more enticing to Kara than getting to sleep early so that she could wake up and do more chores with the Norrises in their barn—she just wanted to be out of the house.

Adrienne spoke again, loud and clear, the suddenness of her voice startling Kara. "Spirit, we have opened our home and called you forth. Give us a sign you are present."

The heavy silence seemed to press down on them from all sides. Kara glanced at her aunt, but Adrienne's gaze remained fixed on the statue, her expression serene yet focused. The statue continued its lifeless vigil, still offering no sign it had heard.

After what felt like an eternity, a faint vibration shuddered through the floorboards beneath her feet. Kara's breath caught as a subtle trembling overtook the statue. The movement was slight, but unmistakable—a resonant quiver was traveling through the stone idol.

She recoiled, panic rising within her. Her pulse pounded in her temples. This was too much. She had to get out, get away—

Yet before she could bolt, Adrienne's hands clamped down on her shoulders in a painful, vise-like grip.

"Steady," Adrienne commanded, her tone allowing no argument. "You mustn't leave the circle."

Kara froze, torn between her fear and her aunt's stern

admonition. She stared wide-eyed as the vibrations grew stronger, the statue shuddering where it sat.

"It's answering our call," Adrienne said, her voice electrified with excitement.

Kara trembled within her aunt's grasp, unable to tear her gaze away as the object convulsed on the floor before them.

Then, as suddenly as it had started, the shaking ceased. The statue went still once more.

Adrienne released a long breath and her grip on Kara relaxed. "It worked," she said, awe tingeing her hushed voice.

Kara stared at the now motionless idol, her heart hammering. She couldn't believe what she had just witnessed. The statue had been lifeless before Adrienne called upon the spirit. But her aunt had been right—something undeniably dwelled within.

Kara felt tears form at the edges of her eyes. She didn't remember the last time she'd been this afraid.

Adrienne called out again, her voice ringing with authority, "Spirit, reveal to us your name!"

Name? Kara wondered. *Why do we want to know that? Why do we care?*

Adrienne's command was met by thick silence.

"Your name!" Adrienne called again.

A soft *thump* sounded on the ceiling above them. Both Kara and Adrienne gasped and craned their necks upward.

"What's that?" Kara whispered. Adrienne didn't respond.

Wait, why is she also spooked? Kara couldn't help but think. For the first time, she wondered if maybe her aunt wasn't entirely in control of the situation.

A second *thump.* Then a third. Finally, Kara realized what she was hearing.

Footsteps.

"Someone's walking around," Kara said, a cold prickle creeping along her skin.

"I'll ask again," Adrienne said. Then, directing her voice to the ceiling, called out, "Spirit, tell us your name!"

In response, the footsteps gradually sped up. Kara tracked the unseen walker's progress as it traversed the same path again and again, circling rapidly around the room in a continuous, counter-clockwise loop.

"Why does it keep going in circles?" Kara whispered through dry lips.

"Circles have power," Adrienne said.

Is it trying to match the circle we're standing in? Kara wondered.

Adrienne's gaze remained fixed above, her expression unreadable. "For the third and final time, spirit, I command you to tell us your name!"

The footsteps grew louder, more substantial as the unseen presence continued its relentless circuits, moving faster and faster around the room above. It was stomping now. The ceiling plaster seemed to flex and stretch downwards, bowing under the weight of something pressing from the other side.

It sounds like it's going to break through, Kara thought.

Then, abruptly, the footsteps stopped. The ensuing silence rang in Kara's ears. Her breaths were rapid and shallow as she waited for what would come next.

Then came an awful scraping sound from above. Kara winced at the noise.

The scratching grew louder and more forceful. She imagined something clawing at the floor in a savage display of power. It didn't take her long to realize that the scraping was moving along the exact same path as the footsteps—a counter-clockwise circle mimicking the ritual space Adrienne had created below.

The ghastly sound set Kara's nerves on edge. She wanted to clap her hands over her ears and block it out, but she didn't dare move. Adrienne's body was taut as a bowstring behind her. Kara glanced over her shoulder; her aunt seemed gripped by anticipation, yet just beneath the surface was a shade of disquiet.

On and on it went, the spirit wearing a rut into the floor above. Kara pictured deep gouges marring the hardwood in that room. Adrienne was peering upward, lips slightly parted, enthralled.

Then the scraping ceased. In the wake of that horrible din, the ensuing silence was immense. She held her breath, muscles locked, every sense straining.

"I think it carved something into the floor," Adrienne whispered. She seemed to take it as a sign of progress. But to Kara, it felt like a violation.

Another heavy *thump,* followed by a second. More footsteps.

Kara listened with growing dread as the unseen footsteps resumed their measured pace above. But this time, they did not trace the same endless loop around the room —these footfalls traveled in a straight line, seemingly moving with purpose.

Kara's mind conjured vivid images of the presence navigating the upstairs hallway, the old, worn floorboards creaking under each phantom step.

Is it coming downstairs? The thought filled her with visceral terror.

But the footsteps went in the opposite direction, away from the staircase.

Then where?

She knew the hallway ended with a dead end and a window that looked out over the side yard.

An agonized groan split the air as the window at the end of the hall was forced open. The footsteps didn't break rhythm as they proceeded toward the window—then started coming from the outside wall of the house.

Kara shuddered, tears burning her eyes. This was too much. She looked to her aunt for some kind of reassurance, but Adrienne was focused on the entity walking down the side of the house, perturbed yet fascinated.

The footsteps continued—as if whatever they belonged to was standing sideways, parallel with the ground, defying gravity. Kara tracked its muffled progress along the wooden siding until they reached the wrap-around porch outside, just on the other side of the living room wall. The footfalls grew louder and more distinct as they echoed on the bare porch boards.

Kara and Adrienne both slowly pivoted, both watching and tracking the movement as it stalked along the porch.

There was a window that looked out over the side yard, and Kara realized that within a few seconds, the spirit would pass by it.

"Aunt Adrienne..."

The steps continued, and just before the spirit reached where it would be visible through the glass, the curtains swished closed of their own accord, as if drawn by an invisible hand.

Kara yelped.

It turned left at the right-angle corner of the porch and approached the window that faced the front yard, and the east. Again, the curtains closed on their own before the entity passed.

As the footsteps continued, Kara finally understood where it was heading—the door. It seemed to take an eternity for it to get there.

The steps ceased their approach just shy of the door. An awful silence descended.

Kara pressed against Adrienne. "I want this to stop," she pleaded in a whisper.

Click. The front door lock disengaged. With a *creak* that made the fine hairs on Kara's neck rise, the door slowly swung open. From their position in the center of the magic circle, there was a short wall blocking Kara's line of sight toward the door. All she could see was the door opened wide.

"Please," Kara begged, the tears running down her cheeks now.

Black smoke poured into the house's entrance area.

Kara stared in horror as the writhing smoke surged through the open doorway. It seemed to move with a sinister purpose, tendrils twisting through the air as it explored the entryway. She pressed against Adrienne, cringing away from the unnatural fog.

"What is this..." Adrienne murmured. The worry in her voice told Kara that her aunt was just as baffled as her.

The smoke continued creeping forward, branching out like the limbs of some foul tree. It probed along the walls, seeming to blindly investigate its surroundings.

Then it drifted closer.

"Adrienne, make it stop!" Kara begged, no longer caring if she disrupted the ritual. This had gone too far.

The blackness came near the magic circle, but started to displace around it, as if it couldn't cross the barrier.

Kara realized her aunt had been right to not let her watch from the couch.

The smoke hovered there, swaying back and forth, like it was testing the barrier.

More of the cloudy substance poured through the open door, amassing just beyond the magic circle's line. Now that it was filling the living room, Kara realized it stunk. Her eyes watered from its acrid stench—like sulfur mixed with rot.

"Please!" she sobbed. She wondered how Adrienne was tolerating all of this so calmly.

Adrienne took a deep, steadying breath. Then she called out in a strong, unwavering voice, "Spirit, you have answered our summons. We thank you for the signs you have shown us tonight. Now we bid you farewell until we meet again."

Yes, Kara thought. *Finally.*

The swirling black fog continued to amass just outside the protective circle, hemming them in. Kara clutched at her aunt's arm, desperate for this nightmare to end. Adrienne hesitated, uncertainty flickering across her features. Kara could sense her aunt's resolve wavering.

"T-try it again," Kara said.

"Spirit, you have shown us a glimpse of your power and presence," Adrienne called out. "Now, by the authority of our ancient pact, I command you to withdraw and trouble us no more tonight."

The writhing tendrils seemed to pause in their endless motions, as if considering her words. For a moment, Kara dared to hope the spirit would obey.

But the smoke began creeping closer once more, probing along the invisible barrier as if seeking a weakness, a way in. Kara recoiled as the foul odor intensified.

"You have tested the bounds of this circle and found them resilient," Adrienne said. "Withdraw at once! There is nothing more for you to do here!"

A low vibration shivered through the floorboards once again. The smoke swirled faster, seeming agitated.

Emboldened by this reaction, Adrienne raised her voice to a commanding shout. "Return now to your vessel!"

She thrust a hand toward the statue. The vibration rose to a violent shudder that shook Kara to her core.

Then, all at once, the smoke rushed inward with a great swirling vortex. It collapsed upon itself, contracting down to a thin black cord that whipped back into the statue's carved mouth. There, it was sucked in, as if the statue were rapidly consuming it, until all of it was gone.

Silence engulfed the room. The statue stood motionless once more. Stunned relief flooded through Kara.

It's... it's over.

Adrienne let out a long, shaky breath. She grasped Kara's shoulders. "It's alright. The circle held."

Kara searched her aunt's face, finding the same lingering fear and disbelief she felt herself. Gone was the self-assuredness Adrienne had worn when they'd first begun this ordeal.

"Can we please never do that again?" Kara pleaded softly.

Kara watched while Adrienne stepped out of the circle. Her aunt moved slowly, as if drained by what they had just endured. Adrienne reached for the stone idol, picked it up, and cradled it in her hands as she studied it in the candlelight.

What... Kara couldn't believe what she was seeing. *How can she even touch that thing after...* Kara had taken the black smoke trying to break through the circle as a threat. *How could she not see it that way, too?*

Kara held her breath, waiting for her aunt to speak, to give some hint as to what she was thinking. Several moments passed in tense silence while Adrienne turned the statue over in her hands. Kara scrutinized her aunt's face again, this time for any hint of regret, any sign that she felt that what had just happened had possibly put them both in danger. But Adrienne's expression remained closed, introspective.

Finally, she returned the statue to the fireplace mantel, its position of prominence overlooking the room.

Kara sagged, a sick feeling settling in her gut. She opened her mouth to object, but the words died in her throat. She no longer had the energy to argue or protest.

Adrienne turned to Kara. "We need to check upstairs."

15

Kara trailed behind Adrienne as they ascended the staircase, nerves still raw. She didn't want to go upstairs; she dreaded what they might find in the spare bedroom, but the thought of waiting alone with the statue was even worse.

The second-floor hallway seemed colder, grimmer than before, as if the spirit's presence had seeped into the very walls. Each step toward the spare room felt heavier than the last. Kara's breath caught when she saw the open window at the end of the hall.

Adrienne moved with calm purpose, showing no indication of fear, and Kara envied her aunt's composure. She trailed an arm's length behind, ready to flee at the first sign of anything she didn't like.

They reached the unused bedroom across the hall from Kara's room. Adrienne grasped the tarnished knob and turned it. The door swung inward with an ominous *creak* that raised the hairs on the back of Kara's neck.

The room beyond was dark—too dark to see. Adrienne's hand went to the switch on the wall. Light filled the space. There were markings of some kind on the floor, though from where Kara stood in the hall, she couldn't make out what they were.

Adrienne stepped inside to examine the floor more closely. Kara remained by the door, arms hugging herself.

Adrienne turned back to Kara. "He answered us."

"What do you mean?"

"Come look."

Kara went to stand by her aunt and peered down. Letters.

UNUZA.

"U…Un…" Kara tried to sound out the foreign word.

"I think it's meant to be read backwards," Adrienne said.

Kara remembered how the footsteps—and the scraping sounds—had come in a counter-clockwise pattern. She tilted her head to get a better look.

AZUNU.

"It's the spirit's name," Adrienne whispered.

Kara winced. Somehow, seeing it etched into the wood made its existence undeniably real. This was no longer merely her aunt's eccentric belief—this was tangible evidence of the otherworldly forces they had awakened.

"Azunu," Adrienne said, as if testing the sound.

Revulsion rose in Kara's throat. She wanted to grab her aunt by the shoulders and shake her, to scream that they had to get the statue—and the spirit within it—as far away from the house as possible.

But she remained frozen beside her aunt, feeling suffocated by the dread that had settled upon her. She could only watch as Adrienne knelt and began using her fingertips to trace part of the jagged "A" with something akin to reverence.

Kara knew then, with chilling certainty, that this was far from over.

16

Kara lay wide awake in bed, her body rigid beneath the sheets. She knew sleep wouldn't come anytime soon that night.

The sound of the thumping footsteps still rang in her ears. When she managed to chase that away, the noises were only replaced by the terrible scraping, the spirit gouging its name into the floor.

AZUNU.

She wrinkled her nose, swearing she could still smell the putrid stench given off by the black smoke as it had surrounded the magic circle, like it was trying to block them in.

Kara pulled the covers up to her chin. As she stared up at the ceiling, mind racing, she realized that perhaps the worst part of this whole thing was that her entire worldview had been brutally shattered over the course of a single night. Things she hadn't believed in just twelve hours ago she now knew to be undeniably real. The spirit world was real. Magic was real. Beings and forces beyond her comprehension existed, contrary to everything she had ever learned from her textbooks and science classes.

She had prided herself on being a skeptic, relying only on provable facts and evidence. But now, the very core of her beliefs had crumbled away. She couldn't deny what she'd experienced, what she'd seen with her own eyes. Azunu's name was just as carved into her mind as it was into the floorboards.

The truth was out there, and she couldn't hide from it. A spiritual component to reality existed, as real and tangible as gravity, whether she liked it or not.

It was almost funny, in a twisted way. She had resented being dragged from her busy city life and forced to spend a boring summer in this tiny town. Now, she *longed* for a boring summer of normality more than anything else.

Kara found it all too much to think about. She needed a distraction, an escape. She rolled over and took her phone from the bedside table, unplugging it from the charging cable. She flipped it open and the bright green fluorescent backlight burned her eyes.

'Hey. You up?' She typed out the message to Cole and sent it. It was just past midnight.

Kara stared at the phone, waiting for Cole's response. A few moments later, his reply popped up on the screen.

'Yep. What's up?'

The smallest bit of relief washed over her; at least now she had something to occupy her mind a little.

'Can't sleep,' she typed back. *'What did you get up to tonight?'*

'Went to church with my mom,' came Cole's reply.

Kara sighed. *Church. Mine and his evenings couldn't have been any more opposite.* While Cole was worshipping the

Lord, she'd been summoning spirits in her aunt's living room. She could only imagine how Cole's mom—or Cole himself—would react if they knew the truth.

It made Kara think about something she had never considered before—if the spirit world was real, as she now knew it to be, did that mean the God that Cole and his family believed in was also real? She'd always written off religion as fairy tales made up so that people could feel better about their own mortality.

But she couldn't be so quick to write anything off anymore. If things like magic circles and spirits existed, then who was to say God and heaven didn't?

I can't be thinking about all this right now, Kara told herself. *It's too much for one night.*

'How was it?' she replied. Never before would she ever have imagined herself being curious about what goes on in church—and she still wasn't—but in that moment, any topic of conversation was a welcome distraction.

'Great. We had a guest speaker who gave a pretty good sermon about standing strong in your faith.'

As Kara read the message from Cole, she could almost detect the enthusiasm in the little letters on her screen. She remembered their dinner at Duke's and how Cole had made it seem like his mother was the driving force behind their church attendance and that he went along to appease her. But now, Kara realized Cole was as invested in his religious beliefs as Debra Turner was—just as she'd suspected.

He followed up with another text. *'Do you go to church?'*
I should've known he'd eventually ask me this.

'No,' she answered.

It took Cole a little longer to reply than usual. When it finally came, all it said was, *'Gotcha.'*

118

Kara tried to think of something else to say so the conversation wouldn't die.

Her thoughts were interrupted by the sound of footsteps just outside her bedroom door.

She gasped and sat bolt upright in the bed, her cell phone dropping from her hand and clattering on the floor.

"Kara, are you awake?" came Aunt Adrienne's soft whisper from the hallway.

Kara took a deep breath to calm herself. "Yeah," she replied, hoping her voice didn't betray how startled she was.

The door creaked open and Adrienne entered. She sat down on the edge of Kara's bed, the old springs creaking.

"I wanted to say something about what happened tonight," she began as she smoothed out the wrinkles in the quilt draped over Kara's legs. "It's clear to me that I made you very uncomfortable, and that was never my intention."

Kara remained silent, sensing this was difficult for her aunt to admit.

"I got carried away without considering how all this stuff might affect someone who isn't as interested in it as I am," Adrienne continued. "I shouldn't have pushed you into participating in something you weren't ready for. That wasn't fair of me."

"It… was definitely pretty intense," Kara acknowledged. That was an understatement, but she didn't want to make her aunt feel worse.

"I know, and I'm sorry," Adrienne said, placing a gentle hand on Kara's arm. "From now on, I won't bring up anything to do with spirits or the statue. You being comfortable here in my home is what's most important to me."

Kara gave a small, grateful smile. As bizarre as her aunt's occult interests were, it meant a lot to hear the woman apologize.

"Thanks, Aunt Adrienne," Kara said. "I appreciate you understanding where I'm coming from. I know you're into all this stuff, but it's just not really my thing."

Adrienne nodded and stood. "I understand. And honestly, all that happened down there... I didn't expect it to be like that. I was too eager and got a little in over my head, and I'm sorry."

Kara remembered how sure of herself Adrienne had been when they'd started, and how her demeanor had shifted to one of uncertain fear.

"Get some rest, sweetie. It's been a long night." She leaned down and gave Kara a brief but heartfelt hug.

"Goodnight, Aunt Adrienne."

"Goodnight, dear. I'll try to be quiet as I clean up everything downstairs."

Adrienne left the room, closing the door behind her with a soft *click*.

Kara lay back against her pillow, feeling a sense of relief wash over her. She was grateful her aunt was so understanding.

And now maybe we can stop obsessing over that little statue.

17

Kara slept fitfully that night, drifting in and out of a restless half-sleep. Her dreams were plagued by nightmares where the statue came to life, growing twisted limbs that contorted as it crawled across her bedroom floor, hollow eyes boring into her.

Kara jerked awake when the neighbor's rooster let out its morning crow. The first light of dawn crept through her room, and relief washed over her as the night's terrors receded. But a lingering sense of dread remained coiled within her—she knew as soon as she went downstairs, she'd end up face to face with that statue yet again.

Kara descended the stairs, steeling herself as the fireplace came into view. Just as she'd expected, the statue sat staring back at her from its perch on the mantel. She forced her gaze away, ignoring the prickle of fear.

She walked over to the window facing the porch to check her aunt's meditation spot, but Adrienne wasn't there.

Kara paused. *That's unusual.*

She checked the kitchen. No sign of her aunt brewing

coffee or chopping up fruit for breakfast. Next, she looked out through the dining room window—Adrienne's car was parked in the front of the house.

Puzzled, Kara crept back upstairs and went down the hall to the master bedroom. She opened the door a crack and peeked inside. Adrienne's sleeping form rested in bed under the covers.

Kara paused in the doorway, taking in the interior of Adrienne's bedroom for the first time. The room was simple yet cozy, with wood-paneled walls and hardwood floors partially covered by a large oval rug.

The mattress was set within an oak frame overlaid with a colorful handmade quilt. Mismatched nightstands flanked the bed, one piled high with books, crystals, and an oil diffuser, the other with only a lamp.

On the wall hung a tapestry depicting mandala patterns. Shelves along the sides displayed an assortment of figurines, candles, and incense holders. Near the window, a small desk held stacks of papers, notebooks, and more books.

Kara retreated carefully, not wanting to disturb Adrienne. *I guess last night wiped her out. If she needs to sleep, then let her sleep.*

She headed back downstairs, deciding to take the initiative and prepare breakfast for her and Adrienne. *It'll be nice to change things up. She's cooked for me so much since I've been here,* Kara told herself.

Cooking wasn't Kara's forte—unlike her aunt—but she could manage a simple breakfast well enough.

Kara cracked four eggs into a skillet, letting them sizzle as she dropped slices of bread into the toaster. The rich smell of the eggs made her stomach rumble. She sprinkled in a dash of salt and pepper, keeping a close eye so they wouldn't burn.

Once the eggs finished, she slid two onto each plate. The toast popped up golden brown, which she added to the plate alongside some cut mango from the fridge. Finally, she poured two glasses of creamy goat milk.

By the time Kara was done eating, Adrienne still hadn't come down. The eggs and toast on the second plate were growing cold in front of Adrienne's spot at the table.

Well, I tried, Kara thought as she got up and washed her dishes in the kitchen sink. *I'll leave it out and she can pop it in the microwave when she wakes up.*

Upstairs, she changed into shorts and a t-shirt. As long as her aunt was going to sleep in, she figured, she may as well head next door and be of use.

And of course, working in the Norrises' barn was the perfect distraction from anything involving the little pest on the fireplace mantel.

Kara stepped out into the humid Mississippi morning. The air was already thick and heavy, hinting at the sweltering heat that would settle in soon.

As she made her way down the porch steps and around the side of the house, she glanced up at Adrienne's bedroom window on the second floor—just in time to spot someone looking down at her before letting the curtain fall back into place.

Kara paused, waiting for her aunt to open the curtain again and maybe wave. But it didn't move.

That's kinda weird, Kara thought as she continued on towards the Norrises' property.

She walked across the field separating Adrienne's home from the Norrises' property, the dew wetting her sneakers. Glenda Norris was already out and gave Kara a smile when she let herself in through the gate. "I think you might be the most consistent help we've ever had."

"Morning," Kara said, forcing a cheeriness that wasn't entirely authentic. "I've decided that it's actually pretty fun around here."

Kara got straight to work, grabbing a bucket and a stool. Martha trotted over and waited as Kara sat down and began squeezing the warm milk into the pail.

The familiar motions soothed Kara's nerves, but despite her best efforts, flashes from the bizarre ritual the previous night kept barging to the forefront of her thoughts.

Focus on the milk, she told herself, moving her hands rhythmically.

Soon, Ed hobbled into the barn. "Mornin', Kara." He seemed delighted to see her. "You here to help out again?"

"I am."

"Well, you're just in time to help me lug these feed bags. They got delivered a few minutes ago."

Kara finished up the milking then followed Ed to the front of the house, where massive bags of feed had been stacked by the delivery guy. Kara grabbed two hefty bags and started carrying them toward the barn. The physical exertion felt good, grounding her. She carried two while Ed carried one, and it reminded her that this work was more than a way to pass the time and distract herself—she had no doubt that Ed would eventually get all the feed bags to the barn by himself, but it would've taken him much longer, and worn him out quickly. As they worked, Ed launched into a long, rambling story about his childhood on a farm. Kara half-listened, making occasional noises of acknowledgment.

After the sacks were neatly relocated, Kara spent the next hour cleaning stalls and reorganizing tools, grateful for the mindless busywork. But despite her best efforts, she couldn't fully relax.

By noon, the chores were done, and it was time for Kara to return home—and the thought of doing so sent tension through her belly too intensely to ignore. Kara wiped the sweat from her forehead as she walked back from the Norrises' barn in the sweltering midday heat.

She stepped inside the air-conditioned home, the coolness washing over her slick skin. Glancing at the kitchen table, she noticed the eggs she'd prepared were still untouched, stone cold.

Kara climbed the stairs and went down the hall to Adrienne's bedroom door. She knocked gently. "Aunt Adrienne? I wanted to check if you're okay. You didn't come down for breakfast."

"Oh, I'm fine," Adrienne replied. "Just needed a little extra rest this morning. Don't worry about me."

Her aunt's voice sounded muffled and distant, and something in her tone was... off. Kara tested the doorknob and found it locked.

"Well, I'm about to make some lunch. So if you wanted to eat, it'll be ready in a few minutes."

"That sounds lovely."

Kara lingered by the door a moment longer, wondering if Adrienne was going to say anything else. When she didn't, Kara went back downstairs.

In the kitchen, she assembled a pair of turkey sandwiches, then sliced an apple for each of them. She poured two glasses of iced tea and carried everything to the table.

As Kara ate, she periodically glanced at the empty

stairwell, listening for the opening and closing of the master bedroom door. The sandwich sat like a rock in her stomach. After thirty minutes had passed with no sign of Adrienne, Kara wrapped up the second sandwich and put it in the fridge.

What's going on with her today? Kara wondered. As she washed the plate and glass in the sink, she realized she couldn't ignore the timing—Adrienne's bizarre behavior happened right after the previous night's encounter. She remembered Adrienne's assurance that they were safe, that the magic circle would protect them. Kara was starting to doubt it had.

But at the same time, I feel fine...

———

LATER THAT NIGHT, Kara lay in bed, the glow of her phone illuminating her face in the dark room as she texted her friends back in Chicago. She had her headphones on, blasting a mix CD on her portable player to drown out the silence that had filled the house that day.

As she'd predicted, her friends didn't believe her when she talked about milking goats and mucking stalls by choice—they'd heard about it from Olivia. Kara promised to take pictures to prove she was actually getting her hands dirty. She'd packed a disposable camera and planned to bring it with her the next time she went to the Norrises'.

The conversation drifted to boys, movies, and all the things they wished they were doing together this summer. Kara missed them all, but chatting with them made it feel like the hundreds of miles between them had momentarily vanished.

When her phone battery dipped below 10%, Kara reluctantly said goodnight, set her phone on the nightstand, and plugged it into the charger. She decided to get a glass of water before sleeping, so she turned off her CD player and removed her headphones.

When she walked out into the upstairs hallway, the first thing she noticed was Adrienne's bedroom door standing open. Looking over the banister, she listened for any sound from her aunt, but heard nothing.

She was halfway down the stairs when she finally picked up on some sounds coming from the dining room. She poked her head around the corner.

Adrienne was crouched down, shuffling through the bottom of the cabinet, various trinkets and boxes spread out on the floor near her. Her back was toward Kara, so she hadn't noticed she wasn't alone. She was muttering to herself in a low voice, though Kara couldn't make out what she was saying.

Kara wanted to go to her and see if she was okay, but stayed frozen in place, spectating instead. Her aunt seemed quite adamant about finding something.

Adrienne gasped, startling Kara.

Her aunt withdrew a small box from the cabinet. Kara leaned forward, curious, straining to see as Adrienne lifted the lid. Nestled inside was a simple silver ring set with a blue stone.

Adrienne delicately plucked it from the box and slid it onto her left finger. She stared down at the jewelry for an inordinately long amount of time. As she did, Adrienne continued whispering, like she was speaking to the ring.

Then Adrienne's shoulders shook and she broke down sobbing. Kara's chest tightened at the sight—she had never seen her aunt so distraught. Instinctively, she wanted to go and comfort the woman. But something held her back—she sensed this was a profoundly private moment she was witnessing.

Adrienne's sobs quieted a few seconds later. Sniffling, she rose to her feet, swiping at her eyes. Kara backed away and crept up a few more steps, hoping her aunt wouldn't catch her spying.

Luckily, Adrienne seemed preoccupied with the ring and her own swirling thoughts. She shuffled past the bottom of the stairs toward the living room, not noticing Kara's presence.

Adrienne approached the fireplace where the statue stood. With trembling fingers, Adrienne worked the tight ring off her finger and placed it at the statue's feet.

Another offering? Kara thought with worry. *Something else that means a lot to you. How many are you supposed to give before it's satisfied?*

Adrienne bowed her head and clasped her hands before the statue. Her lips moved rapidly. Kara wished she could hear what her aunt was saying. Was she chanting? Bargaining?

This was too much for Kara. This time felt different. The necklace had been a heartfelt gift. Now, though, Adrienne seemed... controlled by something outside of herself, as if her usual composure was gone. Like she was desperately placating the spirit within the statue.

Kara went back upstairs and closed her bedroom door behind her, becoming aware of her own tears.

What's happening? I don't like this...

The next morning, after Rocky the Rooster awakened Kara, she went downstairs. She felt herself drawn almost against her will toward the statue on the fireplace mantel. Just as she'd expected, the ring was gone.

And somehow, the statue's stone face seemed to have shifted ever so slightly, its lips now curled into an unsettling smile.

18

Kara stepped out into the muggy morning air. She made her way across the field to the Norrises' barn, ready for her usual chores. The day was cloudy and overcast, threatening rain later.

She had her disposable camera with her, so she could snap some photographs of herself around the barn and prove to her friends what she'd been doing. Kara had wanted to bring her mother's new, fancy digital camera, but her mom had refused, saying she was taking it with her to Europe.

As Kara entered the barn, she called out to Martha. But instead of trotting over like normal, the goat remained lying down, regarding Kara warily.

"Martha? C'mon, girl, it's time for milking." Kara approached, hand outstretched. Martha let out a warning bleat and shifted away.

Kara froze, confused.

"Everything okay in here?" Glenda asked, stepping into the barn.

"I'm not sure. Martha doesn't seem to want me near her this morning."

Glenda clucked her tongue. "Aw, she's just being a stubborn old nanny goat today." She took Martha by the collar, and the goat obediently stood. Glenda led Martha to the milking stand and set her up. Martha seemed perfectly content. "See? Nothing to worry about. Want to take over?"

Kara approached Martha again, but as she got closer, the animal started bleating in alarm and bucking her head.

"Looks like she wants you today," Kara said, backing away to put some distance between her and Martha. The moment she did, Martha calmed down again.

"That's so odd," Glenda said, hands on her hips as she looked down at the goat. "These animals can be crazy sometimes. Why don't you handle the chickens and the eggs while I take care of this?"

Kara headed over to the chicken coop, still feeling perplexed. *Martha hadn't been moody before,* she thought. *Why's she avoiding me now?*

When Kara entered the coop, the chickens scattered, flapping and squawking.

"Whoa, easy," Kara said, taken aback. She approached the nesting boxes to collect the eggs, but the hens pecked relentlessly at her hands, their feathers ruffled. She'd come to understand that getting pecked now and then was normal, but the chickens always surrendered their eggs eventually. This time, however, they refused to let her anywhere near them. After several minutes of attempting, Kara gave up, both her hands feeling as if they'd endured stabs from a hundred needles—and she didn't have a single egg to show for it.

I don't get it. What's going on?

When Glenda appeared in the coop doorway, she asked, "Are the chickens being a little more compliant than Martha?"

"Honestly, not really," Kara said. "It... seems the animals don't like me today."

"It happens," Glenda said. "They have moods just like we humans do. Why not take the day off? I can handle the rest."

Kara wanted to protest—she didn't want to go back to Adrienne's house, but reluctantly admitted to herself that the animals had made it clear: she wasn't their friend that morning.

She walked away from the barn, confused and a little bit hurt by the animals' unusual hostility toward her. She spotted Ed the Goat chewing grass near the gate. "Hey, Ed the Goat. Are you mad at me, too?"

He looked at her, then lowered his head, horns pointed in her direction. Kara jumped back, startled. Ed the Goat let out an aggressive bleat, stomping his hooves.

Kara hurried on, the goat's rejection stinging even more than the chicken pecks.

As she came along the side of Adrienne's house, Kara glanced up at the second-story window of her aunt's bedroom. Again, she saw a figure looking down. Then the curtain fell closed, just like the previous day.

Is she going to spend another day in her room? Kara thought. She rounded the corner of the porch, and froze.

Adrienne sat in one of the rocking chairs, relaxed and seemingly carefree. "Back so soon?"

Kara stared, words failing her. Her stomach suddenly felt hollow.

"What's wrong?"

"Who's in your bedroom?" Kara managed to say.

"What do you mean?"

"I—I… saw someone looking at me from the window. Just now. When I passed. Literally three seconds ago."

Adrienne shook her head. "It's only me here."

"No, I swear. There's someone in your room."

Adrienne seemed amused by Kara's fear, which only frustrated her.

"Let's go see." Adrienne rose and led the way inside.

Kara lingered at the bottom of the stairs, heart pounding as Adrienne walked down the upstairs hall and into her bedroom.

A minute later, Adrienne appeared at the top step and shrugged. "There's no one up here, sweetie."

No. I know what I saw, Kara thought. "Are you sure you checked everywhere? Maybe they hid in the closet."

"That was the first place I looked." Adrienne gave a smile that didn't quite reach her eyes.

"Okay…" Kara said. "If you say so."

"It's just you and me here, as usual." Adrienne then abruptly went back inside her bedroom and closed the door.

Kara frowned. There had been something odd about her aunt's tone that she couldn't put her finger on. Then she realized what it was.

She didn't sound like she was trying to reassure me. She sounded like she was trying to convince *me.*

19

The next day, Sunday morning, Kara got a text from Cole that caught her off guard.

'Hey. Do you want to come to church with me today?'

She paused, surprised at how long she was actually considering it—and feeling guilty about how eager she was to spend time away from her aunt's house.

'Sure. When?'

'I'll pick you up in half an hour.'

Kara rifled through the clothes in her suitcase, wondering what would be appropriate to wear to a church service in Mississippi. She hadn't brought anything too formal. She first put on jeans and a t-shirt, but when she checked herself in the mirror, decided it was too casual. Next was a blue blouse and a plain skirt, but that felt too professional-looking.

I look like Mom when she's going for a job interview, she thought.

Kara settled on a floral sundress dotted with pink roses—it was the nicest thing she'd packed.

She styled her curly hair into a neat bun and applied a touch of lip gloss. She gave herself an appraising look in the mirror. *Presentable*, she decided.

Downstairs, she found Aunt Adrienne tending to some potted plants in the living room. Adrienne looked surprised when she saw her. "Those aren't barn clothes," she said with a smile.

"I'm taking a break from the goats this morning. Cole Turner invited me to his church."

Adrienne's hands clenched. One of the plant's leaves ripped away in her grip. The woman stared at the torn leaf for a moment, her expression suddenly dark.

"You okay?" Kara asked.

Adrienne blinked a few times and seemed to come back to herself. "They go to that nice one on the other side of town, I believe," she said as she dropped the torn leaf and brushed her palm on her dress. "It was big news when they finally finished the new building."

Kara wondered if she'd imagined her aunt's temporary flash of irritation.

Adrienne heard something and looked through the nearby window. "That must be him. Have fun, dear."

Kara stepped out into the humid Mississippi morning. Sure enough, Cole's truck was ambling its way up the long driveway.

When he stopped, Kara opened the passenger door and hoisted herself into the seat. Cole had already begun walking around the front of the truck, but then paused, noticing she'd already gotten herself in, so he returned behind the wheel. He wore khaki pants, a salmon-colored button-down shirt, and shiny brown dress shoes that looked brand new.

"Morning," Cole said, glancing over at her.

"Thanks for the invite," Kara replied.

They set out, and Cole started racing down the empty backroads.

"Are we late?" Kara asked.

Cole chuckled. "Uh… yeah, sorry about that. I waited too long to text you. But I also didn't want to rush you with getting ready."

Kara nodded, turning to look out the window as trees and fields blurred past. The day was bright and sunny, and already hot. It'd be even worse by the time church let out.

As her thoughts drifted, she realized she may have accepted Cole's invitation a bit too quickly.

What if he invites me every Sunday from now on? Then another thought came. *And what if I actually go with him?* She frowned at the idea of her spending the rest of the summer actively trying to find excuses to get out of her aunt's house.

Her mind returned to Aunt Adrienne and her strange behavior over the past few days.

Maybe I shouldn't have left her alone, Kara thought. But at the same time, she needed a break. She'd needed a break every single day, she realized.

"You okay?" Cole prodded, snapping Kara out of her thoughts.

"Yeah, why?"

"You look…" He glanced back and forth between her and the road. "I don't know. Afraid."

"Afraid?" Kara tried to sound natural. In reality, she was.

"Are you nervous about going to church?" Cole asked. "I remember you said you don't normally go, so…"

Kara seized the lifeline that Cole had just provided. "Yeah, I guess I am a little nervous."

Cole smiled easily. "No reason to be afraid. Church is the nicest place on earth. You'll see."

A moment later, he turned right near a sign that read, "Word of Truth Baptist Church." The circular parking lot was crammed full of cars, forcing Cole to park pretty far away. "You okay to walk?" Cole asked. "Sorry. When you get here, even just a little bit late, it fills up fast."

"No problem," Kara said.

Cole killed the truck's engine and she vaulted down from the high passenger seat. They began walking together through the parking lot, the baking pavement reflecting the sun. They were the only ones heading in, so Kara presumed that the service had already started. She noticed Cole walked with long, rushed strides, clearly eager to get inside as soon as possible.

As they went, Kara eyed the massive, modern structure. It looked so much larger now that they were close. *This is the biggest building I've seen in Silver Falls so far,* she thought. Based on the parking lot, it seemed that coming here was the highlight of the week for many families.

I guess that makes me sort of like an imposter, Kara thought. She wasn't there for the right reasons. Those families *wanted* to be there. She was merely using this church as a place to hide. *Maybe God, if he's real, can understand why I'm here.*

Kara followed Cole through the massive glass doors into the church's soaring atrium. The notes of a hymn being sung within the sanctuary drifted out, confirming the service had already begun.

A man in a finely pressed suit stood just outside the sanctuary doors, smiling when he saw Cole. "Good morning, Cole," he said warmly, handing Cole a program pamphlet.

"Morning, Mr. Adam," Cole replied. He turned to Kara. "This is my friend Kara. She's visiting for the summer."

"Welcome, Kara. I'm Adam, one of the deacons here." The kind-faced man shook Kara's hand firmly.

"Nice to meet you," Kara said.

"We're a little late, so I'm guessing the seats downstairs are full," Cole said.

"They sure are," Mr. Adam said.

Cole nodded. "No problem. We'll head up to the balcony."

He led Kara up a flight of stairs to the right of the closed sanctuary doors. They climbed a surprising number of steps, which confirmed to Kara that this building was more like an arena than a traditional church. The balcony area was about three-quarters full of people, all standing and singing along with the hymn.

They walked up some more steps toward a pair of empty seats. As they went, various people on the outside aisle caught Cole's eye, smiled, and waved, two men even leaning over to shake his hand.

After they'd greeted Cole, Kara couldn't help but notice their eyes drift to her—she knew they were wondering who she was.

After they reached their seats, Kara gazed around the expansive church sanctuary, taking it all in. The first floor below was packed, not an empty chair in sight. Everyone stood facing the stage, singing along to the hymn being led by the robed choir and accompanied by piano.

The soaring ceilings and overhead lighting gave the space a modern feel, more like a concert hall than a place of worship. Kara noted the hymn lyrics projected on a large screen behind the choir, so no one had to hold hymnals while they sang.

Beside her, Cole sang under his breath. It was easy to see he was completely in his element here.

As Kara scanned the crowds below, someone among the people caught her eye. While everyone had their attention turned toward the stage, there was a single person who appeared to be looking directly at her.

She's staring at us, Kara thought. Then she recognized the woman—Debra Turner, Cole's mother. Debra was far away, but Kara could still make out the disapproving glare. She could almost *feel* it too, as if it were shooting straight through her.

Kara glanced at Cole, wondering if he'd noticed his mother's harsh gaze. But Cole's eyes were closed, his face serene as he sang. She wondered if Cole had even told his mother that he'd invited her.

Judging by that nasty look, I'm going to guess no, she thought.

After a tense moment, Debra Turner turned away, focusing on the choir. Before long, the hymn wound to a close.

A young pastor strode onto the stage. "Let's hear it for our choir this morning," he said, gesturing to the robed singers. The congregation clapped, polite yet reserved. "And Mrs. Sandy on piano—wasn't she wonderful as usual?" More mild clapping followed as the woman who'd been playing piano by the choir smiled shyly from her bench.

The projector screen changed from hymn lyrics to a simple title card that read, "Announcements with Andrew Harmon, Assistant Pastor."

The pastor glanced down at a sheet of paper he was holding. "I've got a few quick announcements for y'all today. First up, mark your calendars for our summer potluck next Sunday after service. Bring your favorite side dish or dessert to share.

"Next, the women's Bible study group will be starting up their summer session soon. They'll be digging into the Book of Ruth this year and I know it's going to be edifying. See Mrs. Sue after the service if you're interested.

"And lastly, a huge shout out to our high-school youth who'll be heading down to Mexico next week for their mission trip. They'll be helping to build houses for families in need." The pastor started clapping, prompting the congregation to join in. "Please keep them in your prayers. I know God will use them in a mighty way."

Kara noticed several dozen teens seated together near the stage beaming with pride at the acknowledgement. They all looked to be her age.

I wonder why Cole hasn't done one of those mission trips, she thought, remembering that he'd told her he'd never been out of the Mississippi before.

The assistant pastor concluded the announcements and prayed briefly before stepping off the stage.

The head pastor took his place. He was a middle-aged man with black hair, a gentle face, and a calm demeanor.

"Let us pray," he began, bowing his head. The congregation followed suit. Kara lowered her eyes, though her mind was only half-focused on the prayer. She caught snippets of it, something about seeking wisdom and truth from God's word.

After a brief but impassioned prayer, the pastor raised his head again. "Please turn to Acts chapter seventeen," he instructed.

Cole and others around them pulled leather-bound Bibles from pockets on the backs of the seats in front of them. Kara watched as Cole opened the Bible near the middle, expertly and quickly locating the book of Acts and flipping only a few pages to get to chapter seventeen.

Seems like he's done this a lot, Kara noted. She didn't know her way around the Bible at all.

"We're continuing our summer series on the missionary journeys of Paul," the pastor said, his voice filling the cavernous room through a lapel microphone. "Today, we're looking at Paul's visit to Athens."

The pastor began reading aloud a passage about Paul preaching to the Greeks. The screen mounted above the stage displayed the verses in large, easy-to-read print. According to the Scripture, Paul had noticed the city was full of idols and had taken the opportunity to tell the populace about the one true God.

"The people of Athens were steeped in false beliefs," the pastor said gravely after finishing the passage. "They worshipped a pantheon of gods and practiced idolatry through statues and images."

That Paul guy definitely wouldn't get along with Aunt Adrienne, Kara mused, her thoughts almost involuntarily going back to the little statue. She tried to shake the image from her mind, reminding herself that the only reason she was here in the first place was to forget about all that for a short while.

"Paul met their paganism and mysticism head-on with the gospel," the pastor continued, pacing along the stage. He was firm and passionate, but he was far from intimidating. "We too must be bold in proclaiming biblical truth to a lost world. The Athenians clung to 'unknown gods' but we serve the one true God who reigns over all."

"Amens" and tones of agreement rumbled through the crowd.

Kara tried to focus on the pastor's words as the sermon continued, but her mind kept drifting. She watched Cole beside her, enraptured by the message and hanging on to every word.

"Our youth are setting a powerful example." The pastor smiled down at the teens seated nearby. "They'll bring the light of Christ to families in Mexico who desperately need to hear of God's love. I just know he will use them on this trip."

Kara frowned. She was far from a church expert, to be sure, though she couldn't help but wonder why Mexico had been targeted as a location for their mission work. Back in Chicago, her friend Maria's family was from Mexico. People there already knew good and well who Jesus was. They went to church every week, albeit to the big Catholic one near their school.

"The idols in Paul's day looked a lot different from the ones that exist in the modern era," the pastor continued. "Today, we don't literally set up little statues and treat them as gods."

If only you knew... Kara thought.

"These days, we have other things that can become idols in our lives if we're not careful. Are you watching so much football that you're forgetting your family duties? Are you spending too much money at the mall, dipping your toes into unchecked materialism?" He turned to the Mexico-bound teens sitting near the stage. "Are you spending too much time playing video games?" A few of the boys exchanged sheepish glances with each other.

The pastor fell silent for a while as he stared at the stage floor. At first, Kara thought he was pausing for effect, but the silence stretched on for a bit too long. She noticed other people in the congregation exchanging puzzled glances as they waited for him to continue. Cole's eyes were fixed on the pastor, brow furrowed.

The pastor looked up again. "I've just received word from the Lord." He paced the stage, scanning the crowd intently as he continued, "He's told me there is someone here today who has allowed an idol into their life. It's not my place to judge you, but the Lord is calling for you to cast out this idol immediately and return to Him."

He couldn't possibly be talking about... Kara shifted in her seat as the pastor's words echoed through the silent sanctuary.

"The Lord has laid a burden on my heart for you this morning," the pastor said somberly. "You know who you are. The idol must be removed *now* before it takes further hold."

Don't be ridiculous, Kara thought frantically. *There's no way he could know.*

She glanced around, half expecting accusing eyes to be locked onto her. But the congregation seemed just as confused and surprised as she was.

"I urge you to not hesitate in removing the idol." Then he looked up toward the balcony—directly at Kara.

She tried to steady her nerves with slow breaths, yet she couldn't calm the twisting in the pit of her stomach. The pastor's words felt too close, too specific.

A stifling silence filled the sanctuary as the pastor let his admonition sink in. Kara kept her eyes down, and unexpected tears came. Had that really been some kind of divine warning against the statue?

A week before, Kara would've been certain it was a

coincidence. Now, she could no longer make such absolute decisions about what was real and what wasn't.

"Please heed my words," the pastor said, his voice calmer now, but still underlaid with a sense of urgency. His gaze lingered on the upper balcony, as if the "word from the Lord" had hinted that the person in danger was sitting up there. "If you need advice, or prayer, or guidance, please do not hesitate to come to me. I can help you walk in the safety of God's love."

With that, he let the heavy silence linger for a bit longer. "Let's pray," he said, deciding to conclude the sermon. Kara sensed he was wrapping it up earlier than he'd originally planned.

During the prayer, Kara caught Debra Turner eyeing her again. She had a feeling that the woman had interpreted the pastor's dire warning in a similar way. Maybe she remembered the statue Adrienne had taken home from her thrift store that day.

She was already thinking those things about my aunt anyway, Kara thought, remembering how Cole had used the word "witchcraft" at dinner that night. *Now she's probably even more convinced.*

But Kara found herself almost *agreeing* with Debra. It was all too uncanny. Kara got the impression that the pastor really had inferred she'd carried an air of idolatry with her into the church that morning, and he'd been disgusted by that and felt inclined to call it out. It brought tears to her eyes. During the last hymn, Kara had just enough time to wipe them away, managing to do it without Cole noticing.

———

AFTER THE FINAL hymn was done, the crowds started filing out of their seats and heading toward the exits. Kara and Cole descended the crowded stairs. Kara tried to avoid Cole's gaze, not wanting to give away how upset she'd become by the sudden turn the sermon had taken.

When they reached the church's atrium, Kara spotted a sign for the restrooms. "I'll be right back," she said, then rushed off toward the ladies' room without giving Cole a chance to respond.

Kara stood at the sink in the spacious restroom, taking deep breaths as she studied her reflection in the large mirror. The pastor's ominous words still echoed in her mind, and she suspected they probably would for a long time.

She turned on the faucet and splashed some cool water on her face, hoping it would help calm her nerves. As women filtered in and out of the stalls and sinks around her, Kara felt their curious eyes on her back. She avoided meeting anyone's gaze in the mirror. After a few seconds, she turned off the faucet and patted her face dry with a paper towel.

Kara took one more deep, steadying breath before dropping the crumpled paper towel in the trash can and leaving the restroom. The crowds were thinning as people made their way to their cars.

Kara scanned the area for Cole and spotted him several yards away, speaking with his mother. Even from a distance, Kara could see the rigid disapproval in Debra's posture. Cole's head was lowered submissively.

That's my fault, she thought, feeling a pang of guilt.

After a lengthy lecture, Debra stalked off, leaving Cole standing alone and looking dejected. Kara waited near the restroom, giving him a moment to collect himself. Then, after a few minutes, she approached. He brightened when he saw her.

"Hey. You okay?" she asked.

He did a good job at hiding the pain brought on from his mother's lecture and clearly didn't know Kara had seen the whole thing from across the room.

Cole nodded. "Yeah. Ready to head out?"

Stepping out into the roasting mid-morning sun, Kara shielded her eyes, the bright light almost blinding after the dim narthex. She blinked against the glare as they crossed the parking lot, the heat from the blacktop radiating up through the soles of her shoes.

On their walk through the emptying parking lot toward Cole's truck, Kara reflected on how thankful she was that Cole wanted to spend time with her.

Even if his mother hates Aunt Adrienne and me.

———

Cole stopped his truck in front of Aunt Adrienne's house. Kara unbuckled her seatbelt, ready to go.

Earlier, I just wanted to be away from here, she mused. But then, Pastor Craig had gone off about idols while looking directly at her. Now, she wanted this whole church thing to be over with as quickly as possible. *Is there anywhere I can go to feel comfortable?*

"Thanks for inviting me," she said, her hand on the door handle.

"You're welcome." Cole's fingers tapped nervously on the steering wheel. "Maybe again next Sunday?"

Kara hesitated. She hated the thought of sitting through another sermon that felt like a personal attack.

"Um… I'm not sure. I'll have to see how things go this week. My aunt might have stuff planned for us."

"Yeah, no pressure," Cole said quickly. "Just thought I'd ask. Oh, and hey"—he smirked—"let me know how the goat milking goes."

Kara grinned. "Will do." She climbed out of the truck and waved as Cole drove away.

Inside, she started to head upstairs to get changed into more comfortable clothes, but stopped in place, something catching her eye. She turned toward the left and peered into the living room.

The potted plants that Adrienne had been tending to that morning were strewn across the floor, their soil spilled out like dark blood on the hardwood. Leaves and broken stems littered the area, and several of the ceramic pots lay shattered among the mess.

"Aunt Adrienne?" Kara called out, her voice echoing in the eerie silence of the house. No response came.

Heart pounding, she climbed the rest of the stairs, her hand sliding along the banister. The upper floor was quiet, save for the creaking of the old wood beneath her feet. She turned toward Adrienne's bedroom, where the door was slightly ajar.

"Aunt Adrienne?" Kara called softly as she approached.

There was a long pause before Adrienne's voice drifted through from the other side. "Kara? Is that you?"

"Yeah, it's me," Kara replied. *Who else would it be?* She was relieved to hear her aunt, yet also couldn't help still feeling concerned. "Are you okay?"

"I'm fine, dear."

Something was off about the way Adrienne spoke. She sounded… disconnected. Like she was reciting memorized lines rather than having a conversation.

Through the crack in the door, Kara could just make out her aunt's shadow on the wall near the entrance to the master bedroom. It was rocking back and forth.

What is she doing *in there?* she thought.

"What happened downstairs? With the plants?"

The shadow continued its repetitive movement. "Oh, that. I didn't want them anymore. It felt like they were staring at me."

"What—what do you mean?"

"Their leaves." Adrienne's voice was low and monotonous. "Like little eyes. Watching."

Kara swallowed hard. "Are you sure you're alright? Do you need help with anything?"

"I'm fine, dear," Adrienne said again, although her tone was hollow and empty.

"Okay... I'll be here if you need me. I'll clean up the plants, too." Her voice trembled slightly.

Adrienne didn't respond. Her shadow kept rocking.

Kara backed away from the door and returned downstairs. She retrieved a broom and dustpan from the storage closet under the staircase. As she swept up the soil and ceramic shards, Kara listened out for any sounds coming from her aunt's bedroom. But the house remained silent, save for the soft scraping of the bristles against the floor.

Adrienne stayed in her room for the rest of the day.

20

"It's like I have the plague," Kara said. Once again, for every step Kara took toward Ed the Goat, the animal backed two steps away.

Both Ed and Glenda Norris stood nearby, watching the goat's strange, avoidant behavior. They exchanged a glance and shrugged.

"Seems they're still being moody," Glenda said. "It's all right. There're plenty of other things you could do if you don't feel like putting up with the animals today."

Kara frowned. After Adrienne had shut herself in her room all day yesterday, all Kara wanted that morning was to work with the animals—something that felt somewhat normal. Yet once again, they all wanted nothing to do with her.

Kara couldn't help but notice a difference in Glenda's tone. The last time she was there and the animals avoided her, Glenda had brushed it off. Now, she seemed to give it some consideration—as if maybe she was starting to heed their unspoken warning.

Like when your dog doesn't like someone, it can make you suspicious, Kara thought. *I hope that isn't happening here...* She'd be extremely disappointed if the elderly couple wound up asking her to stop coming over. *They wouldn't do that. I'm just being paranoid. Aren't I?*

She spent the morning cleaning the feeding troughs with Glenda. As they worked, Glenda Norris reminisced about a trip she and Ed had taken out west ten years prior. They had packed up the camper they'd owned at the time and drove to the Grand Canyon, sleeping under the stars in national parks and small towns along the way.

"I want to do something like that someday," Kara said, imagining the pictures of the Grand Canyon she'd seen in her textbooks.

"Here's my advice," Glenda had told her. "Do it while you're young. Ed and I didn't travel until we were older, and while we had some good times, I wish we'd started much sooner. These days, we don't get around as well as we used to, so there are some places I would've liked to have seen but probably never will."

When the morning chores were finished, Kara set out back home. When she reached the side of the house, she heard the murmur of voices coming from the front porch. Then she spotted a car that she didn't recognize parked beside her aunt's. She paused and peeked around the corner to check who was there. She saw her aunt standing on the porch looking down at Debra Turner, who was at the bottom of the steps.

"I don't see what the problem is," Adrienne said.

"I would just appreciate it if she stayed away. That's all." Debra was clearly trying to remain calm, but some tension and anger simmered underneath her voice.

Kara kept out of sight around the corner of the porch. *Is she talking about me?*

"I understand your concerns, Debra," Adrienne said gently. "But Kara is my family. I want her to feel welcome here, and your son is doing an excellent job of that. You should be proud of him."

"I just don't think it's *proper*," Debra replied sharply. "You know the trouble kids can get up to. Especially when they spend time alone."

Kara pressed herself against the side of the house, listening to the conversation unfolding on the front porch. She bristled. *Trouble?*

"Kara's a good girl and doesn't get in trouble," Adrienne said. "Neither does Cole, from what I know of him. So what exactly is the issue?"

Debra hesitated at the question. Kara realized her aunt knew precisely what the other woman was implying, but was trying to make her come out and say it.

She knows we're not getting into "trouble," Kara thought. *She just doesn't want Cole to be around someone related to Adrienne.*

"The *issue* is that it isn't the right thing for Cole," Debra finally said.

"Has he told you that?" Adrienne pressed.

"Well… no."

"Then how do you know?"

"Because I'm his *mother!*" Debra snapped. Kara stiffened at the brief outburst. Much to Adrienne's credit, she didn't react at all.

Debra took a long, steadying breath. "I've made my views clear to him, and now to you," Debra said through clenched teeth. "He knows where I stand. I expect you to do the same with your niece."

"I appreciate your concern, Debra, but who Kara spends time with is her decision. I trust her judgment."

Debra huffed in frustration. "Well, I don't. Just keep her away from my son," she said.

Then Adrienne, who Kara had only ever seen as calm and composed since arriving in town, erupted in anger. "How *dare* you!" she screamed.

The sudden outburst startled both Kara and Debra at the same time.

Adrienne flew down the porch steps toward Debra, her face twisted in disgust. "How *dare* you come here and say these things about my niece!"

It was like a dam had burst, unleashing a torrent of rage.

Debra stumbled backward, eyes wide. Kara had never seen her aunt move with such speed or speak with such vitriol. For a moment, Kara thought Adrienne might lay hands on Debra, but the other woman was quick to put some distance between them.

Kara considered rushing out from her hiding spot to get between them, but didn't. She was still too shocked and stunned at what she was seeing—she'd had no idea her aunt was capable of speaking this way to someone.

"Kara is a *wonderful* person." Adrienne jabbed a finger toward Debra. "*Far* better than you ever were or will be. If anyone's a bad influence, it's *you* and your small-minded intolerance."

Debra took another several steps back, alarmed.

Adrienne advanced until she had backed Debra all the way up against her car. "Don't come here speaking ill of my family again. Ever. And if you do, I'll cut you from here to here." Adrienne traced her finger from the bottom of her stomach to her collarbone. "Then, I'll open you up and strangle you with your own bloody intestines."

Kara gasped. *What is she saying?*

Debra's face drained of all color. Her trembling hand fumbled at the handle of her car door.

"I'll tear out your heart and put it on my altar. Then I'll dance naked with the devil all night to celebrate the end of your *miserable* life. Isn't that what you've always thought of me?"

Debra finally managed to wrench open the door and scramble inside her car. The tires squealed as she tore down the driveway.

Kara covered her mouth to suppress the fearful sobs that had burst out. Tears came to her eyes. She couldn't believe what she'd just seen. *Where did that come from?*

After Debra's car disappeared from view, Kara watched as the tension seemed to leave her aunt's shoulders. Adrienne doubled over, hands on her knees, and heaved in deep breaths as if the sudden explosion of anger had exhausted her.

Kara remained frozen in place, almost afraid to let her presence be known and reveal she'd seen the whole thing.

Adrienne then turned and went up the porch steps and into the house, letting the screen door fall behind her.

What... was all that about? Kara wondered. She agreed with Adrienne—Debra had been rude and out of line—but surely it wasn't bad enough for *that* kind of response. When Adrienne had spoken of Debra Turner before, she seemed to understand where the woman was coming from and how that contributed to the differences between them.

Has some conflict between them been building for a while?

Kara wondered. *Did I just see the final straw? Was Adrienne pushed too far this time?*

Despite that, it didn't justify the threat Adrienne had made. That had been far too specific and violent.

No, there's been a change with her now. Even if she was mad, she'd never say something like that to anyone.

Kara went up the porch steps and through the front door, still shaken. She heard muffled sobs coming from the living room.

She rounded the corner to find Adrienne hunched over on the couch, her face buried in her hands as she wept. Kara's heart ached at the sight. This was not the composed, gentle woman she knew.

Adrienne looked up, eyes red and swollen. She studied Kara for a moment before saying, "You saw all that, didn't you?"

Kara nodded.

"Oh god," Adrienne moaned, dropping her head into her palms again. "I don't know what came over me. I've never spoken to anyone like that before." Kara sat beside her on the couch and wrapped an arm around her aunt's shoulders. Adrienne leaned into her niece, seeming to take comfort in her embrace. "Debra had no right to say those things about you. But I shouldn't have reacted that way either."

"I know you were just trying to defend me," Kara said. However, she did agree that her aunt had taken it a step too far.

As she held Adrienne, Kara glanced up at the statue looming over them from its perch on the fireplace mantel. Its empty eyes seemed fixed on the two of them.

You're doing this somehow, aren't you? Kara thought.

Kara pushed those thoughts aside. Her aunt needed

comfort, not wild accusations. She stroked Adrienne's back for several minutes until the woman's sobs subsided. Despite whatever darkness had momentarily overtaken her aunt, Kara knew good still resided deep within.

But still, something had definitely come over Adrienne that wasn't quite right.

21

That night, as she lay in bed, Kara tossed and turned, unable to quiet her restless mind. Sleep evaded her entirely, chased away by the anxiety churning in her gut. She rolled over for what felt like the hundredth time and glanced at the glowing numbers on the digital alarm clock on the bedside table—2:17 a.m. With a frustrated sigh, she sat up and swung her legs over the side of the mattress. She just couldn't shake the feeling that Adrienne was still awake and up to something strange. She'd only caught her aunt acting oddly late at night once—when she'd given her ring to the statue. But after the episode with Debra Turner, Kara had a hunch there was more to come.

She crept out into the dark upstairs hallway, her bare feet making the old floorboards creak. She hesitated at the top of the stairs, straining to hear any sounds coming from downstairs. Very distantly, she heard whispering.

Kara paused halfway down the staircase and crouched, peering through the banister and into the living room.

Adrienne sat cross-legged on the floor in front of the fireplace, rocking back and forth, lips moving in a rapid whisper. Her hair hung loose and wild around her face. For some reason, she'd built a fire in the middle of summer, and already Kara could feel the stuffy, oppressive heat.

Adrienne showed no sign of noticing Kara's presence. Her focus remained fixed on the statue looming above her while she continued her fervent chanting.

Kara remembered the pastor's warning. *"The idol must be removed* now *before it takes hold."*

Adrienne rose. Kara almost started back up the stairs, thinking she'd been discovered. But her aunt's attention remained fixed on the statue.

Then Kara noticed that Adrienne held something. Coldness ran through her veins.

It was a knife from the kitchen—the largest from the block set.

Kara watched as Adrienne lifted her hand toward the statue and began to saw at her palm with the blade. Dark red blood flowed from the wound and dripped first onto the fireplace mantel, then onto the hardwood floor in front of the fire. Through it all, Adrienne did not wince or cry out, as if immune to the pain.

Kara cupped her hands over her mouth, stifling the scream that wanted to burst out. She scrambled up the stairs, wanting to be as far away from what was happening as she could.

She thought back to the night of the ritual, when her aunt had come into her bedroom and promised to stop all of this.

Did she mean she'd only stop involving me? Kara

wondered. Had there been some kind of carefully worded fine print in her aunt's promise? She couldn't remember.

First the food, then the necklace, then that ring that seemed to mean so much to her... now actual blood. What's next?

———

THE NEXT MORNING, Kara descended the stairs, dreading what she might find. She paused at the bottom, peering into the living room. The embers of last night's fire still smoldered in the fireplace, though there was no sign of the blood.

Kara walked over for a closer inspection. It looked like the blood hadn't been there at all—not even the hint of a small smear, nor any forgotten drops.

Adrienne cleaned this all up? With her hurt hand?

That seemed unlikely. Kara had cut herself badly before—wiping up blood was tough, and you almost always missed some.

Kara's eyes rose to the statue, which stared at her from the fireplace. She shivered as an unbidden image came into her imagination—a trail of black, shadowy smoke, like she'd seen the night of the summoning, enveloping and absorbing the blood.

Or maybe I just imagined last night, she thought. *Maybe it was only a very vivid dream.* That would explain the lack of blood. *I really, really hope that's the case.*

Kara decided not to go next door that day. She wasn't in the mood to be attacked by the animals again, and besides, she was tired from the lost sleep.

Adrienne came downstairs around mid-morning. The first thing Kara noticed was the thick, white bandage wrapped around her aunt's palm, instantly shattering any hope that what she'd seen the night before had been a dream.

"What happened to your hand?" Kara asked, trying to make the question sound sincere.

"Oh, just a little cooking mishap. Sliced it with a knife when I was cutting up some fruit."

Kara bit her tongue, swallowing back every one of the questions and accusations rising within her. Her aunt was committed to keeping up this charade.

Adrienne passed through the dining room and disappeared into the kitchen.

Kara wanted to cry. Seeing tangible evidence of her aunt's self-harm brought everything to a terrifying new level.

———

THAT NIGHT, Kara jerked awake, heart pounding. For a moment, she was disoriented, unsure of what had awoken her so abruptly. Then she heard it again.

Thump-thump-thump-thump-thump-thump.

She sat up in bed, straining to hear. The sound was continuous, persistent.

Her chest tightened. This was no ordinary house noise. And it was oddly familiar.

I think I've heard this before. But where?

Sliding out from under the covers, Kara crept toward the closed bedroom door. Working up her courage, she turned the knob and inched the door open a crack. The upstairs hallway was swathed in shadows.

The sounds were coming from the spare room across the hall. Then Kara realized what they were.

Counterclockwise footsteps, rhythmic and hurried.

It's back. It's here.

She bit off a scream. Kara rushed down the hall and pounded on Adrienne's bedroom door. "Aunt Adrienne! Wake up!" she cried.

"Kara?"

The voice had come from behind her. She gasped and whirled around. Adrienne now stood in the hall. Beside her, the guest bedroom door was open—and the footsteps had ceased.

"What's wrong?" Adrienne asked, looking concerned.

"Th-the sounds. From inside there." She pointed.

Adrienne looked into the guest room but didn't seem to see anything concerning. "I'm sorry. I must've made too much noise and woken you up."

Once again, she sounded off, like she was reading deadpan from a script.

"What are you doing?"

"I was just doing some organizing."

Kara scowled. *What's with all these lies?* she thought. "Organizing?"

"Yes. It's a mess in there, as you saw."

"This late at night?"

Adrienne shrugged. "When the motivation hits…" Her flattened tone made her sound like a robot that had been programmed with prepared responses.

Kara wanted to speak her mind, to hurl accusations, yet couldn't find the words. She knew what she'd heard. Why was her aunt stomping around in circles in the middle of the night? Right in the spot where the spirit had carved its name into the floor?

Helpless, she strode away from her aunt's bedroom door toward her room. "I'll just go back to bed." She didn't want to talk about this anymore, and Adrienne clearly had no intention of being forthcoming about what she was doing.

"I think that's best," Adrienne intoned.

Kara walked past her aunt and into her room. As she went, Adrienne only stared at her, a near-empty expression on the woman's face.

22

The next morning, after being woken up by Rocky, Kara went downstairs to find that Aunt Adrienne wasn't home. The living room was empty, the kitchen deserted. Kara looked out the window —her aunt wasn't doing her usual morning meditation, and her car was gone.

Part of her was relieved—it would give her a short break from how strange her aunt had been acting lately. But a larger part worried about what she might be doing.

Kara made herself breakfast, then spent the morning trying to focus on her Biology textbook. Just before noon, she heard the crunch of tires on gravel, so she went to the window. Adrienne's car lurched to an abrupt stop in its usual spot. The woman climbed out, clutching a brown paper bag to her chest. She walked toward the porch, leaving the driver's-side door wide open and the car's engine running.

Adrienne marched straight into the house. "Good morning, dear," she said when she saw Kara. Without pause, she went to the kitchen, pulled out a pan, and unpacked the contents of the bag onto it—a large cut of raw meat. A pool of pink liquid started gathering beneath it. "I got us a roast for dinner." Adrienne's voice was flat. "I'll prepare it later."

"Are there more groceries in the car?" Kara asked.

"No."

"Oh. It's just that… did you mean to leave it running?"

Adrienne paused and stood still for several long moments. "How forgetful of me," she finally remarked, voice still flat, then turned on her heel and strode out of the kitchen. Instead of going to turn off the car, though, she went upstairs.

Okay… Well, I guess I can do it, Kara thought. She stepped outside into the humid afternoon, slipped into the driver's seat, and twisted the key to cut off the engine.

Kara went back inside, closed the door, and leaned against it, frowning. If Aunt Adrienne was going to act strange all day, she wasn't sure she wanted to be around the house. But again, she didn't feel like visiting the Norrises just to be rejected by the animals.

I wonder if Cole's free, she thought. *Maybe we can do something together so I can get away from here for a little while…*

Kara's cell phone was on her bedside table, plugged into the charger. She went upstairs and turned left down the hall, but stopped short of her bedroom door—Aunt Adrienne was already inside her room, studying the crystals on the shelf.

Questions rose up into Kara's throat, but she ultimately kept her mouth shut—and observed.

Adrienne selected some crystals off the shelf and examined them as if she'd never seen them before and was immensely curious about them. Then she brought her nose to the glittering surface and inhaled.

She's sniffing them? Kara thought.

Adrienne then closed both her fists around two of the stones and squeezed. She clenched so hard that her fore-arms trembled, and Kara could hear the crunching from the door. Then Adrienne straightened her fingers one by one, letting the stone shards rain onto the floor.

Kara backed away, heart hammering. Adrienne had been acting strange, but this was something else entirely.

What's gotten into her? she wondered. *What can I do to help?*

Kara waited downstairs until she heard Adrienne's bedroom door slamming shut. She went back upstairs to her room, where she found all but a few crystals destroyed, their remains on the floor.

Curious, Kara picked up one of the few surviving gems. She attempted to snap it in half to see how solid it was. It didn't budge. She applied more force. Nothing. She put it in her palm and squeezed just as Adrienne had, but the rough edges only bit into her flesh.

There's no way, she thought. *How could Aunt Adrienne be strong enough to crush them with her bare hands? And even if she could, why would she want to? She loves these things.*

Kara closed her bedroom door, resolving to stay in there for most of the day. *Maybe if I wait long enough, Aunt Adrienne will get back to normal.*

———

IT WAS late afternoon before Kara poked her head out of her bedroom and peered down the hall; Aunt Adrienne's door was ajar. Distant sounds came from the kitchen.

Kara crept downstairs, her sock-clad feet silent on the steps, then turned left into the dining room. Careful not to make her presence known yet—she wanted to see what her aunt was up to first—Kara peered around the corner and into the kitchen.

Adrienne was rummaging through a drawer, shuffling utensils and tools, searching for something. The sound of rustling metal on metal was grating, but Adrienne didn't seem bothered. Then, as if deciding she wasn't going to find what she was looking for, she slammed the drawer closed harder than was necessary, giving everything inside a final rattle. She then went to stand in front of the roast on the counter, untouched from earlier. She peered down at it for a long time, possibly a full minute, without moving at all.

Why is she staring? Kara wondered.

In a sudden jerk-movement, Adrienne reached for the nearby knife block and took out the largest of the set—the same one she'd used to slice open her own palm.

With an abrupt, violent motion, Adrienne stabbed the roast, the blade sinking deep into the meat with a wet *thunk*. Kara flinched.

Again and again, Adrienne jabbed at it. A soft grunt accompanied each thrust—almost like half exertion, half pleasure. The knife rose and fell in a frenzied rhythm, tearing and shredding rather than cutting.

Kara's stomach churned. This wasn't cooking—it was more like an attack.

Adrienne stopped. The knife clattered to the counter as she leaned over the mutilated roast, her breath coming in short, sharp pants.

Then, with deliberate slowness, Adrienne reached out. Her fingers sank into the flesh, gripping a ragged chunk.

With a swift yank, she tore it free. Adrienne raised the raw meat to her lips, paused for a heartbeat... then shoved it into her mouth. Her jaw worked as she chewed, a trickle of blood-tinged juice running down her chin. She swallowed, her throat bobbing with the effort.

Kara stifled the urge to retch. Unable to watch any longer, she backed away. However, her heel caught on the edge of the rug and she stumbled, her elbow bumping against the wall with a soft *thud*.

Adrienne's head snapped up, then mechanically turned until her eyes locked onto Kara. Kara froze, her stomach feeling hollow.

Adrienne gave a smile that was too wide, too forced. "The roast is almost ready. Only a few more minutes."

The counter was a mess of blood and hunks, nothing resembling a cooked roast. The acrid smell of raw meat hung heavy in the air.

"It's okay," Kara said, swallowing hard. "I'm... not really hungry tonight. I think I might just study for a while and then head to bed early."

Adrienne's smile didn't falter; it remained unchanged, as if sewn onto her face. "Oh. Well, if you're sure. That's fine, dear. Do what you need to do."

Kara nodded, backing out of the kitchen. "Goodnight, Aunt Adrienne."

———

BACK IN HER ROOM, Kara tried to focus on her textbooks, but the image of Adrienne tearing into the raw meat kept intruding. The hours crawled by, and eventually, Kara found herself listening for any sound from downstairs.

The house had gone quiet. She attempted to sleep early, but remained wide awake, unable to relax.

Since she'd skipped dinner, it wasn't long before she was hungry. She didn't want to go down to the kitchen for a snack—she was nervous about what she might catch Adrienne doing next. But the rumbling in her stomach soon became too much to bear.

Just slip in, grab something small, then come right back up, she told herself.

Kara crept down the stairs once more. The living room was dark, save for the flickering glow of the television Adrienne had brought out from where she stored it. Adrienne sat on the couch, her face bathed in the blue light as she leaned forward, eyes fixed on the screen. She didn't blink, didn't move, barely seemed to breathe.

She had put on *Harold and Maude.* But the scenes and characters were moving backwards—she was watching the movie rewind. Her lips moved, as if she were mouthing along with the reversed dialogue.

Hunger forgotten, Kara retreated up the stairs. *If she's not acting normal by tomorrow, I'm going to get help,* she thought as she closed her bedroom door. *I don't know who I could call, but I'll figure it out.* If it came to it, she'd even take Aunt Adrienne's car keys and drive into town herself in search of someone.

Enough was enough. She had a feeling that waiting would only make things worse. She had to do *something.*

23

Kara's eyes blinked open. The bedroom was pitch dark, and she turned toward the alarm clock radio on the bedside table—2:55 in the morning. She didn't remember falling asleep.

Still a couple of hours before the rooster, Kara thought as she rolled over. She lay there for about a minute until she realized she was wide awake.

It didn't take long for her stomach to remind her she'd skipped dinner—and had bailed on getting a snack from the kitchen.

Surely Aunt Adrienne's in bed by now, she thought, hoping that she wouldn't walk in on another one of her aunt's late-night endeavors.

She threw off the covers and headed into the upstairs hall. The master bedroom door was shut. Kara moved quietly, not wanting to disturb her aunt.

She flipped on the light in the kitchen. The mutilated roast was still on the counter. Kara sighed. *If she leaves this out any longer, it's going to rot.* The meat had long since grown cold, and the grease and juices had congealed.

Kara picked up the pan and put the roast in the refrigerator. She returned to the counter, planning to wash the large carving knife her aunt had been using, but as she glanced around the countertop and the sink, she saw it wasn't there. Its slot in the block was empty. Kara wondered if Adrienne had accidentally dropped it, but when she scanned the tiled floor, she didn't see the knife.

Hopefully you're not cutting open your other hand right now, Kara thought. She grabbed a bag of almonds from the cabinet and left the kitchen, turning off the light as she went.

Something captured her attention at the bottom of the stairs before she could go back up. Kara's eyes narrowed as she peered out the darkened living-room window that looked out over the side yard. In the distance, near the tree line, an orange glow flickered against the night sky. She drew closer for a better look, and a few moments later, what she was seeing became unmistakable. The bag of nuts fell from her hand.

"Fire," she murmured. Alarm rose in her chest.

Kara bounded up the stairs, taking them two at a time. She darted to her aunt's bedroom, threw open the door, and turned on the light.

"Aunt Adrienne, there's a fire!" she called out. Her aunt didn't stir underneath the bundle of covers. "Aunt Adrienne!" Still no response. Kara rushed over and flung away the quilted bed covers. "Aunt—"

The bed was empty.

Kara's heart began to pound. *Where is she?*

She spun and raced back downstairs, bursting out the front door and onto the moonlit porch. Kara scanned the surrounding yard and driveway, yet saw no sign of Adrienne.

The orange glow was brighter now, and she could smell the acrid tang of smoke in the night air. It was close to a nearby cluster of trees—too close. One stray ember caught in the breeze could start an even bigger, uncontrollable fire.

There's no way she did this, Kara thought as her pulse pounded in her ears. *Right?*

She ran toward the fire, her feet pounding on the hard earth. The tall grass whipped at her ankles. As she got closer, she realized the bonfire was larger than it had appeared from the window, and farther away from the house than she'd thought.

She stopped short.

Adrienne, dressed in her white nightgown, stood before the raging bonfire. The flames reached high, casting wild shadows across the ground.

"Aunt Adrienne!" Kara cried. "What are you doing?"

Adrienne turned to face Kara, her eyes gleaming in the firelight, though her expression was blank.

Is she sleepwalking? But how—

A distinct sound interrupted her thoughts—a braying.

Kara looked to her left. There, tied to a thin tree trunk about ten steps from them both, was Ed the Goat. He struggled against the short length of rope, clearly afraid of the fire and the heat.

Kara's gaze shot back to her aunt. "What are you doing?" Now her voice was choked by tears.

In that moment when she had looked away, Adrienne had pulled out a large knife—the one from the kitchen. Its sharp blade glinted in the firelight.

Kara's heart dropped into her stomach.

No, no, no. This is all wrong.

"Aunt Adrienne, please," Kara begged, taking a cautious step forward. "Put that down. This isn't you."

Adrienne stared straight ahead, not acknowledging Kara's words. With the bonfire raging behind her, she looked quite frightening, as if she'd risen from the depths of hell.

"Think about what you're doing," Kara continued. "This has gone too far. Let's go back inside and talk."

Finally, Adrienne spoke. "This must be done. We must not anger Azunu—he desires an offering." Her voice was flat and distant. Trance-like.

Azunu. Hearing the name slip so easily from her aunt's mouth sickened Kara.

"Azunu doesn't exist!" Kara cried. "Please, you have to snap out of this!"

"You're wrong." Adrienne seemed angry now. "Even after *everything* I've shown you, you *still* refuse to accept the truth."

"Okay, I'm sorry. Fine, you're right. Azunu *is* real," Kara implored, realizing she'd chosen her words poorly. She searched for anything to convince her aunt to drop the knife and stop what she was planning. "But that doesn't mean you have to do this."

Adrienne seemed deaf to Kara's appeals.

There's no reasoning with her, Kara realized. *Whatever that statue's done to her... she's too far gone.*

"When Azunu makes demands… we oblige." Adrienne turned her empty, hypnotic eyes back to where Ed the Goat was fastened to the tree. She readjusted the grip on the knife.

Kara rushed and planted herself between the goat and her aunt. "You're not doing this. I won't let you." Her own conviction surprised her. She couldn't read Adrienne's expression with the shadows cast from the fire dancing across her face.

"Sacrifices are necessary," Adrienne said. "Move out of our way."

Our. Kara swallowed hard.

Adrienne began striding ahead, knife in hand, eyes fixed on Ed the Goat.

I'm sorry, Aunt Adrienne, Kara thought as she launched herself forward, slamming her body into her aunt with as much force as she could muster.

They tumbled to the ground in a tangle of limbs, Adrienne letting out a surprised cry and dropping the knife. Kara scrambled to pin the woman's arms, but Adrienne thrashed and fought.

"Stop!" Kara shouted.

"Let me go!" Adrienne shrieked, a wild rage once again in her eyes, similar to what she'd shown to Debra Turner.

Not knowing what else to do, Kara reared back and brought her palm down hard across Adrienne's cheek. She could've sworn the slap echoed far into the night. More sobs escaped her throat.

Adrienne froze, eyes wide.

Heart aching and chest heaving, Kara raised her hand to hit her aunt again, but hesitated.

By the light of the fire, Kara watched as the look on Adrienne's face slowly changed. The rage seemed to dissipate. The frantic demeanor faded, replaced by a mixture of confusion and fear.

"Aunt Adrienne?" Kara whispered.

Adrienne looked up at her niece from where she lay in the grass. Kara gazed into her eyes and saw that Adrienne was actually seeing her now.

"K-Kara?" Adrienne's voice was a broken whisper. "What... what's happening? Where are we?"

Kara let out a sharp breath. Her aunt sounded normal again.

"You don't know where you are?" Tears spilled down Kara's cheeks.

Adrienne looked at the bonfire. "What's burning?"

She doesn't know what she was doing, Kara realized. It had all been some kind of... hypnotic trance. In a way, Kara wondered if it was *better* that Adrienne had no memory of what she was about to do.

Kara got off her aunt and helped her sit up.

"I want to go home," Adrienne said. She was crying now, too.

"You are home, Aunt Adrienne." Kara forced her voice to be light and comforting—the opposite of the fearful dread that still filled her. "Come on. I'll bring you to your bed."

Anything to get her away from all this as fast as possible.

As they stood, Ed the Goat brayed. Adrienne seemed to hear him for the first time and looked at him in confusion. "What..."

"Don't worry about that," Kara said, guiding her aunt toward the house. "It's okay. I'll take care of everything. Let's just get you back."

Adrienne looked away from the animal, seeming relieved that she didn't have to think about it.

She clung to her niece as they went. Together, they walked into the house and up the stairs. Kara helped her aunt lay down in her bed.

"I'm so confused," Adrienne murmured.

"Don't worry about it right now," Kara said. "All you need to do is get some sleep."

Adrienne looked up at her as if that had been the best thing she'd heard in a long time. Kara watched as her aunt rolled over and pulled the covers up around her shoulders. Within seconds, Adrienne's breathing slowed to a calm rhythm.

Kara closed the bedroom door and leaned against it, letting out a shaky breath. Her hands trembled from the adrenaline still coursing through her. She clasped her palms together, trying to steady them. Squeezing her eyes shut, she took a moment to think, but had no idea how to even begin making sense of what she'd just seen.

I can't dwell on that right now, she thought. *I need to deal with everything before she wakes up.*

———

KARA PUSHED off from the door and headed downstairs. Under the staircase, she went into the storage closet and rummaged around until she found a large flashlight. She flicked it on to check the batteries; a bright beam appeared. She also spotted an old mop sitting in a blue bucket. Kara removed the mop and took the bucket. She brought it into the kitchen and dropped it into the sink, where she turned the faucet on the highest it would go. When it was full, she hoisted it out of the sink, struggling with the weight.

She went outside, where she saw the bonfire still roaring in the distance. The water sloshed down her leg as she crossed the large yard.

Once she was there, she set the bucket down and rushed to Ed the Goat. "Shhh, it's okay," she soothed, running a hand along his back. Ed trembled under her touch. Kara examined the rope tethering him. She knew she'd struggle to untie the intricate knot, especially with Ed pulling against it in fear.

The knife.

Kara swept the flashlight beam over the ground until she located the blade. She picked it up, but then something else caught her eye that she hadn't noticed during her panic.

The statue. Azunu.

It sat near the bonfire, presumably having been brought there by Adrienne. It was positioned as if it had been supervising everything Adrienne had been doing.

This time, there was something different about it. Before, Kara had gotten the impression that it was watching, a silent observer in the room. Now, it seemed to glare.

It isn't my imagination, she thought. She was done explaining things away. Normally, she averted her eyes. Not this time. Kara met its gaze, furious.

She'd brought the water out to douse the blaze, but now she had a different idea.

"You like to play with fire?" Kara whispered as she picked up the statue. She looked down at it in her hand, and it stared defiantly back up at her. Kara got the feeling that it was reading her thoughts, perhaps even accepting its fate.

Kara tossed it into the bonfire; the bright yellow flames immediately consumed it.

I should've done that a long time ago, she thought.

Kara returned to Ed the Goat—two quick slices of the knife later, the rope split. Ed took several steps back from the fire, clearly relieved to be free. Kara grabbed and held the severed end of the rope so that he couldn't run away.

Kara led Ed the Goat across the dark field between

Adrienne's house and the Norrises' property next door, her flashlight beam bobbing ahead to guide the way. Sweat broke out on her forehead against the thick, humid night air, and her feet swished through the tall grass. Ed stayed close to her side, seemingly aware that she was helping him get home.

When they reached the gate, Kara propped it open with her hip and shuffled Ed through before following and closing it behind them—she didn't want to wake the old couple.

As they approached the barn, Kara saw that its large door was ajar. She was pretty sure that the Norrises wouldn't have forgotten to close it.

Adrienne must have left it open when she came to take him.

She could hear the other goats stirring, bleating softly, likely awakened early from the middle-of-the-night activity.

She led Ed the Goat back to his empty stall, the door of which had also been left open. He rushed inside as if happy to be home, and Kara closed him in. She watched him for a moment, relieved that he appeared unharmed.

As she turned to leave, she paused, casting the flashlight beam over the barn's interior. Kara pictured Adrienne entering while the Norrises slept, moving in that strange, hypnotic trance. She imagined Azunu's whispered commands in her aunt's mind, telling her which goat to take—which specific one he wanted.

Kara left. She latched the door behind her and hoped that the Norrises would never find out about their goat's late-night escapade.

She made her way back across the dark field to the bonfire. The flames leapt and danced with as much life as before. She picked up the bucket and hurled the water. Smoke billowed up as the logs hissed.

The flames shrank, but weren't extinguished. Kara let out a frustrated sigh—they were too big for one bucket of water to handle. She'd have to make multiple trips.

Turning, she began the trek to the house. By the time she returned with a refill, rivulets of sweat trailed down her back from the humid night.

She launched the second bucket at the fire. More smoke and sizzling, yet the flames remained stubborn.

One more should do it, she thought as she ran a hand across her slick forehead.

When she came back with the third sloshing bucket, her arms burned from the repeated hauling. Without waiting to catch her breath, she pitched the water onto the shrinking fire.

The final embers darkened and went out. Smoke drifted into the night sky and the yard plunged into darkness, with only the moon above and Kara's flashlight providing any light.

Kara aimed the beam over the remains of the bonfire. She noticed now that it seemed to be comprised of various sticks, branches, and other bits of kindling Adrienne must have gathered from around the property. Kara imagined her aunt scouring the yard in the dark while in her trance. The mental image sent ice through her.

She directed the flashlight beam into the heart of the doused fire, looking for any sign of the statue. There was nothing there besides ash.

Good.

Kara finally felt a small sense of relief. The thing was gone. Destroyed. She hoped her aunt would now be free from whatever hold it had on her.

24

After the sun rose, Kara checked on Aunt Adrienne every twenty minutes or so. With each peek into her aunt's room, Kara's worry eased a little more. Adrienne slept soundly, her chest rising and falling in a gentle rhythm.

It's all going to be okay now, Kara thought. *I should probably get breakfast ready for when she wakes up.*

Kara made her way downstairs, her bare feet padding softly on the worn wooden steps. In the kitchen, she cracked eggs into a bowl and whisked them with a splash of milk and a sprinkle of salt and pepper.

Maybe I'll suggest we go thrifting, Kara thought as she cooked. At some point, she'd have to admit to her aunt that she'd burned the statue. Perhaps Adrienne could find something else at the store that she liked just as much—and was far less evil. *Hopefully it'll be Cole in the shop today instead of Debra.* After all the horrible things Adrienne had said to the woman, their next encounter was sure to be awkward.

She divided the eggs onto two plates, adding a slice of

buttered toast to each. Carrying the plates to the table, Kara arranged them with care, placing the silverware just so.

She must smell all of this by now, Kara thought. She waited for a bit, then ate her food when Adrienne didn't come down. *Maybe I jumped the gun?*

After eating, Kara went back upstairs to check on Adrienne once more. When she entered the master bedroom, she found her aunt awake and staring at the door blankly, as if she'd been waiting for her to show up.

"How are you feeling?" Kara asked. "I made break—"

"Where's the statue?" Adrienne's voice was weak—but at least she sounded like herself again.

Kara frowned. *Really? That's the first thing on your mind?* "It's gone."

"Gone?" She lifted her head from the pillow.

"Yes."

A fraught expression crossed Adrienne's face. She rolled over in bed, placing her back to Kara and yanking the cover up to her chin.

Kara stepped over to the bedside as she waited for Adrienne to say something else.

Finally, she did. "I want to see him."

Kara wanted to cringe. *Him.* "Come on, Aunt Adrienne. This isn't you. It doesn't make any sense why you're so obsessed with that thing. What about the other things you enjoy? Meditation and cooking?"

"Please. I want to see my statue."

It's like she didn't even hear me, Kara thought. "I told you, it's gone." She felt it was likely better to wait for her aunt to improve a bit before revealing to her that she'd taken it upon herself to burn it.

"You can't get rid of it like you think you can," Adrienne said—her tone had turned into a low growl. Kara gasped and took a wide step away from the bed. Once again, Adrienne sounded like she was speaking with a voice that wasn't her own.

But why? She was just *back to normal.*

"I think he has returned," Adrienne intoned. "I feel it. Go and see." Then she gave a mirthless giggle.

Kara felt guilty for how quickly she rushed from her aunt's bedside and closed the door behind her.

Why is she talking to me like this? Tears of frustration came to her eyes.

Confused and unsettled, Kara went back downstairs to the living room—and gasped.

In the middle of the floor was the statue, bearing no sign at all that it had been burned.

Kara stood frozen, her heart thudding in her chest. It couldn't be. She'd watched it burn. And yet there it was, like the flames had never touched it.

That's impossible, she thought.

The hollow gaze seemed to mock her, as if it knew something she didn't.

It was real. The statue was back, defying all logic and reason. Kara's mind spun with questions. How had it returned? What dark power had allowed it to resurrect itself from the ashes?

And what did this mean for her and Adrienne?

———

KARA SECLUDED herself in the dining room and kitchen. No part of her wanted to go back into the living room at all, nor upstairs near her aunt's room.

I need help, Kara thought.

There was no way around it. Aunt Adrienne was too far gone and too under the influence of the spirit that resided within the statue—which Kara couldn't even get rid of.

But who?

Kara racked her brain as she paced. In her head, she went through the people she came up with one by one.

Mom. No. Kara nearly laughed. There was no way Tracey Mills was going to interrupt her vacation with Robert to talk to her about Aunt Adrienne's spiritualism. She could almost hear her mother now: *"None of that is real, and it's all in her head. Tell her to grow up and snap out of it. You do the same."*

A doctor. No. There was nothing wrong with Adrienne physically, and that was what a doctor would try to find. He couldn't treat her for "bringing a spirit into the house that's making her do crazy things."

Kara sighed and dropped into a chair at the dining-room table. Her mind was drawing a blank. Now that she'd spent a decent amount of time in Silver Falls with her aunt, she realized that Adrienne really was a loner. She didn't have friends she went out with. Her phone never rang with someone checking in on her or just wanting to catch up. Despite all that, the woman kept a smile on her face and seemed happy doing her own thing.

But now, when she needs help, who is there to call? Kara wondered.

She remembered when Adrienne had made a brief slip and told her it was nice having Kara around because she had someone to cook for again. Kara assumed that meant she'd been cooking for a boyfriend who was no longer in the picture.

Does he live here in town? Could he help her?

But Kara had no way of knowing who this guy even was.

Then something occurred to her.

She looked toward the cabinet that stood against the wall just behind the table. The lower compartment was where Adrienne had retrieved the ring she'd offered to the statue.

Was that ring from him? Does she keep other things from him in there?

Kara went over to the cabinet. She knelt down and opened the doors, revealing a cluttered interior. Old books, trinkets, framed photos, and stacks of paper filled the space.

She started removing the contents and arranging them on the floor beside her knees. First was a faded leather photo album stuffed with Polaroids capturing Adrienne during different stages of her life. A younger, carefree woman smiled up at Kara from several of the shots, surrounded by friends whom Kara didn't recognize.

I was right, Kara thought. *This is where you keep your memories.* Maybe there was a clue in there about someone Adrienne was still close to.

Hidden among the clutter was a wooden box. Curious, Kara took it out and set it on the floor. She lifted off the lid. Inside, she found a stack of sketches done in pencil and charcoal. Her fingers trembled slightly as she picked up the first one, realizing that it was a hand-drawn portrait of a younger Aunt Adrienne.

Kara studied the sketch, taking in every detail. Adrienne's wild, curly hair framed her face, free and untamed. Her eyes were closed, lips curved into a soft smile. She looked peaceful, content. Kara marveled at how the artist had perfectly captured Adrienne's warm, caring essence with simple strokes.

She flipped through the rest of the sketches, a collection of candid moments and portraits. In one, Adrienne sat cross-legged in a meadow, picking flowers. Another showed her lost in a book, brow furrowed in concentration. Each sketch reflected pure affection—this artist had seen and known the real Adrienne.

There was a signature at the bottom of each drawing.

Arthur.

Kara ran her fingers over the name, sensing the history and meaning behind it. She imagined a man watching Adrienne, relishing every detail as his hand moved over the page. To her, these sketches told a story of closeness and care.

This guy seems like more than just a friend, Kara realized. *This must be him. Arthur.*

Underneath the artwork, Kara found an open envelope that contained a folded letter inside. As she carefully extracted the aged paper, she felt a wave of guilt for digging through her aunt's boxed-up past. She had a feeling that if Adrienne had wanted to share this part of her life, then she would have done so by now. Instead, she seemed to prefer keeping it all stored away. Kara normally would've never snooped like this, but her aunt needed help. They both did.

The paper only had a few lines of messy writing.

Thank you for reminding me that everything is energy and energy is everything. Thank you for reminding me that there's light in the spiritual world when things seem dark. —Arthur

"Maybe this guy could help me," Kara whispered, but she knew it was only a desperate thought. All she had was a name. She didn't even know how to begin trying to contact him.

Enough snooping. I need a real answer. She returned all her aunt's belongings to the box and put it back into the cabinet.

———

THE AFTERNOON WORE on into the early evening. Kara knew she should check on Adrienne again, but their last encounter had left her on edge. Yet as the hours ticked by, guilt started to gnaw at her. She couldn't avoid her aunt forever. Kara climbed the stairs, each step feeling heavier than the one before.

Taking a deep breath, Kara turned the knob and let herself in. Adrienne still lay in bed, curled on her side and facing away from the door. The curtains were drawn over the window, casting the room in gloomy shadows.

"Aunt Adrienne?" Kara called softly.

Adrienne didn't respond.

Kara approached the bed and put a hand on her aunt's shoulder. She rolled over and looked up at her—and for a moment, Kara thought an entirely different woman had taken Adrienne's place.

Her face was alarmingly pale. Dark circles rimmed her bloodshot eyes. Her hair hung limp and lackluster. A shock of grey had formed at the roots—it hadn't been there that morning. She looked like she'd aged fifteen years in a matter of hours.

"What's happening to you?" Kara took her aunt's thin hand, and the bones felt so prominent. Her jaw had become angular and her cheeks sunken. "This doesn't make any sense."

Something clicked in Kara. *No more.* She couldn't let this go on. She had to intervene.

"It's the statue," Kara said firmly.

Adrienne blinked. "What?"

Even with that single word, Kara could tell her her aunt's authentic voice had returned. *For now. She seems to be fading in and out.* As the woman looked up at her, Kara saw a flicker of the real Adrienne beneath the surface.

"The spirit inside the statue. It's doing this to you."

Adrienne shook her head, almost imperceptibly.

"Yes," Kara said. "I know it is. And I'm going to get rid of it."

This time for good. Somehow...

Adrienne seemed to panic. She tried to sit up in the bed, but struggled, not having the strength. She was suddenly afraid—afraid that her niece might take her statue away.

"Aunt Adrienne, please listen to me. Ever since that night with the magic circle, you've changed. It's like you've become a different person."

Adrienne shook her head, but Kara pressed on.

"We both saw what happened. I think whatever's in the statue is… evil. It's like it's poisoning you someh—." Kara's voice broke. She took a moment to collect herself before continuing. "I saw everything—the chanting, the offerings, you hurting yourself…" She rubbed her fingers along the thick gauze wrapped around Adrienne's hand. "And I want it to stop. This isn't right, or good. You *have* to understand that. You *have* to fight it." Adrienne's eyes glistened with tears. Kara grasped her aunt's wrists and gave them a single, firm shake. "Be strong, like I know you are."

The woman stared up at her for a long time. Her aunt searched her face, and it seemed to Kara like she was internally debating with herself, trying to figure out who she should believe—the spirit within the statue or her own niece.

"What would Arthur say if he saw you like this?" The words slipped out before Kara even fully realized what she was saying.

Adrienne's eyes went wide at the name. Sadness seemed to descend upon her. She looked like she had so many things to say, yet didn't have the strength to get the words out.

Finally, her lips parted slightly. Her voice came out hoarse and weak: "Arthur would say… Lake Silver."

Kara's brow furrowed. "What?"

"Take the statue… to Lake Silver. And throw it in."

She's giving me permission to get rid of it, Kara thought, relieved. She'd do it right now, with no hesitation. But she was unclear about something.

"Why do I have to throw it in the lake?" Kara asked. *Why would that work when fire didn't?*

"The lake is a sacred place…"

Kara then remembered what her aunt had told her when she'd first arrived—the indigenous people who'd once inhabited the area considered the lake to be sacred.

Maybe if the spirit inside the statue is evil, then the sacred spot will… I don't know, get rid of it or something, she thought.

She didn't understand how it was all supposed to work, but it didn't matter. If her aunt was allowing her to get rid of the statue, she'd seize the opportunity.

"I'll do that right now. You just rest. I'll handle this."

Adrienne squeezed Kara's hand with what little strength she had. Her eyes shone with gratitude, and Kara could see her aunt barely emerging from the darkness that had clouded her spirit.

I'll fix this, and then everything can go back to normal, Kara thought.

———

KARA WENT into the living room for the first time since the statue had reappeared. It stood in the same spot, unmoved. Despite being carved from stone, the eyes seemed alive, watching Kara with what she thought was a glint of humor.

The fragments of a plan came together in her mind. She'd toss the statue into the trunk of Adrienne's car, then drive it to Lake Silver. She couldn't remember how to get there, but she could stop and ask for directions from the first person she saw. Surely they'd be able to point her in the right direction.

"We're going for a little ride," Kara muttered.

She went to pick up the statue, but it was far heavier than she remembered.

"What…"

She bent at her knees and tried again to lift it, but it barely budged. Kara groaned in frustration.

She swore that if the thing could talk, it would be laughing at her.

It's like it knows.

Somehow, the statue had become heavier—like some sort of defense mechanism after she'd burned it.

And there was no way she'd be able to carry it on her own. She needed help… and there was only one person she could think to call.

25

Kara went out onto the porch. The afternoon was slipping toward early evening, but it was darker than it should've been at that time—grey storm clouds were brewing in the distance. The humidity was thick and oppressive, and the scent of the coming rain was in the air.

She took her cell phone out of her pocket, searched for Cole Turner in her contacts, and dialed.

He answered on the second ring. "Hello?"

"Hey, Cole. How are you?"

"I'm fine."

He sounded nervous. Kara wondered if his mother had told him about her recent run-in with Adrienne.

"Are you okay?" he asked a few seconds later.

"Honestly... not really."

"What's wrong?"

Kara took in a breath. "You remember that statue, right?" she began. "The one my aunt got from your mom's store? And that we talked about at Duke's?"

"Yeah."

"I want to get rid of it."

Cole was silent for a few moments before saying, "Okay. Why don't you?"

"Well, I tried. And it didn't work."

"What do you mean?"

"I tried to burn it, actually. But it just reappeared back into the house."

"Reappeared?"

She clenched her eyes, regretting using the word.

"Kara, what's going on?"

She hesitated, unsure about how much to reveal to Cole over the phone. He was her friend, sure, but he was also Debra's son. The idea of evil spirits would be very off-putting for him.

Which is reasonable, Kara thought. *Should I be trying to involve him? Maybe this is a mistake.*

But Kara reminded herself that she didn't have time to overthink it. She was out of options. She'd just have to blurt out the truth.

"Look, I don't want to freak you out, but I also want to be honest with you. That statue... isn't normal."

"In what way? You mean like it's creepy?"

"Yeah, but I also know now *why* it's creepy. There's... something inside of it."

Cole was quiet for a moment. "Oh." The simple sound was heavy and meaningful, and Kara understood that he'd picked up on what she was really trying to say.

"Yeah."

"You're sure? How do you know?"

"Well... it's a long story. One that I don't think you want to hear. Look, Cole, I know you don't like this kind of stuff, and I'm so, *so* sorry to be calling you—"

"Kara, it's—"

189

"—but I'm desperate. My aunt needs help. And the only way to help her right now is to get rid of that statue as soon as possible."

"But if it didn't burn, then how—"

"Lake Silver."

He paused. "What about it?"

"I need to throw it in the lake. Aunt Adrienne told me that would work."

"Oh. Why?"

"The lake was apparently sacred to the indigenous people who lived in this area a long time ago."

"Are you asking me to take you to the lake?"

"Yes. If you don't mind." *And to help me carry the stupid thing.*

Cole's silence stretched on and on, her own nerves getting worse with each passing second. She knew it was a difficult decision for him to grapple with—helping her would mean facing supernatural things he'd been taught to fear and avoid. But if he chose not to help her, she didn't know what she was going to do.

"Okay, I can take you out to Lake Silver. No problem."

Kara exhaled in relief. "Thank you," she said fervently. "I *really* need to get this thing out of the house."

"There's a bad storm on the way. Have you seen the clouds?"

"Yeah, I see them," Kara said, biting her lip. "Still... can you come now?"

Cole considered for a few seconds. "I'll head over in a few minutes."

They hung up, and Kara paced back and forth on the porch, counting her steps to pass the time as she waited for Cole.

One… two… three… forty-five… forty-six… forty-seven…

All the while, the sky grew darker and greyer. Light thunder rolled in the distance.

After what seemed like an eternity, she heard the rumble of Cole's truck. The headlights appeared as he turned down the long gravel driveway. Kara paused her pacing at the top of the porch steps.

Cole parked and got out of the truck. "Hey," he said as he walked over. His gait was tense, and she could tell that he was nervous.

"Thank you again for coming."

"No problem," Cole said, nodding and glancing at the house apprehensively. "So… we ready to go?"

"I need your help. Lifting it."

"Lifting it?" he asked, confused.

"Yeah. Come see. I'll show you."

Kara led the way inside. The statue, shadowed in the dim light, still stood in the middle of the living room floor from when Kara had last tried to pick it up.

Cole stared at it warily. "What's wrong?"

"It's heavier now than it was the day Aunt Adrienne bought it."

Cole's eyebrows shot upward. "Heavier? How?"

"I know it sounds crazy, but try to lift it. You'll see what I mean."

He went to stand over the statue, then bent over and took hold. Kara saw his face strain with effort, the muscles in his arms bulging. "Oh wow." He bent his knees and tried again, this time hoisting with all his might, and barely managed to lift the thing off the floor. He started staggering back out to the porch, so Kara rushed to open the door for him.

She watched anxiously as Cole struggled under the weight of the statue. His face was strained, beads of sweat forming on it as he slowly made his way down the porch steps. About halfway to his truck, his muscles gave out, and he dropped the statue onto the ground with a heavy *thud*.

Cole stood doubled over, hands on his knees as he caught his breath. After a few moments, he straightened up and wiped his arm across his forehead. "You weren't kidding," he said between breaths. "That thing's gotta weigh over a hundred pounds now, easy."

Kara nodded, glancing at the statue where it lay inert on the grass. Its carved eyes seemed to glare up at her.

"Yeah… I don't get it either."

Cole looked like he wanted to ask for more information, but then thought better of it. He bent down and wrapped his arms around the statue, grunting with effort as he lifted it again and resumed waddling toward his truck.

"You want it in the backseat?" Kara asked, hurrying to get ahead of him.

"Tailgate," he managed between clenched teeth.

Kara went to open the truck's tailgate. Cole reached it a moment later, where he struggled to get the statue high enough to reach the truck bed, but managed it after a few strenuous seconds.

He leaned against the truck for a moment to catch his breath again.

"You okay?" Kara asked. She slammed the tailgate shut.

"Nothing to it," he said, panting. "I've moved heavier boxes at my mom's store." Kara knew he was just playing it cool, but she nodded in agreement. "Alright, let's get this thing to the lake."

26

They drove down the narrow, winding backroad, flanked on either side by thick woods. Rain began to fall, lightly at first, but turned into a downpour that hammered on the roof. Cole turned on the windshield wipers, their rhythmic swishing the only sound breaking the heavy silence that had fallen between them.

Kara glanced nervously into the passenger-side mirror, which gave her a glimpse of the truck bed where the statue lay. Even with it in the back, she could feel its presence.

"You okay?" Cole asked, noticing her discomfort.

"More or less."

"And your aunt?"

She sighed. "Not really."

"What's going on? Is she sick?"

"Kind of."

"In what way?"

Kara remembered how *aged* Adrienne had suddenly looked, but didn't quite know how to explain that to Cole

—or explain it at all. She quickly decided to answer him another way. "Well... the weirdest thing was a few nights ago..." She told him about hearing her aunt running in circles around the spare bedroom.

If he didn't believe her, he didn't say so. "That's strange. What does it mean?"

"I wish I knew."

Despite what she'd claimed, that was *far* from the strangest occurrence, but it felt like the safest thing to reveal to Cole at that moment. She absolutely did *not* want to tell him about Adrienne slicing her own hand open, or the incident with Ed the Goat.

"And you think it has something to do with... some spirit inside the statue?"

"I just know I need to get rid of it as soon as possible."

After a few more minutes of driving, Cole spoke again. "So that day we went to church and Pastor Craig randomly started talking about idols and spirits..."

Kara kept her eyes fixed on the rain-streaked window. That seemed like a distant memory now.

"Did he mean your aunt?" Cole asked.

Kara lowered her head, ashamed. "I don't know for sure, but probably."

Cole was quiet for a moment. "Right..."

"I'm sorry," Kara said in a small voice. "I never wanted to get you involved in any of this, but I don't know anyone else in town, and my aunt—"

"It's okay. I want to help," Cole said. But there was a note of apprehension in his tone that he couldn't quite disguise. Kara was grateful for his steadfast willingness, despite his discomfort. She hoped that once the statue was gone, this chapter could be behind them.

Although I wouldn't be surprised if he wanted nothing else to do with me after this, Kara thought.

Cole was silent for a long time. Then he pulled the truck over to the side of the road.

"Why are we stopping?" Kara asked, worry shooting through her.

Cole unhooked the cross necklace that dangled from the rearview mirror. He looked down at it in his hand, his fingers closing around it. "Pastor Craig always says that evil spirits are weak compared to God. Maybe we don't need the lake at all."

Before Kara could respond, Cole opened his door and stepped out into the rain. She watched through the rear window as he made his way to the tailgate, his shirt quickly becoming soaked. He lowered the tailgate.

What's he doing? Kara scrambled down from the passenger seat and joined Cole at the back of the truck.

The statue lay on its side, seeming to watch them—daring them to try something.

Cole held out the cross toward the statue.

"Cole, wait," Kara said, her voice nearly lost in the drumming of the rain. "Are you sure about this?"

He glanced at her, raindrops streaming down his face. "Evil can't be in the presence of God," he said, almost as if reassuring himself instead of her. He sounded like he was simply quoting something he'd always been told but hadn't actually experienced himself.

Kara didn't want to do this. Despite her aunt's terrible state, Kara was sure of the instructions: cast the statue into Lake Silver. If Adrienne thought crosses and God would work, then she would've said so. In Kara's mind, what Cole was doing was wasting time—delaying them from reaching the lake. Yet she didn't know how to urge him away from this idea he'd suddenly had.

Cole turned his attention back to the statue. He seemed to search for the perfect thing to say, then a moment later shouted, "By the power of God, I cast you out!"

Nothing happened. The only sound was the continued pinging of the drops on the metal truck bed.

"I want you to leave this statue." Cole's words were undercut by an air of false authority, as if he were unsure of what he was saying.

Again, nothing happened.

"Cole, maybe we should—"

He suddenly gasped and stumbled backward, his eyes wide with terror. He looked around, as if searching for something in the darkness beyond the reach of the truck's headlights.

"What's wrong?" Kara asked. She took a step toward him, but he held up a hand, stopping her.

"Did you hear that?" he asked, his voice shaking.

Kara frowned, straining her ears against the rain. "I didn't hear anything. What was it?"

Cole opened his mouth to respond, but then hesitated. He shook his head and cast his gaze down. "Never mind. It was probably... just the storm."

Kara wanted to press him further, but the look on his face made her hold her tongue. Whatever he'd heard, it had clearly shaken him.

"We should keep going," Cole said, moving back toward the truck cab. "To the lake, like you said."

Kara blinked in surprise at his sudden change of mind. "Um... okay."

His little burst of faith didn't last long, she thought.

She hadn't even gotten her door closed all the way before Cole pressed the gas and jolted them forward, continuing down the darkened road ahead. As they went, Kara glanced over at Cole, taking in the tense set of his jaw and the white-knuckled grip he had on the steering wheel.

What did you hear? she wanted to ask him. *What did it say—*

Something sprinted from the woods on the side of the road, cutting right in front of the truck.

Kara shrieked and braced herself against the dashboard as Cole slammed on the brakes and they fishtailed on the slick asphalt. Cole fought for control of the vehicle, steering them into a controlled skid until they screeched to a halt in the middle of the road.

For a moment, they just sat there breathing heavily, the sound of the rain pounding on the roof deafening in the shocked silence.

"You okay?" Cole asked.

"Yeah," Kara managed. "Did you see…"

Cole nodded, his eyes wide. "It looked—"

"Not like a person," Kara finished for him in a hushed voice. They exchanged a fearful look.

It had been tall, maybe seven feet, and was either dressed all in black or just *was* black. And the way it had chosen right then to dart in front of them… it was almost as if it had been *trying* to make them crash.

"You… you didn't hit it, did you?"

"No."

Kara peered out into the stormy gloom, searching for any sign of the figure they'd narrowly avoided. The headlights illuminated nothing but the road and the surrounding trees. "Let's just go."

"Yeah. You're right." Cole put the truck in gear and straightened out before they proceeded. He drove slower now.

Kara released a breath, willing her pounding heart to calm down.

She cried out again when a sharp sound cut through the cab. Only a second later did she realize it was her cell phone, the jangling ringtone coming from the pocket of her wet shorts.

"Just the phone," Cole said. He'd likely been startled by Kara's yelp.

Kara fished it out of her pocket and flipped it open. Adrienne was calling her. "Hey, Aunt Adrienne. Are you okay?"

"Where are you?"

Once again, her aunt sounded weak, distant. "I'm with Cole. We're going to Lake Silver."

"Why?"

Kara hesitated for a few seconds. "You told me to. Remember?"

"I think you should come home."

Cole shot her a concerned look from across the truck cab.

"I will, I promise, but only after—"

"Come home now. Please."

"I'll be home soon."

"It wants blood, Kara."

Ice ran through Kara, seeming to freeze half the nerves in her body. "Huh?"

"Blood. It wants blood."

Kara swallowed, remembering Ed the Goat. "I know. But it won't get any. I'm making sure of that."

"I think you should come home."

Kara sighed. "Okay. We're coming now." They were close enough to the lake that she could just tell her aunt what she wanted to hear.

The line went dead, as if her aunt had hung up on her. Kara checked her phone screen, and sure enough, the call had been disconnected.

"We're going back?" Cole asked.

"No. Not before dumping this statue."

After getting rid of it, whatever hold it has on Aunt Adrienne will be gone, right? she thought. *Isn't that how it's supposed to work?*

———

COLE STOPPED in an open space off the side of the road.

"Are we there?" Kara asked.

"There's a path through the trees," Cole explained. "This is where people park when they visit. The lake itself isn't too far from here on foot."

Kara stepped out of the truck and onto the soft, damp earth. The rain had slowed to a drizzle, and the air was thick with humidity. She recognized the area—it was the same spot she and Adrienne had parked when they'd gone for their hike.

Cole went around to the truck bed and started hauling the statue, grunting with effort. When he got it close enough to the lip, Kara then helped him pull.

Once it was out, they both worked together to bear its unnatural weight, Cole holding the head and Kara at the base. She hoped wherever they were going wasn't far.

They followed the path as it wound through the woods, their footfalls muted by the layer of pine needles covering the ground. Rain dripped from the canopy of leaves above them, and the trees pressed in close on either side, their branches reaching out like claws.

To an outside observer, Kara and Cole must have looked absurd. The statue they carried was so small that the sight of two people carrying it would have been comical. As they struggled with the statue's unnatural weight, their bodies were forced uncomfortably close together. Their uneven, encumbered steps caused them to stumble, making their foreheads collide more than once.

Then Kara heard a rustling in the underbrush, the snap of a twig. She froze. Cole, noticing her sudden stop, paused and looked at her quizzically.

"Did you hear that?" Kara whispered, her eyes darting to the trees.

"Hear what?"

Then it came again. The unmistakable sound of footsteps crunched through the pine needles, circling them beyond the edge of the path.

"There's something out there," she breathed.

"Just keep going," Cole said.

Kara realized he was right and tightened her grip on the base of the statue. They continued forward, quickening their pace despite the weight of their burden. Her arms ached and her lungs burned, but fear spurred her onward.

They emerged onto a rocky outcropping overlooking Lake Silver. The dark waters stretched out before them, the surface choppy from the heavy winds.

Almost there.

Then Cole stopped dead—and dropped his end of the statue, which wrenched it out of Kara's hands. It slammed down into the leaves and she'd only barely managed to get her toes out of the way.

"No, we're—"

Cole was staring at something behind them. Kara spun around.

A towering figure emerged from the darkness between the trees—the same thing that had nearly made them crash the truck. Kara's thoughts raced back to the night of the séance when she'd seen the shadowy presence—it had been a formless mass, vague and unsettling. But now, it had taken on a distinct shape. It was a tall, jagged silhouette, with edges that seemed to flicker. The sight sent a primal terror coursing through Kara, her mind struggling to comprehend the impossibility of what she was seeing.

Azunu.

It had to be.

She could no longer blame this on a mere trick of the light or a figment of her imagination—a tangible entity had pursued them.

Kara felt rooted to the spot, her limbs frozen. Cole, too, seemed paralyzed beside her.

Then something snapped inside Kara, bringing a surge of adrenaline and determination.

That thing being here doesn't change what I need to do.

She bent over and dug her fingers into the soil beneath the statue's base so she could get her fingers under. She tightened her grip and started dragging it, her muscles straining, working much harder now that Cole was no longer helping her.

With a sudden burst of speed, the flickering shadow closed the distance between itself and Cole. The boy lifted his hands in defense, but a thin, black arm lashed out and struck Cole, who cried out as he was knocked off his feet, tumbling to the ground in a heap a few paces away from where he'd stood.

Kara shrieked when she saw Cole drop, but kept dragging the statue, inch by agonizing inch.

The entity stepped over Cole where he lay and advanced toward Kara.

She shot a look over her shoulder. The edge of the overhang was right there.

Kara mustered every ounce of strength she had left. The stone was unyielding, far heavier than anything she'd ever carried alone before.

The wet sole of her shoe found the edge, slipping on the rock and almost sending her tumbling into the lake. Ironically, it was her hold on the statue that anchored her.

The creature bore down on her. Reached out a hand with narrow, shadowy fingers, ready to grab her.

A guttural cry ripped from her throat. And with a final, desperate heave, Kara rolled the statue over the edge, watching as it plummeted toward the dark waters below. It seemed to hang in the air for a moment just above the surface before it plunged into the lake with a cannonball-like splash.

Kara held her breath and fixed her eyes on Azunu's shadowy form, the hand still reaching for her.

Nothing happened.

The creature remained motionless, its dark silhouette looming over her, cornering her on the edge of the overhang.

A flicker of doubt crept into her mind.

It didn't work. What did I do wrong?

With each heartbeat that passed, a cold dread collected in the pit of her stomach.

A piercing shriek made Kara clasp her hands over her ears; Azunu's shadowy edges writhed and contorted, as if in agony. Sections of black smoke peeled away from his body, dissipating into the air. His form seemed to unravel, losing cohesion. With a final wail that echoed across the lake, Azunu's body collapsed in on itself, imploding into a swirling whirlwind of darkness, returning to his smoky, wispy form.

The pillar of smoke that had once been Azunu arced over Kara's head, moving as if pulled by an unseen force. It streaked toward the lake, drawn inexorably to the spot where the statue had sunk. The smoke hit the water's surface and seemed to be sucked downward, as if the statue itself were a drain pulling everything into its depths. The vortex spun faster and faster, until with a final, violent twist, it disappeared beneath the water.

The lake became still once more, its dark waters placid and undisturbed like nothing had ever happened. Kara stared at the spot where the statue had vanished, hardly daring to breathe.

27

A loud groan came from behind her. She turned to see Cole pushing himself up on his elbows, wincing in pain.

Kara rushed over and knelt beside him, helping him to sit up. "Are you okay?" She gasped when she saw blood running from the side of his mouth.

"Yeah." He gingerly touched the edge of his lip, then spat into the leaves. "What happened? Where's—"

"It's gone," Kara said. "It went back inside the statue. Which is now at the bottom of the lake."

Cole's shoulders loosened as he let out a sigh of relief. "You did it."

"I think so," Kara said, though a tiny sliver of doubt still nagged at her. "I hope so."

No. I did it, she told herself. Adrienne had apparently been right about Lake Silver being sacred. *It wouldn't have disappeared like that if something hadn't forced it to. It's trapped down there now. Forever.*

She helped Cole to his feet. As they headed back down

the path, Cole limped at first, but then was able to walk off the pain. The storm had blown over, so they were no longer pelted by rain.

"You lied. You didn't need me to help lift it after all," he quipped once they were in the truck.

"That's not true and you know it," Kara said. She'd only dragged the statue the final couple of feet. If Cole hadn't come when she called, she'd never have gotten it this far. Despite everything, Kara grinned. It made her happy that even after what they'd just been through, Cole was still willing to make a joke.

But as they started the drive back to Adrienne's house, the humor vanished. Kara couldn't help but sense a dark sullenness fall over Cole. His eyes grew distant and his bloody lip shifted into a frown. He now seemed to be deeply and fearfully contemplating something.

It's all catching up to him, she realized.

The backroads leading away from Lake Silver were completely shrouded in darkness except for the beams of the truck's headlights. Cole's eyes remained fixed on the road ahead. Kara considered asking him what he made of it all, but the heavy silence between them felt absolute. She figured Cole had no more answers than what she could come up with herself.

And while she was grateful for his help, she couldn't deny the guilt that was spreading through her. *He's seen things he never thought he would. Until tonight.* Not only that, but she'd put him in immense danger. For a brief, terrifying moment, she'd been certain that the malevolent presence that inhabited the statue intended to kill them— and would have if she hadn't thrown it into the lake in time. She'd had no clue Azunu would actually fight back.

They'd escaped unharmed, but Kara had a feeling that neither of them had escaped unchanged.

They pulled up to Aunt Adrienne's house. A handful of dim lights were on inside and shone through the windows. A knot formed in Kara's stomach at the idea of going back inside.

But the statue's gone, she told herself. *Everything should be normal now. Right?*

"You alright?" Cole said, breaking Kara out of her thoughts.

"I... I don't know," she answered truthfully.

Cole let out a slow breath. "We probably can't tell anyone about this. They'd never understand."

"You might have a point."

"Will you be okay here?" Cole asked.

That was what she'd been trying to figure out. She still wasn't sure. "Yes, I think so."

I did what Aunt Adrienne told me to do. It's done.

"Call me if you need anything. Or want something. I'm here for you."

"Thank you, Cole. And I'm sorry. For getting you involved in this."

Cole gave a small nod, but didn't respond further.

With nothing left to say, Kara stepped down from Cole's truck, her legs feeling unsteady beneath her. She went around the front, cutting through the bright headlights, and walked toward the porch.

"Kara," Cole called from the rolled-down window. She turned. "I'll be praying for you."

She hadn't been told that many times in her life; it wasn't something she particularly cared to hear. But that night, she found herself grateful. "Thanks."

With that, Kara went up the front porch steps.

'I WILL REMEMBER YOU. You will regret helping her.'

The words echoed in Cole's mind as he watched Kara ascend the front porch steps. Earlier, when he'd held his cross necklace up to the statue, the voice had shot through his head, dark and inhuman. But what had frightened him more was that Kara *hadn't* heard it.

It was talking just to me, he thought.

The creature had repeated the same thing as he'd emerged from the trees by the lake.

'I will remember you. You will regret helping her.'

This time it had been louder, making Cole drop his end of the statue, which had forced Kara to drag it the rest of the way by herself. He'd been so afraid, so immobilized with fear when the entity had struck him down.

She may have saved my life, he thought. *Who knows what would've happened if she hadn't thrown the statue into the lake in time?*

It was gone now. He was safe. And although things felt resolved, Cole knew he wouldn't be the same for a long time. That night, he'd *seen* the things that Pastor Craig had warned about in his sermons. Before, Cole had been confident that he'd never cross paths with anything like what his pastor had described.

"God, thank you for protecting us," he whispered. He took the cross necklace that he kept dangling from the rearview mirror and pulled it over his head. He wanted it close.

Even though it gave him comfort, he couldn't help but remember how it had seemed to fail him earlier. He'd tried to use that cross, yet it had only angered the spirit.

Kara's idea of throwing the statue into the lake was the only thing that had actually worked.

He pushed the thoughts away. *God's plan. God's timing.*

And as he drove, he thanked God again that Kara had succeeded and that the entity was gone. Despite that, the memory of the threat lingered in his mind.

'I will remember you. You will regret helping her.'

28

Cole's truck lumbered down the driveway and the taillights disappeared into the night.

After he was gone, Kara stepped into the darkened entry hall. She was struck by how cold it was inside.

"Why…" she whispered, and even in the darkness, she could see her breath frost in front of her mouth. She rushed to the nearby thermostat. It read seventy-two degrees—the same setting Adrienne had kept it on all summer.

How is it freezing? It wasn't just a bit chilly in the house; it reminded her of stepping outside into a Chicago winter morning.

Kara heard a muffled sobbing.

She went into the living room, where no lights were on. A silhouette lay curled on the floor, crying.

"Aunt Adrienne?"

At the sound of her name, the woman fell silent. She slowly unfurled herself and stood, movements stiff and mechanical.

"Are you okay?"

The sobs ceased, replaced by an eerie silence. Adrienne straightened and planted herself facing Kara. The shadowed outline of her body seemed large and looming.

"I did what you told me," Kara said, as if reminding her that she was supposed to be better now.

Even the usual nighttime sounds that normally came through the windows were muted—the summer insects had hushed, as if they didn't dare make any noise that might irritate Adrienne.

Kara reached over and found the light switch. She flipped it. The living room's overhead light only blinked and flickered, though in the brief flashes, Kara could see Adrienne's vacant stare boring into her, face wet with tears.

What's going on? Kara thought. *I did what I was supposed to. The lake... I watched that monster get sucked underwater...*

"What have you done?" Adrienne said.

"I got rid of the st-statue." Her voice cracked. "You're free now."

"What have you *done?*" Adrienne shrieked.

Kara took a step backward, wanting to turn and flee but also not wanting to leave her aunt like this. "I did what you said!"

"*Liar!*"

Kara winced at the hatred in her aunt's tone. "I swear, I just wanted to help you."

"I told you Azunu demands blood."

In the flickering light, Kara saw Adrienne lift her arm. She hadn't noticed it before, but in her hand Adrienne held the knife—the same one she'd used to draw blood from her palm, and the one she'd intended to use to sacrifice Ed the Goat.

She pointed the tip at Kara.

Not waiting for even a second, Kara turned and rushed toward the front door. It slammed closed by itself, as if by some invisible gust of wind.

Kara pulled on the knob, but it wouldn't give.

"Blood. Blood. Blood." Adrienne chanted.

She wouldn't do this, Kara thought. Her aunt was still inside there. She'd reached her before. She could reach her again.

Kara pressed her back against the door, hand clutching the unyielding knob as her aunt advanced. She searched Adrienne's eyes for any sign of the woman she knew, but all she saw was a cold, empty stare.

"Aunt Adrienne, please!" Kara cried. "You have to fight it, like before."

Adrienne's chanting grew louder as she raised the knife over her head. "Blood—blood—blood."

Kara's mind raced. She suddenly recalled the conversation that had prompted Adrienne to tell her how to get rid of the statue. "Remember Arthur!" she screamed. "What would he think if he saw you like this?"

Adrienne froze, the knife hovering in the air. For a moment, the anger on her face eased. "Arthur?" she whispered.

"Yes," Kara said eagerly. "He loved you. You have to remember."

Adrienne blinked, shaking her head as if trying to clear it. The knife lowered in her trembling hand.

It's working.

Kara softened her own tone as she said, "You wouldn't want him to see you like this."

Adrienne then started to sob again. "It hurts," she groaned. "Make it stop."

That's her. She's fighting through it.

"Give me the knife, Aunt Adrienne," Kara said gently. "Let me help you."

Adrienne studied her niece for several long seconds, as if unsure if she could trust her. "Kara..."

Kara braved a step forward and offered her open palm to take the knife away. "Yes. It's me. You're okay now. You don't need—"

Adrienne sharply shook her head. "Azunu demands *blood.*"

Then Kara watched as Adrienne lifted the knife once more—to her own throat. Without hesitation, she drew the blade across the soft flesh of her neck. A sheet of red cascaded down.

29

Kara sat numbly on the porch steps, staring blankly as police officers and EMTs swarmed the yard. Their voices blurred together into an indistinguishable din. Red-and-blue lights flashed from police cruisers and an ambulance.

She barely registered the uniformed man kneeling in front of her, lips moving as he spoke, his brow creased in concern. Kara shook her head. There were no words to explain. No way they could understand the nightmare she'd emerged from.

Aunt Adrienne. Gone. Just like that. In a flash of self-inflicted violence Kara was still struggling to comprehend.

She wanted to scream, or cry, or lash out, but was unable to. She felt empty. Hollowed out.

Her palms were sticky. There were crimson stains on her shirt and shorts, too.

How did that happen? She couldn't remember.

The officer placed a gentle hand on her shoulder, then

spoke again. Finally, she was able to hear him. "I know this is difficult, but I need you to tell me what happened here tonight."

Kara lifted her head. Her voice came out in a ragged whisper. "You wouldn't believe me if I told you."

PART TWO

21 Years Later

30

Kara walked down the narrow jetway, the humid Mississippi air working its way through seams in the jet bridge as she exited the plane. Every step brought with it a wall of reluctance that seemed to fight against her.

The small airport was just as she remembered it from years prior, yet still felt foreign—it was so different from the bustling hubs she frequented for work.

While she made her way through the terminal, Kara couldn't help but notice that the people around her looked much the same as they did the last time she had visited Mississippi. So unlike the diverse crowds she encountered in Chicago, the Bay Area, or her current home in Boston. Their drawling southern accents transported her back to that summer. Seeing and hearing these people brought up memories she'd worked very hard to suppress.

When she turned a corner to head toward baggage claim, she stopped dead in her tracks. For a brief second, she saw Aunt Adrienne standing right where she'd been at the beginning of that fateful summer, beaming as she waved. Adrienne's colorful, flowing dress and chunky jewelry had made her stand out from the crowd.

Kara blinked and the vision was gone, replaced by a family hustling past, pulling overstuffed suitcases.

Fighting back tears, Kara waited at the baggage carousel. *I knew this was going to be hard,* she thought.

One by one, other passengers from her flight gathered their luggage and headed out. Soon, only a few stragglers remained. Then she was the only one left. Finally, her black suitcase tumbled down the ramp.

She thought back to her arrival all those years ago, when her bag had been the first to come down the conveyor belt.

"I manifested it," Adrienne had said. *"I focused my intention on your luggage being unloaded quickly from the plane. And it worked!"*

The memory jabbed at the middle of Kara's stomach.

She rolled her suitcase over to the rental-car counter. An elderly woman with silvery hair and thick glasses sat behind it, typing on an ancient desktop computer.

"Good afternoon," the lady said. A few seconds later, she finished what she was typing, then looked at Kara with a smile.

"I have a reservation for Mills," Kara said.

The woman nodded and continued clacking away at the keyboard. After what seemed like an eternity, she looked up. "Alright, Ms. Mills, I've got you all set here. Just need your signature on this form, and then you'll be ready to go."

Kara signed the rental agreement and the woman handed over the key. "It's stall number 12 in the economy lot, out that way," she said, pointing toward the exit doors. "Blue Nissan Sentra."

"Thank you," Kara said, taking the key. She hurried to the parking lot, the automated sliding door sighing shut behind her. The thick air wrapped around her the moment she stepped outside.

I didn't miss this heat and humidity at all, she thought as she crossed the asphalt. *Chicago and Boston might have bitter winters, but at least they never get like this.* And nothing beat the Bay Area, of course—it was perfect year-round.

She scanned the rows until she located her rental car. She tossed her suitcase into the trunk and slid into the driver's seat. As the engine sputtered to life, the blast of cool air from the AC offered some relief from the oppressive summer heat.

She reached into her purse and took out the cell phone holder she'd remembered at the last minute to grab from her own car back home. It affixed to the air vent to the left of the steering wheel. Kara set it up and put her phone in the holder, then tapped a few times to where she had saved the address of her hotel. The map came up.

Kara pulled out of the rental lot and onto the main road leading into town. Verdant Mississippi countryside flanked the two-lane highway on either side.

Eventually, the sign appeared, just as she knew it would: "Welcome to Silver Falls, Mississippi - Population 7,124."

Kara's breath caught in her throat as she drove past it, though she kept her eyes fixed straight ahead.

The road widened into Main Street. Kara took in the familiar storefronts lining both sides. They all looked frozen in time. She almost felt like she was sixteen again. *I guess there's a part of me that's also stuck here,* Kara admitted to herself. *Just as unchanged as the buildings.*

Kara spotted the Silver Fields Inn up ahead on the right. She turned on her blinker and eased the rental into an open spot along the curb. Once out of the car, she pulled her bulky suitcase from the trunk and headed inside to check in.

The lobby was small and dim, with worn carpeting and striped, faded wallpaper that looked to be original to the 1960s-era building. Behind the front desk sat an elderly man in a plaid shirt and suspenders, engrossed in a newspaper.

He peered up over his bifocals when Kara approached. "Afternoon. You have a reservation?" he asked in a gravelly voice.

"Yes, under Mills," Kara replied.

He rifled through a stack of papers and nodded. "Yep, got you right here. Room 108, just down the hall and to your left." He slid a brass key across the counter.

"Thank you," Kara said. She headed down the dim hallway, her suitcase bumping along the threadbare carpeting behind her.

When she unlocked and opened the door to room 108, the stale air that escaped indicated the room likely hadn't been occupied for some time. Stepping inside, Kara surveyed the space. The decor was decidedly vintage, with thin bedspreads and heavy drapes that blocked out most of the afternoon sunlight. An old box television was atop a wooden dresser. The bathroom featured avocado-green tile and a simple tub.

Kara set her suitcase on the luggage rack and sat down on the edge of the lumpy mattress. She looked around the room, noting a lightbulb missing one of its frosted-glass globes on the ceiling. Some cracks in the plaster resembled miniature fault lines.

It was a far cry from the sleek, modern hotels Kara stayed in for work conferences and events. But she supposed it was as good as she was going to get in Silver Falls.

I won't be here long, she reminded herself. *Just need to do what I came to do and then leave. This time for good.*

All of this had started from a visit to her mother in Chicago about a month ago. Kara had discovered a letter lying open on the cluttered kitchen table atop a stack of unsorted mail—the bold red letters had caught her eye. The letter was an official notice, terminating the agreement between her mother and her property-management company. It was dated three months earlier.

When Aunt Adrienne died at the end of that summer, her house had passed to Kara's mom, who'd hired some local property managers to operate it as a rental. For two decades, Tracey Mills had received rent payments every month despite never having once set foot in it.

Now, according to the notice, that arrangement had come to an end. When Kara approached her mother about it, the reaction had been swift and angry. Tracey had snatched the paper from her hands and told her to mind her own business.

Kara realized that her mother had been content to keep the house in the family only as long as she didn't have to deal with it. Now, she was refusing to address this issue—whatever it was—at all. Just like how she still refused to address *anything* related to her sister.

Kara had approached her mother the next day after giving her time to calm down. Again, she'd gotten nowhere.

Kara knew her mother's anger stemmed from lifelong issues with her late sister, which would likely never get resolved. In the years following the summer of 2002, Kara had pieced together that her mother harbored deep resentment toward Adrienne. To Tracey, Adrienne had let her mental health deteriorate to the point of taking her own life in front of Kara, leaving her traumatized. Kara, however, held a more nuanced perspective. She understood the full extent of that summer—a truth she hadn't shared with her mother, who, of course, wouldn't have believed a word.

Kara considered putting the old house out of her mind as well. But she knew this notice from the property manager wouldn't be the end of it.

That night back in Chicago, sitting in her childhood bedroom, she'd called her friend Joanna in Boston to ask her advice. Joanna had worked as a real estate agent for a handful of years and now owned a couple of rental properties.

"Sounds like you caught it in time," Joanna said.

"What do you mean?" Kara asked.

"If the house has only been empty for roughly three months, then that's not long enough for anyone to really notice or care."

"Okay…" Kara sensed a "but" coming.

"But if your mom refuses to do anything, then she's going to have problems. That town's local government won't stop trying to reach out. They'll do basic maintenance and inspections, but those costs will be passed to your mom. If she still doesn't act, then there'll be fines and citations. Eventually, they'll foreclose on the home and either sell it at auction or demolish it, depending on its condition."

"I figured… I don't know why Mom thinks this house can just… go away." And it upset her. It was almost as if her mother wanted the memory of Adrienne to disappear as well. Maybe she did.

"She isn't necessarily wrong," Joanna said. "The house *will* go away, but that comes with a massive legal headache she'll have to deal with at some point."

And so here Kara was, summoned back to the town that haunted her nightmares, filled with memories of malevolent spirits and her poor aunt's harrowing descent into madness. She was there to sort out the situation that her mother refused to handle and help her avoid the coming consequences.

Kara wondered if there was more to it. To her, avoiding fines, penalties, and legal pains was well worth the effort, but what about the house itself? Even though Kara had no desire to ever see it again, it still somehow felt wrong to just… let it rot away. It seemed like an insult to Aunt Adrienne. Even if Tracey had no regard for her sister's memory, Kara was different. Since that summer, Aunt Adrienne had always held a huge place in her heart.

Maybe my solving the problem with the house is like some kind of repentance for not being able to save her. Kara shook the unwelcome, intrusive thought from her mind.

Tomorrow, she would meet with her mother's former property manager. The first step was to figure out why they'd dropped Tracey as a client. The woman had refused to talk about it.

"I don't know and I don't care," her mother had told her. *"If you want to dig around, fine, but leave me out of it."*

Before the meeting, though, Kara wanted to take a trip out to the house to see if there was any extensive damage or some other obvious reason her mother had been dropped.

A nagging dread warned her that visiting Adrienne's house would only reopen old wounds she had tried so hard to forget. Memories would come flooding back. As much as Kara tried to convince herself that she was fine, that she had healed, a part of her deep down knew that wasn't true.

Now I'm procrastinating, Kara told herself. She'd learned long ago that when it came to difficult things, it was best to just do them and get them over with—challenging projects at work, uncomfortable conversations, even break-ups. It would only cause more pain and anguish to sit around *thinking* about going to Adrienne's house. Better to handle it.

I only need to go there once. After that, I won't have to return ever again.

———

KARA'S HANDS gripped the steering wheel. She wasn't ready, but the time had come. Her heart raced as she drove down the gravel road leading to her aunt's old house. The fear and resistance grew with every second until the house came into view. The structure stood tall among the ageless oak trees on the expansive land.

When Kara got out of the car, somehow her eyes first went to a distant spot in the field on the side of the house. In her memory flashed an image of the bonfire her aunt had built in the middle of the night, under the influence of the spirit.

She forced herself to look away. She walked up the creaking steps of the porch. Just to the left was where

Aunt Adrienne would sit facing the rising sun during her morning meditations. A porch swing that hadn't been there before creaked in the breeze.

Kara's hands trembled as she slid the key into the lock behind the screen door. With a *click*, the front door swung open. The musty scent of old wood washed over her. She stood frozen on the threshold, overwhelmed. With a deep breath, she stepped inside.

Kara's eyes swept the living room, taking in the emptiness. The last tenants had removed all their belongings, leaving behind faded outlines on the hardwood where furniture had once been. At first glance, the home seemed in remarkably good condition.

Predictably, her gaze was drawn to the fireplace that dominated the nearby wall. She pictured Aunt Adrienne placing that cursed statue on the mantel, as if giving it a position of power over the room. Kara could almost feel its malevolent eyes sweeping the space, observing everything.

She shivered, remembering how the statue always seemed to be watching, like it was silently gathering information. The way its stare had made her skin crawl. And how Adrienne had been oblivious to it all, treating the figure like a houseguest.

I've only made it through the front door, and already being back here is overwhelming, she thought.

Kara tore herself away from the fireplace and moved toward the dining room. As with the living room, it was stripped bare. She pictured the home-cooked food she'd shared with Aunt Adrienne over that fateful summer— and how abruptly Adrienne had stopped eating anything at all.

With a sigh, Kara headed upstairs. Her footsteps

echoed in the empty hall as she walked to the left, stopping outside the first door—the room she'd stayed in. She turned the knob and entered.

It was as bare as the rooms downstairs. But in her mind, Kara could still see the furnishings. The quilt on the bed, the chest of drawers where the statue had suddenly appeared that morning when it all began. She imagined lying awake at night, listening for any sound of Adrienne wandering the house, gripped by a force Kara couldn't understand. She also remembered staying up late texting that boy Cole Turner on her old flip phone, desperately seeking distraction from the terror.

Even now, years later, she could recall the unease that had permeated those long summer nights, the uncertainty of what Adrienne might do next while under the spirit's influence. She'd felt so alone and afraid in this house.

Adrienne's bedroom waited at the end of the hall. Inside, not a stick of furniture was left, but the memories flooded back. Kara pictured Adrienne curled up on that big four-poster bed, blankets wrapped around her. Eyes hollow, skin clammy, hair suddenly grey as if she'd aged a decade. Barely able to speak or eat.

All because the spirit was taking over.

Kara blinked away tears. She'd been just a scared teenager, overwhelmed and unsure of what to do as she'd watched it all happen.

With a ragged exhale, Kara turned and hurried from the room, eager to escape the painful memories. She went back downstairs, where she remembered that she was here to inspect the home, not get lost in the past. There hadn't been anything obvious that had leapt out at her. Tenants and the property manager had maintained everything well over the years.

So what's wrong? Why was Mom dropped as a client?

Kara went back outside onto the porch. The late-afternoon summer air was thick, but it felt better than being inside the house. At least she could breathe again.

She started walking, needing to move and clear her head after being immersed in so many difficult memories. But instead of returning to her car, she found that her curiosity was drawing her to the field—the one she used to walk through to get to the neighbor's property next door. The grass was overgrown, but Kara pressed through it, surprising herself when she remembered the uneven parts of the earth, small and random dips that threatened a rolled ankle. She stepped gingerly when she passed those spots, all the while feeling as if she were gliding through a dream of the past.

Soon, the Norrises' house came into view, looking much the same as before. But the backyard that had once been filled with chickens, goats, and a rooster was now home to a swing set, trampoline, and a playhouse. The old barn was gone, likely torn down years ago. The gate that had surrounded the land was also gone.

There's a good chance Ed and Glenda have passed away by now, Kara thought with a tinge of sadness.

"Can I help you?"

The voice startled Kara. She turned to see a man who looked to be in his early thirties approaching her, suspicion written across his face. Behind him, she glimpsed two young girls peeking their heads out the back door of the house. The man gestured for them to go inside.

"I'm sorry," Kara said, realizing she'd wandered onto this man's property. "I was…" She trailed off, unsure of how to explain herself. The man waited, eyes narrowed. "It's just that my aunt used to live next door." Kara pointed in the direction she had come from. "I visited her for a summer when I was sixteen. I would come over and help in the barn with the animals."

The man's expression softened, but he still looked perplexed. "Well, we bought his place four years ago, and there wasn't a barn." He nodded his head toward Adrienne's house. "Are you moving in?"

"No. My mother owns the property now. I'm just here to… sort out some things."

"Right," the man said.

"Sorry to bother you," she said sincerely. "I was feeling nostalgic, I guess."

The man gave her a polite smile and a nod as Kara started back toward her aunt's old house, the whole time sensing the man's eyes boring into her, likely making sure she was actually leaving.

When she got back, Kara sat in her car for a few moments, letting the rush of emotions from being there wash over and through her. She wasn't certain, but it was possible that returning might turn out to be cathartic in a way.

Speaking of catharsis, there's one more place I have to visit, she thought.

31

ara pulled into the parking lot of the first shop she passed. The interior was modest but homey, and near the front register, she found a decent display of various floral arrangements and potted plants. Kara wasn't sure what she was looking for —how did you choose the right flowers for someone you had tried to save, only to fail?

She settled on a colorful bouquet of gerbera daisies. Their bright, happy faces seemed so out of place, especially given the somber reason she had bought them. Her aunt had always loved vibrant colors.

She used her phone to locate Knox Cemetery on the outskirts of Silver Falls, and it didn't take long to get there. Once parked outside the iron gates, she accessed the cemetery's online directory to look up Adrienne's plot.

The graves were neat rows of stone markers peppered with bursts of color from flowers left by loved ones. Kara wandered among them, following the map on her phone.

And then there it was. Simple. Understated. Just her

aunt's name and the dates of her life. Kara stood frozen, staring down at the grassy plot. Tears blurred her vision as she set the daisies down.

"I'm so sorry," she whispered, her voice strained. "I tried, I really did."

I had no idea what I was up against.

Kara lowered herself to the ground, sitting cross-legged by the headstone. "I was a child, I get it. But I've felt… guilty ever since." The tears were flowing freely now. "I just… hope you can hear me wherever you are. I—I hope you know how hard I t-tried."

She wasn't sure how long she sat there. Finally, she wiped her eyes and stood. The cemetery suddenly seemed very quiet. Peaceful. She felt lighter somehow, like a weight had been lifted from her shoulders.

Then something occurred to Kara. She scrolled through the directory on her phone once more, locating Ed and Glenda Norris' plots.

She plucked two bright gerbera daisies from Adrienne's bouquet and navigated her way between the rows of headstones until she found the pair that marked the final resting place of the older couple.

Kara felt a swell of fondness as she looked down at their names. She still remembered them so clearly—Glenda's warm smile as she taught Kara how to milk the goats, Ed's crinkled eyes and raspy laugh. They had shown her nothing but kindness that summer.

"I never got the chance to thank you both," Kara said, placing a daisy on each grave. She hoped they knew how much their acceptance had meant to her, a girl so out of place. Their barn had become an unexpected refuge amidst the growing darkness.

And you both taught me not to be afraid to try something

new, she thought, remembering the first time she'd milked Martha the goat, the first time she'd gathered eggs, and the first time she'd hauled heavy bags of feed in the heat. That attitude had stayed with her since then and had served her well over the decades, both personally and professionally. *It all started in your barn.*

She turned and made her way back to the parking lot, almost feeling as if the ghosts of her past were watching her go.

32

Kara lingered in her car in the cemetery parking lot, thinking. Besides the Norrises' barn, Cole Turner had been the other positive memory from that summer. On a whim, she pulled out her phone and typed into her maps app the name of the store his mother had owned. According to the listing, Thrift Love still existed. She had a feeling that—much like everything else in Silver Falls—it likely hadn't changed.

I'll pass by on the way back to the hotel, for nostalgia's sake, she thought, although she doubted Cole was still anywhere near Silver Falls.

Kara followed the directions on her phone until she spotted the familiar faded sign for Thrift Love just up ahead. She pulled into the parking lot, empty except for a single truck.

Staring at the shop, she felt a flood of memories come rushing back—walking through those doors with Adrienne that fateful day and browsing the crowded aisles full of dusty relics while her aunt became transfixed by the statue. That moment had set everything in motion.

But that had also been the first time she'd seen Cole. A few days later, he'd called Adrienne's house phone and invited her out for dinner. He'd become her friend that summer, and a welcome distraction from the terrible things that were happening to Adrienne.

He even helped me get rid of the statue, Kara remembered. It had been the first time in a long, long while she'd allowed her memory to go there. She still regretted how she'd involved Cole in such a terrifying night. She wondered if he ever thought about it. Or if, like her, he'd also buried the memory away and refused to think about it.

She didn't know how long she sat there in the car, thinking. Her thoughts were finally broken by movement. A man walked through the door of the thrift shop, then turned around to lock up. He went toward the truck parked on the far side of the lot. As Kara watched him go, she realized he looked familiar. The gait was the same. The body was the same, though a bit heavier than it had once been. He had the same dirty-blond hair, even the cut and style.

It's him, Kara thought, mouth falling open. *He's still here, after all this time.*

Her heart pounded as indecision paralyzed her. Part of her wanted to call out to him, to see if he remembered her after all these years. But another part was afraid of dredging up painful memories. What if he was angry at her for what she had involved him in that summer? Or for the way she'd never answered his texts and calls in the months after she'd left Silver Falls?

Cole was almost to his truck; it was now or never. She had to decide before he drove away, and the decision was made for her.

Before she could overthink it, Kara shifted the car into drive and pulled up alongside him, where she rolled the window down. "Hi."

Cole's hand was on the truck's door handle. "Oh, I just closed down, ma'am, but I guess if you really want, I can —" He paused as slow recognition dawned in his eyes and his words caught in his throat. He blinked slowly, as if he were seeing a mirage.

"Do you remember me?"

"Kara," he said tentatively.

She forced an awkward smile.

"Wow…" He kept staring, and Kara noticed she couldn't quite read his expression. It didn't necessarily seem positive.

"I was driving by and saw you," she continued quickly, to fill the uncomfortable silence that had fallen between them. "And thought I'd come say hi."

"I'm glad you did," Cole said, and finally smiled, which made Kara feel a little better.

Besides being older, he looked pretty much exactly the same.

"What are you doing here?" Cole asked.

"I have to deal with some things with my aunt's old house."

"Right," he replied, the smile fading from his face as his eyes fell to the ground. Although Kara hadn't spoken to him again after that night, she knew Cole must've known what her aunt had done—there was no way the news hadn't gotten around all of Silver Falls.

"Are you in town long?" Cole asked.

"Only as long as I need to be," Kara answered truthfully. "Once this issue is handled, I'll head back to Boston."

"Boston? You left Chicago?"

Kara was surprised he remembered. "Yeah. A lot of life has happened in the past twenty-one years."

"I guess it has." Cole shrugged; Kara could still see that her sudden reappearance had shocked him. "Have you eaten?"

The sun was already setting, so Kara had planned to pick up some takeout and bring it back to the hotel. "I haven't."

"You want to grab something?" Cole offered.

She gave it a moment's thought before saying, "Sure."

A grin spread across his face. "Duke's is still there. You remember?"

"Of course."

"How about it?"

"I'd like that."

"Meet you there." Cole got into his truck and pulled out of the parking lot.

I can't believe it, she thought. A dinner with Cole Turner at the same place he'd brought her all those years ago. Kara started following him there.

As she drove, she felt relieved—maybe her time in Silver Falls wouldn't be completely marred by terrible memories.

————

As Kara pulled into a diagonal parking space at the front of the diner, it was like stepping back in time. The exterior hadn't changed—the building's beige color and the elaborate script on the sign were just as she remembered —albeit faded and weathered.

When Cole emerged from his truck, Kara felt his eyes

sweep over her, perhaps comparing her to the girl he'd once known.

They exchanged an awkward smile before Cole held the door open for her. Stepping inside, Kara recognized the cozy booths, the jukebox in the corner, and the milk-shake machines. It was identical, down to the bubbly teenage hostess greeting them with a handful of menus. Kara realized with amusement that the girl was a dead ringer for the hostess from her memory, as if no time had passed at all.

"Inside or outside?" the hostess asked.

"Outside," Cole said, then he turned to Kara. "Is that alright? We were on the patio last time."

"Fine with me."

The hostess led them out, where the tables and chairs looked the same—not even rearranged. To Kara's surprise, the girl sat them at the same table where they'd been before.

"It's like everything here is frozen in time," Kara said.

Cole chuckled. "Yeah, not a lot changes in Silver Falls." He seemed vaguely embarrassed by that. "But I guess that's part of the charm, right?"

The image of Cole sitting across from her brought another rush. With so much of the past coming back at once, Kara felt she was almost in a dream. *It's all a little overwhelming*, she thought.

"Even the girl looks the same," Kara said as the hostess walked away. "You knew the last one, right?"

"That was like thirty hostesses ago," Cole said, think-ing. "Pretty sure it was Amanda who was working here when we came. She moved after we graduated, went straight to California. Haven't heard from her since, and she hasn't been back." He thought for a moment. "What about you? Catch me up."

"Well…"

Kara ran through the basics for him. She'd finished up high school and gotten a partial scholarship to UC Berkeley. After, she'd done some internships, then took a job in San Francisco as a project manager. Six years later, she'd started at her current company in Boston as a project director.

"That's awesome," Cole said, smiling. "Husband? Kids?"

"Neither. What about you?"

"Um…" Cole shifted in his seat.

Kara listened as Cole recounted his story. After high school, he'd gone to Mississippi State and gotten a degree in electrical engineering. But after graduating, he'd returned home to Silver Falls to continue helping his mother run the thrift shop.

"She got really sick a few years later," Cole explained, his voice growing somber. "Pancreatic cancer."

"I'm so sorry," she offered. Kara's heart ached for him. She remembered how close Cole had been with his mom.

"She's still with us, thank God," Cole interjected quickly.

"Oh, good." She could see it pained Cole to talk about the situation. "How's she doing these days?"

"Holding up, more or less. She can't do much anymore, so I stay with her and take care of her in the evening after working at the shop during the day."

"That's so sweet," Kara said.

"But I don't regret coming back to help her with the store. It's what she wanted. She built that place up from nothing, you know? It meant everything to her. She didn't want to ever shut it down."

Despite what he said, Kara couldn't help but detect a bit of regret behind Cole's words. She'd picked up on how he'd said it was what his mother wanted, but hadn't mentioned what *he* wanted.

"I think that's really admirable," Kara said. "It's amazing how you've kept the store going all these years in her honor."

Cole gave a small, appreciative smile. "Well, it's home. Not always exciting, but home." He laughed. "So yeah, that's my glamorous life story in a nutshell."

Kara smiled back. "Doesn't sound too bad to me."

"Oh, please," Cole said, grinning. "It doesn't compare with what you've done. I bet you even traveled to all those places you said you were going to."

"A few. Let's see… During college, I did a study-abroad semester in London. I loved it there. The history, the architecture, all of it."

Cole listened with polite interest.

"And a few years ago, some friends and I spent three weeks in Iceland. We drove all over, saw amazing water-falls, hiked on a glacier… just epic landscapes everywhere you looked."

"Whoa," Cole said, clearly impressed.

"Costa Rica was another fun place—we stayed in the rainforest. Got to see sloths and monkeys and exotic birds every day. One monkey we came across even stole my sunglasses."

"They can do that?"

"Oh yes. And they will."

"Nothing like that here in Silver Falls," Cole said. "Just

squirrels and possums, who are pretty trustworthy," he joked.

"What about you? You wanted to make it to Germany and Japan."

Cole took in a sharp breath and smiled. "I can't believe you still remember that." Then he shook his head. "Nah, never made it to those places. In fact... I still haven't been out of the country." He paused and thought about it. "Or out of the south in general. I've taken some trips to Louisiana and Florida here and there, but..." He shrugged. "These days, Mama requires a lot of time."

"I understand," Kara said, suddenly feeling regretful she'd shared so much. She hoped Cole didn't think she was bragging.

And he still calls her Mama, she couldn't help but notice. *Is that a southern thing, maybe?*

Kara was relieved when the waitress returned with menus, breaking the awkward silence that had fallen over the table. She noticed the menus looked identical to the ones from over two decades ago, right down to the retro font and laminated plastic covers. As she scanned the options, she saw the prices were still reasonable, especially compared to the overpriced gastropubs and trendy restaurants she frequented in Boston.

"I think I'll have the Light Duke again, just like last time," Kara said, folding her menu closed. "And a vodka tonic, please."

"And your usual, Cole?" the waitress asked, which elicited a nod.

As the girl collected the menus and headed inside, Kara let her eyes drift over the scene. The sun was setting over the building across the street, bathing the patio in a warm orange glow. Although hot and humid outside, some expertly placed fans kept a cool breeze circulating.

"Crazy to be back here," Kara said, breaking the silence.

"Yeah."

She could tell he had more questions and was likely warring with himself internally about whether or not to broach them. Despite the pleasant scene, Kara felt an unresolved heaviness between them. Some pretty insane things had happened when they'd last seen each other, and they hadn't spoken even a single time since then.

"I was worried about you," Cole finally said, apparently choosing to ease his way toward the elephant in the room. "After that summer."

Kara sighed and crossed her legs. "I'm sorry."

"For what?"

"For vanishing."

"Well. You didn't live here."

"I know, but we had each other's phone numbers, and you texted me a few times. I could've at least…"

She hadn't thought about it in a while, but the memories began to creep in. It still was a big blur. The police had come. They'd tried to get the story out of her then, but she'd been too shocked to speak. Later, they'd taken her to the station. She'd waited there for hours. Eventually, one of them handed her a phone, and she was surprised to hear her mother's voice. It had felt like ages since the last time they'd spoken, and besides, back then she hadn't even known it was possible to make a phone call to someone all the way from Europe. Her mother had been hysterical, and the only thing Kara had really understood from that call was that Tracey was cancelling the rest of her trip with Robert and flying home immediately.

At some point—Kara couldn't remember if it was the next day or the day after—a woman police officer had escorted her to the airport in a police cruiser. Somehow her suitcase was in the backseat with her, packed by someone else—all wrong, of course, since they didn't know how she liked it done. She'd been put on a plane and sent back to Chicago. Before long, she'd been reunited with her mother.

The rest of the summer that year was fuzzy, like an old and faded photograph in Kara's mind. From what she remembered, she'd mostly just moped around. Didn't see her friends. Didn't call them to tell them she was home. When she thought about it years later, she realized that she'd been in shock.

She recalled going to speak to someone two or three times. At first, she wasn't sure what was happening; her mother had bluntly instructed her to get in the car because they had an appointment. The therapist had spoken to her gently, like he was trying to ease his way in and gain her trust. Kara didn't have much memory of those sessions, and she and her mother never brought them up again after she'd stopped attending.

She remembered getting a text message from Cole a few days after arriving home, asking if she was okay. She'd never answered. A few more had come as the weeks wore on, none of which she responded to. Finally, one night as she lay in bed, her phone rang, the sound of it almost strange to her after not hearing it ring for weeks. She'd flipped open her phone and seen that it was him. She let it go to voicemail. After that, Cole hadn't tried to reach out again. Over time, he'd joined the rest of the old memories of Silver Falls, vanishing into the background of her memory.

School had started, and that had given her something else to think about. Months had passed. She'd grieved, but slowly the pieces had come back together.

And she'd never told anyone about the statue and the evil spirit that lived inside it.

The waitress returned with their drinks, and Kara took a long sip of her vodka tonic while gathering her thoughts. She could feel Cole's eyes on her, waiting for her to continue.

"I get it," Cole said gently. "I mean, I didn't understand what you were going through at the time. But I wanted to make sure you were okay."

Kara nodded, grateful for his graciousness, but still spotted the flicker of hurt. "I should've reached out. It wasn't right for me to just vanish on you like that after everything you did for me."

Cole looked down and traced his finger over a groove in the wrought-iron metal table. "I'll admit, it did sting. I know we didn't know each other that long, but…" He shook his head. "Sounds silly now, I guess."

"No. It doesn't," Kara said. "You were the only real friend I had here. You listened and you helped me."

"Sometimes I wonder if… that last night actually happened or if it was all just a dream." Cole's eyes searched hers.

Kara's heart skipped a beat at his words. She'd been hoping to avoid talking about that night—which occasionally still crept into her dreams and turned them into nightmares.

She hesitated, shifting in her seat, then took a long sip from her drink to buy herself a moment. "It was real," she said, her voice low. "I wish it hadn't been, but it was."

Cole let out an exhale, sitting back in his chair. "It was

all so crazy. Sometimes it's easier to think it never happened, you know?"

Kara nodded. She understood *exactly* what he meant. There were times over the years when she had tried to convince herself it was all in her imagination. But deep down, she knew the truth.

"I… never told anyone else about that night," Cole said.

"Me neither," Kara admitted. "I just wanted to forget it ever happened. And if you hadn't helped me…" She trailed off, not wanting to think about how things might have ended if Cole hadn't come when she'd called.

"Hey, you were really brave," Cole said. "You did what you had to do to protect yourself and your aunt. Not everyone could have handled that situation as well as you did."

Kara appreciated his reassurance, even if she wasn't fully convinced she deserved it.

But I didn't protect my aunt, she thought. *Everything I did was too little, too late.*

She took another long sip of her drink, hoping Cole would change the subject. Some things were better left in the past. He didn't have time to shift the conversation, though, because their food arrived a few moments later.

As they ate, Kara was happy that the topic turned to more lighthearted things.

They touched on romance. Kara told Cole that she'd dated a few guys during her college years, but those relationships had all fizzled out. She'd gone on a string of unsatisfying dates in Boston, but was currently focused on her career. After that, Cole shared that he had never married and had no kids, but didn't say much more.

Next came hobbies. Kara mentioned she played tennis when she got the chance. Cole volunteered with the youth group at church—the same church he'd taken Kara to; it was still there and going strong.

After they'd finished eating, Cole insisted on paying the bill. Night had fully fallen by the time they walked out to the parking lot together. As they went, Kara had the feeling that Cole was working up the nerve to say something.

Kara followed him to the line of cars in front of the diner. The only sound came from the muted melody of a song blaring on the jukebox inside the restaurant.

As they reached the spot where their respective cars were parked, he turned to face her. "It was great to see you, Kara," he said, rubbing the back of his neck. "I know you're only in town for a little while, but I was wondering if maybe we could meet again before you leave?"

Kara hesitated. "Oh, um... sure," she said, fiddling with her keys. "I have a lot I need to get done while I'm here. But we can try," she added. She knew Cole was just trying to be friendly, but the idea of spending more time together dredged up complicated feelings—and this trip was supposed to be about tying up loose ends as quickly and painlessly as possible.

"I kept your number, you know," Cole said, interrupting her internal debate. He held up his phone, and sure enough, her name and old number were still stored in his contacts.

"Oh wow," Kara said. "Yep, that was my number back then. It's changed a few times over the years."

"Really? Well, mine's the same. Here, type in your new one." He handed her his phone and Kara updated her number.

She smiled when she gave his phone back. "Phones have come a long way since we first exchanged numbers, haven't they?" She opened her purse and took out her sleek smartphone, wrapped snug in a thick case. "But, you know, sometimes I miss my little flip phone. I loved that thing."

"They lasted forever, didn't they?"

"Seriously."

"Maybe we still have free nights and weekends?"

She couldn't help but laugh. That had been *such* a win back in the day.

"Have a good night, Cole," she said, giving him a quick hug before getting into her rental car. As she drove off, she glanced in the rearview mirror, watching his figure grow smaller and smaller until he was just a shadow under the glowing Duke's sign.

33

Cole's thoughts buzzed as he drove home. He could hardly believe that Kara Mills, of all people, had just walked back into his life after more than twenty years. He wanted to see it as some kind of sign from God.

Memories of that summer when they were sixteen—and the huge crush he'd had on her—came flooding back. After she'd left Silver Falls and stopped returning his calls and texts, he'd been devastated. She'd often popped into his mind over the years, and each time he'd wondered where she was and what she was up to.

When MySpace first came out several years later, Cole remembered trying to look her up. But he could never find her profile. The same thing had happened with Facebook and other social media platforms; he would search for her name from time to time, always hoping to stumble upon some trace of her, but she seemed like one of those people who preferred to avoid social media. That, or she kept everything super private.

He hadn't ever had much of a love life. While he'd

watched his handful of acquaintances go out on dates, get girlfriends, and fall in love, he'd found he had to dedicate more time to studying than they did because his college courses had been challenging. When he wasn't studying, he was reading the Bible and at church. And when he wasn't studying or reading the Bible or in church, he spent time with Mama.

Sure, there'd been a few girls he'd been interested in over the semesters, but somehow things had never seemed to work out. He'd never been able to understand why they'd suddenly stop talking to him. Sometimes, he even got the impression they were avoiding him.

But late at night, especially when he was struggling to fall asleep, Kara Mills still crept into his brain. Often, she was accompanied by happy thoughts, like remembering the dinner they'd had at Duke's, or how she'd sat next to him in church that one Sunday. He remembered thinking how *right* that had felt, having her by his side during worship. Other times—if he was being totally honest—the thoughts that came were less pleasing to the Lord. Each occasion, he tried to be diligent and pray them away. It worked about half the time.

And now he'd just relived one of his most cherished memories—a dinner date at Duke's with Kara Mills.

Cole Turner couldn't remember the last time he'd been this happy.

He pulled into the driveway of 117 Chestnut Street, the small home he'd lived in on and off since childhood. The house was dark except for the lamp they always kept on in the living room. Despite the heat and humidity outside, the air conditioner wasn't running—Mama got cold too easily these days, so over the years, Cole had learned to tolerate the stuffiness.

"Cole? Is that you?" Mama called out, the same way she did every evening when he returned home.

"Yes, Mama," he replied. He wondered why she always asked. It would never be anyone else.

He walked through the short entrance hall to the living room, where Debra sat in her favorite corner chair dressed in her faded pink nightgown, which she wore most of the time now.

"You're late." She squinted at the digital clock she kept on the table beside her chair.

"A little." He leaned down to kiss her on the forehead, then sat on the end of the sofa nearest to Mama. The TV across the room played a sitcom rerun. Mama had muted it when Cole had come in, as was her habit.

"Well, where were you?"

Cole sighed. He should've known Mama would press him about where he'd been. She was very attuned to his comings and goings and had become accustomed to a certain schedule. Any time he deviated from that schedule, she grew concerned.

"I stopped by Duke's for dinner."

Mama studied him. "Alone?"

Cole frowned. Sometimes, it felt like Mama could read his mind. "No. I ran into an old friend and we decided to catch up."

"What friend?"

Cole knew Mama was well aware that all of his friends had moved far from Silver Falls long ago. The ones that had gone away to college had never returned, despite saying they would. The others that had joined him at Mississippi State hadn't stuck around much longer after graduating; they'd received job offers and internships in bigger cities. One of Cole's best friends growing up, who'd played on the high-school baseball team with him, had found work with an oil and gas company and relocated to Oman. The last time Cole had spoken with him—years ago—he'd met and married a Lebanese girl and had three kids. He wasn't coming back to Mississippi anytime soon.

"It was Kara Mills," Cole admitted. He didn't like lying to Mama. The Lord also disliked him lying to Mama.

"Who?"

"I don't think you'd remember her. I knew her a long time ago."

"Who is she?" Mama pressed, an impatient edge in her voice. "Remind me."

"I met her when I was sixteen. She was visiting her aunt for the summer. Adrienne Kemper."

Mama blinked several times at the name—the woman hadn't been mentioned in their house since the night *it* happened.

Mama's face hardened. "What on *earth* are you doing with that girl?"

Cole hesitated. He'd known Mama would react poorly. But still, he couldn't bring himself to lie. "She's back for a few days. We wanted to catch up."

But Mama was having none of it. Her face had darkened. "Adrienne Kemper was a witch."

Cole winced. He remembered well how much Mama disliked Adrienne—she'd said so often enough—but at the time, she'd never been quite so vitriolic. Now that she was older and her time was shorter, she was more inclined to unleash her true thoughts.

"A witch and a lover of black magic," she went on. "And there's no doubt in my mind that was the reason she did that to herself."

Cole's eyes were fixated on a brown stain on the carpet—one that had been there for as long as he could remember. He stared at it as he waited for Mama to finish her lecture.

"She spread some of that negative influence to that girl. And you know what Pastor Craig always says: once touched by the devil, the devil never leaves you."

"R-right," Cole said, voice cracking. As much as he hated to admit it, Cole felt Mama had a point. He knew for a fact that Adrienne Kemper had been involved with some dark things. He'd seen some of it first-hand.

"So I don't want you seeing her anymore."

Cole carefully noted what Mama had said. *I don't want you seeing her anymore* was not, technically, a direct order for him to not see her anymore. If—when—they met up again, he wouldn't be disobeying.

"Okay," was all he said, and quickly thought of a way to change the subject. "Are you hungry? I can heat up some leftovers."

Mama bore her hard gaze into him for a few more moments, as if to make sure her point was taken. "I suppose I could eat something. The chicken and potatoes from last night would be nice."

Cole nodded and headed to the kitchen, thoughts of Kara still swirling through his mind.

He put the leftover chicken and potatoes on plates and placed them in the microwave. He wasn't hungry after his burger, but Mama didn't like eating alone, so he served himself a small amount.

When the microwave dinged, Cole removed the food and brought it to Mama, along with a fork and napkin. He set it up on the TV tray that was always near her chair. He then retrieved his own TV tray for his plate.

They ate in silence as they watched television. Cole had seen this episode countless times before and knew most of the lines by heart at this point. But it was Mama's favorite. Years ago, Cole had begun paying a monthly subscription for a streaming service that offered original movies and TV programs that contained no objectionable content at all—no swearing, no violence, no nudity. Of all the wholesome shows on there, Mama would only watch one. She—and Cole—would work their way through the seasons, and once the end of the show arrived, they'd start it back over at the beginning. Cole would never admit it out loud, but frankly, it was torture. There was nothing he could do, though—Mama was used to her routine.

After they'd finished eating, Cole collected their plates and brought them to the kitchen. He scraped off the leftover food into the trash can and loaded the dishes into the dishwasher. He returned to the living room, knowing well what was to come next. Mama already had her Bible out, which she offered to Cole.

Cole sat back down on the sofa and flipped to where they'd left off the night before: Paul's second letter to the Corinthians. As he read aloud in a steady, soothing voice, Mama's eyes drifted closed. Before long, her head nodded forward and her breathing grew deep and regular. Cole marked their spot with a bookmark and set the Bible aside.

Careful not to wake her, Cole took the lightweight blanket from the other end of the sofa and draped it over Mama. Then, he turned off the TV and leaned down to give her another gentle kiss on the forehead. "Goodnight, Mama," he whispered. Even though she had a bedroom, she preferred to sleep in the chair in the living room.

Cole went down the hall to his childhood room, which

hadn't changed much since he was a teenager. His old baseball posters and trophies were still on the walls and shelves; the twin bed with its worn blue comforter was the same one he'd slept in since middle school.

He stripped down to his boxers and got into bed, grabbed the remote control from the bedside table, and flipped on the television that was atop his chest of drawers. The TV was the only thing that had been updated. It was already on his standard channel—he'd usually zone out to sports highlights on ESPN before drifting off to sleep.

That night was different, though. He grabbed his phone and brought up Kara's contact card. It was surreal. He'd lain in that exact same spot twenty-one years ago, texting her. It felt impossible that this *wasn't* God's will.

He wanted to text her, but he knew she was busy and he didn't want to overwhelm her. Besides, they'd just spent a nice evening together. Maybe it would be better to wait a bit to reach out to her again.

Tomorrow, he decided.

34

Kara had arrived at the property-management office fifteen minutes before her scheduled appointment. The lobby smelled of old wood paneling and stale coffee. It was dimly lit with a faded brown carpet that hinted at decades of foot traffic. A lopsided fake plant sat in the corner, gathering dust. The walls were covered in framed stock photos of happy families in front of generic suburban homes. A clock on the wall ticked in the silence.

A door behind a vacant reception desk opened and out stepped a woman. "Miss Mills?"

Kara stood and walked over to her, where her extended hand waited. Kara shook.

"I'm Jean Brewer."

Jean was a petite lady in her late forties with short blonde hair. She wore a navy blouse and a grey coat. Despite Jean's welcoming demeanor, Kara could tell she was on guard. Kara sensed the woman was bracing herself for a conversation that could turn out unpleasant, maybe confrontational—even though Kara had no intention of letting that happen. She wasn't here to argue or plead her mother's case—that ship had long since sailed. No, Kara needed answers, needed to understand why her aunt's home had become such a burden.

Kara followed Jean to a small office in a narrow hallway.

"Coffee? Tea? Water?" Jean offered as she closed the door behind them.

"No, thank you."

Jean went around her desk and sat down in her high-back chair. A modern computer faced her from the corner of the desk, perhaps the only thing in the room that had been updated in the past several decades. Kara sat in the seat opposite the woman.

"I spent the morning reviewing your mother's file," Jean said, taking her mouse and clicking a few times around the screen. "I understand you wanted to discuss our decision to terminate her contract with us."

"Yes."

Jean eyed Kara. "We made our reasoning quite clear in our communications with Ms. Mills. She didn't inform you?"

"Not one bit."

Kara could tell the other woman found that strange— and she was right to think so. Kara was also frustrated by her mother's obstinate refusal to handle the matters involved with Adrienne's house.

"Well, you're listed as a point of contact, so I'm at liberty to discuss these things with you, and I'll be happy to get you up to speed." Jean looked at the computer and scrolled the wheel of her mouse, pupils darting back and forth as she reviewed her records. "In short, your mother's property here in town became too much of a liability for us. There was a high turnover rate of tenants and a very unusual amount of damage that we had to address. Mild wear and tear over the years is standard, of course, but the amount of constant repairs… in the forty years we've been in business, we've never seen such things."

Kara found that surprising, remembering the home's good condition from her recent visit.

"Also," Jean continued, "it took far longer to rent the house than normal, as many prospective tenants backed out when we disclosed the… unfortunate events that occurred there." Jean cleared her throat and moved on to the next point: "Then once we *were* able to secure tenants, we had an incredibly high rate of them breaking the lease and moving out—sometimes without any notice at all."

"And did these people say why they were leaving?" Kara asked.

"Yes," Jean said. As Kara waited for Jean to elaborate, the other woman's lips tensed into a thin line. "They claimed it was 'haunted.' "

Kara straightened. "Haunted?"

Jean nodded regretfully. The way she said the word told Kara that she didn't believe it for one second, but nevertheless, that was indeed the reason the tenants had cited for leaving the home.

"The Smith family moved in in March of 2003," Jean read from her computer screen. "Two kids and a dog. They stayed for about six months before deciding to break the lease, saying the place gave them, and I quote, 'the heebie jeebies.' They also complained about 'strange noises.' "

Kara shifted in her seat as Jean scrolled through more of her notes.

"After them was Jeremy Cauthon. Single guy, some

kind of writer. He lasted only two months. He said he couldn't sleep with all the 'knocking and whispering' that happened late at night.

"Then there was the Walters family. Another couple with three young children. Made it four months before leaving. They reported their kids kept seeing 'things' around the house and wouldn't sleep alone in their rooms anymore. They also claimed there were 'random cold spots' throughout the home that made them feel uncomfortable."

Kara listened with a growing sense of nervousness as Jean listed the strange occurrences reported by past tenants. Though the property manager's tone was dismissive, Kara had a sinking feeling in her gut that these accounts were likely true. Her thoughts were thrust back to the night Aunt Adrienne had conducted her summoning ritual.

Maybe it never left, even after all this time, Kara realized. *Can it really stay for twenty-one years?* She felt a creeping sadness settle upon her. *Did Adrienne's actions affect so many people even this long afterward?*

"It wasn't just the high turnover rate," Jean continued, breaking Kara's thoughts. "As I said, there was the unprecedented amount of damage we've had to repair. Each and every tenant swore they had no idea how these things happened, that it all seemed random. There were strange gouges on the walls. At first, they assumed it had been their kids, even though their children had never done anything like that before. These gouges also appeared when Mr. Cauthon, the single guy, was living there. So... it wasn't the kids." She scrolled a bit more. "There were broken water pipes, sometimes one after the other, at a frequency we'd never seen before. Oh, and here's the strangest thing, in my opinion: a circle of footprints on the second floor." Kara's throat tightened. "Made of some... black or brown substance. But when the tenant tried to clean it, it didn't come up. It was as if the footprints had been burned into the carpet, so it had to be replaced entirely. Look."

Jean swiveled the computer monitor around and, pulled up on the screen, was a photograph taken for documentation. The sight of the footprints threw Kara back decades into the past. It was an image she would've been fine never seeing again.

She immediately recognized the spare room across the hall from the bedroom she'd occupied. The footprints traced the same path the entity had during the séance. The same path Adrienne had been pacing that one night.

Strange noises and broken water pipes were one thing. That could be explained away. This, however... was too precise.

Kara felt dizzy, then nauseous. She gripped the arms of her chair. How could this be possible? *No, it isn't...* Yet Jean had shown her the evidence, stark and undeniable. *It's... it's still there.*

Even after this monster had *killed* her aunt, it remained in her home. Like a warlord who'd conquered a castle. Now, it was terrifying strangers who had no idea what they were walking into. A wave of guilt washed over Kara. How many families had been traumatized because of what she and her aunt had done that night?

"And the footprints occurred with more than one tenant," Jean continued. "What are the odds of this? Police were called each time they appeared, but there was never a sign of any breaking and entering. We still don't know how they got there or what they were even made of." She minimized the photo and brought up another that made Kara look away. "These letters were repeatedly gouged into the hardwood floor in one of the upstairs bedrooms. We'd repair the damage, but then someone would carve the same thing in the same spot. Like the footprints, this happened across different tenants." Jean seemed to notice Kara's reaction, her refusal to look at the picture. "Does this word mean anything to you, Miss Mills? U-N-U-Z-A?" she asked, rattling off the letters.

"Do you believe them, Mrs. Brewer?" Kara asked suddenly.

Jean eyed her for a few seconds. "Believe who? About what?"

"The people who said this house was haunted."

She gave a small laugh and looked down at her desk. "Of course not. There's always a rational explanation for this stuff. Everyone knows that."

I used to think the same, Kara thought. But after the night when Adrienne had summoned the spirit, she'd decided then and there that she could no longer be so sure of certain things.

A long silence fell between them, which Jean Brewer finally broke. "Unfortunately, we always include a clause in our contracts that gives us the right to terminate the agreement with our clients at any time and for any reason. I realize it sounds extreme and unfair, but as I'm sure you know, you'll find language like that in most things you sign. This house is the only instance we've ever used it. It was getting to the point where your mother's property was just costing too much time and resources."

"Okay," Kara said.

In a way, this meeting with Jean had made Kara's decision a lot easier. In a town as small as Silver Falls, odds were there wasn't going to be another property manager to take on the house. And even *if* one existed, they'd likely heard the whispered rumors around town. They'd probably decline—if Jean Brewer couldn't make it work after twenty years, then what made them think they'd get a different outcome?

I'll have to sell, Kara decided. It was a relief, almost. She liked the idea of keeping Adrienne's house in the family, but it just wasn't realistic. Not anymore.

"Is there anything else you'd like to know?" Jean asked.

How to go back in time and change all of this would be nice, Kara couldn't help but think.

"I've heard enough, actually," she said.

35

On her drive away from the office, Kara's mind spun as she processed everything Jean had told her. The property manager didn't believe those wild stories about Adrienne's old house being haunted, dismissing the tenants as superstitious or looking for any excuse to break their lease.

Kara knew better.

She'd lived through that terrifying summer twenty-one years ago. She'd seen the eerie statue move by itself, had watched her aunt spiral into madness under some malevolent influence—even after Kara had thought she'd gotten rid of it by throwing the statue into Lake Silver, the horror hadn't ended. She'd returned home, filled with hope and relief, only to find Aunt Adrienne still trapped in the entity's grip. Even after that night, the entity had never left the house. It had remained there all this time, tormenting every tenant who dared move in.

Those poor people who lived there...

In a way, Kara felt responsible, even though it had been her mother who'd been handling the entire situation.

She'd never told her mother the full truth of what had transpired. Tracey Mills wouldn't have believed it. She wouldn't have entertained for one second any stories about the moving statue, the evil presence, or the ritual that had summoned it. So Kara had kept silent, burying it all within.

Surely Jean must've told Mom the reasons the tenants were leaving when she reached out to her, Kara thought. If that was the case, Kara already knew her mother had been like the property manager—not believing. She could almost hear her mother now: "Fine. Let them go. We can find new people to rent to."

Tracey Mills could be a hard-headed woman. To her, anything and everything was replaceable, and *should* be replaced the moment it stopped serving her. That went for jobs, clients, apartments, and even her romantic relationships.

Kara had never asked about Adrienne's house after that summer, therefore her mother had never filled her in. Kara couldn't help but wonder if she'd heard these stories sooner, could she have convinced her mom the house was haunted? Probably not. Tracey Mills wouldn't listen to such nonsense. As the daughter of two prominent university professors—her father in physics and her mother in cognitive psychology—Kara's mother had been raised in an environment where empirical evidence reigned supreme. From an early age, she'd been taught to question everything, demand proof, and reject anything that couldn't be scientifically verified. Naturally, this worldview had trickled down to Kara throughout her childhood, but the summer of 2002 had shattered her understanding of reality.

Kara followed her phone's GPS to her next planned

stop of the day: the only storage company in Silver Falls. When Kara had learned that her mother had been paying for two decades for a storage unit that likely hadn't been opened once during that time, she'd wanted to explode. It was such a huge waste of money. But Kara knew that in her mother's mind, money's main use was to bury problems indefinitely.

Kara sighed in frustration. Somehow—like so many other things—this issue had also fallen onto Kara's shoulders. She'd have to be the one to go through all the stuff that had been inside Adrienne's house that summer and decide what to do with it—*then* deal with all the dredged-up memories.

Whatever, Kara thought. *Someone has to do it. Besides, it should be simple, anyway.*

The contents of the storage unit hadn't been touched for twenty years, so that told Kara that there was probably nothing worth saving. However, she figured at least *one* final check was in order to see if there was anything sentimental. Kara felt like she owed her aunt that much—owed her something that her own sister wasn't willing to do for her.

Kara arrived and parked near the rows of identical metal units baking in the sun. Her phone then chimed with a text message. It was from Cole.

'Hey. How's it going? What are you up to today?'

She put her phone back in her pocket. Now wasn't a good time to chat. She hoped she'd remember to reply later.

Kara located unit 217 and slid the key into the rusted padlock. With some effort, she managed to pry it open, the hinges creaking in protest. Opening the door released a musty odor.

There sat all the furniture from Adrienne's house, just as Kara remembered it. The sofa and armchairs, now faded from years spent tucked away. The bookshelves, still filled with Adrienne's eclectic collection of books on spirituality, meditation, and the occult. The dining-room table, the surface covered with dust.

Kara's fingers traced over the table's smooth wood, conjuring up memories of the food she had shared there with her aunt.

Kara made her way farther into the cramped storage space. She found several large boxes containing Adrienne's flowing skirts, tunics, and dresses, most of which she remembered Adrienne having worn over the course of that summer.

Kara's eyes fell upon the familiar metal frame of the guest bed, its old quilt still neatly made up. She sank down on the edge of the mattress, the springs creaking under her, then ran her hand over the soft quilt, its fabric worn thin. This had been where she'd tossed and turned, terrified about who—or what—might disturb her in the night. It was also where she'd lain awake, texting Cole Turner just to distract herself from everything that was happening.

She saw Adrienne's bed, its wooden headboard pressed up against the back wall of the storage unit. Kara could almost see her aunt's limp body lying there, weakened by the malevolent force that had invaded their home. Kara shivered at the memory. She'd felt so alone and afraid, desperate to free her aunt from the spirit's grasp.

Kara spotted a small wooden box tucked in the corner. She recognized it immediately. It was where Aunt Adrienne had kept her mementos, one of which—a ring— she'd sacrificed to the spirit in the statue.

Kara lifted the creaky lid. There were the faded Polaroids just as she remembered: Adrienne radiant and carefree, her arms wrapped around a rugged man. Although he didn't smile in the photos, Kara could see the brightness in his eyes.

The boyfriend, she thought. *What was his name?*

As she continued her search, she found an envelope, and inside was a letter—one she'd seen before when she'd snooped through this box. She checked the signature at the bottom.

That's right. Arthur.

Kara thumbed through the photographs, a bittersweet ache in her chest. She wondered why her aunt hadn't wanted to speak about the man when he seemed to have brought her so much happiness. Kara could only assume that it had ended poorly. She'd learned the hard way that no matter how wonderful a relationship was at the start, there was still no telling how badly everything could crash and burn.

At the bottom of the box was a brown envelope, underneath all the pictures and letters. Kara fished it out and opened the flap. Inside was a single paper. She withdrew it and it took her a few seconds to realize what she'd found—a yellowed marriage certificate.

Kara sat back down on the edge of the guest-room bed, staring at the document in disbelief. How had she not known? And did her mother know?

Aunt Adrienne once had a husband and no one ever once bothered to mention this to me?

According to the certificate, Arthur's last name was Briggs.

It was dated a few years before that summer. Still, a marriage would have been so out of character for her free-spirited aunt—she'd seemed more inclined to conduct her relationships without involving pesky laws or the government.

Then something occurred to Kara. She checked the envelope again, but it held nothing else, having only contained the marriage license.

No divorce paperwork, Kara thought. *If Adrienne was still legally married to this guy when she died...*

It could complicate the selling of the house.

But how had her mother been able to rent the place out for over two decades without Arthur Briggs showing up to figure out what was going on with his property?

It's possible he passed away, Kara realized. But still, she was confused. If her mother knew, then why hadn't she said anything?

Kara stepped out of the dusty storage unit, blinking against the bright sunlight. She pulled her phone from her pocket and tapped her mother's contact page.

Tracy answered on the third ring. "Hey. Everything okay?"

"Yeah. I'm at the storage unit going through Aunt Adrienne's things." Kara paused, unsure exactly how to broach the subject. "There was... something interesting in one of her boxes. Did you know Aunt Adrienne was married?"

The line was silent for several seconds. Finally, her mother responded, "No, I had no idea. I knew she dated here and there, but she never mentioned a husband to me."

"Well, I found a marriage certificate in her things. To a man named Arthur Briggs. It was from a few years before the summer I stayed with her."

Tracy let out a thoughtful hum. "That name doesn't

ring any bells. Adrienne was always so private, so I guess it shouldn't be shocking she had a secret marriage."

Private, Kara mused. *More like the two of you were so different that neither of you wanted to speak to the other.*

"It makes me wonder, though," Kara said. "If she was still legally married when she died, then this Arthur guy may have some claim to the house."

"Oh, I wouldn't worry about that," Tracy said dismissively. "If he were alive and interested in the property, he would've shown up years ago when I was renting it out. I'm sure he's long gone."

"Yeah, you're probably right. But still. We… should at least try to confirm it if we eventually have to sell it, shouldn't we?"

"I wouldn't," Tracy said quickly. "But that's me."

Kara heard the unspoken part: *It's your problem now. You do what you need to do.*

Honestly, it didn't *need* to be her problem. She could leave it all alone and let whatever fallout came land on her mother. But she already knew she wouldn't do that. For good or ill, she felt bound by a sense of family obligation. Maybe it was to make up for the lack of it between Tracy and Adrienne.

They exchanged goodbyes, and Kara ended the call. She sighed. This was just another thing to deal with that she hadn't counted on.

Maybe Mom's right. He would've shown up forever ago.

Trying to track him down now might stir up something she didn't want to be involved in. *Like what if he demands back payments for the rent Mom earned?*

But still, confirming that Arthur was out of the picture was the right thing to do. It was very likely that if his and

Adrienne's relationship had ended, they'd gotten divorced at some point, so the whole marriage was a non-issue.

But how do I get in touch with him?

36

ole worked mechanically and on autopilot as he sorted through the box of miscellaneous items, stocking the shelves of Thrift Love with the new additions. Normally, it was easy to focus on this task, but that day he kept taking his phone from his pocket and checking the screen. He'd texted Kara hours ago, and she still hadn't responded.

She already told me she'd be busy, he reminded himself. It was only the afternoon, so there was plenty of time left in the day for her to get back to him.

He climbed onto a foot ladder to put some old books on a top shelf, and he blew away some dust motes that had gathered at the top.

His phone rang.

There she is. Finally.

But it was his mother calling him. He immediately thought something was wrong—she rarely called him while at work.

"Mama?" he answered.

"Cole, you need to come home right now." Her voice was panicked. "Someone's broken into the house."

"What? Are you serious?" After a lifetime of living in the small town, he'd almost never heard of *anyone* being burglarized.

"Yes. Please come home."

"Okay. I'm coming."

Shoving his phone into his pocket, Cole jumped off the ladder and rushed out of the store, not bothering to lock up behind him.

The short drive felt like an eternity, but as he pulled into the driveway, everything seemed normal.

He burst through the front door and hurried into the living room. There, his mother was curled up in her recliner, and when she saw him, she pointed toward the corner of the room.

"I woke up from a nap and there was someone standing right there."

Of course, the space was now empty.

"Are you positive?"

"Yes."

"What did he look like?" He scanned the area and checked down the hall, then the nearby kitchen. Everything seemed as it always was.

"I didn't see him well before he disappeared."

"Disappeared?"

"He moved fast."

Cole had a hunch he knew what was going on. "Are you sure you weren't dreaming, Mama?"

"Of *course* not." His mother scowled at him. "Go check! He couldn't have gone far."

Cole suppressed a sigh. Sometimes Mama "got a bad

"feeling" and asked him to check outside and around the house for a burglar. He always did it to appease her, but he'd never once found anything.

This time was different, however; she'd never called him home from work before.

"Take the gun," Mama whispered.

Cole opened the living-room closet and retrieved his father's old shotgun. Outside, he went through the motions of checking the perimeter.

Though his eyes scanned for signs of a disturbance, his mind was far away. He remembered his mother's last doctor's appointment. At the time, Dr. Hurrell had cautioned him privately that episodes of confusion and delusion were going to become more frequent as the disease progressed.

Cole had nodded stoically as the doctor spoke, but inside he'd been crumbling. His strong, sharp-minded mother, reduced to a state of fear and bewilderment, was almost more than he could bear.

As he made his way around the rear of the house, he felt hot tears fill his eyes. He brushed them away.

God, please comfort Mama. She doesn't deserve this.

As expected, there was nothing amiss. He paused at the front door and steadied his emotions before going inside.

Mama sat on the edge of the recliner, her entire body rigid.

"Nothing there, Mama," he said, and her shoulders immediately sagged with relief. He placed the shotgun back into the closet.

"I swear he was there one moment, gone the next," Debra said, eyes glued to the corner of the room.

"I don't know what you saw, Mama, but we're safe. Would you feel better if I read to you?"

Debra nodded.

Cole sat down in his usual spot on the end of the couch, picked up the Bible, and began to read.

37

That afternoon, Kara sat on the edge of the hotel bed, phone in hand. She scrolled through her contacts to Derek's name. Her finger hovered over the call button as she considered whether or not this was a good idea.

Derek was a police officer back in Boston and a close friend. He'd have access to all kinds of databases and records, but was it ethical to ask Derek to use police resources just to help her clean up after her mother's mess?

Ultimately, her need for answers won out. She pressed call and brought the phone to her ear.

After two rings, Derek's deep voice came over the line. "Kara! Haven't heard from you in a minute. What's up?"

Kara smiled. Derek's warm and familiar tone always put her at ease. "Hey, Derek. I know it's been a while. Listen, I… need a favor."

"Uh oh. What you got?"

"It's kind of a long story, but I'm down in Mississippi trying to handle some assets that belonged to my late aunt. And earlier today and I found that she'd once been married."

Derek gave a low whistle. "Sounds like some family drama."

"Sort of. I'm looking for some information about a guy named Arthur Briggs. That was my aunt's husband. I just need to know if he's still alive. I have a feeling he's not. But if he is, then it'd be nice to have a current phone number, so I can reach out to him real quick."

"Arthur Briggs," Derek repeated. "I don't know, Kara. This… isn't what we're supposed to use the system for."

"I know," Kara said with a sigh. "But it's important, Derek. Please. And also…" She smirked. "I remember you told me once that you run a search on all your sister's new boyfriends, so…"

"Yeah, yeah," Derek replied—she could hear the smile in his voice. "I'll call you back when I have something. Oh, do you have a picture? That could help if there are a bunch of people with the same name."

"I can text you one. Thank you," Kara said, relief flooding through her.

Before she'd left the storage unit, she'd used her phone to snap a few pictures of the Polaroids that best showed Arthur. She sent them to Derek.

About an hour later, she had a reply.

'It's always easier when they have a record.'

Derek's message was followed by a mugshot. The man in the picture, facing both the front and to the side, had aged considerably, but when Kara compared his eyes to the pictures in the Polaroids, she could tell that it was the same guy.

She married a criminal? Kara wondered.

But Derek's follow-up text made her feel a little better.

'He's been arrested numerous times for DWIs. That's the only thing he's done wrong. Lives in a town called Rose Grove in Georgia.'

His next message contained a phone number.

'Thank you, Derek,' she texted back.

So, Arthur Briggs was alive and living in another state. It was a good sign that he and Adrienne had divorced... but still, Kara wanted to be sure.

Her job often required her to call strangers, but in this particular situation, she felt nervous when she dialed the number. The phone rang and rang. Just when Kara was about to give up, someone answered.

"Who is this?" said a gruff voice.

Kara cleared her throat. "Hi. Umm... is this Mr. Briggs?"

"Who is this?" the man repeated, voice even harsher.

Kara winced, but pressed on. "My name is Kara Mills," she began. "I'm the niece of Adrienne Kemper."

Silence lingered for a very long time; Kara even checked her screen to make sure the call hadn't been dropped. "Hello?"

"Is this some kind of sick joke?" the man asked.

"No, sir."

He hesitated for a few more seconds. "What did you say your name was again?"

"Kara. Kara Mills."

He seemed to digest that for a few more minutes. "Yeah. I remember the name."

Kara blinked. "Oh. She mentioned me?"

"Of course. Why wouldn't she?"

Before Kara had come to stay with Adrienne, she'd rarely seen her aunt. It made her happy to hear that Adrienne had still talked about her, even before that summer visit.

"How… uh…" The man's aggressive tone had calmed. "It's been so long. How is she?"

Kara's heart plummeted through the floor. *He doesn't know.* She cleared her throat again and took in a sharp breath. "She passed away, I'm afraid."

The line crackled and Arthur breathed heavily into the receiver. "Oh." His voice was low, yet just in that brief exchange, she could tell the news had crushed him. "So that's why you're calling me."

Kara realized he'd misunderstood—or rather, that she hadn't been clear. "Actually, she passed away in 2002."

She was met by more silence. Finally, she said, "Hello?" There was a *thump* that sounded like he'd set down the phone.

Tears came to Kara's eyes as she waited for him to come back to the phone—she realized he'd stepped away to have a grieving moment.

All this time, and he never knew, she thought. *He still cares for her very much.*

It felt inappropriate to press the man for answers. Asking him if he was still legally married, fishing for if he had some kind of claim to the property. It seemed… wrong.

The phone was picked up again. "Where are you calling from?"

"Silver Falls. In Mississippi."

"Where she lived."

"Yes."

With that, he hung up on her.

Kara sighed and set her phone down. She'd give

Arthur some time, but then she'd eventually have to call him back and get the information she needed.

Not looking forward to that at all, she thought. *Ugh. Alright, enough of this for now.*

That day had been a lot. The meeting with the property manager, then the revelations at the storage unit, then a conversation with her aunt's ex-husband who hadn't known she was dead. She couldn't remember the last time she'd been through that much emotional upheaval in a single day. *I'm definitely going to sleep early tonight,* she thought as she got under the covers and turned out the light.

38

Thump-thump-thump-thump-thump-thump.

At first, Cole thought the pounding noises were a dream. But as he awoke, he realized the repetitive sound was coming from inside the house—from the living room.

"Mama," he whispered, suddenly wide awake and throwing off the covers.

He rushed down the hallway.

In the darkness, he recognized his mother's slender frame. She was walking rapidly in circles in the middle of the room. He hadn't seen her move with such speed and purpose in years.

He flicked on the light, but as soon as she did, she halted her pacing, freezing in place with her back to him. She stood completely still.

"Mama?" He approached her. This was the first time he'd ever caught her sleepwalking.

But how was she moving so fast?

He placed a gentle hand on her shoulder and she recoiled, gasping.

"Mama, it's me."

She turned to face him, and a fearful recognition came into her eyes. "Cole? What's—what's going on?"

"You're sleepwalking, Mama."

All at once, the frantic energy with which she'd been pacing seemed to leave her body. He felt her grow weak against him, so he guided her back to her recliner. She collapsed into it, exhausted, beads of sweat on her forehead from the exertion.

"Mama, are you okay? I haven't seen you move like that in…"

"I'm so tired." She patted her chest as she tried to catch her breath. "Since when do I sleepwalk?"

"Hang on, Mama." Cole rushed into the kitchen and got her a glass of water. She drank the whole thing in a couple of large sips.

She handed the glass back to him. "More."

Cole returned and refilled the glass under the faucet. However, he hesitated before bringing it to Mama. His fingers tightened on the glass as the memories came—this wasn't the first he'd heard of someone bizarrely pacing in circles.

Kara's aunt.

She'd told him she'd woken up once in the middle of the night and caught her aunt rushing around in circles. That had happened a few nights before she'd called and asked him to drive her to Lake Silver.

His shoulders slumped over the sink as he remembered the vile voice in his head after presenting his cross necklace to the statue. He'd tried to be the hero in that moment, and had failed.

'I will remember you. You will regret helping her.'

A cold dread seeped into Cole's bones. After over two

decades, he had all but convinced himself that the voice had been the product of an overactive imagination—a response to the terrifying situation he'd been in.

Why is this happening now? Cole wondered. *Right when Kara had returned to town... did she do something?*

"Cole?" Mama called out.

Taking a deep breath, Cole steeled his nerves and went back to the living room. His mother looked up at him with tired, confused eyes as he handed her the water.

"I'm sorry to wake you up," she said. "I don't know why I was sleepwalking."

"Don't apologize, Mama," Cole said, bending over and kissing her forehead. He checked the decades-old clock on the wall, which had been there since before he was born. It read two minutes after three o'clock in the morning. "You're okay now."

The words had slipped from his mouth out of habit, but this time he wondered if they were actually true. Whatever had been in the statue that night... was it back? Was it here, inside his own home somehow? Had something rubbed off on him when he was with Kara the other night?

It was me who helped throw that statue in the lake, not Mama, he thought. *If it's back, then why would it want to hurt her?*

Now, he wondered if she really *had* seen someone—or something—standing in the corner of the room that afternoon.

Once again, he sat down and took out the Bible and started reading. That night, for the first time in years, the holy Scripture gave him just as much comfort as it brought Mama.

39

The next morning, Kara was scrolling through the day's headlines on her phone as she drank her coffee. The bitter liquid helped clear the fog from her brain. She'd been pleasantly surprised when she learned that the Silver Fields Inn offered breakfast on the first floor. A handful of tables and chairs were set up in an open area opposite the reception desk, though she was the only one there. The food was simple, mostly just pastries, toast, water, and juice, but it was good enough.

An incoming call interrupted her reading. She almost choked on her coffee.

He's calling back?

She tapped to answer. "Hello?"

"Where are you right now?" Arthur asked.

Kara hesitated, caught off guard by the blunt question. "I told you last night. In Silver Falls."

"I mean, *where* in Silver Falls are you?" Arthur clarified impatiently.

Kara bit her lip, unsure about disclosing her location to a stranger. *Is he coming here?*

Normally, she'd be distrustful. But her aunt had married the man, hadn't she? Though that was over twenty years ago. A person could change a lot in twenty years.

"I'm at the Silver Fields Inn," she divulged. Her curiosity was getting the better of her.

"That the one on Main Street?"

So he remembers the town. "Yeah."

"Hmm. Still there after all this time. Okay."

Before Kara could respond, the line went dead.

He sure likes to hang up on people, she thought. Anticipation and uncertainty started swirling within her. What was all that about?

She finished her coffee and was about to head upstairs when her phone vibrated again; Arthur Briggs was calling back.

"Come outside," he barked, then hung up on her for a third time.

Kara decided this was becoming excessive for her—no matter how much this man cared about her aunt, she didn't appreciate or tolerate being spoken to like that.

With a sigh, she went to the lobby window that faced Main Street. An old, red pickup truck caught her eye. It idled in the middle of the road.

Her curiosity drew her forward. She went outside, staying close to the door in case she needed to retreat.

The driver's-side door of the truck swung open and out stepped the man from her aunt's photographs.

He was frail, with tan, weathered skin that was heavily lined. In the Polaroids, he'd had hair, but now what was left of it was nothing more than grey stubble scattered about his scalp. He wore dirty jeans and a plain white t-shirt that hung loose over his narrow limbs. Kara caught sight of a whiskey bottle nestled in the driver's seat of his truck, which reminded her of the DWI arrests that Derek had mentioned.

The man's eyes were dark and piercing—the only part of him that seemed to have life—and she felt very uncomfortable as he scanned her up and down.

"You look like her," he said.

Kara's mother had told her the same thing a few times.

"Where is she?" Arthur asked.

"What do you mean?"

"Is she buried here?" Finally, his voice lost a bit of its edge. And Kara could see a sadness creeping into his eyes.

"Yes."

A nearby horn blared, startling Kara. A car had come up behind where Arthur's vehicle was blocking the road.

"Go around!" Arthur snarled at the driver. They obeyed. Arthur turned to Kara again. "Knox Cemetery?" he asked.

Kara nodded.

Without another word, Arthur got back into the truck, positioned the whiskey bottle between his thighs, closed the door, and drove away.

Kara stood frozen on the sidewalk as Arthur's truck rumbled down Main Street. The brief encounter had left her both uneasy and conflicted. She was amazed that the man had driven through the night to get there, seemingly fueled by alcohol, grief, and a bit of anger. His brusque demeanor had put her off, yet she couldn't deny the deep sadness she'd glimpsed in his eyes when he asked about Adrienne.

With a resigned sigh, Kara walked to her rental that was parallel parked nearby and slid inside. She turned the key in the ignition and eased out onto the road, heading in the same direction Arthur had gone.

———

KARA DROVE along the tree-lined lane leading to the wrought-iron gates. When she arrived, Arthur's red truck was already parked near the curb. Both the front and the rear doors on the driver's side of the truck had been left open.

Kara pulled up behind it and got out of her car. When she approached the truck, she saw Arthur wasn't there; he'd gone inside the cemetery and left his truck doors open.

She passed through the iron gates and started in the direction of Adrienne's grave. As she neared, she spotted Arthur's hunched figure kneeling at her aunt's final resting place. He'd placed a massive bouquet of pink flowers in front of the headstone.

Kara lingered at a distance, watching the man grieve. She had a wave of her own sadness, though she was also confused—had Aunt Adrienne known she was this loved?

Why did it end if this guy still cares so much about her? Kara wondered. *Even after all this time?*

It felt like she'd been standing there forever, but she already knew she'd give this man as long as he needed with her aunt.

Finally, several minutes later, Arthur straightened and started walking toward her. He stopped with about six paces between them and he held her gaze. Kara could see the tears that rimmed his eyes.

"I'm sorry," was all she could think to say.

"How did she die?" Arthur asked. "She would've only been in her fifties."

Kara swallowed, then dropped the heavy word, like an anvil hitting the ground. "Suicide."

The news seemed to choke Arthur up all over again. "No. That's impossible."

Kara only nodded. "I thought the same thing. But I was there. I saw it."

"Saw it?"

"Yes."

"You mean…"

"She did it right in front of me." Admitting it brought the terrible image back in all its vivid detail. Kara closed her eyes, feeling her own tears returning.

"I—I don't understand," Arthur said. "From what I knew of her, she would never…"

"She wasn't herself at the end."

Arthur's jaw flexed as he clenched his teeth. "I want to know everything."

Kara hesitated before responding. This man was asking her to recount the entire story from that summer. It was something she'd never done before.

Am I actually going to tell him everything? she thought. *Will he think I'm crazy?*

But given the way Arthur had acted at the gravestone, she decided he had a right to the truth. All of it. Even the parts that seemed unbelievable.

Kara sniffed, wiped at her eyes, and nodded. "Okay."

"And I'll need a drink if I'm going to hear it." Arthur started walking toward the cemetery gates. "Meet me at Lenny's. I passed it on the way in, so I know it's still there."

He didn't wait for Kara to respond or to even confirm that she'd meet him there. He only stalked back to his truck, its engine roaring to life a moment later. He drove away and, for a second time that morning, left Kara standing on her own.

40

Kara took a deep breath before pushing open the heavy door to Lenny's. The interior was dim, with most of the light coming from neon signs advertising various beers that hung along the back wall. A few dusty ceiling fans spun lazily overhead. The worn wooden floorboards clunked under Kara's feet as she made her way farther inside.

Only a handful of patrons occupied the stools at the bar, nursing drinks in solitude. Arthur sat hunched on the far left, staring into a glass of amber liquid. His shoulders were slumped in a way that radiated defeat. Even from across the room, Kara could see the deep lines of grief etched into his weathered face.

As she approached, the bartender—a burly man with a bushy grey mustache—gave her a nod. "What'll it be?"

"Club soda with lime, please." For her, it was *definitely* too early to start drinking. She was honestly shocked the place was open this time of day.

Kara settled onto the stool next to Arthur just as the bartender slid her drink over. Arthur turned his head to look at her, bloodshot eyes regarding her for a moment before he lifted his glass and tipped back the rest of his whiskey in one swallow.

"Why pay for whiskey at the bar when you have a bottle in your truck?" Kara asked, genuinely curious.

"The bottle's for the road," Arthur said, raising his hand and getting the bartender's attention. He came over and refilled Arthur's glass with another double shot.

"You're not worried about driving drunk?"

"This shit's like water to me at this point," Arthur said, taking a sip. "I could only be so lucky if I get loaded enough to flip my truck."

Kind of morose, isn't he? Kara thought. She wondered what her aunt had seen in him. Likely, he'd been very different all those years ago. In the pictures, even without smiling, he looked happy to be with Adrienne. *Maybe their relationship ending is what did this to him.*

"Ready to talk?" he asked.

Kara sipped her club soda and nodded. Seeing the raw pain in this man's eyes, she knew she owed it to him to share the truth about her aunt's final days, as much as she didn't want to relive them.

"You know… I've never told anyone this story," she said.

"Now's the time," Arthur said.

Then I hope you're ready to hear some crazy stuff, she couldn't help but think. "I'm going to share, but you probably won't believe me."

"What makes you say that?" he asked. Kara wasn't sure, but she thought the man was offended.

"No one would."

"Try me," Arthur said, as if he'd been challenged.

Kara took a deep breath and steadied herself. Though

over two decades had passed, the memories of that summer felt as raw and vivid as ever. She kept her gaze fixed on the condensation beading down her glass as she transported herself back to the events that had changed her life.

"It started with a statue…" Kara began. She recounted how Aunt Adrienne had become enthralled by the weird figurine during a visit to the thrift store. How Adrienne had then become convinced that a spirit resided within it.

When she mentioned that, she noticed Arthur's body tense beside her, but he didn't interrupt.

Does he know where I'm going with this? she wondered before continuing on. Kara detailed Adrienne's attempts to appease the spirit by leaving offerings of bread and water after the statue had moved on its own. The séance where Adrienne had summoned the entity.

The moment she'd finished sharing the events of that night, Arthur hung his head and whispered something under his breath.

"What's that?" Kara asked.

He pressed his fingers into his closed eyes, clearly distressed. "Just… keep going."

She continued with how, after the séance, Adrienne changed: her bizarre mood swings, her uncharacteristically erratic behavior, how she stopped eating and sleeping.

Arthur shook his head.

"By the end, she was barely recognizable," Kara said, her voice strained. "A different person."

"An apt description," Arthur muttered.

Kara watched him for a moment. *He believes every word.* "You seem… not surprised by any of this."

"What happened next?" Arthur said.

Kara was grateful that Arthur believed her, though she knew the story was only getting worse and worse.

She described when she'd discovered Adrienne trying to sacrifice their neighbor's goat; how she'd had no choice but to slap Adrienne as hard as she could, which had briefly brought Adrienne back to herself.

"I burned the statue that night," Kara said. "I thought that would be enough to get rid of the spirit."

Arthur shook his head again, as if already knowing she was wrong. "It was too late."

"Yes. How do you—"

"Then what happened?"

Kara swallowed hard. "The statue came back, some-how. I still don't understand it. I watched it burn, but there it was, back in the house like there'd actually been two of them the whole time. Anyway, in a moment of clarity where she was acting like her normal self again, Adrienne told me to bring the statue to Lake Silver and throw it in. Something about the lake being holy to the Native Americans who used to live near there." Arthur nodded. "So I went to do what she said, but... and I still don't get it, but I swear it's true... the statue suddenly *weighed* way more than it had. Maybe a hundred pounds more. I couldn't even lift it."

Arthur made some kind of noise in his throat, one that suggested to her that the statue violating the laws of physics was somehow unsurprising to him.

"My friend at the time came over and helped me. On the way to the lake, we were attacked by... something."

"Something?" Arthur asked.

She shuddered at the memory. "It wasn't human."

Arthur was staring at her now, having shifted his

complete attention to Kara, his whiskey forgotten. "And then?"

"After we threw it in the lake, I thought it was done and that Aunt Adrienne would be normal again. But when I got home…"

"You got home and…"

"That's when she did it," Kara said. "Right in front of me."

Everything inside Arthur seemed to collapse.

Kara was silent for a few minutes as she gave Arthur time to feel whatever he was feeling. Finally, she said, "I'm only telling you this because it's obvious that you cared very much about my aunt."

"I did," Arthur said. "Still do."

"Then… if you don't mind me asking…" She hesitated, not wanting to overload the man with too many questions, yet she couldn't help herself. "If you loved her, then how did you not already know she was gone?"

Arthur stared down into his whiskey, swirling the liquid as he considered Kara's questions. When he spoke, his voice was low and strained.

"Adrienne and I met by chance when I was spending some time in Mississippi."

Kara perked up. He hadn't answered her question, but he seemed willing to share his own past with Adrienne now. She wondered if his story—much like her own—hadn't often been told.

"I was never expecting to meet someone like her," Arthur went on. "While everyone else around these parts was caught up in their religion, Adrienne had this… openness about the world and its mysteries."

"So you're spiritual like she was," Kara said.

"I suppose you could say that," Arthur said. "I'm a demonologist."

"A… what?" She wasn't even sure that was a real word or an actual profession.

"I guess it's more accurate to say that I *was* a demonologist."

"You… used to study demons?"

"More than study. I fought them."

Kara blinked. *Isn't that from a movie? Constantine?*

"For quite a bit of my life, when people came into contact with demonic entities, they'd call me," Arthur said. "I helped them remove the spirit and restore peace and balance to their lives." He took a sip of whiskey. "That's what I was doing in Mississippi all those years ago when I met Adrienne. I was here working on a long project where a woman had been possessed, and—"

"*Possessed?*" Kara felt herself getting left behind in Arthur's story.

"Yes." He gave her a look that seemed to say he didn't like being interrupted. "You know what that is, right?"

"Uh… yeah, but only from movies."

When she was younger—many years before her summer in Silver Falls—she'd gone to a slumber party with friends. One of them had swiped their dad's VHS copy of *The Exorcist.* She'd covered her eyes with her hands for most of the film. Something about it had disturbed her more than other horror movies. Slashers, zombies, monsters—all of that she could handle. Demonic possession, on the other hand, was a horror subgenre she'd avoided ever since that night.

"It's very real," Arthur said bluntly.

Well okay, she thought.

She remembered the time when she'd thought she

knew how the world worked. After that summer in Silver Falls, she'd decided that she could no longer rule anything out. If this man she'd just met claimed to fight demons and cast them out of people, then as far as she was willing to admit, he was telling the truth.

Because why not? she thought. *I saw so many other unexplainable things, this might as well be true. Vampires and werewolves too, while we're at it.*

"It's dark and dangerous work," Arthur continued. "And this was a big project. The demon was strong, and very attached to the woman. That job kept me around here for a long while—ten months—and that's how I ended up spending so much time with Adrienne. She was like a beacon of bright light in a phase of my life otherwise filled with complete evil." He paused, a hint of a sad smile on his face. "We were so caught up in each other, we eloped after two months. Nothing fancy, just signed some papers at the courthouse. It was a strange chapter for me—a tough, demonic possession situation on one hand, and meeting the love of my life on the other."

To Kara, the image of her free-spirited aunt eloping with this gruff man was both surprising and oddly fitting. "I bet my aunt was interested in your work," she said.

Arthur nodded, his eyes darkening. "*Too* interested for her own good. I tried to protect her from it, but Adrienne was fascinated by it all. She wanted to know everything. Even asked to come with me to one of the sessions, where the local priest and I were going to try to send the demon away."

"Did you let her?" Kara asked.

"Of course not." He took a heavy swig of whiskey before continuing. "However, the entity I was battling noticed I'd developed feelings for someone," Arthur said grimly. "It saw that as a vulnerability."

Kara furrowed her brow. "What do you mean?"

"Demons are horrific creatures. When they're under attack, they fight back, and fight dirty. I've been cut, beaten, and thrown across the room by these spirits. But they know the best way to destroy a human isn't physical, it's mentally and emotionally. This creature knew I'd found a partner in town. He could *smell* it on me. A few days later, he took it upon himself to hurt Adrienne as a warning to dissuade me from continuing the exorcism."

"Hurt her? How?"

"Scratches," Arthur said. "Adrienne woke up one morning with a set of three scratches on her back. I knew instantly what it was and why it was happening. And that I'd made a mistake. When you do the work I do, then it just isn't a good idea to have anyone in your life that you're close to. They're a weakness demons can exploit."

He absent-mindedly rotated his glass on the bar, spinning it round and round. "I realized I couldn't keep Adrienne safe if I continued. So I had to make a choice."

Kara felt a pang in her chest. She could guess what he was about to say.

"You chose to leave," she said softly.

Arthur nodded, his eyes glistening. "For Adrienne's own good. That exorcism ended in success after ten long months, the longest of my career, I believe. But what about the one after that? The next demon would've gone after her as well. And the next one. They all operate from the same bag of tricks."

Kara's heart ached for the grief-stricken man before her. She saw now that he had loved her aunt deeply, despite the physical distance he had put between them.

Leaving her was an agonizing sacrifice he'd made to protect her that still haunted him, even after all these years.

He inhaled a shaky breath. "Looks like in the end, one of those bastards got her anyway."

"What do you mean?"

"That being inside the statue. It wasn't just a normal spirit. It was a demon."

"What's the difference between a normal spirit and a demon?" Kara asked, almost in disbelief that she was even having this conversation. "Is a normal spirit like a ghost?"

"Yes. A ghost is the lingering spirit of someone who is no longer alive. A demon, on the other hand..." He paused, lip curling. "... a demon is an *inhuman* spirit. They've existed for all time, and they become powerful by feeding off of people's fear and negative emotions. Every ancient culture in the world believed in and wrote about demons. They called them by different names, of course, but they're all describing the same basic entity. It's only now, in modern times, that people have stopped believing. Which is a very dangerous mistake."

Kara stared at Arthur, swayed by the sheer conviction behind his words. "Are you sure it was a demon in that statue?"

"Yes. I know how they operate. And Adrienne's behaviors that you described were classic signs of demonic oppression. And what you said about Adrienne pacing in counterclockwise circles... Moving anything backwards or in reverse is a dead giveaway of demonic activity. It symbolizes a mockery or a perversion of what's good and right in the natural world."

Kara had sensed negativity the moment she'd seen the statue. She hadn't ever used the word demon, though.

Then something occurred to her. "When the spirit—or demon, I guess—carved its name into the floorboards, it spelled it backwards."

Arthur's eyes narrowed. As he continued to stare at Kara, she started to get the feeling that she'd said something wrong. Finally, he said, "You're telling me you know the demon's name?"

She hesitated, taken aback by the intensity of his gaze. "Y-yes," she stammered, then cleared her throat. "Azunu."

Arthur leaned back, brow furrowed. "Azunu," he repeated, as if testing it on his tongue. "Don't believe I've ever met that one."

Kara blinked, confused. "What do you mean by that?"

Arthur took a slow sip of his whiskey. "In my line of work, you sometimes encounter the same demon more than once. You get rid of them, and then a few years later, they come back and start haunting some other home, some other family. Which is just as well, I suppose. They have… personalities, for lack of a better word. Tendencies. Patterns. So when you realize you're dealing with one you've already met, then it can make the job easier. You know their weakness." He shook his head. "But Azunu… that's new to me."

Kara stared into her club soda, watching the bubbles rise and pop against the lime wedge. Despite believing everything Arthur had said, she couldn't imagine what his life had been like, what he'd been through. Her encounter with one demon had altered her irrevocably. How had Arthur dealt with an entire *list* of these creatures?

"Would you have preferred it if I hadn't gotten in touch with you?" Kara asked.

Arthur waited a long time before responding, as if giving it some serious thought. "It's better this way. I needed to know." He took a sip. Then something seemed to occur to him. "Although… why *did* you call me?"

"I'm here to decide what to do with Adrienne's house," she explained. "I'm planning to sell it, but then when I saw her marriage license in the storage unit, I knew I had to figure out what the deal was."

"We were only married for eight months. Before I left town, we terminated the legal aspect of our relationship," Arthur said. "So you don't need to worry about that."

"I figured that was the case, but I still wanted to make sure."

"The house…" Arthur straightened up, as if he'd just thought of something.

"What about it?" Kara wondered if he'd ask to go and see it. She hoped not.

"Nothing."

But Kara sensed that whatever had popped into his mind wasn't "nothing."

Arthur drained his whiskey and reached into his pocket to dig out some crumpled bills, which he threw onto the bar. "Appreciate your time."

And with that, he was gone.

41

The doorbell rang at precisely seven that evening, right after Cole and his mother had finished their dinner.

"Who's that?" Mama asked, looking toward the door, seeming both confused and worried. They never had visitors.

"I have a surprise for you," Cole said, rising from the couch. "Someone's coming to see you."

"Who is it?"

He didn't respond, wanting to preserve the surprise. He headed for the entry hall and opened the front door to see Pastor Craig standing on the porch, Bible in hand.

"Evening, Cole," the pastor said warmly.

"Come on in." Cole stepped aside.

Pastor Craig walked into the cozy living room, where Mama sat waiting in her recliner. A huge smile lit up her face—Cole hadn't seen her that happy in a long time. She looked like she might cry. Pastor Craig went to her and clasped both her hands.

"It's so good to see you in person," Mama said. "Watching you on a screen just isn't the same."

"I know," Pastor Craig said. "It's good to see you, too. But community members like you are the reason we stream the services online."

When Mama had gotten weak, Cole had had to convince her that maybe it was time to stop attending church. She wouldn't hear of it, so Cole had gotten her a tablet and taught her how to watch the services live online. At first, she'd detested the idea.

"This isn't church," she'd said, shaking her head at the glassy screen as Pastor Craig delivered his sermon.

"But Mama, think about it. When they do it like this, then all the people that our missionaries reach down in Mexico can also watch the sermons. They don't have to be here in town to hear Pastor Craig."

Mama had appeared to give that some consideration.

Cole had no clue if people in Mexico—or anywhere their church sent missionaries, for that matter—ever watched their sermons. But the notion that they could if they wanted to had helped win Mama over to the idea of online church.

It had taken some getting used to, but after a while, Mama had grown accustomed to Sunday-morning church in her recliner. "Never thought I'd see the day when church would be like this," she'd once said, gesturing to the tablet on her lap. "But I remember watching them put a man on the moon. I guess this is what happens when you start making all this technology."

"What are you doing here?" Mama asked Pastor Craig, drawing Cole's thoughts back to the present.

"Cole and I both thought it'd be nice if I came by for a visit."

"I'm so glad you did. It's been so long since I've seen you in person."

For the next hour, Mama talked Pastor Craig's ear off, regaling him with tales from her childhood. It was her habit that once she got going, she couldn't stop. She'd tell a story, and some detail would remind her of another story, so she'd roll right into that one. As the stories flowed, Cole's mind wandered to the truth of the situation; he'd invited Pastor Craig under the guise of cheering up his mother, but the real reason was that he needed someone to cleanse their home and drive away whatever darkness might be gathering there.

"Oh, this reminds me," Mama said after finishing a story about the time she and her cousin had snuck extra slices of pie from a church bake sale. "Did I ever tell you about when my cousin convinced me to go swimming in the creek, even though my daddy had forbidden it?"

Pastor Craig chuckled. "No, I don't believe you did."

So, Mama enthusiastically launched into the creek story. Cole had heard it many times before and could recite it word for word. He didn't mind, though. The joy on his mother's face as she reminisced warmed his heart. "There we were, up to our knees in that muddy water, our Sunday dresses soaked and ruined." Mama threw her hands up for emphasis, and Pastor Craig chuckled politely. "Needless to say, we caught an earful when we got home."

"I bet you did," Pastor Craig said. "I never knew you had such a naughty streak in you, Sister Debra."

"Only when we were kids," Mama said quickly, as if she didn't want Pastor Craig to get the wrong idea. "The Lord straightened me out very soon after that."

"Speaking of, can I pray for you before I leave?" Pastor

Craig asked. Cole was impressed by how smoothly he could excuse himself.

Mama lit up even more. "I'd love that."

The three of them bowed their heads.

"Heavenly Father, we come before you today to lift up Sister Debra and this household…" The pastor began his petition by asking the Lord for spiritual fortification, comfort, and peace within the home.

After the prayer, Pastor Craig asked, "Sister Debra, would you mind if I blessed your home too?"

"I would be honored, Pastor."

Cole watched as Pastor Craig moved through the house, praying aloud in each room. While he knew Mama would be happy to spend some time with Pastor Craig, this was the specific reason he'd invited the man over.

As Pastor Craig went from room to room, Cole found himself relaxing. The holy words seemed to wash over the home and cleanse the air within.

Pastor Craig returned to the living room when he was done.

"I cannot thank you enough for coming tonight," Mama said. "I feel better than I have in a long time."

Pastor Craig smiled. "It was my pleasure. I'm always here if you need me." He turned to Cole. "You take good care of your mother, now."

"I will, sir," Cole said.

He walked Pastor Craig out, closing the front door behind them.

"Is there a specific reason you wanted the house blessed?" the pastor asked. Cole could tell the man had been waiting for an opportunity to ask, and that the question had been tugging at him.

"I knew Mama would appreciate it," Cole said. It wasn't *technically* a lie, but definitely not the entire story.

Pastor Craig smiled, seeming to accept that. "You're a good son. I'll see you on Sunday, Cole."

After bidding the pastor goodbye, Cole rejoined Mama in the living room. The lamp light illuminated her weary but contented face. "That was a nice surprise."

"I knew you'd like it," Cole said.

They finished up the episode of the television show they were watching, and when the usual time came, Cole retrieved the Bible so he could read to Mama until she fell asleep. He opened it up to the bookmarked spot and froze.

The page they'd left off on had been torn. Three jagged gashes had ripped through the thin paper.

Cole's gut lurched when he saw it.

"Something wrong?" Mama asked.

"No," Cole said as he cleared his throat. He started reading from the next intact page. Luckily, Mama didn't notice that he'd skipped ahead.

———

Cole stirred awake. His bedroom was dark and impossibly cold. The clock on the bedside table read two minutes before three o'clock in the morning. He couldn't explain it, but he somehow knew he wasn't alone in his room.

He scanned the darkened bedroom as he held his breath. Nothing seemed out of place.

But then he saw it. There, in the upper corner, a collection of shadows hovered, a black orb about the size of a beach ball.

Cole couldn't tear his eyes away. He also got the impression that the orb was watching him. As he stared, the orb began to shift and elongate. The shadow stretched and twisted, taking on a more human-like form. Within moments, what had been a floating sphere now resembled the silhouette of a man—the very shadow man his mother had described.

This was the entity that Mama had seen—it had to be. The same one that had threatened him all those years ago.

Knowing that, Cole could only think of a single thing to say. "Leave Mama alone," he whispered.

The response echoed in his head, a telepathic communication.

'No.'

Even after two long decades, Cole recognized the dark, inhuman voice. It was the same as when he'd first heard it—that night when he and Kara had rushed to Lake Silver.

His breath came in sharp, frightened pants. He wanted to sprint from the room, but felt frozen in place.

"Y-you can't be here. The house was b-blessed."

'Your holy man is weak.'

Cole swallowed. "What do you want?"

He braced himself for the heavy voice to invade his brain again. But the entity did not respond. Instead, the black orb faded from view. The temperature in the room went back to normal, and Cole knew the creature had left him alone—for now.

He closed his eyes and began praying, trying hard to muster the faith to believe that God would—and could— protect him from this monster.

42

In the morning, Kara went down to the hotel lobby for breakfast. It offered the same food as the day before. As she ate and had her coffee, she couldn't get Arthur Briggs—and his claims about demons—out of her head.

After Kara had finished eating, she returned to her room and contacted the storage company, asking if they'd be able to terminate her mother's account with them and dispose of everything in her aunt's unit. They confirmed they could, for a fee.

"Great. I'll call you back in a week or two if I decide to do that." Even though she was sure her mother wouldn't have an issue with it, she still wanted to check with her before getting rid of everything Aunt Adrienne had owned.

Then she booked her flight back to Boston, scheduled to depart the next day. She couldn't wait to get away from all the memories. Once she was home, she'd find a real estate agent to help her sell the house as quickly as possible.

So another person can be haunted, the thought slipped into her mind. *But what else am I supposed to do?* Maybe she could tell the real estate agent to strongly suggest to the buyer that they demolish the home and build a new one. *But if they're going to buy it, that means they like the house, right? Why would they tear it down?* Maybe she could insist that the agent only sell to someone who was primarily interested in the land. The thoughts started jumbling up in her head so much that she had to push them away entirely. *I'll decide later. For now, I just need to go. And put all of this behind me.*

Around noon, she packed up her laptop and walked to a nearby cafe. There, she had lunch and another cup of coffee while she caught up on work emails.

Her cell, lying on the table, rang. It was Cole Turner. She realized she'd forgotten to text him back the other day.

It's good that he's calling me now, she thought as she picked up the phone. *I need to tell him I'm leaving.*

"Hey, Cole," she answered.

"Hey. What's up?"

"Getting some work done," she said. "I'm glad you called. I wanted to tell you—"

He cut her off. "Do you want to grab dinner tonight? There's a nice little Italian place just outside of town I think you'd like." His voice was tentative, almost exactly the same as when he'd first called her on her aunt's landline.

Kara heard the intention in his tone. This wasn't a catch-up dinner between old friends.

"That's sweet of you to offer, but... I'm actually heading home to Boston tomorrow morning."

"Oh." He sounded crestfallen. "So soon?"

"Yeah. I got done with what I needed to do here." She traced a groove on the wooden table with her fingernail as she spoke.

"That was fast. When do you think you'll come back?"

Kara hung her head and chose her words carefully. "I don't foresee there being a reason for me to come back here..."

"Oh," Cole said again. An awkward silence stretched between them.

"I'm glad we bumped into each other, though," Kara added gently.

"Me too," he said. Then he blurted, "There's something else I've been wanting to say. I—I haven't..." He cleared his throat. "I haven't stopped thinking about you since that summer. I—I know you have a life in Boston, and a job, but... I can't shake the feeling that... this is meant to be. That *we're* meant to be."

Kara's chest tightened. *You're choosing to do this now?* How could she respond to such a heartfelt declaration? Especially when she'd just told him she was leaving town for good. She struggled to find the words, her heart breaking more with each passing second. "Cole, I'm... flattered, but... I'm sorry, that wouldn't work. My entire life is on the other side of the country."

The complete truth was that even if she had planned to spend more time in Silver Falls, that didn't necessarily make her more open to Cole's intentions. In her mind, he'd been her summer friend. Nothing more.

And even if she *had* been open to a relationship with him... she still wouldn't be able to bring herself to do it. Unfortunately, Cole Turner was too entwined with the memories she'd worked so hard to suppress.

Cole was silent for a long time. In a way, she thought

she could pick up on his quiet resignation through the phone.

"But…" he finally said.

"I'm sorry."

She heard him breathe in a shaky breath. "Okay."

"Take care, Cole." Kara hung up, then set her phone down with a sigh. Guilt shot through her, but the past was the past. It was time to look ahead.

43

Kara jerked awake at the sound of her phone ringing. Blearily, she glanced at the clock—nearly midnight. She fumbled for it in the dark and checked the screen.

Arthur.

"Hello?" she mumbled, half-asleep.

"I'm standing outside your aunt's house right now. You can come over and let me in, or I'll break in. But either way, I'm getting inside."

Kara sat up, suddenly wide awake. "What? Why?"

"Because the demon that killed Adrienne is probably still in the home. And I'm going to remove it."

It took Kara a moment to register what she'd just heard. "Arthur... I don't think—"

"This is happening. You're either letting me in, or I'm going in myself. You choose. What'll it be?"

Her mind raced. "Now? In the middle of the night?"

"Yes."

What in the world? Kara thought. "Don't do anything crazy," she said. "I can be there in fifteen minutes." Maybe if she headed over, she could try and talk some sense into the man.

The line went dead. Kara stared at her silent phone in disbelief.

What the hell have I gotten myself into?

With a frustrated huff, Kara flung away the covers and dressed. She wasn't sure why, but although she'd just met Arthur, she didn't put it past him to break into the house.

Twenty minutes later, Kara pulled up in front of the dark, silent home. Arthur's truck was in the driveway, engine still running. He climbed out as she parked, the glow from her headlights casting his craggy face in eerie shadows.

Kara got out of her rental car. "What are you doing here?" She crossed her arms and stared at Arthur as he approached.

"You said you were going to sell the house," Arthur began, and she nodded. "That's a bad idea if there's a demonic infestation inside."

Infestation? Like termites?

It was as if he'd somehow known she'd wrestled with this very dilemma that morning.

"Right…" She felt ashamed that she'd been considering doing exactly that.

"You can't sell the house in good conscience," Arthur said. "Not as it is now. You can't let someone live here when you know there's danger."

Kara remembered what the property manager had told her. She hadn't mentioned that anyone had been harmed, but from what Arthur had taught her about demons, it seemed like a good bet that if someone stayed in the home long enough, that would change.

If the next owner is affected, then what if they end up doing the same thing as Adrienne?

It was relatively easy for those who'd rented to leave quickly. If someone bought it, though, they'd have a harder time fleeing.

Kara passed him the house keys.

———

As the front door creaked open, Kara hesitated on the threshold. Apprehension gripped her. Arthur, however, strode right in.

The emptiness made the house seem vast. The still, dusty air tickled Kara's nose, and she knew the humidity would quickly become unbearable without the air conditioning on.

Arthur went to the middle of the living room and looked around, his eyes scanning the area as if seeing beyond its physical contents. Kara wondered what he was searching for, what he expected to find. Perhaps he was reliving his memories, like she had done a few days before.

"Do you feel that?" Arthur asked.

"Feel what?"

"The heaviness."

"It's because the AC hasn't run in weeks."

"No. It's more than that."

He approached the fireplace mantel and laid a hand on it, touching almost exactly the space once occupied by the cursed statue.

He remembers where I told him Adrienne kept the statue, she thought.

"I need to tell you something important," he said, his

309

gruff voice unusually gentle. "There's a chance your aunt's spirit never left this place."

At first, it sounded outrageous, but she could both see and hear how serious Arthur was. "What do you mean?"

Arthur turned to her. "Demonic entities have ways of trapping souls, keeping them bound to a location against their will." His weathered face was grim. "If Adrienne's spirit is lingering here, it means she hasn't been able to move on and hasn't found peace."

It was hard for Kara to imagine—it sounded like some unseen purgatory that existed all around them but gave no hint of its existence. "You really think her spirit could still be here after all this time?" And even though it was such an abstract concept, she couldn't help but feel the sadness welling up inside her.

"Trapping souls," Arthur had said. She'd heard it claimed many times before that people's souls were supposed to "move on" to somewhere after death, whether that be the heaven described in the Bible, reincarnation, or something else entirely. She didn't know where these souls were supposed to go, but she somehow knew that Adrienne would have wanted to go there after she passed. And for her to be kept from doing that against her will seemed... sadistic.

"I've seen it before," Arthur said. "A demon gains power over a person in life, then keeps that dominion over their soul in death." His jaw tightened. "After you told me what had happened, I knew there was no way I could leave town."

Kara shivered despite the stale warmth. She thought of her vibrant aunt, so full of light and energy. She hated the idea of the woman's lonely spirit suffering for all this time.

Kara looked back at Arthur, a new understanding dawning. "So that's why you came here tonight. You said you were going to remove the demon, but not because you care about the house. You want to set Adrienne free."

The hard lines of his face softened. "Yes. She deserves to rest in peace. And I have to try."

If Arthur was right and Adrienne's spirit was still there, Kara decided she would do everything in her power to help. She owed her aunt that much.

She met Arthur's resolute gaze and gave a single nod. "Tell me what we need to do."

———

ARTHUR WENT to the bed of his truck and hoisted from it a small table that he'd brought along, which he carried inside and put in the center of the living room. He then returned to the truck, retrieved two simple chairs, and set them up on either side of the table.

"If you had two chairs," Kara said, "then that must mean you knew I was going to come when you called."

"Yes," Arthur said. He placed a large candle in the middle of the table, along with a box of matches.

"Where'd you get all this stuff, anyway?" she asked.

"That thrift shop in town."

"Oh. I know the owner. He's a friend of mine."

"That young guy who's all nervous and shifty?"

"Tall with blond hair," Kara said, offering up what she thought was a more accurate description.

"Yeah, him. I got a bad feeling from him."

Kara was taken aback. "Cole? No way. He's a great person."

Arthur shook his head. "There's something off about him. Believe me."

Kara stared at him, wanting to argue, and even opened her mouth to protest, but Arthur's grave certainty gave her pause.

"Anyway," Arthur went on, striking a match and lighting the candle, "he gave me a good deal on all this shit, so I guess I can't complain. But I also don't think you should be around him anymore."

Kara was stunned. It had been *many* years since someone had tried to dictate to her who she should or shouldn't spend time with. "You know he's the one who helped me carry the statue to Lake Silver that night. Remember, I told you I wasn't able to lift it, so I had to call a friend?" She couldn't keep the defiant tone out of her voice.

Unfazed, Arthur replied, "That's fine. Doesn't mean I'm wrong." He stepped back and surveyed the table, chairs, and burning candle with a nod.

There's no changing his mind. Besides, it doesn't matter. We're not here to talk about Cole Turner. This is about Aunt Adrienne. Focus.

Next, Arthur reached into the bag he'd also taken from his truck and pulled out a flashlight that he set onto the table, then something else that was small and rectangular, which he placed near the flickering candle. Kara realized it was a digital recorder.

"What's that for?" she asked.

Arthur glanced at her as he finished adjusting the device. "It's to capture any sounds that we can't hear," he explained. "Sometimes, when you try to communicate with spirits, their voices come through at frequencies our ears don't pick up. But you can hear them if you slow down or amplify the audio recording afterwards."

At one point, Kara would've scoffed at the notion. Now, she found herself just nodding along with it. *He's probably recorded spirit voices many times before.*

She was willing to indulge him. She remembered the lesson she'd learned the hard way that summer—how reality worked was far outside her understanding. After everything she'd seen and experienced, she couldn't dismiss Arthur Briggs and the claims he made.

Arthur finished adjusting the recorder and took his seat. The candle flame danced, casting flickering shadows across his aged features. His eyes were dark pools in the dim light.

"Let's begin," he said.

Kara drew a deep breath. Apprehension and doubt warred within her as she settled into the rickety wooden chair. "I told you my story, so you already know that the last time I did this, I had a terrible experience."

"You might this time, too." Arthur extended his palms up, resting on the table's surface. After a moment's hesitation, Kara placed her hands atop his. They felt like a bed of calluses. She met his solemn gaze past the candle's trembling light. Shadows danced across the bare walls.

Kara watched as Arthur closed his eyes and took a deep breath. When he spoke, his voice was low and deliberate.

"We are here with the intention of contacting the spirit of Adrienne Kemper," he began. "If she is present, we wish to communicate with her."

Kara felt a prickle between her shoulder blades. The empty house seemed to grow watchful, as if listening.

Here we go again, Kara couldn't help but think. *Hopefully this time will be less crazy than the first.*

Arthur continued the invocation: "Adrienne, if you are here with us, we invite you to make yourself known. Use your energy to interact with our physical world so that we may hear you."

Kara's eyes darted around the shadowy room, straining for any hint of a presence. She realized she was on edge, hyper alert—her last séance had left its mark. But the house remained still and silent.

After a pause, Arthur went on, "Adrienne Kemper, we call upon your spirit. If you are bound to this home, give us a sign so that we may help guide you to the light."

The flickering candle created an eerie dance of shadow on the walls. Kara realized she was holding her breath, half-expecting a dramatic reaction to Arthur's request.

But still, nothing seemed to change in the stale living-room air.

Arthur opened his eyes, appearing unsurprised by the lack of response. "It can take time for spirits to gather enough energy to manifest," he explained. "We'll need to be patient."

Kara nodded. Already she noticed the stark difference in the approach between Adrienne and Arthur. Her aunt had almost approached the séance as an innocent, curious experiment—perhaps that was one reason it had ended so badly. Arthur, on the other hand, came across like he'd done this many times and knew the gravity of the situation.

The older man closed his eyes once more, delving back into the meditative trance. The night pressed in around them through the darkened windows. Somewhere in the distance, an owl hooted through the emptiness.

Kara shifted in her chair as the waiting stretched on. Across from her, Arthur remained still, looking almost as if he were sleeping while sitting upright.

"Adrienne Kemper, I call upon you a third time. If you are here, give us a sign of your presence."

His words seemed to hang suspended in the air. Kara leaned forward, straining her senses for the slightest disruption in the stillness that had settled over the room. She imagined her aunt's whisper-soft voice echoing from a corner, or the brush of a spectral hand across her shoulder... but there was nothing.

The silence stretched on. Though Kara had no idea how much time was actually passing, to her it felt like hours. Her legs were beginning to cramp, and the wooden chair dug into her back. Yet Arthur showed no signs of impatience.

Kara wondered if they would remain like this all night, waiting endlessly for a ghost that would not come. Doubt started to settle in. Still, she remained frozen in her seat, ears straining as she willed some supernatural sign to manifest in the shadowy room.

Just when the stillness was becoming unbearable, Kara felt an almost imperceptible change in the air. The fine hairs on her arms prickled.

"Feel that?" Arthur whispered.

Kara swallowed. "I... I do. What is it?"

"We're not alone." His voice was barely audible.

Kara's heart quickened, but she remained unmoving, palms resting atop Arthur's. He probably felt her hands starting to sweat. The shifting energy lingered at the edge of her awareness. It did not feel threatening, yet it scratched at the boundaries of her perception, demanding acknowledgement.

Now Kara was torn. *Last time, things didn't go well when a spirit showed up,* she thought. She vacillated between two states of mind. Half of her wanted all this to work so she could see her aunt again. The other half—still traumatized by her previous experience—actively resisted Arthur's progress.

"Speak to her," Arthur said, his eyes still closed.

The request caught her off guard.

Speak to her? How? What am I supposed to say?

Arthur seemed to sense her hesitation. He nudged her hand, a silent encouragement. "Your voice will help bring forth her spirit more strongly," he murmured.

Kara's mouth was suddenly dry. It felt strange, almost surreal, to be sitting there in the dark, empty house, addressing her aunt's ghost. But beneath the fear and uncertainty, a flicker of hope stirred.

She drew a shaky breath, gathering her courage. "Aunt Adrienne?" Her voice sounded small and uncertain. "It's me. Kara. I'm here with Arthur Briggs. We... we're trying to reach you."

The words felt awkward, but she kept on. "If you're here, please give us a sign."

Kara paused, straining her senses for any response. The air seemed to grow heavier, the silence more profound.

"Don't just speak to her, *communicate* with her," Arthur pressed.

"What do you mean?" Kara whispered. "What's the difference?"

He opened his eyes and studied her for a few moments. "You lost her without warning. Aren't there some things you've always wanted to say to her but never got the chance?"

Another opportunity to talk to Aunt Adrienne...

A complicated mix of emotions tangled within her—fear, doubt, longing, and a desperate hope that defied reason. She yearned to believe that her aunt was there, listening. That somehow, across the veil of death, they could connect one last time.

"Communicate. Use more than just your voice. Spirits respond to your *energy* more than your words."

There it is again, Kara thought, remembering her aunt's mini-lecture that day in the thrift store. *Energy. I wonder if Adrienne learned that from Arthur.*

Kara took a moment to allow the sad, regretful energy to envelop her. She'd spent decades forcing it away, but that night she let it emerge. "Aunt Adrienne, I… I miss you." Her voice shook, thick with emotion. "There's so much I wish I'd said before…"

She blinked back the sudden tears. The weight of unspoken words, of missed opportunities, pressed down on her chest. If only she'd known then what she knew now. If only she'd been braver, more open, more willing to understand.

"I'm sorry. For everything," she whispered. "If I'd… accepted what was happening to you, then maybe I could've changed it. Maybe things would've turned out differently. But I'm here for you now. So if you're trapped here, if you need help… give us a sign."

Through the tears, she noticed Arthur watching her, his gaze never wavering from her as she spoke. His expression seemed to be made of stone.

The silence stretched on. Kara waited, hoping against hope for some response.

Please, Aunt Adrienne. Be here. Let me make things right.

But the house remained still and quiet, the air heavy with absence.

Kara's shoulders slumped, disappointment and grief welling up inside her. Perhaps it was foolish to think she could reach her aunt after all this time. Maybe some wounds, some regrets, could never heal. Maybe Arthur Briggs didn't know what he was doing after all.

I'm sorry, Aunt Adrienne, she thought, a silent prayer to the darkness. *For everything.*

She searched for guidance or reassurance from Arthur, but his expression remained inscrutable.

Then he drew a deep breath, his face etched with a mixture of determination and something else she couldn't quite place. He was ready.

"Adrienne," he began, "I know it's been a long time. Too long. But there are things I need to say to you that I should've said when I had the chance." His voice was low and rough, yet filled with an unexpected tenderness. "Our time together was short, but it meant everything to me. You were the only woman I ever truly loved, Adrienne. The only one who saw past my walls and *understood* me." His words carried a weight of regret and longing that caught Kara off guard.

Arthur's voice had quivered throughout, and Kara felt his hands tremble where they rested in hers. She realized, with a pang of sympathy, that this confession was difficult for him.

"I didn't show it enough. I was distant, always wrapped up in my work. My obsession with demons came between us, and I'll never forgive myself for that. I should've told you every day how much you meant to me. But I let my own demons get in the way, and I lost you because of it.

I'm sorry, Adrienne. I'm so damn *sorry*. If you're here, if you can hear me... please know that I never stopped loving you. And I never will. Tonight, let us guide you to peace."

The sincerity in Arthur's words was apparent, his gruff exterior crumbling away to reveal a man haunted by the ghosts of his past. Kara realized, with a sudden clarity, that this séance was as much about Arthur's need for closure as it was about helping her aunt's spirit.

She hoped Adrienne could hear his words. That somehow, in the great beyond, the woman knew the depth of Arthur's love and the sincerity of his apology.

Kara and Arthur sat motionless, hands together with Arthur's, waiting for a sign that Adrienne had heard his heartfelt plea.

Then the words came.

"I'm... here."

44

Kara felt her heart leap into her throat as the sound drifted down from the second floor. Two simple words, yet they carried the unmistakable cadence of her aunt.

A dizzying mix surged through Kara—abject terror, overwhelming relief, and utter disbelief at hearing Adrienne's voice after twenty-one long years. It was as if time had collapsed, transporting her back to that fateful summer.

Kara's gaze snapped toward the staircase, the source of the ethereal voice. She half-rose from her chair, her body moving of its own accord, desperate to chase after this impossible connection to her lost aunt.

But Arthur's grip on her hands tightened, his narrow fingers digging into her skin with an almost painful intensity. He anchored her in place, not letting her go.

Confused, Kara looked at Arthur, expecting to see a mirror of her own shock and elation. Instead, she found his face had hardened, the raw emotion of his earlier confession gone. His body was tense and on guard.

Isn't this what we wanted? Kara thought. *To contact Aunt Adrienne?*

But Arthur's eyes remained fixed on the staircase, jaw clenched tight. There was a coiled energy about him, like a snake poised to strike. Kara's confusion deepened, tinged now with a growing foreboding.

Something's not right, she realized.

"I'm... here."

Adrienne's voice came again. It was muffled, as if behind a door, and Kara assumed she was calling out from the master bedroom.

There's something off about it, Kara thought. She'd heard the second time what Arthur must've heard the first; although it was unmistakably her aunt's voice, it sounded stiff and wooden, devoid of the essence that defined Adrienne Kemper.

But wouldn't that make sense? She's been dead for a while now...

After several long moments in which Arthur seemed to consider his next move, he released Kara's hands, got up from the table, and started for the staircase.

Do I follow him? Kara wondered. She didn't want to walk *toward* the uncanny voice, but at the same time, she also hated the thought of being left alone.

She decided to stay close to Arthur. Kara's heart pounded as she followed him up the creaky stairs, each step feeling like a monumental effort. She carried the flashlight with her, but hesitated to turn it on without Arthur telling her to. The air grew thick with tension, a suffocating weight pressing down on her as they approached the second floor.

They came to a stop at the top of the stairs, facing down the shadowy hallway to the closed master-bedroom door. Kara was a half step behind Arthur's left shoulder, so she waited to see what he would do.

"Kara... Arthur..." Adrienne's voice called out again, muffled by the door between them. Kara was sure now that there was something undeniably off about it, a stiffness that didn't quite match her memories of her aunt.

Doubt crept in, insidious and unsettling. Kara leaned closer to Arthur, her whisper barely audible as she said, "Is it really her?"

Arthur's face was grim, his eyes never leaving the closed door. He didn't answer immediately, seeming to weigh his words.

"Watch," he replied. Then, loudly, he said, "Who are you?"

"Adrienne."

Arthur reached into the collar of his shirt and pulled out a necklace that had been hidden from view. He lifted it up and held it with an outstretched arm. Kara saw what dangled from the cord: a cross that looked a bit too large and heavy to be comfortable to wear.

"Who are you?" Arthur asked again, this time more forcefully.

"I am Adrienne. You know me, Arthur."

Kara shook her head. Now that the voice had spoken more at length, she could pick out the subtle difference—though you wouldn't know it unless you'd known Adrienne well.

Arthur took a step forward, his hand steady as he gripped the chain that held the dangling cross. "Who are you?" he asked a third time.

There was a pause, a beat of silence. Then came a response, beginning in Adrienne's familiar tone: "Why, Arthur, it's me. Don't tell me you've forgotten—" But the voice began to change. It warped and distorted, dropping in pitch until it became something else—something inhuman. "—me after all this *time?*" The last word was drawn out in a mocking, guttural snarl that made Kara recoil.

Arthur's expression didn't change, and he seemed unsurprised. "Azunu," he said, his tone low and dangerous. Kara's stomach gave a sickening lurch. "I command you in the name of the Almighty to leave this house and release Adrienne's spirit."

The demon's laughter filled the air, a sound that seemed to come from everywhere and nowhere at once. It reverberated through the empty rooms, echoing off the bare walls until it surrounded them in a cacophony of malevolence.

"You have no power over me," Azunu hissed, his voice dripping with contempt. "This is my domain now. Adrienne's soul belongs to me."

Kara's body was on fire with both fear and anger. She desperately wanted to run away, but also felt emboldened —if this alcoholic old man could stand and confront the entity, she could too.

"Release her, demon," Arthur growled, his voice filled with authority. "And then I will cast you out of this place."

Kara flinched as the bedroom door exploded outward with a tremendous force, as if struck by an invisible battering ram. That same force seemed to surge out from the room and sent Arthur flying backward, his body hurtling through the air like a rag doll. He crashed to the floor at the end of the hallway, landing in a crumpled heap.

"Arthur!" Kara cried out, panicked. She rushed to his side.

Arthur groaned, face contorted in pain. He struggled

to push himself up onto his elbows, wincing with the effort. Kara placed a hand on his shoulder to steady him.

"Are you alright?" she asked, her words tumbling out in a breathless rush. He'd landed hard, and he already looked so fragile.

Arthur nodded, though his jaw was clenched. "I've had worse."

Kara helped him sit up, relieved that he appeared to be in one piece. But her relief was short-lived. With a trembling hand, she aimed the flashlight toward the master bedroom and clicked it on.

The white beam cut through the darkness, illuminating the empty space.

Kara's breath caught.

No...

There, in the center of the room, stood the statue.

It looked exactly as she remembered it—the leering face, the oversized mask on the thin body, the evil aura that seemed to emanate from it.

There's no way, she thought, her mind reeling.

Yet there it was, mocking her with its presence. Kara felt a bone-deep dread that settled in the pit of her stomach.

"That's—that's the statue I told you about," she whispered, her voice trembling. "Arthur, look."

Arthur's eyes narrowed as he took in the accursed object. Then he pushed himself to his feet. Kara helped him to stand. Once he was up, he leaned against the wall, obviously still in pain.

"Are you sure you're okay?" Kara asked, worried. He'd hit the floor hard.

Arthur glared ahead at the little statue. There was a fire behind his gaze that Kara figured had come from him laying eyes on the thing that had killed the only woman he'd ever loved. He looked like he was about to charge the statue and stomp it into the ground in a fit of rage.

But after a prolonged silence, all he said was, "Let's get the hell out of here."

45

Kara followed Arthur downstairs, her heart still racing. The old man dipped into the living room just long enough to snatch up the recorder he'd left on the table—she'd forgotten all about it.

Outside, the humid night air somehow seemed like a relief after the suffocating atmosphere within.

Arthur made his way down the porch steps, his movements stiff and pained. The impact of being thrown down the hallway had clearly taken a toll on his aging body. However, he didn't stop until he was leaning against the side of his truck. Kara went to stand next to him.

A long silence bloomed, and Kara wondered what Arthur was thinking. She remembered what he'd told her —demons fed off fear and negative emotions. Azunu had drawn those in spades from her that night. She was sickened by the thought that he might have grown stronger because of her. And she hated the way Azunu used her aunt's voice so callously. It felt perverse.

"So that wasn't really Adrienne," Kara said, breaking the silence. "But that doesn't mean… do you think she's still in there?" She dreaded the answer, but needed to know.

Arthur nodded, his eyes heavy with sadness. "I'm certain of it. Her soul is bound to that place and she can't move on. The demon is keeping her there."

Kara felt a surge of desperation. "Then we have to go back. We can't just leave her—"

"We will," Arthur interrupted, holding up a hand to stop her. "But not tonight. We need to prepare for a cleansing ritual first. It's the only way to banish this bastard and release Adrienne's spirit."

A cleansing ritual?

"I don't know what that is, but I'm guessing it's kind of like… an *undoing* of what my aunt and I did that night?" The image of the entity floating as a cloud of black smoke tried to occupy her mind the same way it had filled the air around the magic circle, but she pushed it away.

"Yes."

Kara searched the old man's exhausted face. "And you know how to do that? I'm assuming you've done it before as a… demonologist."

"Yes."

"So they work?" She heard the slight desperation behind her words.

Arthur looked at her as if trying to consider her delicate feelings in that moment, but then ultimately decided to give it to her straight. "Most of the time."

She had no idea what the ritual entailed, but to her, it sounded like what was needed. A reversal of a mistake made two decades before.

Kara nodded. "Fine. Just tell me what to do."

Arthur studied her with what seemed to be silent approval. "For now, go home and get some rest if you can. I'll be in touch in the morning."

46

Kara lay in her hotel bed, tossing and turning, her body exhausted but her mind refusing to grant her any sleep. The lamp atop the nightstand remained on, casting a soft glow across the room. She'd been too afraid to turn it off and be alone in the darkness.

The shrill ring of her phone pierced the silence, startling her. She glanced at the clock—six in the morning. When she reached for it, she saw Arthur's name on the screen.

"Are you awake?" Arthur asked.

"I didn't sleep," Kara admitted, her voice weary.

"I want to show you something. Meet me in your hotel lobby." As usual, the line went dead before she could respond.

Kara dragged herself out of bed, her body heavy with fatigue. She freshened up and made her way downstairs. The breakfast area wasn't quite open yet—a young worker was busy setting out trays of food and arranging tables—though she sat down anyway. Instead of protesting, he brought her a cup of black coffee.

About ten minutes later, the main door opened and Arthur came in. He carried a bag with him, the strap over his shoulder and chest.

He sat across from Kara. Without saying anything, he unslung his bag, unzipped the top, and pulled out a laptop that looked to be about a decade old. He opened it up on the table and started clicking with the trackpad.

"You want some coffee?" Kara asked.

"I was up all night reviewing the audio I captured," Arthur said, not answering her question. He spun the laptop around to face her, then went into his bag again and pulled out a pair of headphones. He connected its cable to the auxiliary port and handed them to her.

"What am I listening to?" Kara asked, taking the headphones from Arthur, nervous.

"Put those on and press play."

Kara hesitated for a moment, then placed the headphones over her ears. Her finger hovered over the trackpad. She took a deep breath and pressed it.

She heard her own voice, the things she'd said the night before echoing back to her. But then, just beneath the surface of her own words, another faint sound caught her attention.

Aunt Adrienne's voice—her actual voice—wove through the recording, barely audible. Kara strained to hear, her chest clenching as she recognized the unmistakable sound of her aunt's sobs. It was the same heart-wrenching cry Kara had heard after returning from throwing the statue into Lake Silver—when she'd still thought she'd won.

Tears welled up in Kara's eyes as she listened, the grief

and sadness she had carried for so long rising to the surface. She could almost see Aunt Adrienne, her face contorted in anguish, trapped in a world of pain and despair.

Kara's hands trembled as she removed the headphones, unable to bear the weight of her aunt's suffering any longer. She looked at Arthur, her eyes on the verge of shedding tears.

"She's still there," Kara whispered, her voice cracking. "You were right." The realization hit her like a physical blow, the knowledge that her aunt hadn't found peace, even in death. When Arthur had first suggested it, it sounded terrible, but it still felt like a distant possibility. Now, the harsh reality was undeniable. The guilt and regret she'd carried for so long intensified, threatening to overwhelm her. "For twenty-one *years* she's been there…"

What would've happened if I had never reached out to Arthur? she couldn't help but think. *I never would've known. She would've been trapped there… forever.*

"We're going to get her out," Arthur said. His tone betrayed no sense of doubt at all.

Kara sniffed and wiped at her eyes. "With the cleansing ritual?"

"Exactly."

Kara forced herself to get composed. "Okay. What do you need me to do?"

Arthur thought it over for a few seconds. "Her presence is weak, but it's definitely there. If we could coax her out more, it would give her spirit enough strength to fight against the demon."

"How do we do that?" Kara asked.

"Remember, she draws strength from energy now. So if we had two or three things that brought her positivity

331

and happiness when she was alive, that could help." Kara recalled again her aunt's explanation about the possible energy contained within the baseball at the thrift store. If that were the case, then it made sense that Adrienne's belongings would hold their own energy that her spirit might resonate with. "Do you have anything like that? Any of her things that could help?" Arthur's voice had a doubtful edge.

"Actually," Kara said, "there's a storage unit here in town that has all of her stuff from when she lived in the house." She was glad she hadn't yet given the manager there the go-ahead to dispose of it all.

Arthur's body went ramrod straight. "Are you serious?"

"Yeah. Mom never dealt with any of it. That storage unit is where I found your marriage license."

Arthur looked to the side as he thought for a few moments. Then he nodded. "We need all of it."

"All of it?"

"We're going to move it *all* back in, every stick of furniture there is. Put it exactly where it was when Adrienne lived there. Do your best to remember."

"Are you serious?" Kara asked, though when she looked at him, she could tell that he was. "That'll take all day, maybe even longer."

"Doesn't matter. Setting up her house as it was when she was alive is a *perfect* way to give her spirit the emotional strength it needs to give us an edge."

Kara's heart sank as she realized the magnitude of the task. Moving an entire household's worth of furniture and belongings, arranging it all to mirror the past... it seemed like a huge feat. But beneath the apprehension, a flicker of determination ignited within her. She knew she couldn't leave Aunt Adrienne trapped in that hellish limbo any longer. She'd do whatever Arthur told her to do.

"Yeah, okay. But it's a lot of heavy stuff. And there are only two of us..." She caught herself, not wanting to suggest that Arthur wasn't strong enough for the job.

He took a huge fall last night, yet today seems fine, Kara thought. *Maybe he's in better shape than he looks.*

Arthur seemed to detect what she was implying. "I'm not what I used to be, true. We'll need some help." He considered for a moment. "How about your little friend who runs that thrift store?"

Kara shot him an annoyed look. "You told me not to see him anymore."

"Who else do you know here?"

Kara sighed. "No one."

"Then we're stuck with him."

"I can't just call Cole out of the blue and ask him to give up his *entire* day to—"

"He helped carry the statue to the lake when it was too heavy for you," Arthur said.

"Well, yeah." Kara hated to admit it, but Arthur was probably right; Cole likely *would* come rushing to help her, despite the strangeness of the request.

"Sounds like you have your claws in him and he'd do anything for you. Call him. We don't have time to waste."

———

Kara stood outside the storage unit, her nerves on edge as she waited for Cole to arrive. Arthur was beside her, face impassive. The morning sun beat down on them, and Kara felt beads of sweat sprouting on her forehead.

I hope this isn't too awkward, she thought. She was certain that any pain Cole might feel at her having turned him down the day before would still be fresh.

Cole's familiar truck pulled into the lot. He parked near Kara's rental and got out. "So, moving furniture," he said as he approached them. He shot a sideways glance at Arthur, as if he recognized him from somewhere.

"This is my friend, Arthur," Kara said.

"I was in your store yesterday," Arthur said flatly.

"Right, I remember you." His eyes bounced between Arthur and Kara, as if trying to figure out how they knew each other.

"He dated my Aunt Adrienne a while ago," Kara explained while keeping the truth of their backstory as short and simple as possible.

"Oh," Cole said. "That's nice. How do—"

"We need to get going," Arthur cut in.

Cole stiffened at Arthur's impatience. "Okay. How much stuff do y'all have?"

Kara reached for the latch on the storage unit's exterior. With a quick tug, she pulled it open, sending the garage-style door rolling up on its tracks to reveal the contents inside.

Cole's eyes widened as he took in the sight before him. Stacks of boxes, furniture wrapped in protective covers, and various belongings filled the unit from floor to ceiling.

But then, to her surprise, Cole nodded. "Alright, let's do this." He stepped into the unit and started looking around, clearly already formulating a plan.

Relief washed over Kara, along with a surge of gratitude towards Cole. Despite the strangeness of the request —and her turning down his advances—he was still willing to help. But she also couldn't deny the guilt. In a way, she felt like she was using him. *I'll have to make it up to him somehow,* she thought.

Kara and Cole tackled the heavy furniture first. They lifted a worn couch, grunting with effort as they maneuvered it into the back of Cole's truck. Next were the mattresses and bed frames. She immediately started pouring sweat from the Mississippi heat.

Many items were wrapped in plastic, which Cole removed with a large pocketknife. It was another reason Kara was grateful that Cole was there—she wouldn't have thought to bring anything like that. She'd never even *owned* a pocketknife.

About twenty minutes after they'd started, Cole said to her, "So you weren't really leaving town yet?"

Kara heard something else behind the question—an insinuation that she'd lied to him. "I'd planned to, but I cancelled the flight when this came up," she said, which was actually the truth.

As the two of them worked on the furniture, Arthur had focused on the smaller items. He loaded boxes of knick-knacks and personal effects into the cabs of the trucks and Kara's rental.

When the three vehicles were full, they drove to Adrienne's house to unload what would be the first of many trips.

Kara eyed the house warily once she got out of her car.

"What's wrong?" Arthur asked her.

She glanced at Cole, who had dropped his truck's tailgate and was preparing to unload. He was out of earshot.

"We know there's a demon in there," Kara said. "Is it... okay to go back in?"

"We don't have a choice." With that blunt response,

Arthur opened the backseat of his truck cab and started unloading.

Despite receiving no coddling from Arthur, Kara forced herself to step inside her aunt's home. She stood in the living room, her eyes scanning the space as she tried to recall the exact placement of each piece of furniture. It had been so long, and anxiety filled her when she realized the details were hazy.

Think, Kara, she chastised herself.

Slowly, the memories crept back: the couch against the far wall, the armchair angled towards the fireplace, the shelf stacked with Aunt Adrienne's eclectic collection of books and crystals.

They worked their way through the house, room by room. Kara's fuzzy recollections guided them, each piece of furniture finding its place as if it had never left. The table where she and Aunt Adrienne had eaten, the bookshelf filled with tomes on spirituality and ancient cultures, the rocking chair on the porch.

As Kara and Cole carried the mattress for the master bedroom down the upstairs hall, Kara felt a sudden shift in its weight when Cole abruptly dropped the corner he'd been carrying.

"You okay?" she called from the other side of the mattress. No answer. She set her corner down and looked; Cole was staring through the open bedroom door. The statue still stood in the exact center of the room, right where it had been the night before.

Kara could kick herself. She'd totally forgotten about it.

"Isn't that..." he whispered. Kara went to stand beside him. "But you... you threw it in the lake..."

Kara swallowed hard, her mouth suddenly dry.

Cole turned to her, his expression one of confusion and growing fear. His face had gone pale. "What's going on here, Kara? How is that thing…"

Kara hesitated, her mind racing. She knew she owed Cole an explanation, but the full truth just felt… overwhelming. How could she tell him about the demon that had haunted her aunt and had never left this house? "Umm…"

"I know there are some things you aren't telling me," Cole said, interrupting her thoughts. "Maybe it's time you gave it to me."

Kara shook her head. "Trust me, you don't want to know. It's not something you want to be a part of."

She could see the hurt in his eyes. "I helped you bring it to the lake. And I'm here helping you now. I *am* a part of it." He took a breath and sighed. "Look, I get it. You don't want to tell me everything because of my faith."

"Yeah," Kara said. She felt like Cole had read her mind, but he wasn't dumb. It probably wasn't hard for him to connect the dots.

"Who is this Arthur guy? What does he have to do with this?" There was a slight edge of distrust in his tone.

"He's going to help us get rid of… the spirit. For good this time."

At least I hope *that's the case.*

Cole considered something for a second. "I could call Pastor Craig."

Kara stiffened. She wasn't sure how she knew, but she felt pretty confident that Arthur wouldn't go for that. "Let's do things Arthur's way for now."

"How do you know his way will work?"

She paused. Cole's question made her realize that she'd kind of just swallowed Arthur Briggs's "demonologist" story whole, without much critical thought. It was entirely possible he was lying about everything.

No. My aunt married the guy. I trust her judgement.

But her aunt was also who had summoned Azunu in the first place. Where had her judgement been then?

Kara pushed it all from her mind. She couldn't afford to overthink this, to doubt. She needed her own faith, even if it was different from Cole's.

"So?" Cole pressed. "Can you tell me what's going on? What's *really* going on?"

She couldn't come up with a way to sugarcoat it. "You already know there's an evil spirit in that statue. You saw it. Arthur says it's... a demon. And this demon is what drove my aunt to... do what she did. The demon's still here in the house, so we're going to remove it. Apparently, it's been keeping Aunt Adrienne's spirit trapped here all this time, so she can't move on to the afterlife."

Cole's expression was blank as he took it all in. Kara wondered if he was trying to reconcile what she'd told him through his religious faith, seeking a way to filter it and make it make more sense to him.

"I see..." he finally said.

"What's going on up there?" Arthur barked from downstairs. "We need to be done before the sun sets."

Kara stepped around Cole and went to the statue. The skin on her palms crawled at the thought of touching it, but she needed it out of sight. Again, she chided herself for not thinking about hiding it before Cole came over. She picked up the statue and, relieved that its weight had returned to normal, walked it down the upstairs hall to the spare bedroom—where there had been no furniture that summer, and where Azunu had carved his name into the floor. She opened the door and tossed the statue inside, where it landed with a heavy *thunk*, then slammed the door shut.

———

THE SUN HAD CLIMBED HIGHER in the sky by the time they left the house and headed back toward the storage unit for a second load.

With each piece of Adrienne's old belongings that they moved, with each box carefully placed, Kara felt a sense of purpose growing within her. She was taking action, fighting against the darkness that had consumed her aunt's life. By the late afternoon, she'd allowed herself to feel a glimmer of hope that maybe, just maybe, they could finally set Aunt Adrienne free.

After tucking a rolled-up rug into the bed of Cole's truck, Kara stepped back into the storage unit, her muscles aching from the hours of lifting and carrying. As she surveyed the remaining items, her gaze fell upon Arthur, crouched in the corner, his attention fixed on a particular box—the one containing the mementos of his relationship.

Arthur's hands moved gently over the photographs, the letters. His touch was reverent, as if he were handling sacred relics. Kara watched as he picked up one of his old sketches, his eyes tracing every line, every curve.

Kara's heart clenched when she saw the pain on Arthur's face. The love he'd shared with Aunt Adrienne was still there, as vivid and raw as if no time had passed at all.

She turned away, focusing her attention back on the task at hand and not wanting to disturb the man. This was Arthur's moment—his chance to reconnect with a past he'd thought he'd lost forever. She didn't want to intrude on that.

In more ways than one, Kara realized that reaching out to Arthur Briggs had definitely been the right thing to do.

———

AFTER TWO MORE BACK-AND-FORTH trips to the storage unit and the subsequent unloading, Kara stood in the living room of Adrienne's house, her whole body aching from the day's labor. The setting sun cast an orange glow through the windows, bathing the newly arranged furniture in its light. Cole, his shirt soaked with sweat, leaned against the fireplace mantel.

"I think we're done with all the big items, at least," Kara said, her voice tinged with exhaustion.

Cole nodded, wiping his brow with the back of his hand. "You know, I could go for some food right about now. Should I pick something up for us?"

Despite working all day in the heat, food had been the last thing on Kara's mind. But Cole had a point—they should've eaten something hours before.

Arthur stepped forward, his eyes fixed on Cole. "That's a good idea. But while you're out, I need you to do something else for me."

Cole's eyebrows shot up in surprise—Arthur had barely spoken to him all day. "Um, sure. What do you need?"

"Your thrift store. Go there and bring me *every* holy object you can find. Especially the crosses. I saw a big collection of them when I was there."

Once again, Cole seemed confused, though he didn't

question Arthur. "Alright, I can do that."

The door closed behind Cole, leaving Kara and Arthur alone in the house.

"Holy objects?" Kara asked.

"Demons can't tolerate being in the presence of God. The more holy symbols we have, the better."

"Your cross necklace definitely wasn't enough," Kara said, remembering how Arthur had been hurled backward off his feet.

"After he gets back, you need to get rid of him," Arthur said bluntly, ignoring her comment.

"What? Why?"

"I don't want him here for the cleansing."

Kara shook her head in disbelief. "But he's been helping us all day. He's a good guy, Arthur. He'll be fine."

Arthur's gaze was unwavering. "He was only here because he's the only person you know who could help. Besides, I told you yesterday that I don't feel right about him. He shouldn't be here when we do the cleansing."

Kara was surprised by the sudden anger that flared within her. How could Arthur say that after Cole had spent *hours* in the sweltering heat, lugging heavy furniture and boxes, all without a single complaint? And now Arthur wanted to just cast him aside?

"I can't believe you," Kara said, her voice rising. "After everything he did today—"

"It's to *protect* him, Kara. He showed us he's got a strong back, but he's weak here." Arthur patted his chest over his heart. "And *this* is what's going to count tonight."

Kara wasn't sure what Arthur meant by that, but she already knew from the night before that Arthur's decision about Cole had already been made. And since Arthur was the one in charge, she had to play by his rules. In her mind, she reiterated the same thing she'd told herself before.

This is about Aunt Adrienne. Focus.

But still, the idea of just dismissing Cole didn't sit right with her.

"I'll talk to him," Kara said, her tone softening. "I already promised I'd explain what's going on. He deserves that much."

"Good. After you explain it to him, you can tell him to leave."

———

SOME OF THE remaining boxes that hadn't been unpacked yet were kitchen supplies—Aunt Adrienne's old plates, cutlery, and cookware.

"Will her spirit notice if the kitchen isn't stocked?" Kara asked Arthur.

"I told you this morning," he said impatiently, "we need this place looking as close as possible to how it was when she lived here."

So, Kara hauled the boxes into the kitchen and started filling the cabinets and drawers, the same way as they'd been in her memory. She was exhausted and worn out by that point, and her mind was trying to convince her that these little details wouldn't matter.

Trust Arthur, she reminded herself.

One of the last things she put into place was the knife block, but the largest knife was missing: the same one that Adrienne had planned to use on Ed the Goat—and then used on herself.

Kara stared at the empty slot for a long time, grateful that it wasn't there. *I suppose the police would've kept it,* she thought. She had only fragmented memories of what had happened after the ambulances and police cruisers had arrived.

The last rays of sunlight disappeared behind the trees and the night settled in. About half an hour after heading out, Cole returned with brown paper bags of fast food, the bottoms darkened with grease. In the bed of his truck were black garbage sacks filled with the requested items from the thrift store.

Kara and Cole ate at the newly placed dining-room table while Arthur moved around the living room, placing the crosses and crucifixes. Kara and Cole watched him work.

At one point, Arthur went upstairs with his laptop bag, prompting Kara to wonder why he was bringing it up there. Then she realized she had a few moments alone with Cole.

Now's my chance to do what Arthur told me to do...

Her heart felt like lead. The thought of dismissing him after all his hard work and dedication felt like a betrayal, but Arthur's words echoed in her mind: it was for Cole's own protection. Any appetite that Kara might've had faded. She stared down at the greasy fast food—a half-eaten burger and cold fries.

She took a deep breath and turned to him, her eyes meeting his. "Cole, I… don't want to keep you any longer. You can go home now."

Confusion and hurt flickered across his face. "What? But I thought—I mean, I want to stay and help. With whatever else you need here, Kara."

She shook her head, trying to remain steadfast. "I appreciate that, Cole. More than you know. But trust me, it's better if you go."

"Better for who?" Cole's voice rose slightly, an uncharacteristic edge to his tone. "I won't leave you here. Not with that…"

Demon. He seemed unable to bring himself to say the word aloud.

"It could be dangerous. I don't want you to get hurt."

"I'm not going anywhere, Kara. I care about you, and I care about what happens here. I'm staying."

Kara had never seen Cole so resolute. She pursed her lips and decided to go with the backup tactic. "It's actually Arthur who—"

"You're not the only one dealing with this stuff, okay?"

Cole cutting her off was so abrupt and aggressive that it took Kara a few seconds to process what he'd said.

Her heart rate quickened. "What do you mean?"

Cole exhaled a long breath through his nostrils. It seemed like he was regretting his outburst, that he'd let something slip he hadn't intended. "Mama's been seeing things," he admitted. "At first, I… thought it was just her illness. But I've seen it too. It came as a shadow in my bedroom."

She swallowed hard. "How long has this been going on?"

Cole leveled his gaze at her. "It started the day after we went to Duke's."

Kara felt her insides collapse. There was no way it was a coincidence. *Has Azunu been…* punishing *Cole because of me?*

"Is your mom okay?" she asked. "I'm sure she was terrified…"

"She's fine, at least for now. But one night I woke up and caught her walking in circles in the living room. And

I remembered you'd told me Adrienne had done the same thing."

Kara pressed her hand into her temple, trying to subdue the pounding that had started.

"I invited Pastor Craig over to bless the house. He did, but then after, I found some rips in the pages of Mama's Bible. To me, it felt like a threat."

"Why didn't you tell me about this sooner?" Kara asked.

"I was going to tell you when I invited you out to that Italian restaurant," Cole said, shrugging. "But…"

But I said I was leaving town.

She realized that things were worse than she'd thought. Cole and his mother also had a supernatural problem that needed to be fixed—one that *she'd* brought on.

I need to tell Arthur, she thought.

As if on cue, heavy footsteps descended the stairs and Arthur appeared at the entrance to the dining room. "It's almost time to start."

47

As the darkness outside deepened, Kara and Cole joined Arthur in the living room. There, Arthur's eyes bounced between the two of them, then settled on Kara with a questioning look, as if to say, *What's he still doing here?*

"Cole just told me he's been having his own experiences with the demon."

Arthur turned his hard gaze to Cole, scrutinizing him as if he didn't believe him. "Like what?"

Cole seemed to shrink under the old man's intense attention.

"Tell him, Cole," Kara said.

So, he recounted everything. Arthur took it all in dispassionately.

"He's more involved than I thought," Kara said after Cole had finished. "In more ways than just helping us move furniture."

Arthur studied Cole. The tension in the room was palpable, and Kara couldn't help but hold her breath, waiting for Arthur's response.

"Doesn't change a thing," he finally said.

"What do you mean?" Kara asked, surprised by how unsympathetic Arthur seemed.

"I mean that when we remove the demon tonight, it'll fix his problems too. So nothing changes." He turned to Cole. "You should get the hell out of here."

"I'm not leaving," Cole declared. "I want to help."

Arthur made no effort to hide the way he scanned Cole from head to toe, as if trying to decide if he could *physically* make Cole leave if it came down to it. Kara didn't know Arthur well, but she got the impression that he didn't like to be argued with—especially in a situation like this, the one they were in, where he was the expert.

"You'll be in the way," Arthur said.

"No, I won't," Cole shot back. "After the things I've seen, I have every right to be here. And not even for myself—I'm doing it to protect my mother."

Kara could sense the impasse between the two men. In that moment, Cole's feet might as well have been bolted to the floor where he stood.

Then, to her surprise, Arthur gave a single, sharp nod, his expression unreadable. "Alright, you can stay. But I have a job for you."

Cole's eyebrows shot up, clearly not having expected the old man to relent. "O-okay. What do you need me to do?"

"I want you upstairs in the spare room, where you two put the statue earlier," Arthur explained. "Keep an eye on it during the cleansing. See if it does anything unusual. If it does anything at all, come down and tell us."

But does Arthur actually think it's going to do something? Kara wondered. She got the feeling Arthur was simply trying to get Cole out of the way, to brush him off so he wouldn't interfere with the cleansing.

Cole seemed to sense this, too. "You want me to just… watch the statue?"

Arthur nodded, expression serious. "It's important. We need to know if it reacts during the process."

Kara could see the reluctance in Cole's eyes, how his shoulders tensed. But to her relief, he nodded. "Alright. I can do that."

He disappeared up the stairs, his footsteps echoing in the quiet house.

Kara turned to Arthur. "Do you think it's really going to do something? Or are you just pushing him to the side?"

"Let's get started."

———

COLE CLOSED the door behind him. The entire room was in darkness, and the air within was thick and stuffy. He took out his cell phone and activated the bright flashlight.

The first thing he saw was the statue standing in the center. Staring at him. Cole glared at the slit-like eyes in the mask. The upturned, smiling mouth seemed to mock him. He'd never had many arguments or fights with others before—he tried to always be agreeable—yet Cole couldn't help but think that this was how it felt to come face to face with a true enemy.

He'd been so afraid that night, no matter how hard he'd striven to put on a brave face for Kara. The impossibly heavy statue. The shadow that had attacked him. The voice in his head, threatening him.

He went to the only window in the room. It looked out

over the house's side yard, though it was difficult to see anything in the darkness. Only the white moon and the surrounding stars were visible.

The physical exhaustion from moving furniture was nothing compared to the emotional beating he'd taken that day. His chest felt fuzzy and light. It was a strange feeling, not unlike what he experienced whenever he'd confessed his wrongdoings to God. Usually, when he sinned, he procrastinated and avoided bringing it to the feet of the Lord. He knew hesitating was ridiculous—it wasn't as if God didn't already know his every thought and action. Even though he was called to confess, he still put off doing it—he didn't like to admit weakness and vulnerability. He was very preoccupied with being strong —especially since Mama's diagnosis. Eventually, the weight of the guilt would build and build, and then it would all flood out against his will in a marathon confession-prayer over the course of a long, sleepless night. Afterward, his chest would get that funny feeling, as if it had been unburdened.

It made sense to him that he felt that same way now. He'd finally told Kara what he and Mama had been experiencing. He'd wanted to tell her, but not make her feel like it was all her fault.

Despite the room being physically empty, Cole couldn't help but perceive a looming presence. He turned and aimed his light at the statue. It now peered directly at him, even though it had been facing the door when he'd first come in.

Cole's breath quickened, and he tried to bring it back under control. *Whatever's going on here, God, please protect us all,* he prayed.

He wondered what he was *actually* meant to do in that

room. Arthur's explanation of keeping an eye on the statue made *some* sense, he had to admit. He remembered that night at Lake Silver—he knew what crazy things it was capable of. Still, he couldn't help but get the impression that he was being put on the sidelines.

'You'd do anything for that vile slut, and it's pathetic.'

Cole stiffened at the thought that had come from nowhere. He was instantly revolted in himself. Then, a second later, he realized it hadn't been his own thought at all—the voice had come from the statue.

It was the same voice he'd heard that night at the lake. And the same one that had spoken to him in his bedroom.

Cole's chest thudded. He attempted to take a step away from the statue, but his back was already pressed against the wall.

'You told her about us. Her and the old man.'

Cole closed his eyes and tried to block out the supernatural words. *God, please,* he prayed. *Fill this place with your—*

'Enough! God has no place here!'

Cole winced, startled. The berating voice was sharp, slicing at the inside of his brain like a knife. He opened his eyes again.

'She's using you, Cole. She's always been using you. You're nothing more than a convenient tool for her.'

Cole shook his head, trying to dislodge the venomous words. "No, that's not true," he argued. He recognized the absurdity of his speaking aloud to the statue.

'Think about it, Cole. She left you behind without a second thought all those years ago. And now that she's back, she's only interested in you because she needs your help. Again.'

Cole's hands clenched into fists at his sides, his nails digging into his palms. "She had to leave. It wasn't her choice. And she's here now because she cares about her aunt's house and her memory."

'She's here to sell the house and get rid of everything that reminds her of this place, including you. Once she's done, she'll leave, and this time you'll never see her again.'

As much as Cole tried to deny it, the voice's words struck a chord within him. He couldn't help but sense that there was some truth in them. Kara had already told him that she was leaving and had no intention of seeing him before her flight.

Another distant voice joined the one emanating from the statue. Downstairs, Arthur had begun speaking loudly. Cole could barely make out what the old man was saying: "We come before the spiritual world tonight with a singular purpose."

'She doesn't love you, Cole. You know that. And every minute you waste with her is time Mama spends all alone.'

Cole's fists clenched again. "Leave Mama out of this. Don't talk about her."

'Mama likes it when I visit her at night.'

Cole felt his rage rising. "Stop."

'Sometimes I visit her the same way you visit Kara in your fantasies.'

"Enough!" Cole knew the voice was lying, only trying to get a rise out of him. Still, the mental images came as if forced upon him by some kind of supernatural drug.

'But you can make it all stop.'

Cole blinked. "What?"

'Do you want me to leave Mama alone?'

"Yes… of course."

'Then you must kill Kara.'

Cole felt a wave of heat rush over him. He was aghast

at what he'd just heard. "W-what…" The statue's eyes seemed to glitter with dark delight.

'To get rid of me, you need to get rid of her.'

Cole finally managed to find his voice. "No. I won't do it."

'It's your choice, Cole,' the voice snapped back, as if it had known Cole would refuse. *'But if you don't, then I promise you—I will take Mama's soul.'*

A heavy pressure coiled from the pit of Cole's stomach up to his throat. "W-w-wait…"

'Mama doesn't have much time left. And when she dies, I will drag her soul to hell. Forever. No amount of praying will ever free her.'

"N-no. Y-you can't do that." He couldn't bear the thought of Mama in hell. She'd lived her entire life as a good, God-fearing woman and didn't deserve such a fate. But something about the threat seemed real. Despite himself… he believed it.

'Mama's lifetime of faith in God… all wiped away because you, her only child, would rather spare the life of some girl you hardly know who doesn't care about you.'

"That isn't fair!" The words burst out, and Cole knew in that moment he sounded like a weak, whiny child. He recalled the first thing the demon had ever said to him: *'I will remember you. You will regret helping her.'* Its voice had been silent for over twenty years, but the moment Kara Mills had shown up again, it had returned as well, ready to make good on its promise.

'Kara or Mama,' the demon said. *'The choice is yours. Decide soon, because I'm not very patient.'*

———

ARTHUR MOVED THROUGH THE HOUSE, lighting candles in every downstairs room. The scent of melting wax filled the air. It was all so familiar, so reminiscent of that fateful night when Aunt Adrienne had summoned the spirit into their lives.

No... not the spirit, Kara thought. *The demon.*

As Arthur lit the final candle, Kara couldn't help but feel a sense of déjà vu. The house looked just as it had that night, with the furniture arranged exactly as Aunt Adrienne had kept it. It was as if the intervening decades had been nothing but a dream.

Having the house back how it was all those years ago is affecting even me, so it's sure to make Adrienne feel something too, Kara thought. *Maybe Arthur knows what he's doing after all.*

The two of them came together in the center of the living room. The candlelight illuminated Arthur's face. Kara stood beside him, her pulse rising.

Arthur's voice rang out, strong and clear. "We come before the spiritual world tonight with a singular purpose. We seek to remove hell's demon from this home and to banish the darkness that has taken root here."

Kara wished she felt as confident as Arthur spoke.

Arthur continued. "We invoke the protection of God, of the archangels, and of all spirits of light. We ask that they shield us from harm and lend their strength in this endeavor."

If demons are real, then I guess angels have to be real too, don't they? she reasoned. She'd never considered that before. Angels and demons. Darkness and light. Like some kind of spiritual balance.

Kara closed her eyes, attempting to focus on Arthur's words. As best she could, she pictured the archangels he spoke of, their wings spread wide, swords gleaming. She imagined them standing guard around the house, ready to defend against any dark force that might try to stop them.

But as she tried to draw strength from these images, Kara knew all too well the power of the demon they faced and the depths of its malice. Would the protection of these angels—if they were even listening—be enough? Would their light be strong enough to drive out the darkness?

As if sensing her thoughts, Arthur leaned toward her. "Have faith," he whispered. "We're not alone in this fight."

Kara nodded, drawing in a deep breath. She thought of Cole, upstairs and by himself. Arthur was speaking loudly, so Cole was surely hearing his every word. She wondered what he was thinking now.

"Adrienne," Arthur called out, "we know you're still here, trapped by the darkness that has held you for so long. But you are not alone. You are loved. We need your help. We need your strength and your light to aid us in this confrontation. Together, we can banish this demon and free you from its grasp."

Kara closed her eyes, picturing her aunt's face. Not knowing what else to do, she tried to send out her own silent plea, a message of love and support. *We're here, Aunt Adrienne. We're fighting for you and with you.*

"Muster your energy, Adrienne," Arthur implored. "Help us drive out this darkness so that you can find peace and be free."

Arthur then reached into his bag and pulled out a well-worn Bible, its leather cover cracked and faded. He began to pace through the house, his voice ringing out as he recited Scripture from memory. "The Lord is my light and my salvation—whom shall I fear? The Lord is the stronghold of my life—of whom shall I be afraid?"

Kara followed close behind, a crucifix from the thrift store clutched in her hand. She was surprised by how it brought her comfort. That night, it wasn't just a piece of wood and metal—it felt like a tangible source of strength and protection.

Is this what true faith feels like? Kara wondered. She'd never put much—or any—stock in the power of prayer or holy objects, but during this spiritual battle, she couldn't deny the effect it was having on her.

As they moved from room to room, Arthur's voice grew stronger, more impassioned. "When the wicked advance against me to devour me, it is my enemies and my foes who will stumble and fall. Though an army besiege me, my heart will not fear; though war break out against me, even then I will be confident."

Kara's heart raced as they entered the kitchen, the site of so many of Aunt Adrienne's culinary experiments. She could almost smell the herbs and spices. But now, with Arthur's words filling the space, it felt different—sanctified, somehow.

As they circled back to the living room, Arthur's voice reached a crescendo. "The Lord will rescue me from every evil attack and will bring me safely to his heavenly kingdom. To him be glory forever and ever. Amen."

"Amen," Kara whispered, the word slipping out automatically.

Kara then followed Arthur up the stairs, her heart pounding along with each step that creaked under their feet. When they reached the upstairs hallway, Arthur's voice rose once again.

"And the great dragon was thrown down, that ancient

serpent, who is called the devil and Satan, the deceiver of the whole world—he was thrown down to the earth, and his angels were thrown down with him."

Kara's skin crawled at the mention of the serpent. She couldn't help but think of the statue with slit-like eyes that seemed reptilian.

Arthur paced the length of the hallway, his steps measured and purposeful. "And he said to them, 'I saw Satan fall like lightning from heaven. Behold, I have given you authority to tread on serpents and scorpions, and over all the power of the enemy, and nothing shall hurt you.' "

Kara's eyes were drawn to the closed door of the spare room, where Cole was keeping watch over the statue. *Is he okay in there?* she thought, a knot of worry forming inside her. *We haven't heard from him. That's a good thing, right?*

Arthur continued, "The God of peace will soon crush Satan under your feet. The grace of our Lord Jesus Christ be with you."

As they walked, Kara couldn't shake the feeling that they were being watched. She glanced over her shoulder, half expecting to see a dark figure lurking in the corner. But there was nothing, only the flickering shadows cast by the candles on the floor.

Focus on what Arthur's saying, Kara told herself as she turned her attention back to Arthur's words, trying to draw courage from them. She couldn't ignore the growing feeling that something was building, gathering strength, so she tightened her grip on the crucifix.

But the prickle at the back of her neck persisted, and she found herself looking around again.

Still nothing. Just shadows. Or were they? One dancing on the wall now looked very human-like.

My imagination, she chided herself. She forced her gaze forward, determined to concentrate.

"No weapon forged against you will prevail, and you will refute every tongue that accuses you. This is the heritage of the servants of the Lord, and this is their vindication from me, declares the—"

Arthur stopped short as a sudden chill swept through the hallway, a cold so intense it took Kara's breath away. She shivered, goosebumps springing up across her skin.

"Do you feel that?" she whispered.

"Something's here," Arthur said, looking around. "Spirits require energy to manifest. That's why they make everything feel so cold."

"Is it Adrienne, or…"

"Could be either," Arthur said.

"It's me." Adrienne's voice.

Kara gasped and reflexively pivoted to face the closed door of the master bedroom. Arthur did the same.

But Kara only gritted her teeth. It was the same voice from the previous day. She wouldn't be tricked again.

"Demon," Arthur spat toward the door. "In the name of God, we command you—"

"You failed me, Kara. You let me die. It's all your fault."

The words, spoken in Aunt Adrienne's voice, were like a sword to Kara's heart. She felt the weight of two decades' worth of pain crashing down upon her. The memories she had tried so hard to forget and forgive herself for came rushing back with a vengeance.

"You were always so *selfish*, Kara," the voice said, dripping with contempt. "So wrapped up in your own little world, your own desires. You're just like your mother—it's only ever all about *you*."

Kara shook her head, trying to block out the accusations. But they kept coming, relentless and unforgiving.

It's true, a small, insidious thought whispered in her mind. *You failed her. You could have saved her, but you didn't.*

"I was suffering, Kara, and what did you do about that? *Nothing.* You were too busy flaunting your ass for Cole Turner. You'd rather spend time with the neighbor's goats than your own family. The poor Norrises believed you wanted to help them, when really you were only *using* them as an excuse to leave me all alone."

"Don't listen!" She barely heard Arthur through the self-loathing haze. "It's not her. The demon's trying to get into your head."

Tears stung Kara's eyes. *I tried. I did everything I could,* she wanted to scream.

"And then, that night... you had the chance to save me. But you were too weak, too much of a coward." The voice took on a mocking, almost gleeful tone. "You let me *die,* Kara. You *watched* as I opened up my own throat, and you *watched* as I bled out on the floor, and you did *nothing.*"

A raw sob escaped her mouth. The memory of Aunt Adrienne's lifeless body, blood pooling around her, came rushing back with sickening clarity. She felt her knees buckle, the weight of each accusation too heavy to bear.

"It should have been *you,*" Adrienne hissed. "You should have been the one to die that night, not me. But maybe... maybe it's not too late for that."

It was all too much. Something broke inside Kara. "I'm s-sorry!" she cried out, then rushed away from Arthur's side and fled down the stairs.

———

SHE BOUNDED through the front door and out onto the porch. There, she cried harder than she ever had as everything that she'd worked so hard to suppress came spilling out in the worst kind of way.

Kara's crying wracked her body, her tears blurring her surroundings.

She didn't notice Arthur's presence until he was standing directly beside her.

After a while, Kara took a shuddering breath, trying to compose herself. "I messed everything up," she said, her voice hoarse.

Arthur shook his head, his expression one of soft understanding and regret. "No. I should have warned you about what might happen." He sighed and leaned against the porch railing. "Like I told you... demons find our deepest fears and regrets. They use those emotions to demoralize us and break our spirits. It's their way of resisting when we try to remove them."

It worked, Kara couldn't help but think as she wiped at her tears, trying to process Arthur's words. *There's no way I'm going back in there.*

"Even though I knew it wasn't really her... it still felt like it was, somehow."

"Because the demon is tapping into some very powerful emotions," Arthur said.

Kara nodded. "I've carried all this... *shit* for so long. You know? Hearing it out loud, in her voice... it was too much."

"That's exactly what the demon wants. But you have to remember—it's lying. None of what happened was your fault. You did everything you could for your aunt." He paused. "Believe me, it wouldn't be saying all of that if it weren't afraid of us."

Kara drew in a deep breath as she tried to let Arthur's words sink in. It was hard—so hard—to release the guilt she'd harbored for so long. But she knew he was right. She couldn't let the demon win, couldn't let it use her own pain against her. And now she understood what Arthur had meant when he'd said that what they were doing required strength from the heart.

"Thank you," she said softly. "For explaining, and for being here with me."

Kara turned at the sound of the screen door opening. Cole came out onto the porch, his face full of both fear and concern.

I forgot he was still here, Kara realized.

"Are you okay?" she asked, her voice shaky from crying.

"I should be asking you that," he said. "I heard everything up there."

"I'll be fine," she said, attempting a reassuring smile. "I just need to pull myself together." Of course, it wouldn't be that easy. The demon's words, spoken in Aunt Adrienne's voice, still echoed in her mind, jabbing at the wounds she'd tried so hard to conceal. Even so, she knew she'd eventually have to go back inside the house and face the entity again.

"We should take a break," Arthur said, his tone gentle but firm. "This won't be a quick process, and we need to pace ourselves tonight."

Kara nodded, grateful for the reprieve. She wasn't sure she could face the demon again so soon.

"It's going to be a long night. Why don't you go get us all some coffee?" Arthur said to Cole.

Cole shot Kara a look, one that said he was hesitant to leave her after what she'd just experienced.

"You're the local, so you know the closest place," Arthur added.

Cole's jaw muscles tensed, but he ultimately nodded and went down the porch steps to get into his truck, then drove away.

"You said this wouldn't be a quick process," Kara said. "Do you think it'll at least be faster than ten months like the last time you were in town?"

Arthur only headed back inside the house and up the stairs.

———

KARA LINGERED ON THE PORCH. She leaned against the railing, eyes closed, trying to steady her breathing and calm her racing thoughts. *If only Mom could see me now...* She already knew she'd never tell her mother about any of this.

The buzz of her phone startled her. It was a text from Cole.

'Forgot to ask—what kind of coffee do you like?'

Despite everything, a small smile tugged at the corner of her mouth. *Always so thoughtful,* she mused as she typed out her response. *'Latte with oat milk, please. Thanks.'*

She hit send, then paused, realizing that while she was usually in the mood for coffee, right now that wasn't the case at all. Her stomach was in knots, and the thought of consuming anything at all made her nauseous.

Her phone buzzed again. *'What about the old man? What does he want?'*

Pushing herself off the porch railing, she headed back inside. She found Arthur sitting at the dining room table, hunched over his laptop, headphones on. He seemed engrossed in whatever he had up on the screen, his forehead tight in concentration.

What's he doing? she wondered.

Kara approached him. "Hey, Arthur?" No response. She stepped closer, raising her voice. "Arthur?"

He glanced up, noticing her for the first time. But instead of removing his headphones, he lifted an impatient finger at her, then turned his attention back to the screen.

She returned to the living room and responded to Cole. *'He's grumpy right now and won't answer me. Just get him a black coffee. Old people normally like that.'*

Kara then sank down onto the couch, her eyes drawn to the flickering candles that still illuminated the space. After a moment, she realized she felt a lot better than she had earlier. She thought about telling Arthur that she was ready to try again, and that it might be a good idea to do so while Cole was gone. With any luck, maybe they could succeed and finish before he got back.

"Come here," Arthur said, his harsh voice directed straight at her.

Although she detested his tone—and the way he usually spoke to her in general—Kara felt herself comply. She rose from the couch and went into the dining room.

"Sit."

She sat in the same chair she'd occupied when eating with Adrienne that summer. Arthur had somehow chosen the spot where her aunt had always been. He spun the laptop so the screen faced her and handed her the headphones, just as he'd done that morning. The same audio app was pulled up.

"What am I listening to this time?" Kara asked.

"Press play," was all Arthur said.

Kara sighed, then placed the headphones over her ears and clicked the play button. At first, there was only static, a hissing white noise. But then, a voice emerged from the crackling—a man's voice, distorted by whatever manipulation Arthur had done to the audio track. She struggled to make out the words: "No, that's not true."

She recognized Cole talking. His voice was joined by another—dark and guttural, with an otherworldly quality that gave her chills: *'Once she's done, she'll leave, and this time you'll never see her again.'*

Cole's speaking to Azunu, she realized. *But... when?*

Azunu's true voice slithered through the headphones and seemed to scratch at her soul like nails on a chalkboard. It was somehow far more unsettling than when he'd been mimicking Aunt Adrienne.

'She doesn't love you, Cole. And every minute you waste with her is time Mama spends all alone.'

Was this just a little while ago? she realized.

'But you can make it all stop. Do you want me to leave Mama alone?'

"Yes… of course."

Kara pressed pause on the audio and ripped off the headphones. "What is this? What's happening to Cole?"

Arthur's expression was grim. "The demon is trying to tempt him in order to turn him against us."

"Against us?" Kara asked.

"Did you listen to the whole thing?"

"No. I couldn't…"

Arthur nodded his head toward the laptop, beckoning Kara to continue.

Filled with apprehension, she put the headphones back over her ears and pressed play.

'Then you must kill Kara.'

The direct order was a bomb dropped on her heart.

"W-what…" Cole stammered.

'To get rid of me, you need to get rid of her.'

"No. I won't do it." Despite the noble words, Kara couldn't help but hear the lack of conviction in Cole's tone.

'Mama's lifetime of faith in God… all wiped away because you, her only child, would rather spare the life of some girl you hardly know who doesn't care about you.'

Then, the audio track ended.

Tears once again came to Kara's eyes as she slid the headphones off. "That's why you sent Cole upstairs. You had your recorder planted up there."

"And thank God I did," Arthur said, sliding the laptop back over to himself. "This demon is trying to get him to hurt you and threatening his mother if he doesn't."

Kara shook her head. She'd already felt guilty for getting Cole involved, but she'd had no idea that Azunu was actually *speaking* to him. *Should I be… afraid of him?* She dismissed the notion. "Don't worry. He'd never hurt me."

"Are you sure?" Arthur pressed. "How well do you *really* know this guy?"

Kara paused before responding and thought about it. The time they'd spent together didn't add up to that much in the end.

"Still," she said. "He wouldn't."

"Not even for 'Mama'?" When Kara didn't respond, Arthur only grunted. "When he gets back, you stay inside. I'm going to have a talk with him."

This time, Kara didn't protest.

48

Cole's hands gripped the steering wheel tightly as he navigated the familiar roads. The rich aroma of coffee filled his truck's cab. His mind replayed the demon's words over and over, like a broken record. The choice it had presented to Cole was clear, and it tore at his very soul.

Kara or Mama.

The weight of the decision pressed down on his chest, making it difficult to breathe. He couldn't fathom the thought of harming Kara. Yet the idea of his mother suffering, tormented by the very entity that now haunted his thoughts, was equally unbearable. Cole's eyes darted to the rearview mirror, catching a glimpse of his own reflection. The man who stared back at him was drawn, his face clouded with uncertainty and fear. He didn't recognize himself.

Am I really considering this? he thought.

He remembered the voice's words: *'Kara or Mama. The choice is yours.'*

For a fleeting moment, he considered turning the

truck around and not going back to that house. *If I'm not there, then I can't do anything that I'll regret, right? But then what about Mama?*

Maybe Kara's friend Arthur was Cole's only hope. Could the old man actually remove the entity like he claimed? If he did, would that mean Mama would be okay? But as quickly as the thought came, doubt crept in. Arthur wasn't a pastor. As far as Cole knew, only true men of God could cast out demons.

Then again, hadn't Pastor Craig's house blessing failed?

Cole's thoughts turned inward. What if the choice wasn't real? What if the demon's beckoning was nothing more than a twisted game designed only to confuse him?

That must be it, he thought. But the entity had already demonstrated its ability to reach Mama—both appearing to her and influencing her behavior. *No... this is very real.*

He pressed the knob on his radio and the Christian music station came on. The soothing melody and the lyrics of a praise-and-worship song were a temporary balm for him.

"In Your presence, I find my might,
Your love surrounds me, holds me tight,
In Your glory, my soul shines bright,
With Your strength, I'll always fight."

Cole mouthed the words; it was one of his recent favorites. But as the song progressed, something changed. The singer's voice remained the same, sweet and melodious, but the lyrics were altered.

"To get rid of me, you need to get rid of her,
Even though you want to hold her tight,
To get rid of me, you need to get rid of her,
It is the only way, and you cannot fight."

Cole's eyes widened in horror, not quite believing what he was hearing. He focused on the radio, waiting for the chorus to come around again, to confirm if he'd actually heard what he thought he had. But the song played on as usual.

"In Your presence, I find my might,
Your love surrounds me, holds me tight,
In Your glory, my soul burns bright,
With Your strength, I'll always fight."

The sound of Cole's ragged breathing filled the cab, his vision blurring with unshed tears. *I know what I heard,* he thought. *I'm not crazy.* He blinked rapidly, trying to clear his eyes so he could see the road again.

God, please help me, he prayed, desperately seeking guidance. *I can't do this alone. I need your strength, your wisdom. Show me the way.*

When he arrived back at the house, he parked next to Kara's rental car and the old man's truck. He picked up the cardboard tray that held the three cups of coffee and got out from behind the wheel. But he stopped short when he realized Arthur was standing at the top of the porch steps, arms folded, glaring down at him.

Cole froze. He and Arthur stared at each other for several long moments, neither of them speaking.

What's going on here?

"You've made a new friend, haven't you?" Arthur finally said.

Cole's stomach shifted. The old man's piercing gaze seemed to bore right through him, as if he could see the very thoughts that plagued Cole's mind.

He knows, Cole thought. He considered confessing everything. The urge to pour out his heart—to seek guidance and help from someone who might understand what had been happening to him—was almost overwhelming. But as he opened his mouth to speak, the words caught in his throat, trapped by invisible chains of fear and guilt.

If I tell him, it means I've chosen Kara over Mama, he realized, a cold dread settling within him. *I can't choose right now. Not... not yet. I need more time.*

Cole swallowed hard, forcing a look of confusion onto his face. "I don't know what you're talking about," he lied, his words sounding hollow even to his own ears. He'd never been good at lying. He'd have to pray for forgiveness later.

"Are you hearing a voice telling you to do things?" Arthur went on, ignoring Cole's denial entirely. "Things that you normally wouldn't ever think to do?"

"No."

As Arthur continued to study him, Cole noticed something in his periphery. A shadowy figure stood in the dining room window, peering out at him—the same figure that had appeared in his bedroom a few nights before. The same one that, two decades before, had struck him across the face and sent him to the ground.

'I will remember you. You will regret helping her.'

"Do you see him now?" Arthur pressed, commanding Cole's attention once again.

Cole swallowed. "See who?" He ventured a quick glance back at the window. The shadow was gone.

Arthur's expression was unreadable, but Cole got the sense that the old man didn't believe him.

"Come," Arthur ordered.

49

Kara watched nearby from the dining room as Arthur escorted Cole back inside the house. Arthur gestured toward the couch, and Cole sat, placing the tray of coffees on the nearby table.

Arthur went to stand in front of him. Despite his slender and frail frame, the older man could come across as imposing when he needed to.

Cole hung his head like a scolded schoolboy.

"There's no shame in what you're feeling, Cole," Arthur said, his tone softening. "The demon knows our weaknesses, our deepest fears, and desires. He'll use them against us. He'll try to twist our thoughts and manipulate our actions."

Cole's shoulders slumped, his eyes downcast as he listened to Arthur.

"You said earlier that you heard the demon mimicking Adrienne's voice and the terrible things it said to Kara," Arthur continued, glancing in her direction. "You heard those accusations, and the guilt it tried to make her feel. You should expect the same. But you must remember—

everything it says is a lie. Every promise, every threat... It's all meant to deceive and destroy."

Cole nodded, but remained silent with his gaze fixed on the floor.

"Whatever it told you, whatever it promised... do not believe it." Arthur's voice took on a harder edge. "You *cannot* give in to its demands, no matter how tempting they may seem."

Kara felt a pang of sympathy for Cole as she watched him absorb Arthur's words. In that moment, Cole reminded her of Adrienne after she'd been under the demon's influence for a while. He looked like he wore a withered outer shell that was somehow strong enough to keep his true self subdued and muted.

Cole finally met Arthur's gaze. "I understand," he said, his voice barely above a whisper.

But even as he spoke, Kara could see the doubt in his eyes and the fear that lingered beneath the surface. *He doesn't believe Arthur,* she thought.

"Good," Arthur said. "We'll continue what we started in just a few minutes."

With that, Arthur turned away and went into the dining room. He paused as he passed Kara, seeming to notice her distress. "You alright?"

Kara folded her arms and dropped her voice to a whisper so only Arthur could hear. "You were right. I... I don't want him here. He... that thing told him to kill me."

"I understand," Arthur said. "But I'd trust him even less if he were out of my sight now. Once the demon is gone, he won't hear those voices anymore."

Kara didn't like it, but she had no choice but to believe Arthur. "In that case, let's get this done."

THE THREE OF them reconvened in the living room.

As Kara stood there, she couldn't help but feel the tension that seemed to pulse between her and Cole. It was as if something previously connecting the two of them had shattered, an earlier trust broken by the demon's insidious whispers.

That was probably its goal, she thought as she glanced sideways at Cole, trying to read his expression, though he avoided her gaze. *He was told to kill me, and he didn't immediately refuse...*

Arthur's voice cut through her thoughts, "In the name of God, the Father Almighty, maker of heaven and earth, I call upon the angels and spirits of light to aid in this battle against the forces of darkness," he intoned into the stillness of the room. "Saint Michael the Archangel, defend us. Be our protection against the wickedness and snares of the devil. May God rebuke him, we humbly pray." He paused for a moment. "We're here for you, Azunu. You've been posturing like you're powerful for all these years, but we know the truth now. We do not fall for your tactics. You are nothing more than one of hell's many *rats.*"

Arthur paced around the room, waiting and listening to the silence for a few moments before continuing, his voice growing louder. "You hide behind your tricks and illusions, whispering lies and half-truths to those who are vulnerable. But we see through your charade and know how pathetic you truly are. You wouldn't have to rely on these gimmicks if you weren't scared, if you didn't already know that God has given us dominion over you."

What is he—

But Kara's thought was interrupted when one of the

cross statues on the fireplace mantel flung itself toward Arthur, the older man dodging just in time. The cross smashed into the far wall, breaking into pieces. Kara yelped at the sudden attack; Cole gasped beside her.

Arthur seemed unperturbed by the near-miss. "I've seen your kind before, Azunu," he spat. "I know all about the hierarchy of hell. And you... you're one of the bottom-feeding scavengers."

Another cross from the coffee table lifted itself into the air and hurtled toward Arthur. Once again, he pivoted out of the way and allowed it to shatter against the wall.

He's provoking the demon, Kara realized.

"A lowly *parasite*, fueled only by the misery and pain of others. You think you're strong, but you're just a desperate *runt*, clinging to any shred of relevance you can find. I've fought *dozens* of demons who were more powerful than you, *far* more favored by the devil than you'll ever be. And I've beaten every single one of them. To me, you are *nothing*."

The foundations of the house around them started to shake. The walls rattled and the floorboards trembled beneath Kara. She heard the dishes in the kitchen fall out of the cabinets and smash onto the floor. Some of the candles tipped over and extinguished, plunging parts of the room into darkness.

Kara held her arms out, trying to keep her balance as the violent shaking threatened to knock her off her feet. Terror gripped her heart at the image of the entire house crashing down on top of them.

Is that his plan? Kara thought. *Would Azunu destroy the house and kill us all rather than be beaten?*

Arthur seemed unfazed by the sudden upheaval. He stood firm, as if the tremors couldn't touch him. His voice rose above the din, unwavering and defiant. "Is that all you've got, Azunu?" he shouted. "You think I haven't seen this before? You'll have to do better!"

As if in response to his challenge, the shaking intensified. Kara heard the groaning of wood as the walls strained against the unnatural forces assaulting them. Cracks appeared in the plaster, snaking their way up to the ceiling.

Kara realized something had to be done, otherwise the entire house would come down. Before she knew what she was saying, her voice rang out clear and strong: "In the name of Jesus Christ, I command you to leave this place!"

To her utter shock, the house stood still. Silence lingered around the three of them.

Arthur and Kara looked at each other. In the faint candlelight that remained, she thought she saw a look of approval on the man's face.

Cole's eyes darted between Kara and Arthur, seeming to search for both explanations and reassurances. "Did it work?" he whispered. "Is he gone?"

A heavy *thump* came from the ceiling above. Then another.

The three of them craned their heads upward. Kara already knew what was coming before it happened, as the terrible memory from that fateful night bubbled up again.

Thump-thump-thump-thump-thump-thump.

The footsteps above them accelerated into a frenzied pattern. She remembered what Arthur had told her—that the counterclockwise direction was significant and symbolic to demonic entities.

The steps receded, then started moving down the hallway with a deliberate, almost taunting slowness. Every creak and groan of the floorboards above seemed excessively loud to Kara. She felt the heaviness and darkness of the memory overtaking her. But then she realized what was happening.

It's doing this on purpose. Recreating that night.

The upstairs hall window creaked open.

Resist the fear.

The footsteps tracked down the side of the house, each *thump* landing hard against the exterior wall. She pictured the entity—in whatever form it had taken—crawling along the outside like some sort of oversized insect.

And then it was on the porch, the old wooden boards creaking under the weight of the unseen presence as it approached the nearby living-room window. Last time, the demon had closed the curtains as it had passed to keep from being seen.

But now, there were no curtains.

For a brief moment, Kara caught a glimpse of Azunu in his manifested form, exactly as she remembered it: a tall, jagged shadow, its edges seeming to flicker. The shadow moved out of view as it drifted past the window.

Kara looked to Arthur, hoping for some sort of guidance or consolation, but the old man's expression was unreadable, his eyes fixed on the window where the entity had just been.

Beside her, Cole was trembling, his face a mask of fear in the candlelight.

Azunu's shadowy form passed by the second living-room window.

As the demon approached the front door, Kara's mind flashed back to when the door had swung open of its own accord, unleashing a billowing cloud of black smoke into the house. The memory was so vivid, so visceral, that for a moment she felt as if she were sixteen and reliving it all over again.

That night, the magic circle her aunt had drawn onto the floor had protected them. Now, they had nothing.

The anticipation was unbearable as she watched the front door, waiting for the inevitable.

Beside her, Cole was visibly shaking.

Arthur, on the other hand, seemed almost unnaturally calm. He stood firm, his gaze fixed on the door, as if daring the demon to make its move. There was a determination in his eyes, a resolve that Kara wished she could borrow just a fraction of.

The seconds ticked by with agonizing slowness. Kara's pulse pounded in her ears and her breath came in shallow gasps.

Please, she prayed, though to whom or what she wasn't sure. *Let us get through this.* She tried to find that same burst of resolve she'd had less than a minute earlier. It seemed to have already flamed out entirely.

The front door creaked open, the sound echoing through the stillness. The black, shadowy figure stepped across the threshold, its movements deliberate and unnaturally fluid. As it turned to face them, Kara felt a wave of pure, unadulterated terror wash over her.

Azunu towered over even Cole, his body a mass of shifting shadows that seemed to absorb the flickering candlelight. The edges of his form were jagged and ever-changing, as if the demon were unable to maintain a cohesive shape in this physical realm.

But it was the demon's face that haunted Kara. Where eyes should have been, there were only deep, endless voids, pools of darkness that drew you in. What appeared to be his skin was a sickly ashen color, stretched taut over a skeletal frame.

Cole's breath came in short, ragged gasps. Even Arthur, who had seemed so unshakable before, took a small step back.

For a long, agonizing moment, they stared at each other, human and demon. Kara could feel the weight of Azunu's gaze upon her; the black eyes seemed to watch all three of them at the same time.

Then Azunu extended his arm. His skeletal fingers unfurled and dropped two things onto the floor at his feet. There, now lying on the hardwood surface, were the necklace and ring that Adrienne had given to him two decades before.

Arthur's wide eyes were fixed on the pieces of jewelry, clearly recognizing them. Kara realized what the demon was trying to do—attack Arthur's psyche where it most hurt, the same way it had done to her.

Don't get distracted, Arthur, she thought. She wanted to say the words aloud, but they stuck in her constricted throat.

Then Azunu extended his other hand, mimicking the motion he'd just made with the first. His fingers uncurled, and the statue that had started this entire nightmare dropped to the floor between them. It landed upright with a heavy *thud*, facing Kara, Cole, and Arthur. Despite all the revulsion the statue had caused within Kara, it seemed almost unremarkable now that Azunu had emerged in his manifested form.

"Enough," Arthur barked as he tore his gaze away from Adrienne's jewelry. "In the name of God, I command you, Azunu, to leave this home!" His words echoed through the room, ringing out with strength and authority. "By the power of the Holy Spirit, I banish you to—"

Arthur was suddenly lifted off his feet and sent slamming hard against the living-room wall. Kara gasped, her hand flying to her mouth as she watched the man struggle against the invisible force that held him pinned in place.

Arthur fought back, his voice strained but still strong as he continued his desperate invocations. But Azunu's power was too great. Arthur was wrenched upward along the wall until his head smashed against the ceiling with a sickening crash that brought an abrupt end to his prayers.

Kara could only watch as Arthur's limp body was pulled along the ceiling, flush against it. It seemed like he'd been knocked unconscious.

Do something, Kara, she thought. *But what?*

Then she noticed the demon had turned its attention back to her and Cole again.

'Kara.'

She felt a sudden, intrusive presence in her mind, icy threads worming their way into her thoughts. The sinister whisper was the same one she'd heard on Arthur's recording. And for the first time, the demon was speaking directly to her.

'Give yourself to me.'

Azunu's voice echoed through her consciousness with a sickening clarity. She tried to push him out, to force up some kind of mental barrier, but his presence was overwhelming, suffocating.

'Give yourself to me now, and I will release your aunt's spirit.'

The offer hung in the air, both tempting and terrifying. If she could free her aunt, even at the cost of her own life, wasn't that a price worth paying?

'Yes,' the demon beckoned. 'It is.'

He can read my thoughts, Kara realized.

Then memories of that summer flooded her mind—they came so suddenly that she suspected they were being forced there by Azunu. She once again felt the fear, the confusion, the helplessness. She'd been so unprepared for it all, since she'd only been a teenager.

'You failed her, Kara.'

In her mind's eye, Kara pictured Adrienne lying in bed, looking so very ill and as if she'd aged a decade in mere days. She remembered the sorrow, the terror, and the stubborn denial that anything was wrong. The mental images consumed her so much that she lost all sense of Arthur and Cole; it seemed she and Azunu were alone together.

Kara's resolve faltered under the weight of Azunu's words and the crushing guilt that threatened to consume her.

'It's what you deserve,' the demon whispered.

"Maybe," Kara said aloud.

'Then say the word, and it all ends. Everything will be made right.'

Kara wavered in indecision. Azunu was mercifully silent, anticipating her reply. The price was steep, but it would ultimately grant Adrienne the liberation she deserved.

———

COLE FROZE as he faced the same entity he'd encountered that night at Lake Silver. Azunu now stood before them. The room crackled with an unholy energy, and the temperature had immediately dropped.

Then Arthur was suddenly levitated off the floor. It was as if an invisible hand had grasped the man, lifting him effortlessly into the air. Cole winced when he slammed against the wall, and again when Arthur's body dragged along the ceiling, limbs dangling like a marionette being manipulated by a sadistic puppeteer.

'You failed.'

Azunu's venomous accusation barged into his mind, the demon's fury evident.

'Your mother now belongs to me.'

Cole's throat constricted. "Please don't," he begged.

'You had your chance.'

Tears fell from Cole's eyes as he imagined his mother's suffering while her soul was forever lost in the demon's clutches. She was screaming. She was in pain. Cole didn't know where the crystal-clear thoughts came from— maybe they were directly put there by Azunu.

'She'll suffer for the rest of time in a place where your god has no power.'

"I'll—I'll do anything," Cole heard himself say. The weight of his failure pressed down on him, threatening to crush him.

'No. You are too late.'

"Please!"

'Then do it now,' Azunu commanded.

Cole's hand went to his pocket and wrapped around the pocketknife he'd carried with him every day for years. He looked at Kara—her eyes remained fixed on the demon. She was unaware of the battle raging within him. There was no indication that she'd heard him respond to Azunu. In fact, she might've even forgotten he was right beside her.

Maybe he's speaking to her, too, Cole thought. *Telling her to do the same thing to me...*

'*Now!*'

Deep in his heart, a distant voice pleaded with him to resist the darkness—tried to make him understand that what was being asked of him couldn't possibly be the will of God.

'*I will not wait any longer.*'

Cole closed his eyes and thought of Mama.

———

IN A DISTANT CORNER of her mind, Kara remembered what Arthur had said: "Demons lie."

Then she realized something else. *He's playing on my guilt and regret.*

'*You could have saved her,*' Azunu cut in, as if trying to interrupt her thinking.

No, she thought. Then she said it out loud. "No."

She pictured Adrienne as she had been before the demon's influence—kind, loving, full of life. *That* was the Adrienne she wanted to remember, not the twisted, tortured version Azunu had created. This true image of Kara's aunt gave her back her strength.

"You're lying," she said, her voice stronger now. "You won't release Adrienne, no matter what I do."

She felt Azunu's grip on her mind loosen ever so slightly.

"I will not give in to you," Kara declared.

Azunu did not protest. He only met Kara's determined gaze with his blackened, pit-like eyes. She clenched her fists, expecting the demon to react, to attack, to do anything.

Why isn't he moving? she wondered. *What is he waiting—*

There was a swift movement to her right. Then she felt like someone had hit her in the stomach, and a dull pain followed.

She turned. Cole was there, too close, and his expression was one she'd never seen from him before—he seemed so empty. She felt the strength she'd worked so hard to muster rapidly leaking out of her.

She looked down. Cole's hand gripped the hilt of his pocketknife, which was now pressed against her stomach.

What...

Before she could comprehend what was happening, her knees gave out and she crumpled to the ground.

50

Kara's eyes fluttered open, the bright sunlight streaming through the windows and illuminating the room. She squinted as she slowly sat up.

Looked around.

She was alone.

Cole, Arthur, and even Azunu were gone. The house was entirely empty, devoid of all the furniture they'd brought in earlier.

She tried to remember what had happened.

He stabbed me.

Her hand flew to her stomach, expecting to find a gaping wound, but there was nothing. No pain, no blood, only the smooth fabric of her shirt.

Am I dead?

A flicker of movement caught her eye. She glanced up toward the living-room window.

On the other side of the glass, looking in at her, was Aunt Adrienne.

She was just as Kara remembered her that summer—

radiant, face lit up with a gentle smile. She seemed at peace.

Kara's heart leapt in her chest. She scrambled to her feet, ignoring the lingering disorientation as she rushed to the window. Her hands pressed against the glass, as if she could somehow reach through and touch her aunt.

So I am dead.

'No.'

Kara gasped when she heard her aunt's voice in her mind—her *real* aunt. It was not a soulless mimic this time. It was really her.

I'm not dead? Kara thought.

'Not yet.'

Adrienne's smile widened. She seemed to shine with warmth.

Kara's fingers curled against the glass, her forehead resting on the cool surface as she tried to make sense of it all. She closed her eyes, taking a deep breath to steady herself.

'You need to wake up.'

"So this isn't real," Kara whispered. Cole, Arthur, and Azunu—*that* was all real.

'Go now.'

———

KARA BLINKED AWAKE as the illusion vanished all at once. The familiar surroundings of the house greeted her. It was nighttime again, and the furniture was back.

She'd somehow made it to the couch. As she tried to sit up, a searing pain tore through her abdomen, forcing a gasp from her lips. Her hand went to the source of the agony, and her fingers brushed against the hilt of the knife still embedded in her flesh.

Fighting through the pain and the rising panic, Kara managed to pull herself into an upright position on the couch. Her eyes darted around the room. She spotted Arthur on the ground at the living-room entrance, unmoving. Cole was gone.

The demon was crouched down, right where she'd been standing when Cole had stabbed her. At first, Kara couldn't comprehend what he was doing, but then it registered.

Azunu was licking her blood off the floor. The wet, slurping sounds filled the room.

With a shaking hand, Kara gripped the knife hilt, braced herself, then pulled it out, a scream tearing from her throat the moment the blade slid free.

Azunu snapped his attention to her, freezing in place where he was crouched.

Kara felt warmth flowing from her stomach wound, so she clamped her hand over it.

Not knowing what else to do, she hurled the knife at Azunu. The demon swiped his long, thin arm through the air and batted it away.

Casting her gaze around the room, Kara spotted the remaining cross statues Arthur had set up earlier on the coffee table in front of her.

Holy objects.

Kara lunged for the table, scooping up one of the crosses. With a cry of desperation and defiance, she hurled it at Azunu.

To her surprise, the cross passed through the demon's shadowy form—and also caused Azunu to recoil with a hiss of pain. Emboldened by this reaction, Kara snatched another cross.

"In the name of God, I command you to leave!" she shouted, her voice raw as she threw the second cross. It, too, found its mark, making the demon stumble back.

Kara's mind raced, trying to recall the words Arthur had used earlier when he'd tried to banish the evil entity. She grasped a third cross—the last one within reach—and her hand shook as she raised it high.

"By the power of the Holy Spirit, I cast you out!" The cross flew forward, striking Azunu once more. The demon's form shuddered, his shadowy edges flickering.

"Kara!"

She turned at the sound of Arthur's voice. Beside him on the floor was the crucifix she'd been carrying with her all night. In one swift move, Arthur shoved the cross toward her; it skidded across the hardwood, coming to rest at her feet. She bent over to retrieve it, ignoring the white-hot agony that flared in her stomach at the sudden movement.

Her fingers closed around the cool metal of the crucifix, and she felt a surge of strength flow through her. She turned to face Azunu, holding the holy symbol aloft.

"Leave this place and never return!" Kara commanded, her voice ringing out with a vigor she hadn't known she possessed. "And let Aunt Adrienne go!" With a final, desperate effort, she hurled the crucifix at the demon.

The moment it struck Azunu, he began to unravel like wisps of smoke caught in a strong wind. An inhuman shriek filled the air as the demon's essence was torn apart.

Kara watched as Azunu's form dissipated and faded into nothingness.

The house fell silent.

Is he gone? she thought. The energy she'd gathered for her last stand had faded all at once, and she knew she wouldn't be able to get it back again. There was nothing left. The pain in her stomach pulsed. A wave of dizziness hit her.

If he isn't, then we've lost. Because I can't...

The temperature in the room increased. The heaviness in the air let up.

A rattling sound drew Kara's eyes to the other side of the living room, near where Arthur still lay. The statue trembled. Kara braced herself, waiting for what was to come next.

Then it disintegrated, miraculously falling into particles no larger than grains of sand.

That was when she knew. Azunu was gone.

51

"Arthur?" she called.

He only groaned in response. It seemed he'd also given all he had left.

He hasn't gotten up, she thought. *How badly is he hurt?*

"I'll… I'll call for help," Kara told him as she fumbled for her phone, her fingers slick with blood. Each movement sent a searing jolt of pain through her stomach, but she gritted her teeth and managed to make the call. Her voice was weak as she croaked out her location before the phone slipped from her grasp and clattered to the floor.

She trudged over to Arthur, knees bent and struggling to stay upright. She tried to lower herself down next to him, but something gave out, and she dropped, jarring her wound and making her clench her jaw.

Arthur reached out and gripped her thigh with surprising firmness. "You did it," he said, voice low and pained. A dark trail of blood ran from his scalp down the bridge of his nose.

Kara clasped her hand over Arthur's. "Are you okay?"

He kept his gaze fixed on hers for a long time, as if

seriously considering the question. He seemed unwilling —or unable—to move any more than that.

"I don't know," he finally said.

Kara wanted to say something to reassure him, but couldn't find the words—or the strength. Her eyelids were heavy, the pull of unconsciousness becoming harder to resist with each passing second.

The wail of sirens eventually came from the distance, then grew louder until they were almost deafening. Red and blue lights danced across the walls.

One benefit of a small town, she managed to think. *The police come fast.*

Before long, the room was filled with unfamiliar faces. Gloved hands pressed against her wound, stemming the flow of blood as they hoisted her onto a stretcher. Through the haze of pain, Kara caught a glimpse of Arthur being loaded into a separate ambulance.

And just beyond the ambulance, near the collection of trees at the front of the property, Kara spotted someone standing there. She craned her head to get a better view. When she did, she realized it was Aunt Adrienne's form, watching her.

Is it real? she wondered. *Am I seeing things?*

Adrienne lifted her hand in an affectionate wave. Then, her aunt's form began to glow a brilliant white light, obscuring her features. The light floated off the ground and ascended into the starry night sky.

Kara watched in awe as it rose. Despite its brightness, what she was witnessing still seemed to be only for her. None of the police or paramedics around her noticed it at all.

The light that had been her aunt then vanished. The

very next moment, the stretcher on which Kara lay was lifted into the back of the ambulance.

Kara let herself believe her own eyes. What she'd seen had been very real. And now she knew that Aunt Adrienne's spirit was free.

———

THE RIDE to the hospital was a blur of motion and muffled voices. An EMT hovered over Kara, his hands working deftly to treat her injury. Kara's mind drifted, the events of the night playing out as a movie in her head: the demon's taunting whispers, Cole's betrayal, the knife plunging into her flesh. It all seemed like a nightmare.

The harsh fluorescent lights of the emergency room jolted Kara back to reality. She squinted against the brightness, struggling to focus on the doctor standing at her bedside. He was middle-aged, with kind eyes and a reassuring demeanor. He said he was sending her directly for a CT scan. A moment later, a man in grey scrubs appeared, and the doctor told him something about "penetrating abdominal trauma." Kara was then rolled to another part of the hospital. The grey-scrubbed man was joined by a second similarly dressed colleague, and together they used the sheet beneath her to transfer her onto the table of a donut-shaped scanner.

The scan only took a couple of minutes before she was sent back to the ER. The doctor returned with good news —the knife had missed her bowels and other organs.

As he prepared to stitch her wound, the doctor's voice was gentle, almost conversational. "Were you attacked?" he asked, his tone carefully neutral.

Kara swallowed hard, the word sticking in her throat.

"Yes," she managed. The admission made it real—the gravity of what had happened hit her like a physical blow.

The doctor nodded, his expression sympathetic. "The police will want to talk to you after I'm done," he said, his hands never faltering as he worked to stitch the gash in her stomach.

"Okay." Kara closed her eyes, tears leaking from beneath her lashes. "How's Arthur?"

"He hit his head pretty hard. We sent him for some CT scans, but thankfully, everything seems fine. Just some cuts on his scalp and he'll be sore for several days."

The doctor finished his work and left. The nurse came in and checked her vitals before leaving her alone again.

A few minutes later, the curtain of her room was yanked aside, and there stood Arthur, looking ridiculous in an oversized hospital gown that gaped open at the back. A thick bandage had been taped to the dome of his head.

"Listen to me." His voice was low and urgent. "When the police come, *don't* tell them about the demon."

Kara blinked several times. "But... what do I say?"

"The truth. Just not all of it."

Before Kara could ask anything else, a nurse appeared behind Arthur, not even trying to hide her annoyance. "Sir, you need to return to your room. You shouldn't be walking around—you're on fall precautions." She took the old man by the arm and ushered him out.

If Arthur hadn't been sent away, Kara would've argued with him, told him that she refused to lie to the police. But as Kara rehearsed the story in her head, it dawned on her how strange it would come across. *Yes, Officer, we were there to perform a cleansing ceremony to remove a demon from the house and release my aunt's spirit that was trapped there. And it worked!*

Kara reluctantly admitted to herself that Arthur was right—the police would never believe the truth. Trying to convince them would be a near-impossible task. This was a reason she'd never told anyone about what had happened that summer with Adrienne. Worse, they'd likely think she was covering something up. They might even become suspicious of her.

Exhaustion caught up with her, and Kara felt herself slipping. But before she could fall asleep, the curtain to her room slid open and the nurse asked her if she would talk to the police now. Kara nodded.

Two uniformed officers came in, a man and a woman, both of whom carried an air of concern. The male officer —a tall, broad-shouldered hulk with a greying beard— stepped forward. "Can you tell us what happened tonight, miss?"

"I was preparing my late aunt's house for sale," she began, her voice shaking slightly. "Arthur and Cole were helping me."

"Cole Turner?" the female officer asked.

Kara nodded. "Yes."

Everyone knows everyone in this small town, she thought.

The officer jotted down notes. "And then what happened?"

Kara hesitated, the memory of Cole's betrayal still fresh in her mind. "Then Cole stabbed me."

The accusation hung heavy in the air. She watched as the officers exchanged a glance.

The man sighed, his expression almost resigned. "Can't say I'm surprised," he muttered, shaking his head.

Kara frowned. "What do you mean?"

"My guys have had some run-ins with him before. A couple of stalking and harassment complaints when he was at Mississippi State, but we went easy on him back then. He's behaved himself since, but I hate to say, I always knew something like this would eventually happen. There's always been something *off* about that guy." He turned to Kara. "Any reason Cole Turner would want to hurt you that you're aware of?"

"I don't know," Kara said. It was partially the truth.

The officer hesitated before he continued, "Is it possible he had romantic feelings for you?"

In a small town, everyone really knows you, Kara thought again.

"He did recently admit that to me, yes."

The officer nodded, as if that was all he needed to hear. "Similar story as the young ladies at Mississippi State." He tilted his head toward the room on the other side of the wall. "And your friend? Arthur, I believe? Did Cole hurt him as well?"

Kara's mind worked fast for a response. "No, Arthur fell while chasing Cole after... it happened."

"Okay." The officer looked at his partner. "You want to bring Turner in, or me?"

"I'll do it," she said, expression grim. "Gladly." She disappeared through the curtain.

AFTER THE POLICE LEFT, the ER doctor explained to Kara that while he was confident both she and Arthur would be fine, he was going to admit them both to stay for a day out of an abundance of caution.

"Just for observation," he added.

Kara was transferred to an inpatient room with maroon floor tiles and white walls. A small, flat-screen TV was mounted in the corner, and her window overlooked the parking lot. When the food arrived, she eyed it with little enthusiasm: a rubbery chicken breast, a lump of mashed potatoes with congealed gravy, and some kind of gelatin dessert.

When her nurse came in to check on her, Kara asked about Arthur. Thankfully, the nurse showed Kara how to use the phone by her bed to call Arthur's room.

"Hello?" he answered in his usual gruff way.

"How are you holding up?" Kara asked.

"They're refusing to bring me whiskey," he spat. "What did you tell the police?"

"Exactly what you told me to," Kara said. "The truth, except for the parts they wouldn't believe."

"And they bought it?"

"They seemed satisfied once they heard what Cole did." That reminded her. "It… looks like you were right about him. I'm sorry for not taking your warning seriously."

Arthur let out a low growl. "He was weak. He believed the demon's lies."

True to the ER doctor's word, Kara and Arthur were both discharged early in the morning after spending one full day and night in the hospital. When they stepped outside, the sun was just beginning to peek over the horizon, bringing with it soft hues of pink and orange. The woman behind the reception desk at the hospital's entrance had called a cab to bring them back to Adrienne's house, where they'd left their cars.

Arthur's gait was slightly unsteady. Yet despite the bandage on his head and the exhaustion etched into his features, there was a sense of resilience and stubbornness about him that Kara couldn't help but admire.

The taxi pulled into the ER parking lot. Kara and Arthur got in and were silent for the duration of the short ride back to Adrienne's house.

The sun had fully dawned by the time they arrived, indicating it was going to be another hot and clear day.

Once out of the cab, Arthur limped straight to his truck.

"Thank you," Kara called after him. "For everything. I'm glad I got to meet you."

Arthur only grunted. "And I appreciate you deciding to call me."

Kara could tell Arthur Briggs had long ago fallen out of practice when it came to exchanging pleasantries. She didn't mind. She knew he was grateful.

Arthur climbed into his truck. He started the engine and drove down the gravel road, out of sight a few seconds later.

Kara looked up at Aunt Adrienne's house. The air around the old structure seemed lighter, cleaner somehow. She felt no fear, no dread. The malevolent presence that had haunted its walls was gone.

"It's over," she whispered to herself.

And Aunt Adrienne's spirit was free and at peace.

With a final nod, Kara got into her rental car. She could now put it all behind her—this time for good.

NEVER MISS A NEW RELEASE
AND GET A FREE NOVELLA!

My novella Nanny is FREE and exclusively available to members of my Reader Group. To join, type this web address into the browser on your phone or computer and enter your best email address:

https://rockwellscott.com/free-book/

You'll receive an email with a link you can click to download Nanny directly to your computer, phone, or ereading device. You'll also be notified when I release new books.

A NOTE FROM ROCKWELL

Hey there.

I would like to thank you for spending your valuable time reading my book. I sincerely hope you enjoyed it.

As you may know, reviews are one of the biggest things readers can do to support their favorite authors. They help get the word out and convince potential readers to take a chance on me.

I would like to ask that you consider leaving a review. I would be very grateful, and of course, it is always valuable to me to hear what my readers think of my work.

Thank you in advance to everyone who chooses to do so, and I hope to see you back in my pages soon.

Sincerely,

- Rockwell

ALSO BY ROCKWELL SCOTT

A Haunting in Rose Grove

A malevolent entity. A violent haunting. A house with a bloody history. Jake Nolan left it all behind, but now he must return.

Jake has it all — a new home, an amazing girlfriend, and nearing a promotion at work. Best of all, he feels he's finally moved on from the horrors of his traumatic past. But when he learns that his estranged brother, Trevor, has moved back into their haunted childhood home, Jake knows his past is not quite finished with him yet.

Jake rushes to the old house in Rose Grove — a small town with a tragic history — to pull his brother from that dangerous place.

But it's too late. There, he finds Trevor trying to make contact with the spirit that tormented them years ago.

And Trevor refuses to leave. He is determined to cleanse the house and remove the entity. But the supernatural activity becomes too much to handle, and Jake knows they are both unprepared for the fight. Worse, the entity targets Daniel, Jake's young nephew, and wants to bring him harm. And when the intelligent haunting shows signs of demonic infestation, Jake realizes they aren't dealing with a mere ghost.

Jake attributes the evil spirit for driving his parents to an early grave. Now it wants to claim the rest of the family, and the only way Jake and Trevor will survive is to send the entity back to hell.

A Haunting in Rose Grove is a supernatural horror novel for readers who love stories about haunted houses and battles with the demonic — the truest form of evil that exists in our world.

ALSO BY ROCKWELL SCOTT

The Tenth Ward

Meet Randolph Casey—university professor by day, demonologist, ghost hunter, and paranormal investigator by night. And he's about to take on his most dangerous assignment.

Rand has seen better days—his ex is getting remarried, and a persistent "non-believing" university auditor is threatening his job. The last thing Rand needs is to take on a new ghost hunting case. But when a desperate couple approaches him about their terminally-ill daughter, Georgia, who claims a ghost is visiting her hospital room at night, he can't seem to turn them away.

Rand figures that banishing Georgia's ghostly intruder will be a routine matter. All he needs to do is guide the lingering ghost to the afterlife. But when the ghost returns with a vengeance, attacking Georgia and terrorizing other hospital wards, Rand realizes this is no benign spirit, but an evil demonic entity. He's faced such monsters before, but never one so complex, so aggressive and violent. If he doesn't unravel its ancient origins and discover how to banish it back to hell, a hospital full of people will fall victim to its destructive agenda.

The Tenth Ward is a supernatural horror thriller for readers who love stories about hauntings and battles with the demonic—the truest form of evil that exists in our world.

ALSO BY ROCKWELL SCOTT

The Gravewatcher

Every night at 3 AM, he visits the graveyard and speaks to someone who isn't there.

Eleanor has created an ideal life for herself in New York City with a career that keeps her too busy, just as she likes it. But when she receives an anonymous message that her estranged brother Dennis is dead, her fast-paced routine grinds to a halt. She rushes to Finnick, Louisiana — the small, backward town where her brother lived and temporarily settles into his creepy, turn-of-the-century house until she can figure out how he died.

But that night, Eleanor spots a young boy in the cemetery behind Dennis's house, speaking to the gravestones. When she approaches him, Eleanor's interruption of the boy's ritual sets off a chain reaction of horror she could have never prepared for. The footsteps, the voices, and the shadowy apparitions are only the beginning.

Eleanor learns that the boy, Walter, is being oppressed by a demonic entity that compels him to visit the graveyard every night. She suspects Dennis also discovered this nightly ritual and tried to stop it, and that is why he died. Because there are others in Finnick who know about Walter's involvement with the evil spirit and want it to continue, and they will do whatever it takes to stop Eleanor from ruining their carefully laid plans. Now Eleanor must finish what her brother started — to rescue the boy from the clutches of hell before he loses his soul forever.

The Gravewatcher is a supernatural horror novel for readers who love stories about haunted houses, creepy graveyards, and battles with the demonic - the truest form of evil that exists in our world.

ABOUT THE AUTHOR

Rockwell Scott is an author of supernatural horror fiction.

When not writing, he can be found working out, enjoying beer and whiskey with friends, and traveling internationally.

Feel free to get in touch!

Instagram
https://www.instagram.com/rockwellscottauthor/

Facebook
www.facebook.com/rockwellscottauthor

X
@rockwell_scott

www.rockwellscott.com

rs@rockwellscott.com